# SONS OF DARKNESS
# SONS OF LIGHT

# SONS OF DARKNESS
# SONS OF LIGHT

## BY
## MARY
## LA CROIX

*Edited by Patricia Wertheim Abrams*

A.R.E.® PRESS • VIRGINIA BEACH • VIRGINIA

A.R.E. PRESS
67th Street and Atlantic Avenue
P.O. Box 595
Virginia Beach, VA 23451

Copyright © 1987 by Mary LaCroix
Published by arrangement with the author
ISBN: 87604-202-7

First A.R.E. Press Printing, July, 1987.

Printed in U.S.A.

NOTE TO THE READER:

Appendices have been included at the back of the book which describe and illustrate the relationships among the many characters in the novel. Also included are maps and other illustrations which provide further background to the story.

Mary LaCroix's earlier novel, THE REMNANT, creates the setting for SONS OF DARKNESS, SONS OF LIGHT. THE REMNANT tells the story of the Essene Community, the birth of the Messiah Jeshua, His ministry, crucifixion and resurrection.

## Acknowledgment

I would like to acknowledge the contribution made to this novel by my friend and editor, Patricia Abrams. Her editorial expertise, insight, and knowledge of the era and its people were invaluable to me in preparing *Sons of Darkness, Sons of Light* for publication. Her unfailing encouragement and understanding made me believe it could be done. Thank you, Patricia.

Streaks of lightning will flash from one end of the world to the other, growing ever brighter until the era of darkness is brought utterly to an end. Then, in the era of God, His exalted grandeur will give light forevermore, shedding on all the Sons of Light peace and blessings, gladness and length of days.

THE WAR OF THE SONS OF LIGHT
AND THE SONS OF DARKNESS

DEAD SEA SCRIPTURES
English translation by Theodor H. Gaster

Dedicated to Dave and Jaunda
and the American Farmers

# PART I
# JERUSALEM

# Chapter 1

Lucius was surrounded by flames. Behind him the Lower City was a raging inferno; before him yellow, red and blue tongues of fire hungrily licked at the Temple walls. The heat was agonizing, searing his skin and sucking out the air from his shrinking island of safety. He labored for breath. His heart pounded and his eyes bulged with terror.

He flung his head back, casting his eyes upward, searching for any avenue of escape. Great billows of black smoke obscured the sky, filtering the sunlight into an ominous glow. Frantically he looked down to the Temple wall, hoping against hope to find a break in the fire, and then his belly revolted in horror.

An obscene row of crossed beams stood planted along the wide walkway at the top of the wall, starkly outlined against an indifferent brilliant blue sky which rose up beyond the holocaust. Mercifully the flames distorted the faces of those hanging there. He did not know them, he did not know the crucified, he could not know them. He tried to tear his eyes away, not wanting to see, not wanting to know.

Insidiously the flames crawled upward, casting an ever brighter glow until he saw the faces clearly and opened his mouth wide, screaming a long, terrible scream of denial. The sound was lost in the roar of the fire.

Lucius awoke with a lurch. He was drenched with sweat and gasping for air, every muscle tensed for flight. His eyes, wide and wild, swept the garden for a means of escape until, nearly at once, he realized where he was—the fire was a dream and he was safe in his father's garden.

He fell back against the cushioned settee. A nightmare. But so real! He could remember every detail as if he had actually been there. It was Jerusalem in flames. Lucius had never been south to Jerusalem, yet he saw it clearly: the tiny, box-like houses, the great stone Temple with the wide promenade at the top of the wall. He squeezed his eyes shut, remembering what stood at the top of that wall.

Who were those crucified? In the dream he knew them, but now, did not. He had never known anyone crucified. Indeed he had never seen any execution carried out by the dreadful Roman death machine.

Lucius' terror subsided. His muscles relaxed and his heartbeat returned to normal. It was, after all, only a dream. He watched the sun sink out of sight behind the circle of mountains that ringed Laodicea and the dream faded, replaced by the memory of the real afternoon he had so recently spent in Vesta's arms. A smile played at his mouth. His eyes drooped partly closed and he gazed through a shadow of dark, thickly-curled, long lashes that brushed his cheeks and gave him more the look of an innocent, pubescent lad than that of a man now thirty. He breathed deeply and squirmed with pleasure as the garden's perfume affected his senses like an all-conquering aphrodisiac.

Vesta! Even to think her name warmed his loins though he left her couch only hours before. He thought of the night they had met at the Governor's palace when her beauty bedazzled his wits. Tall, golden, regal, a cousin to the Caesars, she had floated before his eyes like a Greek goddess, tantalizing his senses until it had been impossible to disguise his visible lustfulness. As all Greeks, Vesta was an ardent admirer of proportion and form, particularly admiring the beauty of the human body, and Lucius' finely-honed, athletic body and exotic Jewishness had attracted her immediate attention. She had laughed at his lust and teased him unmercifully, then playfully led him to her chambers

where with great merriment she had guided him into
delights he had never before known.

Philippi's booming voice brought Lucius out of his
reverie. He swung his legs to the ground and sat up,
watching with a surge of affection and pride as his
father strode across the lawns toward him.

Philippi was tall, muscular, flat-bellied; his closely
cropped curls were without a trace of gray and belied his
fifty years. He still moved with the grace and power of
an athlete, his unaging body testifying to his belief that
exercise, proper diet and an uncluttered mind were the
true paths to a long and happy life.

Lucius' mother, Merceden, followed not far behind,
bearing a tray with a pitcher of wine and ornate silver
goblets. The evening breeze molded her blue linen
*chiton* to her still firm and slender body, outlining her
long, finely shaped legs. Her thick, silver hair was piled
neatly at the crown of her head, like a halo that set off
the dark, olive glow of her skin. She put the tray on a
granite table before the settee and sat next to Lucius as
Philippi drew up a seat for himself.

"Did you go to the fields today, Father?" Lucius
asked.

Philippi took a long draught from the goblet
Merceden had poured and nodded. "The crops look
better than ever before. A bountiful year if all continues
well. Jesua is a good overseer."

Lucius agreed. His sister, Lucia, was fortunate to
have wed Jesua. He might be slightly overweight and
somewhat dull, but he was kind and malleable and
devoted to Lucia and the children.

"Did you see any damage from the earthquake?"
Lucius asked Philippi.

"No. Oh, a few mud slides, but the men had that
cleared away in short order. That quake was nothing,
only a tremor."

Lucius frowned, remembering the quake and the
sudden, unexpected eclipse of the sun the day before,
and the sense of dread and foreboding he felt then and
even now could not be entirely shaken.

The sound of a child's high-pitched wail came from

the house. Merceden listened, then sighed. "Such a day. Lydia spilled her milk and Antonius refused to eat his fish. Now neither child will go to bed and Lucia is in tears. I wish Jesua would take a firmer hand."

"My dear," Philippi chided, "raising children is a woman's work, not a man's. Jesua has to attend to his own duties. Lucia is just overly emotional due to her condition."

"Three children in as many years would try anyone's patience," Lucius snorted.

"At least Jesua stays at home and performs his duty as a husband, as his children attest, instead of roaming the world in search of I know not what and sowing his seed in any fertile field he might find," Merceden retorted.

Lucius' face darkened and his voice carried a tone of warning. "Let us not enter into that argument, Mother."

Merceden flushed and bit back the scathing response which flew to her tongue, then channeled her anger in a different direction.

"Where is Nimmuo? I never know where she is or what she is doing from one moment to the next. You really must speak to her, Philippi. It's unseemly for a young woman to go about unattended as she does. Lucia never caused me such worry. Nimmuo is sixteen. She should be betrothed, even wed by now. You indulge her too much."

"Now, now, my dear," Philippi soothed, "Nimmuo is young and high spirited. She's a good child and you needn't worry."

Merceden refused to be mollified. She was still angry with Lucius, but it was safer to vent that anger on an old, well-worn argument with Philippi than to risk alienating her son. "It was a mistake to agree to let you choose a husband for Nimmuo. I should have realized that even in this matter you would let her have her way and choose for herself."

"Be that as it may, you did agree," Philippi glowered. "You made the decision for the three older children and I shall choose for Nimmuo. As yet I've not met anyone who is worthy of her, but when I do, it will be my decision."

Lucius was relieved when a servant appeared and summoned them to the evening meal. He had heard this argument many times before and it bored him. He was never worried when his parents volubly disagreed for, in truth, they enjoyed it. It was when they lapsed into cold, isolated silence that Lucius became alarmed. They had done so when Antonius died, and their withdrawal from one another had been more than Lucius could bear.

The death of Lucius' brother, Antonius, a few years earlier had been a great blow, shrouding the family in unfamiliar grief and bewilderment, replacing the previous gaiety and love. Merceden had taken to her room, her Jewish sense of Heaven's Will accepting the fact in dry-eyed silence. Philippi had wept and raged and would not be consoled. His son had set out for Rome with friends to visit relatives, and had never returned. To have a son slain in battle he could have understood, but to die of disease without even a physician to attend him was an affront to Philippi's Roman sense of order and justice. He was not even allowed the comfort of weeping over his son's body, for Antonius lay buried in foreign soil with only a few prayers muttered by his companions to accompany him to the Elysian Fields.

Lucius had fled his father's rage, his sister's tears and his mother's stony acceptance. His own grief made Laodicea intolerable and he had taken to wandering aimlessly from city to city, Philippi's name and Roman citizenship granting him freedom to go where he pleased without interference. He had worked for his bread. He sold ale for the innkeeper of a small tavern, taking great pleasure in the nightly brawls with the peasantry who sought the oblivion offered by sour wine to forget their miserable existence. He had signed on as a ship's hand and learned the ways of the sea. He lived for a time in a small fishing village and learned the difference between a day's catch and a hungry belly at night. He used his strong, young body to assuage his grief by day, and a soft, willing girl to banish his loneliness by night. His muscles hardened with physical toil, his skin turned copper and tough from the sun. He let his beard grow until he looked more like his Jewish mother than the son of a Roman equestrian. Every few months he returned home to assure Merceden of his health and safety, and it was during one of those visits that he had met Vesta.

For a time Vesta had quenched his strange restlessness, her eager body and quick wit fulfilled his need for excitement. The fact that Lucius was betrothed to Merceden's niece in Judea in no way deterred their passion, for it was commonplace among the Greeks and Romans to enter into casual liaisons regardless of marital status. They never spoke of marriage, even when Vesta discovered she was carrying Lucius' child, but Merceden had reacted with outrage. Her strict Jewish upbringing considered such behavior sinful, a breach of the Law which clearly stated that a man should cling to his wife and become one flesh. It mattered not to her that the marriage contracts had been signed years before when the girl was just a babe or that Lucius had never yet met her; Merceden refused to acknowledge either Vesta or her child.

Lucius and Vesta delighted in their son, Pebilus, lavishing the child with love and affection but seeming boredom soon claimed Lucius anew and he found the days intolerable. With Vesta's wisely given blessing he left Laodicea, once again without purpose, reveling in each day's delight, and searching out diversion and pleasure wherever he found them. He made his way along the coast of the Great Sea until at Sidon he heard of the unrest in Judea, of the Zealots who plotted revolt, and of a miracle worker in Galilee who performed wonders to behold. His mother's brother, Thomas, lived in Capernaum on the shores of the harp-shaped Sea of Galilee, so Lucius turned inland across the lush, rolling hills and fields where, unbeknown to him at the time, his destiny lay waiting to greet him.

The table had been laid in the atrium and glowed invitingly beneath the flickering torchlight. Lucia and Jesua already reclined at one side of the wide board, and the elusive Nimmuo gave a final touch to her shining curls before expansively greeting her mother, thereby averting a scolding for being late. Lucius aided her in the ploy by quickly pulling her to the wide couch opposite Lucia and Jesua while declaring his ravenous appetite could wait no longer.

Servants filed in with bowls of water to pour over the family's hands in keeping with the tradition of Merceden's piety. They wiped their hands on small linen cloths and Merceden raised her palms and intoned the blessing of Adonai, King of the Universe, over the food as Philippi in turn poured a libation to his gods.

No guests joined them at table so the meal was simple and nourishing as Philippi preferred: fish, some cheeses, a variety of vegetables and light and dark breads, enhanced by a mild, sweet, cinnamon-scented red wine beholden to the family vineyard. A large bowl of fruit sufficed for dessert, consisting of figs, dried apricots, raisins, and apples preserved through the winter in a cold cellar beneath the house.

They ate with leisure. The table conversation revolved around the state of Philippi's vast holdings, and Lucius thought again how fortunate they all were that Lucia had wed Jesua. With Antonius' death, Lucius was now Philippi's sole heir, and he wanted nothing to do with agriculture. Jesua, on the other hand, was a true farmer. Nothing gave him more pleasure than a bountiful harvest, the result of his own careful planning and nurturing.

Lucius let the drone of their voices float past his ears until he heard his mother say, "You should take an interest, Lucius. One day the farms will be yours and you will know nothing."

Lucius laughed. "I'll be old and decrepit by then. At any rate, I have no enthusiasm for crops and livestock. Promise me, Jesua, that even if you divorce my lovely sister you will not leave me to the fate of playing the farmer."

Philippi had followed the conversation attentively. "Lucius will have enough to do looking after my other interests," he said pointedly.

Lucius threw up his hands in mock horror. "To be buried among dusty ledgers full of nonsensical figures is even worse! I leave that to Nimmuo's husband, provided any thinking man will have her," he teased.

Philippi frowned. "What do you intend to do then, my son? Surely not remain a wanderer all your life."

Merceden had watched for an opportunity to speak on this subject for weeks. "I received a letter some months ago from my brother Luke in Judea. He had high praise for you, Lucius. He wrote that you have an eloquent tongue and the gift of healing in your hands."

Lucius squirmed in discomfort. The conversation had suddenly taken a turn he had no wish to explore. His mother had no idea what Luke had meant by the gift of healing.

When Lucius had first arrived in Capernaum, he found not only Thomas, but, to his delight, Luke was also there. His uncle, Luke, was a physician and had lived in Philippi's household during the years he attended the celebrated Academy of Physicians and Healers in Laodicea. Luke had never married, but moved about wherever his services were needed, so it was no great surprise to find him in Capernaum. What had surprised Lucius was to find that both his uncles were devout followers of the Nazarene, the wonderworker whose fame had drawn him to Capernaum in the first place. Thomas was even numbered among the Nazarene's inner circle of twelve.

Thomas had introduced Lucius to the Nazarene, Jeshua ben Joseph, and Lucius had been overwhelmed by the presence of the man. Not only was he impressed by Jeshua's marvelous physique and extraordinary handsomeness, but the man exuded an impelling air of authority, holiness, and compassion for his fellowman. Jeshua's blue-gray eyes had gazed into Lucius' own with such knowing that Lucius had flushed and ducked his head, feeling as if the man looked directly into his soul and laid bare all his transgressions. Lucius recoiled from that gaze. He even shrank from the touch of Jeshua's hand which sent tremors racing down his spine. For the first time in his life Lucius was speechless. He stammered like an awkward schoolboy caught in the act of breaching some rule, and then had fled, confused and bewildered by his own behavior.

For a time Lucius stayed back along the edge of the crowds, watching and listening and trying to sort out the many emotions which roiled within him. He made friends with a group of young men whose passions lay with the Zealot party. Their leader, Judas Iscariot, was one of the twelve intimates. They burned for the day when the yoke of Rome would be lifted from their necks, and looked to the power of the Nazarene to aid them. They hailed Jeshua as the Messiah, the prophesied son of David who would one day rule over all of Israel as the instrument of the One God. Lucius felt sympathetic to this group of eager young men. Battle plans and skirmishes and the fight for a cause he could understand, but after a time he began to wonder if they all were not chasing the wind.

Was not Jeshua's message one of love and peace? He taught his followers to turn the other cheek when struck by an enemy, and to forgive seventy times seven times those who had done them an injustice. "Blessed are they who show mercy, blessed are the peacemakers, love your enemies and pray for them, treat others as you would have them treat you "—hardly the message of a man preparing for war.

Jeshua's mercy extended beyond the border of Israel. A Roman centurion's son was snatched from the brink of death by a spoken word; a Samaritan leper was healed in a trice. Was not he, Lucius, son of a Roman, proof of Jeshua's disregard for race or creed?

When the multitude of souls crying out for relief became so numerous that no one person could heal them all, Jeshua had chosen seventy-two men to aid him in this work, laying his hands upon them and giving them the power to heal and dispel demons in his *name*. A controversy had raged when Jeshua numbered Lucius among them. Some questioned Lucius' Roman parentage, arguing that only those of pure Jewish blood should be called to the work of the Lord. But Jeshua had silenced their objections, saying, "The harvest is rich but the workers are few," and had laid his hands upon Lucius, blessed him and sent him on his way.

A gift of healing in his hands! Could Merceden understand what that truly meant? No, Lucius decided, at least not yet. Why even he, whom Jeshua had tapped to apply the gift, was uncertain about its full power. So he responded to his mother as if healing depended only upon treatment of the physical body, although he knew otherwise.

"Years of study among herbs and ointments and raw bloody wounds have little attraction for me," he said, lightly.

"I thought not," Merceden sighed, then attempted another suggestion. "I hear from my cousin, Rachel of Tarsus, that her son, Saul, is now in Jerusalem attending a Rabbinical school where students and sages of the Torah are studying under the revered Raban Gamaliel."

"Mother!" Nimmuo cried. "Lucius doesn't wish to become like that bandy-legged, self-righteous fanatic!"

"You are impertinent," Merceden chided. "He needn't become like Saul. I only suggest that since your grandfather was a respected member of the Pharisees there would be no obstacle to Lucius enrolling in a rabbinical school. Luke had mentioned the eloquence of Lucius' rhetoric. He would make a fine teacher of the Law."

Philippi interjected. "Now, if teaching is to your liking, what about the Greek academy in Alexandria? There you would have a vast array of subjects to explore before deciding where your interest lies. You could be a philosopher, a great historian like Tacitus, or a writer on any subject you chose. You have always shown a skill with the stylus. How many journals have you filled since you were but a lad?"

Lucius forced a laugh, trying to quell the near panic he felt. He did not know what direction he wished his life to take, and he had given the matter lengthy consideration. In Galilee he had been content only to follow Jeshua, but where would Jeshua lead, and what

place would Lucius have at his side? He had come to
realize that open confrontation with Rome would be
futile and, even if not, on whose side would he fight? He
was Roman by the blood of his father, and Jewish by
the blood of his mother. To fight for one was to betray
the other, yet the strength of Jeshua ben Joseph's love
was such that Lucius would abandon all for him.

After the seventy-two had given their reports of the
healings they had accomplished among the many souls
who had responded to the new message they taught,
Lucius had returned to Laodicea. He intended to bring
Vesta and Pebilus back to Judea to hear the word of God
spoken by Jeshua of Nazareth, but Vesta had laughed
at this new superstition and refused to journey to
Galilee. Lucius and Pebilus had gone alone, and Lucius
would never forget the sense of profound humility and
gratitude he had felt when Jeshua had placed his hands
upon Pebilus' golden curls and blessed him.

They had followed Jeshua for a time, watching the
crowds who groaned in ecstasy at his message of hope,
and saw the miracles he performed. Jeshua's words and
actions had spun in Lucius' mind until he was
perplexed and confused. When Jeshua retired to Perea
for a time of rest and prayerful solitude, Lucius had
come home, to think, to ponder, to try to bring order to
all his jumbled thoughts and emotions.

Lucius sipped at his wine to disguise his nervousness,
saying lightly, "I've only been home a few weeks. Am I
so tiresome you wish me gone already?"

Merceden was immediately contrite and reassuring.
"Of course not, my dear. We are overjoyed to have you
home with us. Forgive us. We were only showing our
love and concern for your future."

The subject was dropped. They finished the meal with
light-hearted banter and retired early to bed.

Lucius did not return to Vesta's villa, but spent the
night in his own house. The conversation at table had
disturbed him and he wanted to think without the
distraction of Vesta's sharp wit and enticing body to
lure his thoughts to other things.

He lay awake a long time, thinking about what had

occurred in Galilee, about his dream of that afternoon, and the earthquake of the day before. Was there a connection? He shook his head in the dark. His thoughts were too jumbled, too disconnected to make sense of them.

He lit a lamp and reached for papyrus, a split reed and ink. He wrote in his journal late into the night until his lids grew heavy and his eyes too blurred to read and he extinguished the lamp and slept.

The next morning Lucius awoke sluggish from too little sleep. He saw the pile of small scrolls scattered on the floor beside his bed where he had abandoned them the night before, accounts of his experiences with Jeshua in Galilee and the disturbing report of his nightmare. He picked them up and tucked them away in his secretary alongside many other journals, thinking he would read them another time.

He called for his man servant. A bath restored him. The servant then trimmed his beard and helped him to dress, guiding his arms into a short, pale blue tunic and girding it with a pure silver belt. He picked up a mantle, richly embroidered with silver trim at the hem, and adjusted it across Lucius' shoulders to complete the ensemble. Fruit and bread sufficed to break Lucius' morning fast and he emerged from the house into brilliant sunlight.

The sky was a sea of blue without a cloud in sight. Lucius stopped for a moment, breathing deeply of the fresh clean air as he gazed upon the city laid out at his feet.

Laodicea was indeed a gem of the Roman Empire. Set in Phrygia south of Sardis and east of Ephesus, it lay in the path of the main trade route running from the Great Sea to the lands of the East. White plastered houses capped with golden straw-thatched roofs sparkled like orderly rows of jewels, and clay tiled houses gleamed like burnished copper in the morning sun. Looking over and beyond the city, Lucius saw Laodicea's famed black sheep drifting across greening hillsides streaked with freshets cascading down to join the wide river on the valley floor as it wound its way through the city streets bringing life and refreshment to all who lived there.

Philippi's house nestled in the hills that arose on the eastern edge of the city. His neighbors were the magistrates, politicians and wealthy men of commerce who guided the affairs of the city. Their homes, as his own, were fashioned of granite and brick, built by the toil and sweat of hundreds of slaves and servants so their masters could escape the heat and din of the city and enjoy the view from a high vantage point. Broad stone stairways led from the uppermost manse to the floor of the valley, lined with flower beds and tall, pruned trees that formed a canopy high overhead. Wrought-iron, wood and granite benches graced the tiers at well-planned intervals, allowing strollers to stop and rest and gossip with friends and neighbors.

Lucius descended the staircase and followed the hard-packed streets through a more modest section of homes until he entered the heart of the city.

Even at this early hour the marketplace teemed with merchants from every land, hawking their wares in every known language, buying and selling and bargaining for prices while the natives traded their famed black wool and happily banked all the foreign coins that they then lent out at exorbitant interest.

Lucius waited for a caravan of braying asses to pass then threaded his way across the square toward the street of the weavers. He ignored sellers who called to him to examine their wares, dashing their hopes that the well-dressed young nobleman might leave a few coins.

The weavers were the largest society of craftsmen in Laodicea. Many communal shops lined the street and Lucius wrinkled his nose at the acrid smell of raw wool. He found the shop he sought and entered.

A woman approached, her face veiled according to the custom among the working class. She began to offer assistance then, recognizing him, raised her veil and spoke his name.

"Lucius! Have you come to buy? You should have sent word and we would have brought our wares to you."

"Shalom, Rhea. No. I came to see Jehul. Is he here?"

"In back. Come. I will show you."

Lucius followed her through the shop, picking his way around rolls of vividly dyed carpets and ducking his head to avoid the colorful blankets that hung from the rafters. Her husband, Jehul, was untying a bale of wool and the stench made Lucius' eyes water.

"Jehul! You have a guest," Rhea called.

Jehul stood, his face registering surprise. "Lucius! Shalom. What can I do for you this fine morning? Are you lost?"

Lucius laughed then glanced at a number of women who stood in rows before bowls of yarn, their arms upraised as their nimble fingers twirled the yarn into thread on spindles that spun at their feet. He stepped closer to Jehul and said in a low tone, "I wish to speak with you on a private matter."

Jehul nodded. "Come to the house and share a glass of brew with me."

Lucius followed him through the back door at the shop and looked up the street with approval. The tiny, box-like houses set in orderly rows behind the shops were in good repair, the door-yards and street free of the clutter and filth that was common on streets of less prosperous craftsmen. The weavers of Laodicea were counted among the best and wealthiest in the world. The fine quality of their wool brought a far higher price than elsewhere so they lived more comfortably than most artisans.

Jehul led Lucius to one of the houses, stopping outside to wash his hands with a strong smelling soap, then motioned for him to enter.

Lucius took a seat at the heavy plank that served as a table and watched his host pour the dark brown beer into two heavy glasses. Jehul was short and stocky. His straight black hair was held away from his face by a piece of wool rolled into a band and tied at the nape of his neck. His eyes were dark, serious, wide-set, his lips thick and sensuous. He wore the common striped breeches and wide sleeved, dun-colored shirt. He was quiet, thoughtful, a man to trust and lean on in times of trial.

He handed Lucius a glass and raised his own in toast. "To life!" He took a long draught, then wiped his mouth with the back of his hand. "Now. What can I do for you?"

"I want to know more about the Nazarene," Lucius said, steadily.

"Ah. What can I tell you? You were there. You saw and heard, more than I. Did he not call you as one of the seventy-two?"

Lucius nodded. "There's still much that I do not understand."

Jehul sighed. "Who does? A man of God, a prophet— who can understand these things?"

"Do you believe he is the Anointed One, the Messiah? Will he rule over Israel?"

Jehul shrugged and stared into his glass as if to find the future foretold in the dregs at the bottom. When he answered, he spoke slowly, choosing his words with care. "Some of us plan to go to Jerusalem for the Feast of Shavout. Iscariot and his followers looked for Passover just past to be the turning point, when the Master would assert himself and wrest the reins of authority from old Annas and his many sons and sons-in-law. We've heard nothing. We'll see when we get there." He raised his eyes. "Come with us."

Lucius felt a stir of excitement. He thought of Vesta and Pebilus, and of his parents' dismay if he were to leave again so soon, and yet if he were to discover more of Jeshua ben Joseph, then Jersualem would be the place to do so.

"When do you go?" he asked.

"Soon. A few days."

Lucius stood and laid a hand on Jehul's shoulder. "I'll let you know."

For the rest of the morning Lucius wandered preoccupied through the marketplace, his mind filled with all the advantages and disadvantages of returning to Judea. When he bought a frail gold bracelet for Vesta, he smiled ruefully to himself, realizing that he had made his decision and that he bought the bauble to forestall an argument.

The sun was rising to its zenith when he retraced his steps of early morning, but this time he used a different staircase, one that led to Vesta's royal villa.

A servant admitted him and bade him to wait in the vast entrance hall while she went to summon her mistress. Vesta appeared almost immediately and greeted him with an embrace. She kissed him full upon the mouth, her breath sweet, her body soft and supple as it molded itself to his own.

Lucius stiffened against the sudden rush of desire that Vesta evoked, and gently disengaged himself from her arms.

Vesta stood back, feeling a slight sting of rejection, but smiled brightly so Lucius would not know. "So serious on such a glorious day," she said airily. "Really, my dear, you Jews are sometimes quite tiresome with all your gloom and heavy thoughts. We Greeks know how to enjoy ourselves."

Lucius ignored her pointed barb and said, "I have a matter to discuss with you."

Vesta laughed. "I might have guessed from your somber expression. Come to the atrium. At least I can enjoy the sun."

Lucius followed her, irritated that he could never win in one of Vesta's battles of wit.

Vesta reclined upon an upholstered couch and smiled seductively, well aware of the impact she had upon his senses.

She was tall and slender as a reed. Her white silk *chiton* clung to her body like another skin, outlining her long legs and gently curving thigh, molding itself to her full high breasts where it fell away just enough to show the dark shadow of cleavage. Her hair was a golden mass of curls, piled high, with springy tendrils falling over her brow and in front of her ears. Her eyes were large and blue and teasing, fringed by thick pale lashes that had been carefully curled. She dipped sparingly into her paint-pots, wisely allowing her own translucent skin to weave its charm.

Vesta shifted her body to the far side of the wide couch, making room for Lucius beside her, but he

refused her subtle invitation and sat instead on the edge
of a fountain in the center of the atrium.

"I've decided to go to Jerusalem for the Spring
Harvest Festival, Shavout," Lucius said quickly.

Vesta's seductive smile remained frozen upon her
face, but her voice was brittle. "Really. How nice."

Lucius recognized her tone and quickly invented a
ploy to deter her temper. "I thought to make it a family
trip, taking Nimmuo, Lucia and Jesua. Nimmuo has
pleaded with me to take her to Jerusalem, and Lucia
needs some time away from her children. The wheat
will be harvested by then and it is a perfect time for
Jesua to go."

"How thoughtful," Vesta purred sarcastically.

"Come with us, Vesta, you and Pebilus. It would be a
wonderful opportunity for you to get to know my family,
and they you."

Vesta's cheeks reddened. She fixed a disbelieving
gaze upon Lucius, thinking, his Hebrew family
welcoming me! How absurd! His mother deplores my
existence and even shuns our child!

Vesta was determined that Lucius would never guess
at the pain his family's rejection caused, or how she
loathed to have him leave again. She forced a laugh and
said, lightly, "You must be joking, Lucius. Do the Jews
have a sense of humor after all? I have little desire to
cultivate a friendship with your family and I am sure
they feel the same way. As for Jerusalem, I am told it is
filthy and overcrowded, that the stench of garlic and
cheese pollutes the air. A most unfit environment for a
child. Go if you wish and enjoy yourself. I'm sure I can
find amusements enough to satisfy me while you are
gone."

She swung her legs from the couch, turning her face
away so Lucius would not see the deep disappointment
that dignity and pride would not allow her to reveal. "It
is time for our son's nap. I promised him a story. Would
you like something to eat? I'll call a servant to serve
you."

Lucius shook his head. He had known it was hopeless
before he asked, and in a way was relieved that she

refused to go. She would never understand his quest for the world of Jeshua ben Joseph, and her presence in Jerusalem would only hinder him from his goal. "I'm not hungry and have some things to do. I'll come back later this evening."

Vesta did not look at him. She made an excuse, thinking if he must leave, to let it be swiftly. "Not tonight, Lucius. I have, as you know, further reports to finish before sending them to Rome."

"Tomorrow then," Lucius said.

"Perhaps."

Vesta disappeared into the house, leaving Lucius to grind his teeth at being so summarily dismissed. He felt diminished and chafed at Vesta's insinuation that he could easily be replaced by others and that her work held precedence over his company. He took the forgotten bracelet from his money pouch and dropped it onto a table, then left the house without turning back.

# Chapter 2

Aboard the LIBER

. . . and it is the first day since sailing out of Ephesus that I have felt at peace to write.

The weather holds favorable. We should reach Ptolemais in less than a week. The seas have been calm and the crossing smooth. The great Roman merchantman that carries us toward Judea cuts through the seas with barely a tremor, bearing a full load of lumber and over one hundred passengers, not counting the crew.

Our vessel has a length to beam measure of four to one. The hull, made of cedar, is brightly colored in bands of red and blue; the ship's interior is pine; and the steering oars, of fir, are painted yellow. The sails are linen—a squaresail, a topsail above the main, and a bowspritsail set on a short raking mast forward. The lines are made of hemp. While there is a cabin aft for the boatmen, we passengers sleep on deck—no hardship in this fair, mild weather—but tents are erected at night to provide privacy for the women. We obtain water from tanks in the hold, and eat mostly meat and steamed grain cooked over a fire in a carefully protected enclosure.

I have a fondness for the sea more than can be said for my fellow passengers, whose grey faces attest to their stomachs' distress. For the most part, they are Jews going to Jerusalem to attend the Festival of Shavuot, and the blood in their veins is the blood of shepherds, not men of the sea. It is no doubt my father's blood that makes me immune to the illness.

I am grateful for this time at sea. With Nimmuo and Lucia occupied by new friends among the Jewish passengers, and with Jesua busily watching over Lucia, I have been free to think and to plan for our arrival in Jerusalem.

First I shall try to find Thomas and Luke. If they are still following the Nazarene, I shall no doubt find them in Bethany. If they are not there, Jeshua's cousin, Martha, will know where they are.

I wonder what the political climate will be in Judea. Not good, I imagine; it never is. The many Jewish sects are forever disagreeing among themselves about how to fulfill the Word of God. The wealthy, privileged Sadducees, who hold majority rule in the Temple, require strict adherence to the Pentateuch as Law. The Pharisees, rabbis of the people, argue that observance of the Laws of Moses—to separate the clean from the unclean—is open to the changing times and they formulate additional laws aimed at sanctifying every aspect of daily life. The Essenes, whom Jeshua and his followers favor, strive to live an even purer and less contaminated life by forming close communities where simplicity of living and rigid discipline attempt to overcome material and fleshly temptation. They incur the hostility of more traditional Jews, because they observe the holidays according to their own calendar and have introduced their own rituals.

Not all of the many sects are interested in religious debate. Zealot radicals concentrate their activities on politically overthrowing foreign rule. But Rome maintains the tenuous peace with an iron fist, and all the sects rally together in their abhorrence of Roman rule.

These are frenzied times. Some of the Jews say it is indeed the End of Days foretold in prophecy. Everyone awaits the coming of the Anointed One, the Messiah promised by the prophets, who will usher in the Kingdom of God on earth and end this period of trial and tribulation. Many false prophets have risen and fallen.

Most Jews believe that the Anointed One will appear only when Israel has attained a state of perfect obedience to God's will. But the Essenes believe that they are the Remnant who have already prepared the way. Some claim Jeshua ben Joseph to be the Messiah who will bring a new revelation, institute a new covenant between God and His people, overthrow human government and rule by the Word of God. Jeshua and his followers have brought much animosity upon themselves from the more orthodox Jews as they continue to deviate from traditional values. After all, Jeshua has openly consorted with Gentiles, dispensed with certain rituals and has broken the sacred Sabbath laws on occasion. Some of his own sect of Essenes even find Jeshua's actions questionable, particularly his brother, James, a pious lad who spends most of his time on his knees in prayer.

I am not sure what I believe, but I've seen and heard enough from the Galilean to want to know more. Surely, also, to find out from him my place among the seventy-two. I will find him first, and then I will decide for myself.

*　　*　　*　　*　　*

They debarked at Ptolemais and joined a group of Jews who had come overland from Antioch. Nimmuo was piqued that they did not tarry in the bustling port city, but her good humor was soon restored when she found that the Antioch Jews included a golden haired lad of about her own age.

His name was Stephen. His father, who had died before he was born, was a Greek, accounting for his mass of golden curls. His mother was Jewish. He had been studying at a rabbinical school in Antioch since he had reached the age of manhood and was now on his way to Jerusalem to visit his mother and attend the Feast.

Stephen did not wait for a proper introduction, but simply approached Nimmuo and imparted all this background information in a rush of excitement. Nimmuo seemed not to notice his lack of etiquette. She laughed at his boyish exuberance, allowed him to take her arm and lead her to meet the rest of his party. Lucius frowned. Merceden had spent the days preceding the journey impressing upon him his responsibilities toward Nimmuo, and the thought of informing his mother that his headstrong sister's heart had been captured by an impoverished young Greek was not pleasant even to contemplate, but he soon realized that Stephen was no threat to Nimmuo's innocence. He treated everyone with the same open friendliness, whether they were male or female, rich or poor, young or old, Jew or not. He had the face of a cherub and an air of innocence and youthful eagerness that was irresistible. He charmed everyone, even Lucius. By the time they camped for the night and Lucius heard the boy speak, he realized that Stephen's attraction was a deep and abiding love of God which flowed out to his fellowman.

Stephen's companion, Philas, was a different matter. He was tall and dark, with a full, sensuous mouth and knowing, mocking eyes which shone with open invitation. He flirted openly with all the women, whether married or not, and spoke to them with thinly disguised seduction. Lucius intended, at the first opportunity, to warn Nimmuo to keep her distance, and was relieved to see that she had already correctly assessed his character and responded to his overtures with cool aloofness.

After a hectic day of buying supplies, the caravan of pilgrims from Laodicea and Antioch set out at a leisurely pace across the lush green hills of Galilee. They were in a holiday mood, singing and dancing along the dusty road. The women exchanged advice on food preparation and child-raising, while the men discussed the fundamentals of their various trades. They looked forward to the Feast, to the excitement of being in the Holy City, and to seeing friends and relatives, some of whom they had not seen for years.

They camped beneath the stars at night and the men took turns telling tales before the campfire. Some of their stories were of their people of old, others were of the Nazarene. Those who knew Jeshua ben Joseph told all that they had heard and seen until his name became familiar to every tongue.

They were, for the most part, poor people, oppressed on every side. They had waited for the promised Messiah for centuries, and the thought that the Hope of Israel might be found in the carpenter's son was awesome even to contemplate. A sense of expectancy hastened their steps until they reached Sepphoris and learned he was dead.

Crucified! Lucius reeled with shock and refused to

believe it.

The holiday mood vanished. They pushed on toward Tiberias with a sense of urgency, eating as they walked, oblivious to the burning, relentless sun, the sweat that soaked their shirts and the dust that stung their eyes and clogged their throats.

They reached Tiberias and hired boats to take them across the sea and learned from a boatman that Jeshua had been betrayed by one of his own, taken in the night, accused of tyranny against Caesar, condemned and hung up on Golgotha.

Lucius thought he could not bear it until the boatman continued, "On the day of the Sun, some women went to the tomb but found it empty. The stone had been rolled back and all that remained were the grave clothes. The Master had risen. He appeared to the whore of Magdala and then to the others. He's been here to the Sea of Galilee. I've seen Him myself. I know!"

This report was harder to believe than the news Jeshua was dead! But somehow, deep in his heart Lucius felt it was true.

They landed at Hippos on the far shore of the Galilee, then followed the east bank of the Jordan in order to avoid the hostile land of Samaria. They crossed the Jordan at Jericho and began the steep, arduous climb over the ridge of mountains toward Jerusalem. They stopped to rest at the final crest of the ridge where they could see Jerusalem spread out before them. The Temple soared above the city; its gold-plated Court of the Priests reflected the sun like tongues of fire and seemed like a torch beckoning weary travelers toward the gates. The city lay ringed behind it, palaces and public buildings standing stark amid a jumble of small houses thrown this way and that as though bowing low in submission.

The descent to the Kidron Valley was a blessing after the torturous climb, but the valley floor was airless and shimmered with heat. Lucia and Jesua had planned to stay with Jesua's relatives in Jerusalem so Lucius left them where the road turned toward Bethany. Nimmuo insisted on going with Lucius. Jesua's relatives held little enticement for her. She guessed by his description that they were no doubt of the poorer class whose accommodations would be meager and their conversation dull. Lucius was in no mood to argue, particularly in that hellish stretch of landscape, and, with a curt nod, consented to take her with him.

It was a long walk. The road wound around the Mount of Olives, uphill and down. Nimmuo struggled to keep up with Lucius' long strides and wondered if she should have gone with Lucia, after all. By the time they reached the village, she was exhausted and her throat so parched with thirst that she literally ran to the well which stood in the center of the village. Lucius waited while she slaked her thirst, then pulled her along a hard-packed street to a large house nestled at the foot of the Mount.

"This is the house of Lazarus and his sisters, Martha and Mary. They are cousins of Jeshua. He tarried here when he came to Jerusalem and their house is a meeting-place for all of his friends. I expect to find Luke here, and if not, they will know where he is."

A servant hurried toward them, smiling and gesturing expansively. "Welcome to my master's house."

Lucius wondered how the man could seem so happy considering the tragedy that had occurred to this house. He said gruffly, "I am Lucius, nephew of Luke the physician and Thomas, followers of Jeshua, with my sister, Nimmuo."

The servant led them onto a wide porch that stretched the entire breadth of the house. A maid-servant brought water and and washed their feet while the other servant disappeared to summon his mistress.

The maid was drying Nimmuo's feet when a tall, portly woman of an indeterminate age appeared and greeted Lucius with formal dignity. Her eyes were unfriendly and deep furrows creased the center of her brow. Nimmuo thought she was a most formidable looking woman and scrambled into her sandals as Lucius repeated the explanation of who they were.

Martha turned toward Nimmuo, her stern countenance softened and her eyes became warm and motherly. A smile struggled to appear but soon fled, as if shy and unaccustomed to public appearances. For some unaccountable reason, Nimmuo felt sorry for her and she stood on her tiptoes and impulsively kissed her cheek.

Martha was startled. She flushed and scolded Lucius in an attempt to hide her embarrassed pleasure. "She is just a child, Lucius. How could you take her away from her mother and bring her so far from home!" She turned to Nimmuo. "Come, dear, you must be famished and wearied to the bone. A bath and a fresh change of clothes will restore you, then a hot meal and you can rest for the afternoon."

She began to propel Nimmuo toward the back of the house when she suddenly stopped and whirled to face Lucius, her eyes wide in wonder.

"Lucius! Lucius of Cyrene! The Holy One Himself must have inspired you to come to Bethany. Mariaerh is here!"

Lucius' mind drew a blank and he stared at Martha in puzzlement.

"Are you not betrothed to Mariaerh, daughter of Marh and Jochim of Ain Karim? They are here, staying with Thelda, my friend and neighbor who is a kinswoman of Jochim's."

Lucius' was shocked. For one desperate moment he wanted to flee, but his feet seemed rooted to the floor. Martha did not wait for him to answer, but rushed on, obviously delighted at the opportunity to impart such joyful news.

"The family came to Jerusalem before Passover to register Mariaerh who has reached marriageable age," Martha explained to Nimmuo, who was struggling against shouting out with laughter at Lucius' look of total dismay. "The Romans require this for taxation purposes." Turning to Lucius, Martha added, "With all that has come to pass since then, they have chosen to stay and wait for Jeshua's return. What a wonderful surprise they will have when they return from the city this evening!"

Lucius was absolutely speechless. He knew he should respond but he could not seem to move. Nimmuo came to his rescue, swallowed her mirth, and said as politely as she could manage, "Marh is our mother's sister. Due to the distance that separates our families, we have never met our cousin Mariaerh. What a coincidence that she would be here. I'm sure Lucius is most anxious to see her."

Lucius choked, then sputtered. "Of course. Yes. I had never considered the possibility."

"You'll have your chance this evening. They will all be here for the Lord's feast."

Martha led Nimmuo through a curtained doorway, and Lucius staggered to the nearest bench and dropped down upon it. He was stunned. His last thought in coming to Judea had been Mariaerh. The marriage contracts had been signed years before when he had reached the age of adulthood, but he had given it little thought then and even less thought through the ensuing years. He pictured the scene which would have occurred if Vesta had agreed to come with him to Jerusalem. Vesta would no doubt have found the situation highly amusing, but the Judeans would not. He groaned aloud at the outrage such an event would have caused among the pious Jews.

Then his shock turned to anger. A stupid tradition! Perhaps marriage contracts served a purpose in ages past, but this was the modern day and a man should choose a wife for himself, if he even wanted one which Lucius did not, at least not at this time. Why had his father indulged Merceden in this outdated custom! Was he, Lucius, not a Roman as well as a Jew? It was true that even among the lower Roman classes they still in some cases held to this nonsense, but the educated, thinking class had abandoned it long ago. Lucius was even angry at Nimmuo who had escaped this trial simply because she was her father's favorite!

Lucius paced up and down the long entrance hall, his mind filled with back thoughts caused by his fury. Then he remembered a sentence casually injected among all of Martha's excited babble. If the girl came to

Jerusalem to be polled for taxation, that meant she was a mere fourteen years of age, far too young to be wed to a worldly man more than ten years her senior. A reasonable enough argument to delay his fate. He felt somewhat soothed by the thought and by the time a servant summoned him to a lavishly laid table, he had regained his composure enough to treat the subject with casual interest. But when Martha left them alone for a moment to call her brother, Lazarus, away from his beloved scrolls, Lucius pulled Nimmuo aside and whispered warningly into her ear. "Say absolutely nothing of Vesta to these people. If you think our Mother is vehement upon this subject, then multiply her piety ten-fold and imagine the furor it would cause!"

Nimmuo opened her eyes wide in mock sympathy, caressing Lucius' cheek and saying, "Dear brother. Of course I'll keep your secret. I would not distress you for the world."

Lucius wanted to shake her, but at the same time knew she would keep her word. He and Nimmuo had always been of one mind and were devoted to one another, though neither would condescend to admit it.

Lazarus emerged from his library and embraced Lucius, murmuring, "Peace be with you, dear friend," as he kissed him on both cheeks. He turned to Nimmuo and took both her hands in his. "And this is Nimmuo, at last. We've heard so much about you, child, but your uncles' praise did not do you justice. She is charming, Lucius."

Nimmuo smiled with pleasure. She had received many compliments from men before, but none had been delivered with such candor and sincerity. Lazarus was little taller than herself. His smile was infectious and his eyes shone with warmth and affection. He bore an air of childlike innocence and secret joy, and Nimmuo liked him immediately.

Martha bustled them to the table where they dipped their hands in fragile bowls and Lazarus gave thanks for the food and the company. Nimmuo followed Lucius' lead in profusely complimenting each dish which deserved every accolade it received, sensing Martha's

need for reassurance over her cooking skills. When the
initial edge of their hunger had been dulled, Lucius
finally had the opportunity to ask about Luke and
Thomas.

"They are in the city," Lazarus explained, "they go
each day, for our Lord Jeshua commanded that they
wait there for baptism by the Spirit."

"Luke and Thomas now live with us," Martha added.
"All of the Galileans have come with their families to
live in Jerusalem. The Twelve, except for James and
John, are here in Bethany. Jeshua's mother and
brothers have joined Zebedee's household, as have the
Other Mary's family. His sister Ruth lives with Marcus
and Josie. Each evening we gather here to eat together
and share in blessing the bread and wine as Jeshua did
when we ate with Him last."

"Tell us what happened, how Jeshua died. I only
know what the boatman told me," said Lucius.

Lazarus wiped his fingers, then folded his hands in
his lap. A shadow of pain crossed his face and he gazed
down at the table. Martha answered for him, for it was
obvious that he could not bring himself to speak of that
time.

She told them of Judas Iscariot's treachery and how it
resulted in Jeshua's arrest. She wove a tale of horror
and nightmare, told with bitter anger and condemnation for all who took part in that infamous act. Lucius
clenched his fists to stop them from trembling with the
rage he felt for the torture and suffering Jeshua had
endured, and for the anguish and despair the family
and all those of the Essene sect had felt at that time. He
fought back tears when Martha related how Ruth and
her husband Philoas had raced from Sidon, only to find
it was too late; her brother lay in a tomb.

Lazarus raised his head when Martha came to the
end of her tale. His face was eager and he continued the
story with growing excitement. He told of the women
finding the empty tomb, of Jeshua appearing to Luke
and Philoas as they walked to the village of Emmaus.
He took them through all the forty days that had passed
since that fateful feast of Passover, and Lucius' rage

and grief evaporated, replaced by overwhelming awe.

How could Jeshua have suddenly appeared in the midst of a locked room, or eaten with his friends on the shores of the Galilee! Lucius was deeply moved by Lazarus' account of the day on the Mount when five hundred souls saw the carpenter's son raised into heaven before their very eyes.

Lazarus ended his story with Jeshua's last words. "You will receive power when the Holy Spirit comes down on you; then you are to be my witnesses in Jerusalem, throughout Judea and Samaria, yes, even to the ends of the earth."

They were silent. Lucius lay back on the couch, emotionally drained. It was all fantastic, not to be believed, but he knew it was true to the depths of his soul.

Lucius left Lazarus' house, climbed to the top of the Mount of Olives and stood looking out across the Kidron Valley at Jerusalem rising ghostlike through the blue afternoon haze. The city seemed beautiful, tantalizing, offering hope and the promise of love, a soft breast for the weary, a refuge to the lost, all the lures of a beautiful woman. But he knew that stripped of her adornments one found lust and passions, discontent, cunning, faithlessness and danger. He felt repulsed, yet drawn. He gazed at the narrow road winding from the Mount to the city walls. His mind's eye could see the parade of torches licking the black night sky in a sinister snakelike dance on the night of Jeshua's betrayal. Beyond Jerusalem lay Golgotha, the Place of the Skull, and not far away, the tomb where he had lain. Would the Holy One take revenge for Jeshua? Once before He had regretted creating man and had vowed to wipe him off the face of the earth. Would He do so again?

Lucius turned again to the Mount upon which he stood. It was here, or nearby, where Jeshua had risen. He promised to return. Would it be here, or in Jerusalem, the place of defeat transformed into victory? When would He come, today, tomorrow, a year, a decade? Even He seemed not to know. And what would come to pass in the meantime? War and earthquake and famine and storm; treachery, panic, false prophets, chaos in darkness. Who could endure? Would any survive? Was there a righteous Noah to save, to replenish the race with his seed? Lucius sighed, engulfed in a sea of sadness. "You are to be my witness, even to the ends of the earth." Jeshua's words promised time, a delay of the end, as Noah was granted time for building his ark. "The meek shall inherit the earth." So the earth would survive, and the meek upon it. How many? Who would hear the testimony of the Elect? "He who has ears to hear, hear!" Would Philippi hear? Merceden, Vesta, Lucia and her brood? Would Jerusalem hear and cast out the Sons of Belial who nursed at her breast?

The shadows grew long. Lucius shivered and started down the Mount. His thoughts raced ahead . . . the meeting with Mariaerh . . . forming questions to Thomas and Luke . . . leaving the End Times to God.

# Chapter 3

It was nearly nightfall when Lucius reluctantly pushed open the gate and entered Martha's courtyard. He paused for a moment, searching the gathered company for a maid who might be Mariaerh, but saw no one who answered her description.

The guests were Jeshua's relatives and most intimate friends, most of whom he knew, so he soon forgot his dread of meeting Mariaerh in the excitement of renewing acquaintances. The women were carrying dishes and laden trays to the tables when Martha sought him out and breathlessly informed him that Mariaerh had arrived.

Lucius was vastly relieved when he saw Mariaerh. She was as young as he had guessed, a pretty maid with the dark, sunkissed coloring of most Judeans. Enormous jet black eyes dominated her slender face, and her hair was pulled back, dark, shining, falling in waves down her back. She was small, with narrow shoulders and long, tapering hands. Her breasts were still developing and her hips, hidden beneath a full skirt, seemed slim as a boy's. She was staring at him, eyes wide with shock and mouth agape, almost in horror. She recoiled and turned crimson when Lucius' eyes met hers, and she immediately cast her gaze downward while her hands fluttered together, clutching one another so tightly her knuckles turned white.

Martha practically dragged Lucius toward Mariaerh, much to their profound embarrassment, and she introduced him to Mariaerh and her parents, Marh and

Jochim. Lucius was moved to compassion by the maid's distress and said, as gently as possible, "I'm sorry that we meet in such an abrupt way, Mariaerh."

Mariaerh managed a tremulous smile, but still did not speak nor raise her eyes.

Lucius directed his speech to his aunt and uncle in order to give her time to recover and was surprised to hear his own voice proclaiming a lie to ease her confusion.

"Had I known you were in Jerusalem, I would certainly have sent word of my pending arrival. Our journey was decided upon impulse, or else my mother would surely have written had there been time. I planned to send a messenger to Ain Karim to tell you I was here and then to visit you there if I would be welcomed."

"Of course, we would welcome you, Lucius." Marh managed. "It is just such a surprise. We are delighted that you are here! Your mother and father are well, praise God? And your sisters?"

Nimmuo had been standing at Lucius' side, hugely amused by the situation, and Lucius pulled her forward, saying, "This is Nimmuo, and my other sister, Lucia, and her husband are with us also, in the city with Jesua's relatives."

Nimmuo dutifully kissed her aunt, then slid her arm around Mariaerh's waist and supported Lucius' lie. "It is wonderful to find you here, Mariaerh. We thought we would be forced to wait until the Feast to meet at last, but here you are! This is my first journey of any kind and I was so excited, but how much better to see the sights with a friend my own age rather than with a watchful, older brother."

The Twelve arrived— Jeshua's most trusted circle of intimates. With them were Thomas and Luke and Lazarus' younger sister, Mary of Syrus, whose beauty made Lucius' senses reel. A flurry of greetings brought the awkward meeting between Lucius and Mariaerh to a conclusion.

Martha called them to eat. Tables had been set up in the garden, illuminated by torches thrust into the ground. The Twelve sat together at one long table that was placed at right angles to the others. All seemed to know their proper place and Lucius grinned at Nimmuo's surprise when Mariaerh led them to the far end, knowing it was a novelty for his sister to be considered the least on a list of guests. Nimmuo was further amazed to see that the women assisted the servants in bringing and serving the food. Merceden would be mortified to ask a guest in her house to help with the meal.

Mariaerh also saw Nimmuo's surprise and explained, speaking low and avoiding meeting Lucius' eyes. "The Poor believe there is no class distinction among souls, that servant and master are of equal importance in the eyes of the Father, and that the most menial task is necessary to the good of the whole. Jeshua set the example himself at the last supper he ate with us. He washed the feet of The Twelve while admonishing them to do the same for others."

A sudden silence fell over the garden. Peter, the leader of The Twelve, stood in the place customarily reserved for the host. Wine and bread had been placed before him and, when all were seated, he stood and lifted the cup, blessed it in Jeshua's name, drank and passed it along to the others. He did the same with the loaf. This was a ritual that Lucius had never before seen, but he followed suit and watched as even the servants and children received their share.

When the last one had partaken of the seemingly symbolic meal, a servant bore the cup and the remains of the loaf to Peter who again intoned a prayer, then the silence was broken.

Lucius was puzzled. This was an unfamiliar ritual to him. He asked Mariaerh to explain.

Mariaerh blushed and spoke without looking at him, directing her words to Nimmuo.

"On the night before he died, our Lord took bread and wine, blessed it and gave it to us to eat, saying, 'This is my body to be given for you. Do this as a remembrance of me.' It was only later when we realized the significance of his action. The Elect have long practiced a similar ceremony in anticipation of the Messiah, and Jeshua's declaration that this was his body and blood was a confirmation that he was indeed the Holy One sent from God."

Lucius found Mariaerh's explanation sobering. He felt suddenly ashamed, as if by partaking of the bread and wine he had somehow invited Jeshua to discover all of his misdeeds. He resolved that the next time he came to table to share in this food, he would make sure there were no lies and deceit on his soul.

The meal progressed as any gathering where family and friends come together in affection and love. The children reclined with their parents which surprised Lucius, for he was accustomed to having the young fed first and then sent off to bed. Then he remembered Jeshua's great love for children and the hundreds he had seen blessed by Jeshua on the roadways of Galilee. He recalled his own son's reaction when Jeshua placed his hands upon the boy's head and blessed him. Pebilus' face had shone with joy and he had looked upon the Master with total devotion, even though he was hardly more than a babe.

When the women had cleared away the remains of the meal, Peter again stood before them and led them in prayer and the singing of hymns. Lucius watched him with admiration, finding it difficult to understand how a man of such obvious humble origins could come to hold the position of honor and authority that Peter enjoyed. His lack of education and training in the arts of oratory seemed not to matter, for he spoke with clarity and forcefulness, and the conviction of his faith could not be denied.

When Peter finished, others of The Twelve read from the Holy Scriptures, quoting the prophets of old, interpreting their words and pointing to recent events that had brought those prophecies to fulfillment. Lucius listened closely, awed by the tale that began to unfold.

The prophet, Malachi, forsaw the return of Elijah, a sign that the Promised One was soon to follow. Philip told of John the Baptiser, born to Elizabeth in the twilight of her child-bearing years, of the vision John's father, Zacharias, saw as he attended his temple duties, and the subsequent period of muteness he endured until the squalling fore-runner was brought forth from his mother's womb and the Holy Spirit loosened Zacharias' tongue and prophesied the destiny laid for his son.

James ben Zebedee traced the life and growth of John, of his youth at the City of Salt—the monastery and school established by the Remnant on the cliffs above the Salt Sea—of his tutoring by the gentle monks, and of John's travels into Egypt where he absorbed the knowledge offered by mystical men of great wisdom.

He told of John's years in the desert, of his zeal for the Lord which led him to live clothed only in animal skins beneath the open skies and forego the luxuries of the world. He told of John's mission, of his call for repentance through the outward sign of baptism by water, and of his declaration of One who would come after him to baptise the faithful in the Holy Spirit.

Young John ben Zebedee called to mind the words of Isaiah, Micah, Hosea and Jeremiah. He wove the tale of Mary chosen on the stair as a vessel for the holy seed, of her visitation by a messenger from the Divine and of all that Messenger told to her. He related the miraculous advent of the child in her womb, and the journey to Bethlehem in compliance with Caesar's edict.

Then John nodded toward a woman who had helped serve the meal, a woman work-worn and bent, but whose face was alight with joy. She told of the night of Jeshua's birth, of the star and the music and the heavenly peace, and her voice quavered with awe in the telling.

Andrew bore the burden of telling the horror that followed and, in his forthright, fisherman's manner, recounted the visit by the Magi to Herod, Herod's rage and his systematic slaughter of innocent babes.

Judith, the leader of the sect, muffled a sob. Indeed did Rachel mourn for her children. Lucius swallowed a a lump in his throat, knowing there was more than one woman here tonight whose son had been sacrificed for a cause.

Andrew finished his narrative, telling of Mary and

Joseph's flight into Egypt and of those who went before and after, suffering the pain of exile in order to protect the One they had sought for so long.

The hour grew late. Babes already slept in their mothers' arms and the Saints parted to go to their beds. Lucius spoke privately with Jochim and suggested that, for the time, Mariaerh remain in her father's house until his own future was more in order. Jochim seemed somewhat puzzled by the fact that Lucius was not eager to share a bed with Mariaerh but agreed, thinking it must be the influence of Philippi's Roman blood.

The Twelve lingered in the garden. Lucius bade them goodnight and failed to notice their strained response or the questioning look in their eyes.

*　　*　　*　　*　　*

## Home of Lazarus in Bethany

*I write this account by the light of a candle, for the hour is late but my heart and mind are too full to entice sleep to my eyes, and the thin, straw pallet upon the floor does little to beguile my body to the same pursuit.*

*We abide in the house of Lazarus, Nimmuo and I, a large and comfortable home for so small a village as Bethany, but filled to capacity with Jeshua's family and friends. I am allotted a small alcove at the back of the house, furnished with naught but the uninviting pallet and an ancient table and stool, but sufficient for my needs. Nimmuo fares better with a larger room, though it is far from that to which she is accustomed.*

*I feel privileged to be counted among this company. Many I had met when last I visited this land and, along with them, followed the Nazarene, but on this night I was blessed to meet the Lord's mother. I shall attempt to describe this wondrous lady, but words are inadequate to convey the beauty of her person and the sense of awe she inspires.*

*Mary. To be in her presence is to be with Jeshua. The same golden-red hair; the same blue-gray eyes, fathomless depths of love, and wise beyond description. The face of an angel. Her skin is flawless. The hand she held out to me seemed carved of the finest* porcelain and her voice held a poignancy, like the sweet, haunting note of a shepherd's pipe drifting from the hills on a warm, still night. She said to me, "Peace be with you, Lucius. My son spoke to me of you. He considered you his friend." All of my bones seemed to melt. I could not speak, emotion choked me. I wanted to throw myself at her feet and pay her homage. She is beyond compare!

The others in Jeshua's family I was already honored to know. His brothers, James and Jude, are so unalike in appearance and temperament that it is difficult to believe they are brothers. James could be a twin to Jeshua in appearance, but is thin and pale where Jeshua was robust and bronzed by the sun. Jeshua delighted to mingle among the people and enjoyed life, while James spends most of his time on his knees in isolated prayer. Jude and their sister, Ruth, are said to resemble their father with dark eyes and hair and olive skin. Philoas, wed to Ruth, is a Roman. Their union caused a scandal at the time until Jeshua blessed the marriage by performing the ceremony himself.

I was shocked by the appearance of Zebedee. When I saw him last, just a few months past, he was boisterous and exuberant, striding through the land with authority and command. He has aged, become old. His step has lost its spring and his hair is now gray. The forceful, booming voice I remember so well now quavers, ravaged by grief. He is brother to Mary, the Lord's mother, father to James and John of The Twelve and was a follower from the time of the Lord's birth. A mortal blow to see one beloved condemned to death. The women of his family support him and watch over him; his wife, Salome; his daughter, Naomi, who is not wed, and his daughters-in-law, Abigale, wife of James, and Lia, widow of his eldest son who was slain while defending the Baptiser.

Mary's sisters were here, Josie, wife of Marcus and mother of John Mark, and Salone, wed to Zuriah. Their cousins, Elizabeth and the Other Mary, came with them. Alphaeus, who has four sons numbered among The Twelve and is brother to Jeshua's father, was also a member of this company of guests. My own uncles, Luke and Thomas, greeted me with their usual affection and were greatly surprised by our unexpected visit.

I have at last met Judith, the first female leader of the Essenes and a legend among the sect. She is the most revered of all the

Saints, with the exception of the Lord's mother, and is, upon first meeting, a formidable woman—stern of countenance, with eyes as blue as the Galilee that make a man uneasy beneath their searching gaze until, upon closer examination, one discovers the humor that lies hidden there. She was Jeshua's teacher so must be near to fifty years, but her skin is taut and fresh as a maiden's and her hair, though streaked with gray, is thick and glows with vigor and health. She speaks candidly, quite disconcerting when one remembers her ability to know one's innermost thoughts. Her husband, Justin, is a Roman and the loving banter between them is not unlike that of Merceden and Philippi.

The most startling of all the prominent personages I encountered this night was Mary of Syrus, sister to Lazarus and Martha. A more beautiful woman I have yet to see, a woman the gods would war over. She seems innocently unaware of her allure, moves with a quiet grace and humility and it is difficult to believe that once she was known as the whore of Magdala. She was forgiven her trans-gressions and healed from error by Jeshua himself, obviously the reason for the deference and respect paid to her by the others.

I have grown weary enough to attempt the pallet. I go into the city tomorrow with The Twelve and must try for a few hours of sleep. I also met my betrothed on this night.

\*    \*    \*    \*    \*

# Chapter 4

Lucius arose early despite his few hours of sleep. He was eager to see Jerusalem and ignored his stiffened joints and aching back that resulted from lying on the thin, straw pallet. It was not yet dawn, but he hurried to the water jars that were in back of the house and poured water over his hands, quickly intoning the prayers that were customary among the Essenes.

Nimmuo found him there and pleaded with him to take her and Mariaerh with him to the city and, since The Twelve were already convening at Martha's gate, he consented, fearing they would leave without him if he took the time to argue with her.

Mariaerh was waiting at the gate when they passed Thelda's house. She flushed and lowered her eyes when Lucius spoke to her and looked to Nimmuo for confirmation that she was welcome to join them. Her behavior irritated Lucius for a moment until he saw how The Twelve and his uncles greeted her with delight. She was obviously a favorite among them which would pave the way for his own acceptance into the elite of the sect.

There was little distinction made between a betrothal and a marriage among the Hebrews. It was commonplace for a child to be born before the actual marriage ceremony was performed, for a man was as free to exercise his connubial rights over his betrothed as he was over his wife. If he wished to set aside his betrothed, it resulted in the same humiliation and social stigma as a divorce within a marriage.

Lucius had no wish to subject Mariaerh to that fate,

but neither did he intend to comply with the archaic tradition of a marriage contract, made between families when children were far too young to know their own minds. He would have to find some way to circumvent the issue, though for the moment he could think of no solution. He had gained some time with his suggestion that Mariaerh remain in her father's house and could only hope that Jeshua would return before he was forced to take further action.

It was a leisurely walk to the city and they had not gone far when Lucius noticed that The Twelve, Peter especially, treated him with cool aloofness, responding when he spoke with only a curt reply and looking past him with obvious disapproval. Lucius was bewildered and wondered how he had earned their displeasure. He finally drew Luke aside and asked, "What have I done? I seem to be very unpopular this morning."

Luke seemed embarrassed. He kicked at a stone in the road and answered without meeting Lucius' eyes. "It's Mariaerh. They question your intention regarding her. They remember that you brought your son to Galilee."

Luke was more bewildered than ever. "What has one to do with the other?"

Luke sighed and groped for words to explain. "It's a question of adultery," he said lamely.

Lucius nearly choked. "Adultery! Those marriage contracts were signed when I was only a lad and Mariaerh nought but a babe. Did they expect me to be a eunuch? I suppose you would have me believe that they have never lain with a woman who was not their wife!"

Luke tried to placate Lucius' anger. "Jeshua taught that even if a man looks at a woman with lust, he has already commited adultery in his heart. They follow the Master's teaching and have set aside their carnal ways."

"And am I not to be allowed the same privilege of correcting my past transgressions?" Lucius asked, bitterly.

"It's not that, Lucius. They fear you will set Mariaerh aside in favor of your son's mother. Such action would cause enormous distress for Mariaerh and her parents."

"I have no intention of setting Mariaerh aside," Lucius declared, though feeling a pang of guilt. "Why do they think such things!"

"Does Mariaerh know of your son?"

Lucius was amazed. "Why should she? Who would tell her, except, perhaps, the pious Twelve! Do they tell their wives of their infidelities?"

"Try to understand their position, Lucius. Will you never return to Laodicea? Will you never take Mariaerh home to your father's house? No one here will reveal your secret, but what of the future?"

Lucius thought for a moment, then said, "According to your own teaching, Jeshua promised to soon return, that the age of chaos is upon us. I don't know if I will ever see my own city again, or my son. If this comes to pass, the question has no substance, if not, I will worry about it at its proper time. In the meantime, you can tell The Twelve that I will see to my own affairs!"

The day was spoiled for Lucius. He quickened his pace and rejoined Nimmuo and Mariaerh, but had no inclination for conversation. He felt unjustly treated by those who spoke so freely of love and forgiveness. Their charge of adultery was nonsense! Every man he knew took his pleasures where he found them and no one thought a thing of it. True, Merceden had been scandalized by his involvement with Vesta, but she was a woman and his mother. He would not expect otherwise.

His thoughts went around and around, growing blacker with each passing moment. If the charge of adultery were only a ruse to hide some other motive for their disapproval, what was it? The only answer that came to his mind was his parentage. His father was Roman. It was Rome who condemned Jeshua to death on the cross, a criminal's sentence, reserved only for those who did not enjoy citizenship in the Empire, and he was being made the scapegoat for Rome's injustice!

By the time they reached Jerusalem, Lucius had convinced himself that his assessment was right. He grew more furious by the moment and decided that his only course of action was to return to his own city at the first opportunity. He would stay for the Feast to avoid disappointing Nimmuo and Lucia, but then he would insist that they go home. As for Mariaerh and her family, they would have to face the fate The Twelve thrust upon them. It was out of his hands!

They reached Jerusalem and entered the city through the Golden Gate that led directly onto Solomon's Porch and then to the Court of the Gentiles. In spite of his mood, Lucius gasped at the grandeur before him.

The Temple was immense. Roman-style white marble columns soared aloft, supporting a gold leaf roof that shaded the many wide steps that led to the Women's Court. The morning sun set fire to the gold and reflected from the marble in a blinding blaze of light. The Court of the Gentiles was a turbulent sea of colorful booths and market stalls, filled with men of every race discordantly hawking their wares.

Lucius was dazed by the throngs and the noise and the chaos and disarray. Priests were everywhere, accepting the offerings, mediating disputes, admonishing, encouraging, interpreting the letter of the Law. Clusters of young men trailed after their favorite Rabbi, arguing volubly over fine points of the Law, their faces eager, their hands flying in widely exaggerated gestures.

Lucius marveled, allowing himself be carried along by the crowd until someone clapped a hand on his shoulder and he turned to find Stephen and Philas behind him.

"We were watching for you," Stephen shouted in Lucius' ear. "The Laodiceans are this way."

Lucius made no attempt to make himself heard above the roar, but simply nodded and kept a tight grip on Nimmuo and Mariaerh as he followed Stephen through the melee.

The Laodiceans were clustered in a far corner where the noise was at a more reasonable level. He introduced Mariaerh as only his cousin, stubbornly refusing to call her his betrothed. He saw Mariaerh's surprise, then flush of embarrassment, but in his present mood he cared little for her feelings.

Stephen guided them through the Temple, explaining the rich symbolism in its structure—details overlooked amidst the overwhelming crush of buyers, sellers and petitioners at their daily ritual. But they could barely hear him over the din.

At midday, they left the Temple. They bought food and drink from merchants whose booths vied for space outside the Temple walls, and once refreshed, set out to see Jerusalem.

The city fascinated Lucius, unlike any other he had ever seen. He stared in wonder at the massive buildings erected by Herod. The four-towered Fortress Antonia was a sight to behold, though it lost its appeal when Lucius remembered how Jeshua had suffered there. The hippodrome was as grand as any Lucius had ever seen, and the theater could hold thousands. They followed the viaduct to Herod's palace and Lucius wondered if Caesar himself lived as well.

The Upper City was as beautiful and well-planned as Laodicea. Graceful homes of Roman and Greek architecture flanked wide, paved avenues, proudly displaying their owners' appreciation for form and color with meticulously planned gardens profuse with blooms. The people they met in the streets were richly dressed. Even the servants wore fine quality linens that were fashionably cut and bespoke their master's affluence. Stephen explained that the Roman magistrates lived here, as did wealthy Jews and men of commerce from many lands.

Lucius did not speak to Mariaerh all day. Whenever there was a lull in Stephen's discourse or there was no spectacle to admire, he nursed his anger and fed his sense of having been wrongly judged. Philas delighted in the opportunity for a possible conquest and flirted outrageously with Mariaerh, but Lucius ignored the affront. Indeed, he hoped the girl would fall in love with Philas and then he would be free!

Mariaerh was bewildered and confused by Philas' seductive manner. Most of the time Philas' provocative illusions were beyond her understanding, for her sheltered upbringing in rural Ain Karim had given her no social experience with the opposite sex. She tried to be polite for he was, she thought, a friend of Lucius', and it was a wife's duty to be respectful and solicitous to her husband's friends, but instinct told her that Philas was overreaching the bounds of friendship. She yearned to tell him so, but feared if she were rude, Lucius would be all the more angry. She struggled to smile and make a passably intelligent remark occasionally, but mostly she was kept busy trying to avoid Philas' wayward hands.

She did not understand why Lucius was so angry. It could not be the attention paid to her by Philas, for his anger had emerged before they had reached the Temple. He had not even told his friends that they were betrothed. She thought she must have done or said something to incur his wrath.

There was no one to whom she could turn. All of the young people in their party had come from large cities, and Mariaerh felt like an ignorant peasant in the company of their urban worldliness. She risked laughter and ridicule if she told any of them, even Nimmuo, of her plight. She longed to go back to Bethany, but she knew she would never find her way and feared the unknown horrors that could befall a maid alone.

Stephen led them to the Synagogue of Roman Freedmen which he himself attended before he had gone to Antioch. It was built with funds donated by wealthy Jews throughout the Diaspora for the use of their countrymen who did not speak the native Aramaic. It was a low, rectangular structure, erected of polished white limestone with marble columns supporting a deep, roofed porch that ran the breadth of the building. The furniture inside was richly ornate. The ark that held the precious Torah was gilt with gold, the lectern intricately carved by the finest artisans in the world. The seats were designed for comfort and ease of visibility, and the archways leading to storage and school rooms were panelled with cedar and polished to a burnished glow.

The Temple was the Abode of God and all the pomp

and ritual and sacrifice took place there, but the synagogue was the center of Jewish life throughout the world. It was here that all community problems were discussed and solved, business transactions conducted, funerals performed and schools maintained for the instruction of young and old alike. It was not dominated by priests. Any man could speak his mind or expound upon the Law. Women, of course, were not allowed to speak and were isolated from the men to their own section, but they played an important role in the social life of the synagogue.

The Synagogue of the Freedman was the last place of importance Stephen wished to show them. Lucius wanted to avoid the crush at the Temple and Stephen gave him directions to the Fountain Gate which led to the road to Bethany. After agreeing to meet in the Temple Court the next day, Lucius parted from the others and led Nimmuo and Mariaerh through the maze of narrow, winding streets in the Lower City. The houses there seemed to Lucius like weeds, growing up in any unused crevice without any apparent thought or planning. Some sections were so poor that he wondered how anyone could survive there. His stomach revolted against the stench of despair.

He found the Fountain Gate with little trouble and once they left the city, Lucius strode ahead, leaving the girls to keep up with him the best they could.

Nimmuo was furious with Lucius. He had been disagreeable and rude all day, and his treatment of Mariaerh was unforgivable. If Philas had tried to work his charms upon herself as he had upon Mariaerh, Lucius would have thrashed him soundly. She had never seen Lucius act in such a manner before. His anger was obvious, but the cause of his anger eluded her. She dared not question Mariaerh, who looked close to tears already, and if she did weep, in his present mood, Lucius would no doubt respond even more harshly.

They walked the entire way in silence, and left Mariaerh at Thelda's gate with mumbled, strained good-days. As soon as she entered the house, Nimmuo turned on Lucius.

"What on earth is the matter with you? I have never seen you treat anyone so cruelly. What could Mariaerh have done that you behave so indifferently toward her?"

Lucius was taken aback. "Mariaerh? She has done nothing. It's the others. Luke told me this morning that the Elect remember when I brought Pebilus to Galilee. They accuse me of adultery."

Nimmuo's eyes widened. "Adultery! Why Lucius, that's silly!"

"I warned you that the Essenes were an overly pious sect."

"I know, but adultery is a serious charge. Surely they know the difference between a youthful affair and adultery! Uncle Luke cannot possibly be so unjust."

"Not Luke, or Thomas," Lucius said quickly. "Only the others. You see now why I am angry. I cannot stay here as I had planned. They would never accept me. I would always be on the outside of their circle. To be truthful, I think their charge is only an excuse. It is so ridiculous, it must be. I think it's my Roman blood to which they object. We'll leave for Laodicea as soon as the Feast is over."

"What of Mariaerh?"

Lucius sighed. "I'm sorry for Mariaerh. She's the innocent victim of The Twelve's hatred of Rome and of our mother's meddling! I cannot stay here and I cannot take her to Laodicea. She has been schooled in the same pious attitude as the others of this sect. Can you imagine my telling her about Vesta and Pebilus? That would be more hurtful than if I break the marriage contracts. That is why I told no one that she is my betrothed. The fewer people who know will cause less embarrassment to her later."

Nimmuo groaned. "What an impossible situation!"

They had reached Martha's house when Nimmuo suddenly said, "What of the Nazarene?"

Lucius started. In his anger and self-pity he had forgotten about Jeshua. He desperately wanted to be in Jerusalem when Jeshua returned, to again be in His presence and feel the peace and love he had once known there. He wanted to have a place in the Kingdom Jeshua would establish on earth when He returned. If only he knew the day and hour of His coming! He had no answer for Nimmuo.

That evening The Twelve seemed to have changed their attitude toward Lucius for they treated him in a friendly manner. Luke drew him aside and told him that he had explained Lucius' position to them and that they were willing to accept Lucius' word, a fact that Lucius found to be poor comfort. They retired early, and Lucius dreamed that the Master returned and set him at his right hand while the others chafed with jealousy at a sign over Lucius' head that proclaimed him Jeshua's friend.

The entire village, every man, woman, child and servant, gathered the next morning to carry the first fruits of the grain harvest to the Temple to commemorate the giving of the Law to Moses. By the time the sun peeped over the Mount, they had formed a long, winding line, singing and weaving in time to the music, an undulating river of humanity flowing a course toward Jerusalem. Lucius found himself caught up in the holiday spirit and danced as well as any while Nimmuo and Mariaerh danced by his side and laughed at his light-hearted antics. They were delighted and relieved by his mood even though they did not know what had occurred to change it. It was a new day, a feast day, and all the angers and hurts of the day before were set aside.

Most of the people of Bethany went only as far as the Temple where Jeshua's followers left them and continued on to the home of Josie and Marcus in the Upper City. The streets were crowded with pilgrims. The outer city walls were ringed by a city of tents, raised by Jews from all over the world who had come for the Feast. Even at this early hour people had begun to pour through the western gates and make their way through the Upper City to the Temple below.

The Elect walked against the flow of the crowd, speaking little as they wove in and out to avoid colliding with those they met. Lucius expertly guided Nimmuo and Mariaerh through the surging mass until at last they arrived at Marcus' gate.

A waiting servant held open the gate, then locked it securely behind them as John Mark came bounding across the lawn, crying, "Welcome! Peace be with you!" He then slid to a halt in front of Nimmuo where he formally bowed, first to her and then to Mariaerh. The girls laughed and John Mark grinned, pleased to have elicited the response he sought. "Everyone is in the upper room," he said. "Come. I'll take you there."

They climbed a narrow staircase at the rear of the house and John Mark knocked discreetly at a thick wooden door. His brashness had fled. His face was serene and his voice subdued. The door opened without a sound and he ushered them into an atmosphere of peace-filled holiness.

All who gathered at Martha's house each evening were there, plus many others, some Lucius recognized as those of the seventy-two. Some were apparently deep in prayer, while others spoke in quiet tones with one another. Lucius was struck by the vast contrast between the quiet reverence found in this room and the clamorous din he had experienced in the Temple.

At the arrival of The Twelve, speech ceased and those in prayer raised their heads. Lucius found a place for himself and the girls. They joined in the singing of hymns and listened as The Twelve read the appropriate words from the Torah. Then Peter raised his arms in prayer and asked them to enter the silence, to become one in mind and spirit as they prayed for Jeshua's speedy return.

Heads were bowed and eyes were lowered. Silence fell over the room, and time and space became non-existent as the Saints stilled their minds to become one with the Lord.

The congestion in the streets beyond the house increased as more and more pilgrims spilled through the gates to take part in the Temple festivities. The crowds were joyous, infected by a sense of expectancy and high excitement and the volume of their voices rose as the momentum of their emotion grew.

Within the upper room Lucius heard the outside clamor with clarity. His eyes were closed, his body completely relaxed and floating on waves of total peace, yet he was acutely aware of all his surroundings. He heard the whisper of the gentle breeze, even though the windows were tightly closed and locked, and later, could pinpoint the exact moment when its lullaby changed, grew and expanded until it became a mighty wind, a roaring, thunderous power that Lucius heard and felt to the core of his being. He felt no fear. His eyes slowly opened and he watched with curious detachment as tongues like fire descended from above and came to rest on the heads of The Twelve.

The Twelve convulsed as if struck by lightning. Their faces became suffused with bliss. Their arms thrust aloft of their own volition, and they burst forth in rapturous phrases of praise. The great upper room rang with their joy. The others joined in, their voices blending and melding in one harmonious song. Their ecstasy bloomed uncontained, and they surged from the house as though of one body and spilled into the garden below.

The throngs in the streets heard the wind and gathered in front of the house which seemed to be its source. They peered through the gates and watched in amazement as those in the house came singing and dancing through its doors. The crowds came from all over the world, yet they understood the hymns and proclamations poured forth by the Galileans, and they trembled in fear and awe. They were dumbfounded and confused. They began to murmur among themselves and to exclaim over the phenomenon taking place before them. Some sneered and accused the Elect of consuming too much wine, but others felt the power of the Holy Spirit stir in their hearts and pressed close to the wall to hear.

The Twelve advanced to meet them. They heard the charge of drunkenness, and Peter raised his voice and addressed them. "You who are Jews, indeed all of you staying in Jerusalem! Listen to what I have to say. You must realize that these men are not drunk as you seem to think. It is only nine in the morning!"

The crowd quieted. Peter continued, his voice ringing with forceful conviction and his words a clarion call to faith in Jeshua of Nazareth as the promised Messiah.

Lucius listened to Peter in awe. He spoke as skillfully as any orator Lucius had ever heard, and he had listened to some of the greatest in the world. He addressed them as "Men of Israel," a subtle reminder of the convenant they held with God. He called upon the prophet Joel to explain the wonder they witnessed this day. He reiterated the life and works of the Nazarene, proving by the power He showed to be one approved by God. Their attention won, he addressed them as "Brothers," abandoning his pose of authority and speaking to them as an intimate friend, calling to mind the words of their own beloved King David who foretold the resurrection of the Anointed of God, then witnessed that all those with him had seen David's vision fulfilled.

Who could disbelieve what the rough fisherman proclaimed with a tongue of such eloquent power! Lucius was fascinated, remembering Peter as he had known him in Galilee, coarse, ignorant, awkward—and now! What power transformed him? Suddenly Lucius realized with shock that Peter was speaking that mixture of Greek and Latin that was peculiar only to Laodicea. He knew that Peter could not speak his tongue! What voice spoke? He searched the faces of the crowds and saw that they too understood everything Peter said no matter what language they called their own. Surely Jeshua continued His work from on High!

When Peter had finished his discourse, the crowds began to clamor for admittance into the brotherhood of faith, pleading for baptism for remission of their sins. The Holy Spirit moved the Elect to honor their request. Under the Power of the Spirit, The Twelve set aside the sect's rule for baptizing only in clear, flowing water, and ordered that large jars of water be brought from the house. They prayed over the jars, purifying their contents by their newly-found power, then, dipping their hands into it, began splashing it onto the heads of the repentant in Jeshua's *name*.

The Saints worked tirelessly all day in aiding The Twelve. They kept the water jars filled. They organized the repentant into twelve lines, recording their names, accepting their gifts, cataloging and storing the goods for future use. They prepared the initiates for what lay ahead, the long period of instruction into the sect, the sacrifices to be made, and the commitment of heart and soul to follow the Way of the Lord.

Jesua and Lucia were among those baptized, as were Jehul and Rhea, Stephen and Philas, nearly all who had been in the caravan. Those in the upper room who had not previously been baptized by water, joined in the lines and bowed their heads to the cleansing bath, Mariaerh among the first, with Lucius and Nimmuo close behind her.

By late afternoon, more than three thousand souls had been baptized into faith, and the jubilant, weary Remnant gave thanks unto God.

# Chapter 5

That night at Martha's, the evening meal became a celebration. Never before had their prayers been intoned with such fervor. It felt as if their reverent "Amens" soared aloft on the wings of angels. When Peter broke the bread and blessed the wine he was filled with a new understanding of the ritual he performed, and before passing the bread and wine to the others, he reminded them of Jeshua's words that so many had found to be stumbling blocks. " 'For my flesh is real food and my blood real drink. The man who feeds on my flesh and drinks my blood remains in me, and I in him.' Today we have witnessed the meaning of our Lord's words, for surely He dwelt within us this day."

They passed the bread with loving hands and drank from the cup as their eyes brimmed with tears. The hymns sung that night were songs of thanksgiving, transcending the garden walls with resounding, swelling joy.

"In the mouth of Thy servant Thou didst open, as it were, a fount, and duly set on his tongue the words of Thy Law, that through the understanding which Thou givest to him, he might proclaim them to human mold, and serve as the interpreter of these things to dust like myself."

From his place at the end of the table, Lucius observed the festivities with a sense of destiny fulfilled. His heart was full, his mind at peace. He knew that he could never leave, that his wandering was over, his restless search at an end. His own ears had heard Peter speak the Laodicean dialect, even though he knew that Peter could speak only Aramaic, and then with the Galilean slur. He needed no further proof that Jeshua would keep all of his promises, that soon He would return, and he, Lucius, would be here to greet Him. He bid a silent final farewell to Vesta and his son, to his mother and father whom he felt he would never meet again in this world. He felt no grief, only a sadness, a melancholy acceptance of what was meant to be, then turned his thoughts to Jeshua and gave himself heart, body, and soul to follow the Way of the Lord.

When the meal was over and the children put to bed, the Elect gathered again in the garden to plan what the dawn would bring. The night was soft. A full moon joined with the flickering torches to bring them light, and the stars bent close to hear. Judith stood before them, tall, strong, the leader of her people as promised long ago. The Elect sat silently before her, pouring out their love toward the one who had led them to see this day. She turned her loving gaze from one to another until her eyes came to rest upon Mary. Her face softened, her voice was a gentle caress.

"I am reminded this night of the day a blessed maiden was chosen upon the stair, a child pure and spotless in body and soul from whose womb would come the Messiah. It was a day of death, and a day of life. A day of seeing the old pass away and a new day begin. Then came the years of preparation and waiting. Waiting for the seed to take root and grow until finally it burst forth in full bloom as Jeshua came to claim his own."

Her eyes then left Mary and swept over them all. "In recent weeks we again experienced a passing away of the old and the emergence of the new. We groaned in horror and despair as we saw our Lord lifted up, then rejoiced in exaltation when He appeared to us alive again. The promise of ages had been fulfilled. The first-fruits of the resurrection harvest had been reaped. Then we entered into another time of preparation and waiting, preparing our hearts and minds to reach one accord as we waited for our Lord and Master to build His Tabernacle within us. Today this has come to pass. Our Lord Jeshua now rules from His rightful place at the Father's right hand, using us, His servants, as His body to fulfill His mission on earth until He comes again in the flesh, as promised that day on the Mount. We are blest among all generations.

"We now must prove ourselves to be worthy of this blessing. We have known since the days of our founder Samuel that the Last Times would one day come upon us, that the Sons of Belial would be cast into the pit and the People of God would reign. The Holy Spirit has led more than three thousand souls to join forces with us in our battle against the Sons of Darkness and I see more being added to our ranks day by day. Our task is clearly laid before us!"

Judith paused. They all held their breath, tense and waiting to hear what they were to do. She suddenly relaxed her pose as Prefect and Leader, bending her body toward them and twisting her face into a grimace of feigned bewilderment. She turned her palms upward in a dramatic gesture of mock helplessness and asked in a tone of seeming desperation, "What are *we* to do with them?"

The Elect exploded into gales of laughter. Nimmuo clapped her hands and whispered to Lucius, "She is wonderful. I have never known anyone like her."

"Nor I," Lucius laughed, "nor I!"

When their laughter subsided, James ben Joseph raised his hand for recognition. Judith called his name and he stood.

"I think the answer is obvious. We admit them into the Brotherhood like any other initiate. Our Rule provides exacting methods for the admittance of new members. We need only follow its dictates."

"In ordinary times I would agree," Judith answered. "But these are not ordinary times. We do not know the exact hour in which the Master will return, but I believe the hour grows short, that there will not be the years necessary for an initiate to become a full member of our congregation according to the Rule. Also, neither Mount Carmel nor the City of Salt is in any way prepared to accommodate three thousand. These people for the most part are not native Judeans, but come from all over the world. They have no homes here, no way of providing bread for their tables or clothes for their backs. Most do not even speak our language. Only a few of those qualified teachers at Mount Carmel and the City of Salt are able to speak a foreign tongue, and even if they could, there are not enough to teach three thousand and more."

Peter stood. "We must also remember that Jeshua ordered that we wait for Him in Jerusalem."

"Yes," said James ben Zebedee, "but only until the Holy Spirit came down upon us, then we were to be His witnesses not only in Jerusalem, but in all of Judea and Samaria, and even to the ends of the earth."

"Does this mean that we are to travel the world over, or that the Spirit will lead souls to us, here in Jerusalem as we witnessed today?" Matthew asked.

No one answered. It was unthinkable to be away from Jerusalem when Jeshua returned. Few if any of The Twelve had ever traveled beyond the borders of Palestine and they recoiled from the thought of entering the hostile Gentile world. They shifted uneasily in their seats and stared at their hands until Judith decided the matter for them.

"We will concentrate for now on the problems at hand. The Spirit will guide our future actions. These people now burn with their newly-found zeal, they hunger for knowledge and understanding. This we must provide immediately before their ardor cools and Belial tempts them back to their old ways and we are charged with losing the souls drawn to us by the Spirit through our lack of haste in action."

"The Temple is the only place suitable to preach to so large a number," said Peter. "If we preach the Lord's word from Solomon's Porch and refrain from speaking such things in the Court of Israel, the authorities will likely ignore us."

James ben Zebedee agreed. "That is true enough. Every day I hear nonsense spewed forth by false prophets of doom and they are left alone, knowing their disciples will soon abandon them when their prophecies fail to come to pass. Let them think we are in the same mold. They'll learn soon enough who we are and that we speak truth, but by then it will be too late for them to act against us."

The hour grew late. They were all exhausted, drained by the events of the day. After The Twelve agreed to meet at Solomon's Porch at the ninth hour, Judith bade them good night and they quickly found their way to their beds.

*     *     *     *     *

### Home of Lazarus in Bethany

Each day we meet to organize the multitude baptized on the day of the Feast. Disputes are numerous, often resulting in heated arguments between the leaders. They are of many minds, each clinging to old ways of thought and reluctant to embrace the new.

James, the brother of the Lord, resists any change in the ancient traditions, fearful lest we destroy the very foundations upon which they stand. He argues for strict adherence to the Essene Rule, declaring it to be the origin of unity which holds the sect together as one heart and mind. Many of the long-time members agree.

Peter and James ben Zebedee argue for the relaxation of the Rule, pointing to Jeshua's own occasional setting aside of the Law when human need took precedence. Young John ben Zebedee reminded them that Jeshua was now The Way by repeating the Master's words, "People do not pour new wine into old wineskins. If they do, the skins burst, the new wine spills out, and the skins are ruined. No, they pour new wine into new wineskins and in that way both are preserved." John's analogy is wise. To force the old rigid Rule upon the new initiates would be more than their newly-born faith could bear. We risk losing the lambs that the Shepherd has brought into the fold.

My admiration for Judith is boundless. Her keenness of mind is equal to any man's and her insight into human nature is unsurpassed. She leads with wisdom and authority and, when dissensions arise, calls us to enter the silence, to wait for that small, still voice to speak. Each time we return to the conscious world with minds united, proof that Jeshua leads his flock from on high.

Many initial difficulties have been resolved. The initiates could not continue to live in tents outside the city walls or pay the costly price of an inn. The Elect gladly opened their homes to as many as possible but they could not absorb three thousand. We have appointed overseers to discover the vocations and talents of each newcomer and then to find them a place to work and live where they can use their gifts for the benefit of all.

Teachers have been appointed from among the Elect, both men and women, while others come from Mount Carmel and the City of Salt to aid us. Classes are divided according to age and knowledge, and interpreters assigned where needed. Young girls have been charged to care for children under ten years of age while their elders attend class or work at their trade. Some of the women offered to care for the aged and infirm who cannot be left alone to guide them in useful endeavors.

Food, clothing, household utensils and other goods are distributed from the common fund. Cooks have been appointed to prepare the communal meal in various parts of the city and experienced members of the Elect conduct the blessing of bread and wine.

Jonas and Susane, with Luke's aid, will see to the health of the new initiates. They worked together in Capernaum to relieve the suffering of the poor, and now join forces again. Jonas, like Luke, is a physician. His wife, Susane, is a childhood friend of the Lord's sister, Ruth.

Order has been established, though much remains still to be accomplished. Jesua and Lucia have returned to Laodicea for Lucia could not bear to remain forever separated from her children. Jehul went with them, but only to sell his weaver's shop and bring the proceeds back for the use of The Way, as have others. Nimmuo remains with me. The prospect of never again seeing my own city or my loved ones fills me with sadness, yet not with regret for I eagerly await Jeshua's return.

\*　　　\*　　　\*　　　\*　　　\*

Lucius labored among the Elect with unflagging zeal. His family, Vesta, even his son seemed to fade into a shadowy past where he remembered them with nostalgic affection, but they had no bearing upon the life laid out before him. He felt reborn, a new man. Gone was the soldier of fortune whose restless feet sought out the pleasures of the world, who could find no purpose, no goal, but only an aimless wandering as he bided his time on earth. Now he looked forward to each new dawn, eager for each day's labor in preparing for Jeshua's return. His commitment was total, his determination to become closely affiliated with the Intimates of the Lord was boundless, forcing him to submit to the subtle pressures brought to bear by the sect and bring Mariaerh to live in Martha's house as was fitting for one betrothed.

For all his desire to please the Elect and to be accepted as a trusted equal, Lucius had no intention of consummating his marriage or of undergoing a formal ceremony. He rebelled against being forced to accept a wife who was not of his own choosing, yet he dared not express his feelings openly lest the Saints charge him with walking in the stubbornness of his own heart. He found reasons to explain his behavior to them. But what to do, what to say to Mariaerh? He had to be rid of this problem.

He asked Mariaerh to walk with him upon the Mount of Olives where he could speak with her in privacy. The Mount was a cool respite from the punishing heat in the city where Lucius had spent the day acting as interpreter to those assigned to find homes for the initiates. The long days of summer had just begun, and a strong southwest wind had blown all day, parching man and beast alike with dry, desert air.

Lucius was tired and irritable, his energy drained by the heat and the frustration of trying to bring understanding to people who spoke in different tongues. He dreaded the unpleasant task of telling a fourteen-year-old girl that he could not, would not, take her to be his wife, but for days he had been unable to think of little else. He kept going over and over what he would say and how he would present his position with as much kindness and gentleness as possible. However painful, he simply had to dispense with the problem to be free to do the work of the Lord.

He chose a wide sloping path winding through a grove of olive trees that offered shade from the late afternoon sun. They spoke little, and Lucius tried to break the awkward silences by frantically searching his mind for any tidbit of news that he thought might interest a girl of fourteen, but Mariaerh was so shy and quiet in his presence that he could not fathom what lay in her mind, if anything, and the effort only added fuel to his already smoldering anger.

Mariaerh walked somewhat apart from Lucius, wondering why he had suddenly invited her to walk with him. She had accepted his invitation reluctantly, fearful of being alone with him lest she somehow arouse his anger again. She had not forgotten his unconcealed wrath that day in Jerusalem, and still felt that in some unknown way, she had been its cause. She sensed his resentment toward her and believed that he was disappointed in her, that somehow he expected someone much more beautiful and worldly than she. Mariaerh was determined to do everything possible to please him, to prove herself to be a worthy wife. She kept her gaze on the path before her, taking care not to stumble and appear clumsy, and spoke only when Lucius' comments demanded a response so he would not think of her as an empty-headed, chattering female.

Mariaerh's lack of conversation and careful reserved manner irritated Lucius. The girl never spoke unless forced to do so, and she kept her distance as if he were someone unclean. He tried to guess what her reaction would be to his proposal, but she kept her face averted and offered no clue as to how she might feel. Finally his patience came to an end. He forgot his well-planned speech and blurted out his decision without preamble, his voice harsh and authoritative, leaving no quarter for mutual discussion.

"It is not fitting that you should continue living with your parents in Thelda's house. When we return I wish you to gather your belongings and bring them to Martha's where you'll share a room with Nimmuo."

Mariaerh was stunned. "With Nimmuo?" she stammered.

Lucius did not hear her. He spoke quickly, covering his embarrassment and guilt at deceiving the girl with gruff impatience. "It is foolish to even consider building a home and family when Jeshua is expected to return at any time. No one knows what lies ahead, and Jeshua himself warned that it would be difficult for those found to be with child or with a babe at the breast. You will be under my protection and authority as deemed by Law, but you need have no fear that you will be numbered among those unfortunates who will suffer when the end is upon us."

Mariaerh was so shocked she could not speak. It felt as if her world had come to an end already. She had been schooled from infancy to believe that the sole purpose for her existence was to make a home for her husband and to bear his children and rear them in such a manner as to bring honor to his name. Her mind did not absorb Lucius' explanation. She only grasped that she was being rejected out of hand and she reeled in humiliated despair. She turned away from him, unable to bear having him witness her shame.

When Mariaerh made no comment or objection to his plan, Lucius took her silence to mean that she understood and agreed. He felt a great weight lifted from his shoulders, and was vastly relieved that there would be no ugly scene or lengthy argument as there would have been if Mariaerh had been Vesta. He regarded Mariaerh with new eyes. Perhaps she was not as vacuous and mindless as he had thought. He shaded his eyes with his hand and looked at the sun.

"It grows late," he said light-heartedly. "The Twelve will soon return from the city and I am anxious to tell them of the progress we made today. Come."

He started down the Mount without waiting and Mariaerh stumbled after him. She was trembling so she could hardly walk. She struggled to keep up with him, brushing away the tears that ran down her cheeks and swallowing the sobs that threatened to humiliate her further. Lucius' mind was intent on what he would say to Peter and paid her little mind until they reached Thelda's house where he said, "Bring your things when you come for the evening meal. Nimmuo will gladly welcome you."

Mariaerh waited until he was out of sight, watching the long shadow made by the setting sun that followed him, then wept as if her heart would break.

# Chapter 6

Mariaerh's move to Martha's house was accepted routinely and the few comments that were made only lauded Lucius' self-sacrifice and charity toward another. Mariaerh's fear of public shame and gossip disappeared, but the pain of rejection remained, as did her grief at being forced into a state of perpetual virginity. Each babe she saw was like a sword piercing her heart, and she fought against the envy that eroded her soul.

Lucius was highly pleased with himself. He thought he handled the matter extremely well and gave thanks to God whom he credited for the inspired solution to his dilemma. He basked in the warmth of the Saints' approval, and grew self-confident, offering opinions and suggestions without fear of reproof or ridicule.

Once Mariaerh ceased to pose a threat to his personal life, Lucius' attitude toward her changed, and his manner became relaxed and easy going. Her unobjecting compliance freed his conscience from the tortures of guilt, and the very sight and thought of her no longer aroused his anger. He saw her as a comely child, shy and malleable, certainly obedient, and without a trace of the rebellious independence that Nimmuo often displayed. He enjoyed his role of guide and protector, and fed on a sense of self-importance instilled by having absolute authority over another. He believed that Mariaerh was as content and pleased with the status of the marriage as he himself, for her conduct gave no evidence to the contrary. With his marriage firmly established on mutually agreeable terms, he dismissed Mariaerh from his mind and turned his full attention to The Way.

As all new initiates, it was required for Lucius, Nimmuo, and Mariaerh to attend classes to learn the tenets and creed put forth by the Essenes. Lucius rebelled at this requirement, feeling that as one of the seventy-two he should be exempt from this rule. He felt himself to be a knowledgeable citizen of the world, certainly better educated than most of the Disciples. He argued before The Twelve that it was sufficient for him to go to the Temple each day and hear them preach, but they disagreed. James, the brother of the Lord, was the most adamant. Ever zealous in preserving the Rule, he fought for its strict adherence at every turn and only direct interference by the Spirit would change his mind. Once more the dark shadow of doubt loomed in Lucius' mind and he again felt it was his Roman blood that influenced the leaders and not his need for instruction. John and Jude tried to convince him that this was not the case. John subtly chastised him for his lack of humility.

"It is true that you knew the Lord and observed his works and heard his words for yourself. But there are other things you do not know, things of the world of spirit that are kept secret until the soul is able to bear it. Do not let self-pride stand in the way of your growth in spirit."

Jude was more direct. "We need you, Lucius. The Twelve preach Jeshua and Him crucified. That you know already. The fact that Jeshua chose you himself is proof of your worth, but we need more than your gift for languages. Are you content to be merely an interpreter? Come, man. Think! When Jeshua returns He will reign over the whole world. We need leaders, men who understand the ways of that world and can bring it into one accord with the Spirit. You know the letter of the Law, but what of the spirit, the hidden meaning that lies behind the Law?"

Lucius was mollified, even flattered by Jude's argument and allowed himself to be persuaded, but when he learned that he was assigned to a class taught by Martha of Nicodemus, he questioned Jude's sincerity. He expected to be placed under the guidance of one of the celibate teachers from Mount Carmel or the City of Salt, possibly even James, the brother of the Lord, and it was a blow to his pride and dignity to learn that his teacher was Martha. He considered it demeaning to be taught by a woman, a public admission of his intellectual inferiority. He was also disgruntled to learn that Mariaerh and Nimmuo would share in his instruction, a further indication that he was no more highly thought of than the females in the sect.

The first morning that they walked to Martha's house in the Upper City, Lucius was sullen and short-tempered. He quarreled with Nimmuo over the arrangement of her hair and rudely remarked on Mariaerh's lack of haste. The girls exchanged knowing glances and tried to avoid antagonizing him, but it was difficult to maintain subdued decorum when they felt such excitement over their first day in class.

Jerusalem was just awakening when they entered the Fountain gate. The streets were nearly deserted and they walked quickly, unhampered by the crowds of merchants and buyers who would fill the streets at a later hour. They found the house without difficulty and Mariaerh stared in awe, feeling out of place in the midst of such unfamiliar luxury. Nicodemus' home bespoke his wealth and prestige. It was large and tastefully furnished with objects from all over the Greek and Roman world. The large receiving hall was lined with graceful couches—the cushions were so soft and plush a girl might sink out of sight if ever she dared to sit upon them, Mariaerh thought. Tall, alabaster vases filled with a profusion of blooms gave the hall an airy, outdoor look and, although there were no statues or busts of human likeness in keeping with the Jewish faith, huge murals depicting rural scenes were painted on every wall. Martha welcomed them, wearing a lovely gown cut from lush, expensive fabric, and Mariaerh noticed immediately that its flowing lines hid a blooming womb.

Martha led them to a smaller chamber off the great hall to meet the others in the class, and when Lucius saw that there were no Judeans and only foreigners in the group, he was further convinced that his Roman blood testified against him.

They numbered sixteen in all. Most of them were young people who had journeyed in the caravan from Ptolemais: Stephen and Philas, a young man called Phillip, a newly married couple, Sylvia and his wife Jeseuha, and two girls whom Nimmuo had befriended, Lydia and Helene.

They were intelligent, curious young people, privileged to come from families where education was affordable and to live in cities where it was easily attainable. They grew up in the midst of the pagan world where attitudes of thought and morality were often in direct opposition to the traditional views birthed to them by their Jewish heritage—a continuous confusion, a continuous attraction!

The Greeks around them emphasized physical beauty, believing that bodily perfection mirrored the divine. They loved the arts and the challenging allures of philosophy, and could timelessly embrace the hours debating the virtues of one theory over another. Pleasure in all forms was the goal to be attained, and the suggestion of sin in pursuit of pleasure was unthinkable.

For the Romans, law, justice, and social order were most esteemed. They saw themselves as a race born to rule, and revered the lawmaker Solon as one of the gods. Austerity in behavior and excellence in physical performance were of the highest priority, demonstrated by their numerous public games, gymnasiums, and their invincible legions which were the pride of the Empire.

To a Jew, his religion was his life, his goal to attain salvation, redemption. Survival as a race and a culture in such an enticing milieu was a never-ending struggle. Compromise was often necessary. Relenting to the mighty force of Rome was sometimes the only way to avoid an early grave. He depended on the Law to save him from total absorption into the Gentile world, an absorption that would lead to the loss of his soul. Had not God commanded him and his brethren to be "a nation of priests" serving His Name? Had not that same fidelity to the Torah sustained his ancestors as they wandered in the desert wilderness of Zin, as they remained intact despite the might of the Babylonian armies under Sennacherib, despite dispersion and destruction of the Holy Temple by Nebuchadnezzar, not to mention the recent hated rule of the Greek-Syrian, Seleucids? He zealously looked to follow every precept of the Law, and performed every ritual with such compulsion that the very performance stood in danger of becoming an end in itself where the spiritual meaning might too easily be lost.

The soul cried out in anguish, grieved by the lack of knowledge that portended her death. Life without meaning was useless. The struggle simply to survive was in itself obscene. Many gave way to defeat and adopted the ways of the world, but others gave heed to the cry of their souls and searched for a way back to God.

The young people in Martha's class were among those who longed for the purpose of life. They believed that the Nazarene pointed the Way, that the Saints held the key to the Law. They were avid for knowledge, eager for life, and dedicated.

Martha was fully aware of the conflict these young people experienced. She and Nicodemus walked that precarious tightrope between the Jewish and Gentile worlds, placating Rome, pleasing the Temple priesthood, while living the life of the Spirit. So she knew the difficulties her students would encounter in trying to set aside attitudes and customs permitted in their homelands and replace them with new actions and restraints dictated by the Saints. To bring the passions of flesh under spiritual control was no easy matter, particularly for the young so newly awakened. Martha realized that the reason for doing so must be more enchanting than experiencing the passions themselves. She began her instruction by telling of the time before time.

"All souls were created in the beginning as companions to God, to live in the highest heavens, the Empyrean, in perfection and bliss with the Almighty. The world below was not formed to be their dwelling place, yet once they beheld its beauty, they desired to experience what they saw and entered the realm of the earth as sojourners in a foreign land. God had endowed the souls with His gift of free will and so did not prevent them from distancing themselves from Him. Once in the world, souls became so enamored of pleasures that they slowly forgot their beginnings and gradually knew nothing but an innate longing, for what they remembered not.

"Know that this took place over eons of time and not all souls left their true abode. When those souls who chose to remain with God saw the distress of those in the earth, they sought to rescue their kindred and rekindle the memory of their true nature and self. God gave their leader the Adamic pattern, the most perfect channel by which to experience the earth in the flesh. Lo, the first Man made his appearance. God warned Adam not to become entrapped by the world, but temptation was great and soon even Adam had lost his way.

"When God saw the state into which Adam had fallen, He was moved with compassion for the plight of the souls. He sent death to the world as a mode of escape whereby souls could leave their body of flesh and enter a state of repose and reflection before entering again to meet that which had been their undoing. For what had been created as perfect was now imperfect, and only by regaining their original state could the souls reunite with God."

It was sobering to think of oneself being eons and eons of age, wandering lost in an alien world without a map as comforting guide. Lucius remembered how Jeshua often referred to himself as the good shepherd, come to gather the sheep who were lost, and he now felt the full impact of the Master's words.

Every day Lucius and the girls made the short trip to

the city to sit with Martha and learn the ways of the soul. Lucius' admiration for his teacher grew steadily, and he regretted that he had previously questioned the decision of The Twelve in assigning him to Martha's class. She wove the story of the souls' creation and their subsequent sojourns in the earth with consummate skill. Her explanations were clearly stated, her patience limitless. No question or statement put forth by her students was treated with scorn or disdain, which led to freedom and exploration of ideas, and to lively and thought-provoking discussions. At the end of each session, they were emotionally and intellectually exhausted but eager for the next class to begin.

Lucius also quickly learned that each member of the group was as knowledgeable and quick-witted as he. Mariaerh especially astonished him. At Bethany she was shy and quiet, seldom expressing opinions or entering conversation, but at Martha's she was clearly a leader, offering insights that had not occurred to the others, displaying a sense of humor that Lucius had never seen before, and using her humor to explain complex concepts.

After class the students would go to John Mark's home to assist in carrying out the work of The Way. His home became a center for initiates as new believers were added daily, many of them friends and relatives of the original three thousand. The faithful were beginning to come together, a gathering of people awaiting the Messiah's return.

The students' tasks varied. There were records to be kept, the multitude to be fed. Every talent was used. Classes were held to teach the young a useful trade and to improve the arts of homemaking. Young girls were taught the life-giving value of foods and the healing properties of herbs and spices. Young couples contemplating marriage were encouraged to hear the true meaning of the union of souls and to practice those ideals for fulfillment in their shared life. They were also taught to nurture the spiritual growth of a child as well as to care for the child's physical well-being.

Mariaerh resented the fact that because of Lucius'

bewildering stance she was denied the opportunity to join other young couples in preparing for sacred marriage. She never complained or in any way showed the disappointment and bitterness she felt. Whenever she and Nimmuo were assigned to care for children she hid the ache in her heart and tried not to think that her own child would never be among them. She found refuge in the sect's teaching: was she perhaps deprived of a home and child as atonement for some past transgression?

It was not easy. When she saw others entering into marriage and bearing children, she was devastated by a sense of injustice. Everyone showed excitement and joy over such events, but then regarded Lucius' actions in not marrying and having children as laudable. It was bewildering and Mariaerh could make no sense of it. When Jehul returned from Laodicea with the news that Lucia had borne another son, Mariaerh's anger at Lucius' joyful reaction bordered on hatred. His public concern for her was a lie! He made no secret of his affection for his sisters. If he truly believed that these uncertain times boded ill for a woman with child, why did he not groan in distress when one he obviously loved faced such a time of trial? Instead he laughed aloud in happiness and gave thanks and praise to God! There was no one in whom Mariaerh felt she could confide, for everyone seemed to agree with Lucius. She suffered in lonely isolation.

The days fell into a routine pattern of classes, assisting in the work of John Mark's home, or meeting at Solomon's Porch, in the Temple precinct, to hear The Twelve preach. Then, home again in the late afternoon to share in the evening *Agape,* a feast of love, a word adopted by the Saints from their Greek-speaking brothers. It was a perfect description of the evening meal. To join together in the breaking of bread and the drinking of wine that denoted the body and blood of the Lord, was an act of love, love of one another, love of the Lord, and most of all, of Jeshua's love for them. The ritual was performed with solemn devotion and piety, a reverent act of faith performed throughout the city wherever the Saints convened. It was inspiring to think that when the cup was raised in Bethany, it was also raised at Mount Carmel and the City of Salt, and in homes throughout Jerusalem. They were one in thought and one in purpose, and their pleading cry, "Lord, Come!" resounded with one voice.

Autumn was deep upon them. The days were wet and chill, the nights bitter cold, and the walk to the City and back became an uncomfortable duty. Stephen invited Lucius and the girls to stay at his mother's house on the Sabbath days and attend the Synagogue of Freedmen with him and others in the class. Lucius accepted gratefully. The tiny synagogue in Bethany was overcrowded with the poor and the old rabbi who presided there delivered the familiar expositions of the Torah. Lucius knew them all by heart. Since joining the Essenes he had come to have a new understanding of the Law, and the possibility of a new Covenant on hand. He hoped the intellectual atmosphere in the rich Synagogue of Freedmen would match the rising expectations of his soul.

Stephen's mother Veronica lived in a tiny, box-like house set against the outer city wall not far from the synagogue. She was an elderly woman, of sixty years or more, whose luminous light brown eyes were startling against their background of pale, translucent skin and snow white hair that framed her narrow face in gently curving waves. She was of medium height, quite thin, and with a look of fragility that hinted at years of failing health. Her facial features were a mirror of Stephen's. Her eyes held that same bemused, ethereal quality, ever-smiling lips and a clear melodic voice that called to mind angels.

Autumn yielded to winter, and throughout the long, raw winter weeks Veronica's abode served as the meeting place for the young Greek-speaking followers of The Way. Each late afternoon when classes were over and assignments in aiding the Saints were finished, the tiny house would reverberate with youthful exuberance. The girls hurriedly prepared the evening meal, simple fare, but ample thanks to the communal stores maintained by the sect. They took turns in blessing the bread and the wine, the girls as well as the boys, for God did not recognize Jew or Greek, male or female, but all were one in the Lord.

When the tables were cleared, Stephen took his harp and led them in hymns of thanksgiving, a joyful chorus in praise of God, drawing them together in a fellowship of love. Veronica told them tales of events she had witnessed when she followed the Baptiser along the Jordan, then later of Jeshua ben Joseph as he rested with friends in Bethany. Lucius told of being one of the seventy-two, and of the healings he had performed by the power of Jeshua's *name*. Mariaerh spoke of the last days when Jeshua rode into Jerusalem, a king on the back of a colt, only to hang like a thief from a tree.

They were often joined by older believers who had known Jeshua from the time of birth. One of their favorites was Sara whose father had owned the stable where Jeshua was born and had witnessed the night of the Star. They begged her to repeat the story over and over again, never tiring of the wonder and awe her tale evoked. They shuddered at the coarse drunkenness displayed by the rabble that night, and laughed at the ruse her father employed against the Roman guard. They sighed at the poignancy of simple shepherds who looked on the babe, and gasped at the splendor of the exotic Magi. Their eyes widened in wonder as they imagined the star and the music that came from its light, but the best was the babe with his silken brow and eyes that mirrored a soul Divine.

When Ulai and Pathos came to break bread with them, they learned the story of Mary and Martha and Lazarus ben Syrus, how Mary had run away from the home she had loved and fallen into sin and disgrace until she was healed by the Lord himself with words of loving forgiveness. They thrilled to the story of Lazarus' fever, of his death and recall from the grave. Ulai repeated Lazarus' own tale of experiences in that period of inter-between, when there rose that quickening and movement within, and the Voice that had called, "Lazarus—Come forth!"

They then understood why Lazarus was so feared and hated by the Temple authorities. Was he not living proof of the authenticity of the Nazarene? To admit that Jeshua raised Lazarus from the dead was to admit the possibility that he was indeed the Anointed One— condemned and crucified. It would be chilling to consider that perhaps an error had been made. So Lazarus remained in Bethany, secluded from the High Priest Caiaphas' vengeful eye lest he be moved to violence.

The weeks of winter passed in peaceful solitude. The seas raged beneath the winter winds, slowing commerce and trade to a standstill and discouraging all visitors from coming to Jerusalem. The rich and influential fled the freezing city for the temperate air and healing springs of Jericho, leaving the hushed, empty streets to the poor who had nowhere else to go.

The Twelve preached undisturbed from Solomon's Porch, each week drawing new members from the Jews who remained in the city. Winter was a time of suffering and hardship for the city's poor. Food and other supplies that normally flowed into the city slowed to a trickle causing prices that few could afford. When the rich abandoned the city there was no longer a market for the goods produced by the masses and their looms and churns and ovens and dying vats all stood idle. Sickness raged through the hovels in the Lower City, brought on by the cold and lack of food. Men fled the misery in their homes, unable to bear their children's hungry cries or the fear they saw reflected in their women's eyes. They came to the Temple in search of hope and found it in the Nazarene.

The minor priests who were left in charge of the Temple affairs paid little attention to those that surrounded The Twelve and so did not notice that their followers grew in number. Even some Romans listened and joined, particularly those who had been on duty during Passover week and had seen the dignity and majesty of the one they had led to the cross. A groundswell of new thought, new awareness, new faith was being born. It was a ground-swell so subtle and deep

that neither Jewish nor Roman authority, finding
comfort around smoking braziers in their fine houses or
fleeing to the warmth of the sun in Caesarea and
Galilee, realized what was happening.

The poor knew. For every convert who believed the
witness of The Twelve, there were a hundred who did
not. They had no faith in a Messiah who died like a
common criminal, supposedly rose to heaven, and
promised to return with a golden age for all. They were
freezing and hungry and sick today! All summer they
had watched as foreigners moved into their midst,
opened new shops and robbed them of their livelihood.
They did not want more cheesemakers, weavers, and
other merchants adding their wares. The "Nazarenes"
as they were known were well-fed, wore warm clothing,
and had what seemed an unending source of supply.
Jealousy and resentment sprouted among those who
had none. They looked with suspicion upon those who
spoke in a foreign tongue and greeted one another in
such obvious friendship and love. What did they have to
be so joyful about? They watched as the Nazarenes
gathered together to share their evening meal and
wondered what went on behind their closed doors.
Rumors of strange rites and abominations began to be
whispered among the Judeans and they wondered if
their own mean existence was a punishment from God
for harboring such sinfulness in the City of David. A
ground-swell of hate also grew.

The Saints were too lulled by the euphoria of
expecting the Master's return to notice the glares they
received from men in the streets or to hear the cries of
ridicule shouted by children. If they did see or hear, they
brushed it aside as an isolated incident caused by
ignorance and dismissed it from their minds. They lived
in a world of their own making, a world of friendship,
sharing and love, and the outside world revolved
around them unheeded. They no longer worried about
business matters or where they would live or what they
would eat or wear. What Rome or Herod or Caiaphas did
was no longer of any concern, for all that secular world
would soon pass away when Jeshua came to claim His

own. They were of one thought, one mind, to await the Day of the Lord. They were a secret community of Saints who walked in a world doomed to destruction, but were not of it. They were a family, Brothers and Sisters in God, the Elect, the Chosen Ones, safe and secure under the guidance and shield of the Lord.

The cold wind blew. An occasional blanket of snow wrapped the city in cozy silence. Martha gave birth to a baby girl and the Saints rejoiced in peace.

# Chapter 7

The mending in Mariaerh's lap lay idle. She sat in
Martha's garden with her hands folded and her face
turned up to the sun. She allowed her mind to drift and
her senses to absorb the warmth, and aromas and
sounds of spring.

Blessed peace and privacy! She could not remember
when last she had been completely alone. Probably not
since she had left Ain Karim more than a year ago. A
twinge of guilt edged its way into her thoughts for she
had lied to obtain the luxury of a day spent alone, telling
Lucius and Nimmuo that morning that she did not feel
well and so could not go with them into the city. It was
not totally a lie. She was tired. The strain of maintaining a pose of cheerful acceptance while her heart and
mind rebelled in angry resentment had sapped her
strength, both physically and emotionally.

It had been a difficult winter for Mariaerh. The
Saints' joy over the birth of Martha's daughter,
Rebecca, had been hard enough to bear, but Jeseuha's
whispered confidence that she was also with child was
an even worse blow. Jeseuha was only slightly older
than Mariaerh and had been wed only a short time
longer. It was not fair that she and Sylvia should have
such happiness while Mariaerh was forced into a sham
of marriage. All winter Mariaerh had watched as love
matches evolved, betrothals and weddings took place,
and babies appeared amid glad celebrations. Even
Naomi glowed under the tender attention paid to her by
a carpetmaker named Cephas, and Naomi at age thirty-
three was considered a spinster by all.

Mariaerh did not understand Lucius. She had done everything she could think of to please him and gain his notice. She had been obedient to a fault, avoided any conversation that might lead to a quarrel, had personally seen to his every need and had comported herself exactly to his dictation, all to no avail. No longer did she believe his disinterest was because she was plain and undesirable. She knew she was as comely as any, even more so than many. During the last few months her girlish figure had bloomed into womanhood, and she was aware of the openly admiring glances she evoked from young men and old alike.

At one time Mariaerh had wondered if Lucius hid some physical abnormality that prevented the natural physical urge of a man to lie with a woman. Then she had come to suspect that he occasionally visited the city brothels with Philas and other young men in their group. The realization that she was being rejected in favor of a depraved harlot had infuriated her, but still she held her counsel and never acknowledged that she knew.

Why did Lucius reject her and refuse to live a normal married life with her? The only reason Lucius had given was to protect her from suffering the tribulations that would precede Jeshua's return. She did not believe it! Even James, the brother of the Lord, who was the most pious of them all, was rumored to be interested in Suphor, a girl who served as a maid in Zebedee's house. Susane and Jonas had wed. All The Twelve were married except John, and the friendship between John and Mary of Syrus was said to be growing deeper each day, a match promoted by the Lord's own Mother. If all those who had been the closest to Jeshua showed no fear of the coming days, then why Lucius, who was not even in that inner circle of original followers? And why did they all condone and applaud Lucius' actions when they did not do so themselves?

Her thoughts circled around and around. The pile of mending at her feet slowly shrank as her hands automatically performed their task. A maid servant brought her morning meal to the garden where she ate in grateful solitude. She spent the day undisturbed except when Lazarus joined her for a short while until Martha called him away. For a fleeting moment Mariaerh had considered unburdening her heart to him, even though he was a man. One simply did not think of Lazarus as either male or female, for his saintly demeanor transcended the barrier of gender. He was the kindest, most gentle person she knew, and his quiet, humble manner invited confidences, but she knew he would be of no help to her in this problem She needed solid, practical advice, and Lazarus saw only the ideal and not the realities of life.

There was really no one who would understand. Certainly not Nimmuo whose devotion to Lucius blinded her to all his faults. Mariaerh's mother believed her to be happy and safe in Lucius' care, and to shatter that impression and cause her worry seemed cruel. The only one she would completely trust not to betray her was John Mark, and one simply did not speak of such things with a member of the opposite sex.

Mariaerh was so lost in thought that she did not notice Martha's approach and gave a start when Martha laid her hand upon her shoulder.

"Goodness, child! I didn't mean to startle you." Martha bent and scooped up the pile of mended clothing and exclaimed, "Why you've nearly finished! You've done a fine day's work, Mariaerh. Are you feeling better?"

Mariaerh blushed and lowered her gaze, embarrassed by the lie she had told. "Yes. Thank you, Martha. I think I only needed a day of rest and the sun."

Martha shaded her eyes and turned her face toward the setting sun. "Jeshua once said, 'Put off your shoes and your clothing and suffer the Angel of Sunlight to embrace all your body. Then breathe long and deeply, that the Angel of Sunlight may be brought within you and shall cast out of your body all evil-smelling and unclean things which defiled it without and within. None may come before the face of God whom the Angel of Sunlight lets not pass. Truly, all must be born again of Sun and of truth, for your body basks in the sunlight of the Earthly Mother, and your spirit basks in the sunlight of truth of the Heavenly Father.' "

Mariaerh smiled. "The Angel of Sunlight. That's a lovely thought, though I fear I would create a scandal if I removed my clothing."

They laughed. Martha sat down on the bench next to Mariaerh with a bundle of mending in her lap. "It is well to separate ourselves sometimes from all company and from the cares of the world. Our Lord did so often, going off alone to refresh both body and spirit. I sometimes wish that I could follow his example as Mary and Lazarus do, but there are always matters of the house pressing for attention, and I never seem to find the time."

Mariaerh laid her hand over Martha's and said gently, "I think your body and soul find refreshment in the service you perform. You make this home a haven from the world for all of us. We would be lost without you."

Martha was confused and embarrassed. Seldom did anyone recognize the nourishment behind her efforts. She felt a sudden surge of affection and gratitude for the young girl at her side. She knew Mariaerh was troubled, but why? It seemed to her that Mariaerh had the ideal situation, the protection and security of a husband without having to submit to marital vows. If she had known a man of sensibility like Lucius, she might have considered marriage herself. She wanted to help Mariaerh, so she forced her shyness aside, determined for once to share aloud the wisdom she carried within. She spoke at first with hesitancy, unable to look at Mariaerh.

"I know something troubles you. You needn't say what," she added quickly, "it is none of my concern, but whatever it is, you can use your will to bring about change." She paused as if to gather new courage then continued. "There is nothing that can supersede the will of man, for such are the gifts to the sons of men. There is today, every day, set before us good and evil, life and death. We must choose. We are conscious in a living world, aware of suffering, of sorrow, of joy, of pleasure.

These are the price one pays for having will, knowledge. But do not count any condition lost. Make each situation the stepping-stone to higher things, remembering that God does not allow us to be tempted beyond what we are able to bear and comprehend, if we will but make our wills one with His. For we can say yes to this, no to that. We can shape our lives by the very gifts that have been given into our keeping. In meeting every error, every trial, every temptation, whether mental or physical experiences, the manner and purpose and approach should ever be in the attitude, 'Not my will but Thine, O God, be done in and through me.' "

Martha stopped abruptly, suddenly humiliated at venturing to tread where not invited. She gathered the bundle up in her arms and stood, saying, "Goodness! Look at the time and a thousand things to do before the others return from the city!" She took off at a trot toward the house, leaving Mariaerh speechless behind her.

Mariaerh was astounded. She had never heard Martha speak so many words at one time before, and had never guessed that such thoughts lay buried in her heart. She watched Martha's sturdy figure hurrying toward the house, then ran after her, calling, "Martha, wait!"

Martha stopped. Mariaerh caught up with her and through a choked voice and with eyes brimming, said, "Thank you, Martha. Thank you very much."

Martha could only nod, then went on into the house.

Mariaerh felt more joyful than she had felt in months. Somewhere in Martha's words lay a clue to solving her dilemma. She would have to think about what Martha said, but the future no longer seemed quite so bleak.

Spring saw the return of the rich to the city and the streets surged with life once again. The warmth of the sun performed its miracle of healing. Coughs disappeared, new strength flowed through veins of the winter weary, and hope and optimism were re-born.

The sea calmed. Trade and commerce resumed. The animosity of Jerusalem merchants toward their Greek-speaking neighbors abated as buyers for their wares increased and the spectre of starvation was arrested for a time. They listened with interest when The Twelve preached the Messiah from Solomon's Porch, and were moved by the power with which they spoke. No one could deny their sincerity. Their courage and conviction of faith was respected, but to think that a lowly Galilean carpenter's son was the long awaited Anointed One was difficult to accept. Some believed, others did not. Most reserved judgment, afraid to believe in case they were wrong, and afraid not to believe in case they were right, for The Twelve's use of sacred scripture as testimony to the truth of their words was a powerful argument.

The tide of pilgrims that converged on the city for the Feast of Passover again brought an influx of new believers to The Way. It was easier for Jews raised in the pagan world than for native Judeans to accept the concept of an incarnate god who could die in the flesh then rise again. The king of the Roman gods, Jupiter, was the son of the god Saturn. He had brothers and wives and children, and was depicted in statues as a man of flesh. Greek-speaking Jews, while not believing that Jupiter was a god, lived in the shadow of his many temples and were daily confronted by his image, and so were not shocked by "God become Man."

Native Judeans were outraged! Except for matters of business they shunned all intercourse with Gentiles. Allowing no pagan images and gods to enter their city, their minds were totally unprepared for such alien ideas. To say that the One God, Creator of All, would have need to beget a son was nothing less than blasphemy. It was not long before the majority in The Way spoke Greek.

A packet of letters was delivered to Lucius by a Laodicean who came to celebrate Passover. It was the first time in nearly a year that Lucius had heard from his family. He recognized Philippi's bold scrawl and his mother's carefully drawn hand. Longing gripped him. Just holding the letters in his hand brought a rush of memories—lush green hills dotted with flocks of fat, black sheep, fertile valleys patchworked in green and gold, and the city itself, clean and orderly, alive with laughter. So different from Jerusalem, moaning in misery and stuggling for life amid the stark, bleak hills of Judea.

The letters from Philippi, Merceden and Lucia were addressed to both him and Nimmuo, but one letter, whose handwriting Lucius failed to recognize, bore only Lucius' name. He broke the seal on the others first and read with delight, hearing their voices in the words they wrote. Philippi demanded that they forgo their nonsense and return home at once. Merceden admonished them to eat well, comport themselves in an appropriate manner, and not forget they were Jews. Lucia bubbled with news of her brood and wailed over the loss of her figure. She looked like a matron!

Lucius laughed aloud and could hardly wait to share them all with Nimmuo. He set them aside and opened the last. It was from Jesua, short, to the point, apologetic. Lucius paled as he read. He gripped the scroll in his fists and began to tremble with anger.

Vesta had given birth to a son, his son! Jesua was not so bold as to say it was his son, but from the date of the child's birth there could be no doubt. Vesta had even given the child a Hebrew name, making certain Lucius would guess whose spawn he was. Thaddeus!

Lucius felt sick. His head spun. Why had she not told him? He counted back from the birth date to the day he had sailed from Ephesus. Surely she had known! He felt betrayed, duped. If he had known he never would have come to Jerusalem, certainly not have stayed. Had he known he would never have accepted Mariaerh as his betrothed, would have told them all that he had a wife and sons at home. In his anger and hurt it never occurred to him that one son or two made little difference and that the decision he had made regarding one would have been the same with two. A blow had been struck at his pride, at his very manhood, for he had been made the fool by a woman!

Lucius' impulse was to return home immediately, to

confront Vesta with her lie by omission and see the son whom he never knew existed. He quickly abandoned that idea as he imagined Vesta's mocking laugh and her smug satisfaction that her ploy had worked and brought Lucius back to her bed. No! He would not allow any woman to control him and force him to act against his will. He would stay where he was and Vesta be cursed!

Lucius burned Jesua's letter and said nothing to anyone, not even to Nimmuo. He forced himself to join Nimmuo's glee when reading about the others and to act as if nothing were wrong. He refused to allow himself even to think of Vesta or of his sons, and threw himself into the new life he had carved for himself. His anger and wounded pride made it easy to dispel Vesta from his mind, but his sons were not so easily banished. They crept into his thoughts at odd moments without invitation, causing a dull ache to settle in his breast. He began to wonder if other sons would fill the void in his heart, and he looked at Mariaerh with new interest.

Jeshua had not returned. On the anniversary of His ascension some of the faithful gathered at the place on the Mount where He had been taken up. All day they watched and waited and prayed, until the sun went down on their vigil and they trudged home beneath the twilight sky, His coming again delayed.

Why had He not returned! Judith came down from Mount Carmel and met with The Twelve, the Elders, the Remnant who had seen it all. Her presence gave strength, her wisdom understanding. She stood before them with her hands outstretched as if in blessing. "Be not weary that He apparently prolongs His time, for as the Master has given, 'As to the day, no man knoweth, not even the Son, but the Father and they to whom the Father may reveal. I go to prepare a place that where I am there you may be also. I will come again and receive you unto myself.'

"The cry in the hearts and souls of us who seek His way is to hasten that day. Yet, as He has given, in patience, in listening, in being still, may we know that the Lord does all things well.

"The merciful kindness of the Father has, in the eyes of many, delayed the coming, yet the Son prepares the way that all men may know the love of the Father. And as we would be channels to hasten that glorious day of the coming of the Lord, then we must do, with a might that our hands find to do, what will bring to pass the greater manifestations of love for the Father in the earth. For, into our keeping, and to His children and to His sons, has He committed the saving of the world of the souls of men. As He has given, 'Who is my mother? Who is my brother? Who is my sister? They that do the will of my Father who is in heaven, the same is my mother, my brother, my sister. I leave thee, but I will come again and receive as many of you as have been quickened by manifesting in your life the will of the Father in the earth.'

"For centuries our forebears dedicated their lives to the labor of bringing about conditions necessary for God to enter the world. We saw this fulfilled in our own generation. When our Lord spoke to us of the last days, the days preceding His coming again, He assured us, 'The present generation will not pass away until all this takes place.' Our labor is not finished. Like our fathers before us, we too must make clear the way.

"Hence know that, as our minds, our activities, long more and more for the glorifying of the Son in the earth, for the coming of the day of the Lord, He draws very nigh unto us. Hasten, O Lord, the day of thy kingdom in the earth!"

The Remnant was strengthened and comforted. Their purpose was redefined. They were shepherds in Jeshua's stead. He delayed His coming until all the lost sheep were gathered into the fold, and they must bring the Word wherever it would be received in the world.

The Saints' rededication and renewed enthusiasm for the tasks laid out before them gave Lucius a welcomed respite from brooding over Vesta's deceit and the keenly felt separation from his sons. He threw himself into the work of The Way, planning with the Elders each day's events, finding homes, distributing goods, mediating disputes, acting as an interpreter, and a myriad of other duties that prevented his mind from wandering home to Laodicea. Only at odd idle moments did thoughts of Vesta and her children enter his mind and he considered the idea of lying with Mariaerh, but those moments were fleet and soon disappeared and he made no move to act upon them.

Mariaerh hoped that after the meeting of the Elders, Lucius would realize that if Jeshua's coming was to be delayed then there was no longer any reason to refrain from having children. Her desire for a child and to be recognized as Lucius' wife—in the complete sense of marriage—was so great that she convinced herself it would come to pass. With the present situation, she had no appropriate place in the sect. She was betrothed but not wed. She was a wife, but not wife. Neither was she a young girl free to flirt and laugh and join in the activities of Nimmuo and her friends. Such behavior was unseemly for one betrothed. She imagined the attention and respect she would receive from others once they learned a child grew in her womb. She saw herself accepted into the married women's circle as one of them, not as a girlish intruder who could not fully share in wifely concerns. She day-dreamed how the child would look and feel and smell until her arms cradled the expectation. Her mind's eye saw Lucius looking proudly at his son, treating her with tenderness and maybe even love as the mother of his child.

Mariaerh wanted Lucius to love her. When she saw an intimate exchange between husband and wife, her whole body longed for such intimacy to come to her. To see Sylvia put his arm around Jeseuha's waist and support her up a stair filled her with a sense of loss. Even the naked lust in Philas' eyes when he spoke to a pretty girl sent a stab of grief to Mariaerh's heart for she had never evoked such a look from Lucius. Perhaps now that would all be changed.

Mariaerh watched for some sign that Lucius had a change of mind but saw none. In fact he seemed more remote towards her and more taken up with concerns of the Way than ever. She tried everything she could think of to gain his attention. She dressed with care, arranging her hair in the style Lucius suggested for Nimmuo, and chose garments of modest cut and subdued color that she thought his piety would approve. She spoke sweetly to him at all times, anticipated and provided for his every need before he asked. Lucius did not notice.

One night Nimmuo stayed at Stephen's house and Mariaerh was alone in the tiny room they shared. She convinced herself that Lucius would surely come that night to claim her. She lay on her pallet in tense anticipation of his approach. Her blood raced with fear at the unknown sensations she was sure were about to overtake her and her nerves thrilled with almost unbearable excitement that finally the dreamed-of moment was upon her. By dawn her body ached with waiting and her heart was deluged by despair. Lucius did not come and Mariaerh's dreams dissolved in her tears.

For the next few days Mariaerh walked through her daily routine in a listless haze of futility and self-pity. She was crushed by a sense of total aloneness in the world. Nowhere to go. No one to turn to. Even her prayers were dry husks, empty words flung into the void of indifferent space until her natural resources of youthful resilience refused to indulge her anguish. Martha's words on the use of the will entered into battle with her despondent thoughts. She came to realize that nothing she could do would bring about a change in Lucius, so change must come from within herself. If the life she had planned for herself was doomed not to materialize then a new plan must take its stead. No longer would her every thought revolve around Lucius. No longer would she simply exist for the day when a child grew within her. She would find a new purpose for her life in the earth. If no one offered her a place in The Way she would create one for herself.

Acceptance replaced defeat; despair turned into resolve, and her need to be loved she turned into a deliberate effort to give love, not to a man, but to mankind. She put away her girlish dreams and locked the door on her childhood. Mariaerh had grown up.

# Chapter 8

When God made known to Moses His intent to meet with him face to face on Mt. Sinai, He instructed Moses to tell the people that they were to prepare and sanctify themselves, cleansing of all iniquity. Those same conditions, according to The Twelve, again had to be met for God to enter the earth in the flesh as Jeshua, the child borne by the virgin, Mary. Now the challenge was once more before the Nazarenes, to call all Israel to put away sin, to turn their hearts and minds to the One Crucified, that the Way may be made for Him to come again.

The believers took up the challenge gladly. They threw themselves into the task with fearless zeal. The Holy Spirit was with them and no authority on earth could deter them from fulfilling their purpose. Those who were God's would hear, those who were not would turn a deaf ear. The sheep knew their Master's voice, and the Remnant spoke in His stead.

Up until now The Twelve had confined their preaching to Solomon's Porch, and their acts of healing and of casting out demons had been reserved for the faithful, performed quietly and out of the public eye for fear of censure and retribution by the Temple authorities. Now their new insight and understanding of purpose made them bold, and their desire to hasten the Coming of the Lord over-rode their fear. The increase in believers and the success of the wonders they performed in Jeshua's *name* were all signs for them that the Holy Spirit was with them, and they emerged from the shadows of obscurity and lit their lamps of truth for all the world to see.

Old Annas, Caiaphas and other Sadducean leaders had paid little attention to the city's poor and the foreign pilgrims who gathered around a group of ill-dressed men on Solomon's Porch. They did not know who they were nor did they care as long as they caused no disturbance. Any rumors they heard of a Messiah or of miracles performed they dismissed out of mind, for prophets and healers arose in the land with maddening regularity and the less attention paid to them, the sooner they disappeared. Their followers were usually the poor and uneducated, ignorant wretches too lazy to study the Law and ready to follow any charlatan who promised them free bread. Only if the situation got out of hand and threatened the precarious peace with Rome was intervention necessary, which had happened in the case of the Nazarene. Then one day it did get out of hand and Caiaphas was forced to take action.

Peter and John had come to the Temple to meet with the others at three o'clock and had waited to enter the Beautiful Gate while a group of people ahead of them placed a cripple at his usual spot to beg for alms. The man was well known in Jerusalem. He had been born with deformed limbs and his only means of livelihood was to beg. Every day for nearly thirty years, kind-hearted friends had carried him to the Temple at its busiest hour, then carried him home again at the end of the day. When he held out his box toward Peter and John, Peter had automatically reached into his pouch for a coin then stopped as though frozen to immobility. A charge of energy coursed through his veins. He felt cold, then hot. His skin tingled and all his senses were heightened. He glanced at John and saw that he experienced the same sensations, and he knew that Jeshua wanted this man healed. Without a word exchanged, both men fixed their gaze upon the beggar and Peter commanded, "Look at us!"

The cripple's eyes lit up. People seldom spoke to him, they only dropped a coin and went on their way. He hoped this time he would maybe get more.

Peter said, "I have neither silver nor gold, but what I

have I give you! In the *name* of Jeshua, the Messiah, walk!"

Peter took him by the right hand and pulled him to his feet. The beggar cried out in fright, then realized that he was standing, without aid, on his own feet! He stared at Peter, then at John, his mind unable to comprehend what was happening. Then he took a tentative step. He could walk! He began to jump and skip and kick out his legs. For over forty years his legs had been nothing but useless sticks, and now he could walk!

He burst through the gate onto Solomon's Porch, shouting and crying and praising God, dragging John by the hand behind him. His shouts brought the crowds running and they stared in astonishment, stupified at the sight of someone they had seen nearly every day of their lives as a hopeless cripple now dancing ecstatically before their eyes. Women began to scream hysterically. Men pushed and shoved to be able to see. More and more people came running until a great crowd engulfed the three.

Lucius was with the other members of The Twelve and several believers of The Way at a far side of Solomon's Porch waiting for Peter and John to join them when they heard the outcry at the Beautiful Gate and saw people running across the court toward the site of the disturbance. They wondered among themselves as to what was happening but at first stayed where they were until the size and excitement of the crowd was so great that curiosity impelled them to see for themselves. By the time they reached the gate the crowd was so dense they could not see and no one on the outer fringes seemed to know any more than they. Not until they heard Peter's voice booming out over the crowd did they realize that the near riot had to do with their own. They tried to push through to the front of the mob, but no one would relinquish his place. Others had run in from behind them and they were hopelessly trapped in the midst of the crowd.

At the first sign of trouble the Temple police had sent word to their captain, but everything happened so quickly there was no time to prevent the crowd from amassing. The captain took one look and immediately went to Caiaphas.

Caiaphas walked out onto the porch off the Holy Place where he could view the entire Temple area. When he saw the size and frenzy of the mob, he feared he would soon have a riot on his hands. He called for some priests and a few of his Sadducean friends to investigate. "Go with the captain and find out what is going on down there, and if need be, arrest the instigators."

The captain assembled his men and marched quietly up to the edge of the crowd. Peter was calling for quiet, raising his hands and shouting over the din. Finally the mob saw that he wanted to speak and a hush fell over the court.

Lucius strained to hear and see. His heart pounded and his palms were wet. Fear of being crushed and concern for what Peter had done to cause such madness brought the taste of copper to his mouth. Peter's familiar Galilean slur resounded in his ears.

"Fellow Israelites, why does this surprise you? Why do you stare at us as if we had made this man walk by some power of holiness of our own? The God of Abraham, of Isaac, and of Jacob, the God of our fathers, has glorified His Servant Jeshua, whom you disowned in Pilate's presence when Pilate was ready to release him. You denied the Prince of Life. But God raised him from the dead, and we are his witnesses. It is his *name*, and trust in this *name*, that has strengthened the limbs of this man whom you see and know well. Such faith has given him perfect health, as all of you can observe."

One of the priests groaned. A Sadducean muttered, "In the name of the Most High! I thought we'd rid the land of this scourge!"

They had let Peter and John continue to speak to see how far they would go, but when they proclaimed the resurrection of the dead, it was all the Sadducees would tolerate.

"Disperse the crowd!" one growled. "Arrest those two. Throw them in jail for the night and we'll deal with them tomorrow."

The captain urged his men forward, ordering the

crowd to go on about their business, using their clubs to convince the reluctant to obey.

Lucius felt himself roughly shoved to one side and tensed for a fight. His fear was gone. A rush of madness pumped into his blood and the lust for battle coursed through his veins. He drew his fist back, but before he could swing, his wrist was caught in an iron grip, an arm wrapped around his neck from behind, and he was yanked from the crowd like a child's rag doll. He was pulled backward, stumbling and struggling to keep his feet. He was blind with rage, choking from the pressure upon his throat. When they were far from the melee, his enemy released him and he swung around with the intent to kill and looked into the face of Saul.

"What are you doing?" Saul rasped. "Have you gone mad? Why do you turn against the Temple police?"

Saul! His cousin from Tarsus! Lucius stared down at the short, balding youth before him and knew it could be no other. The same hollow burning eyes, crooked nose, and slightly deformed hips and thighs that he remembered from when they were children. A wave of annoyance and acute dislike washed over Lucius. Even when they were children, the younger, smaller Saul had badgered him into wrestling matches that Saul invariably won. He showed surprising strength for one his size, was wiry, agile, quick as a snake and as hard to hold. Now he had bested Lucius again.

Lucius emitted a sound of sheer disgust and spun away from him. He saw the captain of the guard and the Sadducees leading Peter and John away as the rest of the guard used their clubs and whips to scatter the crowd. He lurched forward, his impulse to rescue Peter and John, but again Saul caught his arm and held him back.

They struggled. "Calm yourself, cousin!" Saul ordered.

Lucius was livid with rage. "Let me go, you fool! Can't you see they are taking them away?" His eyes searched frantically for some help from his friends but they were helplessly lost in the crowd. He saw Peter and John disappear through a door in the wall and his body sagged. Too late. Nothing could be done now.

When Lucius stopped struggling, Saul released him and asked increduously, "What have you to do with that rabble?"

Lucius spat. "Rabble! You were a fool when we were young and a worse fool now! You were always so holy, so pious, so damned proud of your superior intellect that you never learned to listen with your heart. If you would, you'd never dare to call them rabble!"

"And you were always an incurable romantic, out to do good! As superior and self-righteous in your kind heart as I in my knowledge!" Saul shot back. "Why did I always win when we fought? Because big, strong handsome Lucius took pity on his lesser cousin!"

Their shouting caught the attention of one of the Temple police. Saul saw him watching and lowered his voice. "We're creating a scene. Let us get away from this place and talk in private."

"No!" Lucius growled. "I go to my friends."

"Heed my words, cousin. Keep away from that sect. They'll bring you naught but trouble, both from men and God!"

"Men maybe—not God!" Lucius retorted. He stalked away, trembling with rage.

The crowd was gone. Only a few clusters of men and priests remained to discuss the event that had taken place. The booths and stalls were closed, deserted. An eerie quiet hung over the courtyard where just a few moments ago all was chaos. Lucius took a deep breath to calm his anger and clear his mind. He was alone, separated from his friends and suddenly felt very vulnerable. He walked quickly across the vast empty court and fled through the nearest gate. He sprinted down the steps then paused to get his bearings. He had come through the Triple Gate, near to the wall and the Kidron Valley. His impulse was to turn left, to leave the city and go to Bethany where it was safe and secure, but logic told him the others would not leave the city while Peter and John were in custody. He turned right and followed the narrow, twisting streets toward John Mark's home in the Upper City.

Mariaerh was waiting for him in Josie's garden, and when Lucius came through the gate, she ran toward him, crying, "Lucius! Praise God! We were so concerned when you weren't with the others."

She did not touch him, though she wanted to throw her arms around him and hold him close in her relief to see him safe.

"You needn't be concerned, I can take care of myself."

Lucius spoke gruffly to hide his own relief at being safely among his friends at last. He gave no explanation about how he became separated from the others, ashamed of both the fear he had felt and the fact that Saul had prevented him from acting in Peter and John's defense. He had no wish to describe his cousin Saul to the Saints. The Elders distrusted his Roman blood as it was, and if they knew that a fanatic young Pharisee who hated them with blind bigotry was his kinsman, Lucius feared they would distrust him all the more. He decided not to mention the incident even to Nimmuo, for she would find it highly humorous that Saul had bested him again.

He questioned Mariaerh, his tone curt, impatient, as though angry that she delayed him with her childish fears when he was anxious to join the others. "The others are here then?"

His tone made Mariaerh feel foolish. "Yes. Marcus and Nicodemus have gone to question other members of the Sanhedrin to learn what Caiaphas intends to do, and Philoas has gone to the Fortress Antonia to tell Barrian what has happened and to solicit his help if need be."

"Who is Barrian?"

"He's in charge of the Fortress and is a friend. Everyone else is in the upper room, praying for Peter and John."

Lucius turned abruptly and strode toward the house without a further word. Mariaerh watched him with dismal defeat. Again rebuffed. As a wife she was not even allowed to show concern for her husband's safety. She would not resort to tears of self-pity! If that is what Lucius wished, she would never worry over him again.

She squared her shoulders and went into the house, refusing to show any reaction when Nimmuo flew down the stairs and into Lucius' arms. Mariaerh ignored them and went up the steps without waiting, but tucked the scene away in her heart to fester with so many others.

The Way spent a sleepless night in prayerful vigil. A meal was served, but few could eat. Marcus and Nicodemus returned. John and Peter would appear for trial before the Sanhedrin in the morning, and Philoas came back to report that Barrian sent some of his men to make sure that they would not be mistreated, but Barrian warned Philoas that he could only interfere at a critical point, and that any punishment short of death decided upon by the Temple authorities he would have to allow.

The Sanhedrin met in the Hasmonean Palace that stood next to the western Temple wall by the bridge that spanned the Tyropoeon Valley. Only members of the Court and disputants were allowed entrance so The Way was forced to wait for news in the upper room. It was a long day. The tension was nearly unbearable. The newer converts were optimistic, convinced that Jeshua would not allow any harm to come to the one he had named as the "Rock," or to John whom he had loved above all others. The Saints were not so confident. They remembered believing that God would not allow the death of His son, but Jeshua had hung on a cross.

It was late afternoon when Marcus, his father, Cleopas, and the others who were authorized to attend the trial returned to the house in jubilation, with Peter and John beside them. The Council could do nothing. Before their very eyes the cripple whom they all knew had surely walked. To punish Peter and John for healing would cause an outcry from the people and a far worse disturbance would occur than the day before. They let them go, but not before warning them never to speak Jeshua's *name* or teach about him again, to which Peter and John had answered, "Judge for yourselves whether it is right in God's sight for us to obey you rather than God. Surely we cannot help speaking of what we have heard and seen."

The Way rejoiced. Josie served a great feast. They ate, and sang hymns, and gave thanks unto God. The Holy Spirit had borne witness against their enemies. The sheep were returned to the fold.

\*      \*      \*      \*      \*

## Home of Marcus in Jerusalem

The Twelve continue to preach from Solomon's Porch, but the people fear to join them, even though they hold them in great esteem. Caiaphas' spies listen each day and the Temple police stand ready, their clubs and whips a visible deterrent to any who might voice agreement with The Twelve. Away from the eye of authority, people bring their sick and lame into the streets, so convinced of Jeshua's power that they think even if Peter's shadow should happen to fall across them, they will be healed. Their faith is justified.

We meet in secret. We draw the sign of the fish in the dust or whisper "Peace be with you" to indicate our faith. We do nothing to draw attention to ourselves, but live as inconspicuously as possible. We work at our trades, go home to our families when our work is finished. We attend the synagogues and keep all feasts like our unbelieving neighbors, blending unknown into the fabric of life in Jerusalem. We are like the yeast in a lump of dough, no one knows it is working until the dough rises up, then none can deny its existence.

The numbers of believers quietly grow. People from neighboring towns bring their sick and possessed, receive healing for body and soul then return to their homes as believers. The common fund grows accordingly and many who own property or goods sell them and lay the proceeds at the feet of The Twelve.

Not all is well. Dissension has arisen among us. Divisions have begun to emerge though we strive to maintain our unity.

We are a diverse sect. We transcend the barriers of rich or poor, male or female, master or slave, Greek-speaker or Hebrew. It is natural that those who speak Greek and those who speak Hebrew or

Aramaic should gravitate toward those of their own tongue, also natural for the young people to form their own group. The Elders' personal knowledge of Jeshua and the memories they share of those times of trial and joy serve to create a gulf between them and the initiates who do not have those memories to draw upon. The initiates, lacking in knowledge and experience, regard the Elders as figures of authority and feel themselves to be at a disadvantage and not as equal in the eyes of the Lord.

Standards for morality have become an issue for debate, particularly concerning those who attend the Synagogue of the Freedmen. These people are, for the most part, the wealthier and more socially prominent of the Greek-speaking Jews who have mingled freely in the Gentile world and have adopted many of the attitudes and social customs of their Greek and Roman associates. While they believe Jeshua to be the Holy One sent from God and willingly give of all they have, old habits of thought and deed are difficult to set aside.

Those who give most offense are the young. The more pious Judeans are dismayed by what they see as the lack of proper decorum displayed by those raised in the midst of Greek culture and thought. They are shocked by the openness of speech between young men and maidens and deplore the intimate license which is taken as a matter of course. They are more forgiving in their judgment of the young men, but are scandalized that some of the maidens also seek the pleasures of the flesh. They exhort the young people on the virtues of a chaste mind and body, reminding them that the body is the Temple of the Lord, created as the channel by which souls might enter the earth, but their exhortations more often than not go unheeded.

In days past, all questions were referred to the Rule of Discipline which covered every contingency of social conduct and laid down a precise procedure to govern any problem that might arise. The Remnant was then vastly fewer in number, imbued with the tenets and creed of the sect from earliest childhood, and the Rule was readily accepted and enforced. The Essene temple compound at Mount Carmel had then served as the heart of the believers, pumping the life-blood of faith and encouragement to all the brothers in the cities and camps. If the people could not come to the

Mount for spiritual refreshment, they sent their supervisor, and the network of communication and unity remained unbroken. In later years, the establishment of the City of Salt on the shores of the Dead Sea further served to bond them into an all-inclusive disciplined community where each person's talents and labor were freely given to the glory of the whole.

Now the sheer number of followers and the fact that they no longer live in closely knit groups but are scattered all over Jerusalem and Judea make the communal Rule of the Essenes virtually impossible to enforce. The old Rule is no longer valid, the old practices are no longer feasible. With Jeshua's coming, the heart of the sect shifted from Mount Carmel to Jerusalem. With His death, The Twelve now serve as Jeshua in His stead. Many new followers look particularly to James ben Joseph for guidance, his piety and physical likeness make him seem an embodiment of the risen Lord. We must formulate new rules, create a new order, slowly, as questions arise and solutions are sought in agreement of all.

It is often discouraging and frustrating. We struggle for unity, to maintain our oneness of purpose and thought, but just when the day seems darkest, an initiate appears who seems to have the Law written upon his heart and, in that day, we give thanks unto God.

Barnabas is such a one. He is my kinsman, so too of Thomas and Luke and Saul. His given name is Joseph, but The Twelve call him Barnabas, "son of encouragement." Barnabas is a Levite from Cyprus. When he heard in his own city of the risen Lord and that He will soon come again, he sold his farm and, with Marcia, his wife, gave the proceeds to The Twelve. They are eager for instruction and have adopted the teachings with consummate joy as if their souls knew all the truths and only needed their ears to remind them. Would that they were all like Barnabas!

Our trials are not all internal. The non-believers in the Synagogue of the Freedmen take great pleasure in baiting us. Our young people have become a challenge to the more worldly youth. They taunt our young men for what they call their lack of manhood, going so far as to call them eunuchs in an attempt to shame them into unchaste behavior, and they court our young women with flattery and promises of love. We are accused of being weak and too fearful of censure by our elders.

All of us who meet in Stephen's house resist associating with those non-believers and, by doing so, have become a particular target for their ridicule and scorn. Stephen tries to reason with them, to share with them the joy we find in following the Lord, but they laugh at his "man made God" and say he is either mad or consumes too much wine.

Nimmuo matches them taunt for taunt. They have learned to avoid her sharp tongue and, recognizing that I am equal to any mischief they might invent, pay her the respect that is her due. Mariaerh recoils from any disturbance and avoids the Synagogue, even in my company.

Philas revels in the contest. He enjoys debate and relishes pitting his wit and silvery tongue against opposition. He also relishes the young women and allows himself to be seduced and to seduce without a qualm. While aware of the Elders' thought on such matters, he counters their judgment by arguing if God had not meant the body to be used for pleasure, then why is it so pleasurable?

The Elders' cannot fault his defense of The Way. He listens with unfeigned interest to the non-believers' side of the issue, then demolishes their view with logic and reason in a manner they can accept without rancor. He is a valued speaker and has changed more attitudes and thought than does Stephen with his unyielding demand for purity. The Elders implore him to use self-discipline when associating with the opposite sex, and he solemnly promises to do so until the next pretty face banishes all such promises from his mind.

\*     \*     \*     \*     \*

## Home of Stephen in Jerusalem

The Greek-speaking initiates complain to The Twelve that the women who distribute the goods favor their Hebrew-speaking friends with the choicest portions while they are given the least. They have lived in poverty all of their lives and their minds are consumed with thoughts of how to provide bread for the table. The Way now provides for all their needs, but worry is addictive and old patterns of thought do not easily die. Out of habit they count each loaf they receive and weigh each cheese in the palm of their hands. They watch what their neighbor receives and compare it in quality and size to their own. They ask that The Twelve oversee the distribution of goods themselves to assure it is done in fairness.

These people do not know what they ask! Already The Twelve arise before dawn and labor until dusk. They mediate disputes, visit home altars, lead groups in prayer and instruction and preside over meetings where they are called upon to settle questions of faith and creed. I wonder that they have time left for preaching or healing!

The Twelve have chosen seven Deacons to oversee the distribution of goods. I have been overlooked, though am as qualified as any. Stephen is, of course, the first choice and a right one. He is without doubt a leader and loved by all. Neither Greek nor Hebrew would ever consider him to be less than perfectly honest and he has been made the keeper of the treasury over all. Philip, too, was an easy choice, held almost in the same esteem as Stephen, and Sylvia portrays the ideal of balance between earthly concerns and those of heaven.

I even understand their choice of Philas, though his election resulted only after great debate. His conduct and excesses with young females was a serious strike against him, yet he is popular and trusted by the Greek-speakers. The Twelve hope that this new responsibility will inspire him to change his ways.

The last three are women. Duors is a longtime friend of John and Thomas. Archar was recommended by Martha of Nicodemus and, it is hoped, Jacobean will be an influence for chastity among the young, for she is, herself, overly pious. I have no quarrel with the appointment of women, but I do believe my own qualifications and experience take precedence over theirs. I can only think that once again my parentage and former life testify against me.

*       *       *       *       *

# Chapter 9

The failure of The Twelve to include Lucius among the deacons was a devastating blow. He knew that Thomas had presented his name for consideration, and he took the rejection as a personal rebuff. His qualifications were obvious. His education, social standing, and experience with men of all walks of life were certainly far superior to those who were chosen and clearly marked him as a man well able to assume a position of leadership. He had worked hard for The Way, accepting every assignment willingly and had even submitted to the Elders' insistence that he attend Martha's class. They could not deny his dedication and zeal for the Lord, and still they had passed him over.

It made no sense. He could not fathom their reasoning unless it was again his Roman blood. The fact that Justin and Philoas were also Roman was of little comfort, for Justin had wed the Prefect of the sect, and Philoas the Lord's own sister.

With Stephen, Philip, Sylvia and Philas all engrossed in performing their new duties, Lucius found himself again on the outside of a circle of intimate friends. His visits to the Synagogue of the Freedmen became rare, nor did he go to Veronica's house as often as he formerly had for it pained him to hear the deacons' account of their work and to witness the high esteem in which they were now held.

Before deacons were chosen, Lucius had been the one others had looked to as a guide and instructor. He was the oldest and most experienced, and the fact that he was one of the seventy-two sent out by Jeshua himself carried a great weight of influence over the others. Now the young people turned to the deacons for a final decision or clarification on a point of doctrine and Lucius felt reduced, subtly edged aside and ignored.

He began to spend most of his time with Barnabas and Jehul. After the morning class at Martha of Nicodemus', he would leave Nimmuo and Mariaerh to their assigned tasks and make his way to the Lower City where gradually he became immersed in the daily life of the poor.

Lucius had lived among the poor before on his wanderings through the land, but his attitude then had been one of adventure, knowing that at any time he wished he could return to the ease and opulence of his father's house. He had lived among them, but not as one of them. His father's name and Roman blood had been a shield against oppression, and the pouch of coins hidden next to his skin in the folds of his cloak assured him of a bed for the night and a meal to fill his belly. His commitment to The Way had closed the doors on that security. His father's name was now a disadvantage, his pouch of coins had long since left his side to join the treasury of The Way. His only path for return to his former life was to renounce the Lord, impossible for him to do.

Lucius for the most part lived wth Barnabas and Marcia throughout that winter, returning to Bethany only two or three times a week, and then only to keep up appearances. He felt again the joy to be found in hard physical labor. He worked in Jehul's weaver's shop, hoisting heavy bales of fleece whose acrid smell brought tears to his eyes and coated his hands with an oil that even the strongest soap was hard pressed to remove. His hands became stained from the dyers' vats and his clothes reeked of sour cheese. He itched from making carpets and his hands bled from making tents, and he reveled in it all.

He came to love his new friends. Their raucous humor was coarse with bold irreverence and made Lucius laugh until he ached and tears rolled down his cheeks, and their simple faith and homespun ways touched him to the heart.

At three o'clock they set aside their chores and went to Solomon's Porch to listen to The Twelve preach. For Lucius this was the highlight of the day, to hear the Word as the new initiates heard, with wonder, awe, and ever-growing faith, then the chance to add his own knowledge and to explain The Twelve's meaning as they walked back along the winding streets to work again until the sun went down. At the close of the day when muscles ached and bones were weary, The Way would gather now here, now there, as many to a box-like house as space would allow, to share in the *Agape*.

Those who met regularly in Barnabas' house were Jehul and Rhea, Naomi and Cephas whose carpet shop was nearby, and Jonas and Susane who had come to live in the Lower City since the greater portion of those who needed their healing gifts were the chronically ill and poor. The four young couples had become close friends and included Lucius as one of them. If they wondered why he never brought Mariaerh to join them, they tactfully did not ask, but accepted him without question.

There were others who joined them, on a less frequent basis, each bringing some donation to the meal so always there was more than enough and no one went home hungry. Lydia was a weaver in Jehul's shop and had come with them from Laodicea. Sylvesta and Celia, both skilled musicians, played the harp while Naomi sang. Carvette and Agnosta were artists; Phoebe taught the properties and effects of color; Sachet a cook; Salome a lacemaker; Pasquarl and Eleiza, sister of Nathaniel, one of The Twelve, both served with Jonas and Susane as nurses, and many more gathered in fellowship to serve and follow the Lord.

When Lucius first began to join them for the evening meal, they had given him the honor of presiding over the blessing of bread and wine, an honor he had accepted as his due. After only a few weeks of living and working with them side by side, Lucius found himself embarrassed to be the chosen one each time. He came to realize that every adult who came to eat was as worthy as himself to perform that sacred rite, all were priests of the Lord. He declined the honor and took a place among the others, only presiding when his turn came about.

One day in Martha's class he listened as she taught the purpose for the souls' entry into the realm of the earth.

"Know that the purpose for which each soul enters a material experience is that it may be as a light unto others . . . not as one boastful of self or self's abilities in any phase of the experience, whether mental or material, but rather living, and being in that spirit which is ideal. Do not merely proclaim or announce a belief in the Divine, and promise to dedicate yourself, but consistently live in accordance with that belief. And know you, the test, the proof is long-suffering and not grumbling about it. Rather, though you be persecuted, unkindly spoken of, taken advantage of by others, you do not attempt to fight back or do spiteful things; that you be patient, first with yourself, then with others; again that you not only be passive in your relationships with others but active, being kindly, affectionate to one another. Remember, as Jeshua said, 'Inasmuch as you do it unto the least, you do it unto me.' As oft as you contribute then to the welfare of those less fortunate, visit the fatherless and the widows in their affliction, visit those imprisoned rightly or wrongly, you do it to your Maker.

"It is the 'try' that is the more often counted as righteousness, and not the success or failure. Failure to anyone should be as a stepping-stone and not as a millstone."

All through the winter months Lucius tried to improve his relationship with Mariaerh, but she was not responsive to any of his awkward overtures. He refrained from demands or orders, instead invited in a kindly manner, but Mariaerh consistently refused, just as kindly, but also firmly. He had tried to entice her by appealing to her desire to help others. He related the great need for service among the poor, but Mariaerh resisted, saying, "I'm sorry that I cannot help you in your endeavors, Lucius, but I have my own work to do."

Mariaerh was assigned to caring for the very young, and Lucius would stop by for her on the nights he returned to Bethany. Sometimes he made it a point to arrive early, to stand unnoticed and watch as she crooned a lullaby or told a story, or performed some task that saw to the children's needs. His heart would ache for his own sons. A curly head would evoke visions of Pebilus in his mind. He saw the tenderness and love that Mariaerh extended to all those little ones and he longed to have her hold his child in her arms.

He did not know how to approach her. His stubborn pride refused to let him humble himself, to admit that he was wrong or to confess his need for her and for a child. Fear of condemnation by the Elders and of rejection by Mariaerh restrained him from telling her the truth that lay at the root of his former conduct. Frustration drove him to seek solace in any young girl who would lend her body for temporary warmth and comfort, but they proved a poor substitute for the desire of Lucius' heart.

The winter proved to be unusually hard. Cold, drizzling rain quickly turned to sleet and then to snow, coating the city in a layer of ice. Walking was sometimes next to impossible. Falls were commonplace, and broken bones numerous. Frigid winds slipped through every crack and the limestone houses were as cold as tombs. Coughs and fevers ravaged lungs and took their toll on the young and old. Shrill cries of mourning were heard nearly every night while every dawn brought the sight of funeral processions, freezing, grieving families slipping and sliding on the icy streets as they went to bury their dead.

Luke moved in with Jonas and Susane and they worked around the clock, sleeping when they could, catching a nap here and there and eating on the run. Lucius worked with them, straining to understand an unfamiliar dialect and then to interpret the source of pain to Jonas or Susane. He bandaged broken legs and applied cold cloths to fevered brows. He held screaming patients in his grip while Luke applied the knife, praying that the sufferer would faint and oblivion would banish such agony. He mixed herbs and medicines, quickly learned to diagnose disease and to set a bone. It all came so easily to him that he wondered, had he not perhaps learned these skills once before?

The power of healing he had received from Jeshua as one of the seventy-two had not departed as he had feared might happen once he left to return to Laodicea. He found his hands and his eye's-touch, combined with prayer, could ease a searing pain and diminish a raging fever. His heart cried for the afflicted. He moaned with grief at the sight of a dead child and gathered a distraught mother into his arms and whispered soothing words in her ear. He thought then of his own sons, fed and warm under Vesta's tender care. They did not need him, these people did.

He saw the Crucified One in every suffering face, and came to know deeply in his heart the true meaning of Jeshua's words, "Whatsoever you do to the least of these, you do to me." Each time he alleviated someone's pain, he carried a bit of Jeshua's cross. Each time he cooled a fevered brow, he wiped the blood caused by a crown of thorns. He wept from weariness. He ached from a lack of sleep, but his heart knew peace, the peace that passed all understanding. His own petty trials faded into shadow, forgotten, drowned in the sea of others' need. He learned what it meant to serve.

The Elect spread out throughout the Lower City, bringing succor to any and all, whether believers in the Messiah or not. James ben Joseph came to help and his striking likeness to Jeshua reminded them all of when the Lord walked in the flesh, a light of hope in a darkened world. It was greatly due to James that the animosity toward The Way was not as great as it had been the winter before. The people revered James. He was Jewish as themselves. He spoke their tongue, cared nothing for earthly goods, and was not a threat to their tenuous economy. He asked nothing for himself, dressed as poorly as they. He knelt by the side of the sick for hours without complaint and promised them a life beyond this vale of tears.

The Jews knew he was a monk of the pious Essenes and that the Temple authorities condemned the sect as heretical outcasts. They did not care, for they saw living proof of his holy ways. When James preached the Anointed One risen in flesh from the dead, a stumbling block for the average Jew, he did so in the form and manner of a saintly priest in the Court of Israel, a form familiar and without threat to their own beliefs. Besides, who could forget the miracles his brother performed?

Spring came. Blessed sun and warmth and health, arriving early as if the Almighty One, Blessed be He, repented sending a winter so harsh and unrelenting. Those who survived brought gifts of thanksgiving to the Temple priests and turned their hearts from death to life. The city came alive. The rich returned, the seas opened, the marketplace swarmed with buyers. The cycle of life had again come full circle.

Spring came, but Jeshua did not. Again a group held vigil at the place where He arose, but this time in an attitude of commemoration rather than in hope that He would come that day.

A wedding feast was planned for Naomi and Cephas, and The Way was eager with anticipation. Mariaerh was among the married women who helped with the preparations, and, as the day drew near, she became caught up in the frenzy of activity.

Naomi's mother Salome was ecstatic; her only daughter to be wed at last! She invited everyone she knew and insisted that everything be perfect. For days a steady stream of musicians and entertainers paraded through the house displaying their talents for Salome to choose whom she thought was best. Fabric sellers and seamstresses argued volubly among themselves over the most appropriate color and cut, forcing Naomi to stand for hours on end with silks and linens held under her chin until her mother was finally satisfied.

Cooks tried one food preparation after the other until Martha of Syrus decided to bring an end to the experimentation and took over the kitchens herself. Salome moaned over the shabby condition of her home after years of neglect when they had all been occupied with following Jeshua, and demanded that painters and

artists and carpenters be brought in to restore its
beauty. Extra gardeners were hired, for most of the
festivities would take place out of doors. Tables and
benches and settees were necessary to accommodate so
many guests, and the courtyard rang with the sounds of
hammers and saws, and over all was heard Zebedee's
thundering voice as he stormed and bellowed and raged
over the upset in his house and the money spent on such
frivolity.

Mariaerh had never had so much fun. Throughout the
year she had offered her services in whatever tasks the
married women performed until they had come to
accept her presence as a matter of course. She was
delighted when Salome asked her to help with the
wedding, and later when Mary, the mother of the Lord,
requested her aid in making Naomi's wedding dress,
she nearly wept for joy. To make the bride's gown was
the most honored task in all the preparations, and was
usually reserved for close members of the family. While
Mariaerh was unusually skilled with a needle and
thread, she never dreamed she would be asked, for she
was not related in any way. She felt humbled and awed,
and so nervous she could not sleep. Her place in The
Way was forever secure.

The first day that Mariaerh was to begin her work at
Zebedee's she was almost physically ill with anxiety.
She arose early and dressed with care, trying to be as
quiet as possible to avoid awaking Nimmuo. She tiptoed
through the receiving hall to the jars outside the door
and shivered as she splashed the icy water over her face
and hands and intoned her morning prayers. The house
was just beginning to stir and she went to offer her help
in the kitchen, anything to busy her hands and make
the time go faster.

The walk to the city seemed to take forever. Nimmuo
was in high spirits and babbled incessantly over the
glories of spring, but Mariaerh was too full of her own
thoughts to pay her any attention. The sky was clear,
birds sang. The whole earth seemed impatient to shed
its winter brown and burst forth in a new garment of
living green, but Mariaerh hardly noticed.

Class that morning seemed never to end. The girls teased her mercilessly over her sudden rise in esteem, and John Mark solemnly swore to defend her from his tyranical aunts if need be. Their taunts were all good-natured and Mariaerh laughed along with them, but she wished they would stop for she was nervous enough without their teasing. Even Lucius was impressed. When John Mark and Philas offered to walk with her to Zebedee's, Lucius intervened, saying he would escort his wife through the city himself. Mariaerh was surprised and a little disappointed. Being alone with Lucius was always a strain and on this day in particular she would much rather have had the easy companionship of the other two friends. However she said nothing, and once they were alone, was even more surprised when Lucius said, "You bring honor to me with this assignment, Mariaerh. I am pleased."

Mariaerh knew he was trying to compliment her, but his attempt was so blundering and condescending that it made her angry. Why must he always judge everything about her in the light of its reflection upon himself! She was a person in her own right, a soul as individual as he and not just an appendage of Lucius of Cyrene. His rejection of her had certainly made that clear!

She drew her shawl closer around her shoulders and said coldly, "I'm sure it was only my skill with a needle that prompted Mary to request my services, not the intent to bestow honor on anyone."

They walked the rest of the way in silence; Mariaerh seethed with anger that Lucius had spoiled the excitement of the day, and Lucius wondered what he had said to upset her. At Zebedee's gate, he tried again. "I'll come back for you later so you needn't walk back to Bethany alone."

"If you wish, though I'm sure I'd be perfectly safe. You really needn't bother."

"It's no bother. I'm happy to do so," Lucius said quickly.

Mariaerh nodded and left him. Lucius turned back toward the Lower City thinking he would never understand the ways of women.

Salome met Mariaerh at the door and ushered her into a small room at the top of the house where the Lord's mother, his sister Ruth, Elizabeth and Mary of Syrus were already at work. Mariaerh returned their warm greeting shyly and Mary of Joseph tried to put her at her ease, but that first day Mariaerh's tongue seemed cloven to the roof of her mouth. She sewed virtually in silence, measuring each stitch as if someone's life depended on their uniformity and was weak with relief when Elizabeth called a halt for the day's activity.

After a few days Mariaerh relaxed and began to enjoy herself. Her awe of the holy women passed and she realized they were as other women. Mary of Joseph delegated the tasks, Elizabeth cut, Ruth and Mariaerh sewed seams and hems, while the two Marys worked the embroidery. The intricate detail stitching with real gold threads, Mary of Joseph reserved for herself. Once she handed it over to Mariaerh to try.

Mariaerh was aghast. "Oh, Mary, I can't!" she wailed. "I haven't had nearly enough experience. I might ruin it!"

"Nonsense, child," Mary laughed. "I was younger than you when I sewed the purple for the veil in the Temple at Mount Carmel."

She could not refuse the Lord's mother. She took the piece with shaking hands. Her palms sweat and her tongue worked against the inside of her mouth. She gingerly took a few stitches and then gave it back to Mary, quickly, as if the silk were on fire.

They all laughed at her and Mary hugged her. "So little courage, Mariaerh," she teased. She examined the few stitches closely. "See! You did very well!"

"Mother is easy to please, Mariaerh," said Ruth. "She always said I did well. Josie was the one to watch out for. She made me rip out more stitches than I put in."

Mariaerh knew that Ruth referred not to Mary's sister, John Mark's mother, but to Josie, Mary's handmaiden who lived with them since before Jeshua was born, and still did.

The days passed in easy companionship. They

worked hard. Mariaerh's fingertips became calloused from pushing the needle but her heart sang with happiness. Elizabeth's younger sister who was called "the Other Mary," Mary's sisters Salome and Josie, and Lia, Naomi's widowed sister-in-law, worked in an adjoining room on the bridesmaids' dresses and the two groups were often back and forth, solving one another's problems and exclaiming over the progress made. Mariaerh felt completely at home with them all. She had expected to find them quite somber and pious, given to prayer and devout conversation, but instead they were gay, spoke of ordinary, daily things, no different from her mother's friends whom she had known in Ain Karim.

There was a difference though. Never did Mariaerh hear an unkind word spoken against another. Never did she witness anger, pique or envy. The newer members in The Way called them the "Holy Women" and so they were. A wellspring of deep abiding love was always present among them. They uplifted one another, supported, comforted, encouraged one another. They lived the Word, the Gospel of the Lord, in every act and in every word that left their tongues.

Mary the Mother of the Lord set the tone. Her beauty and gentle mien were unforgettable. Just to look upon her loving face banished every adverse thought and emotion that lurked in anyone's mind and heart. Mariaerh found it hard not to stare. When Mary touched her it brought tears to her eyes and a melting warmth spread throughout her entire being.

On numerous occasions Mary's hands would suddenly become still and drop to her lap. Her face would glow, become almost transfigured. A smile, so poignant, so loving, would play at her mouth and her eyes seemed to melt into pools of ecstasy. The whole room would feel filled with warmth, an unseen light. All conversation and movement would stop until after a few moments Mary would take up her needle and begin her conversation wherever she had left off as if nothing exceptional had happened.

The first time Mariaerh witnessed that profound

occurrence she had been shaken to the depth of her being. Ruth had casually stood and motioned Mariaerh to follow her to the garden where she ladled cool water from one of the jars and gave it to Mariaerh to drink.

"Don't be frightened, Mariaerh," Ruth had explained gently. "You'll see this happen often. Mother and Jeshua are as one mind, one soul. I believe she is in constant communication with Him. It's as though she lives on two levels of existence, one here with us and the other, there with Him. I cannot understand or explain how this is so, but I know that it is. Sometimes their oneness becomes more overt, or noticeable, though those words are hardly adequate to describe it, and Jeshua's presence is felt and known by all who are near her."

Mariaerh's chin had trembled. She was close to tears from a sense of profound gratitude and privilege. She even felt humbled to be on such intimate terms with Ruth. She had ventured to ask, suddenly shy at even speaking to Ruth, "And you are His sister. Does He ever come like that to you?"

Ruth smiled and put her hands on Mariaerh's face as though to reassure her that she, Ruth, was an ordinary human being. "Yes. Though not with the intensity that He manifests to Mother. He comes to any and all who call Him and are able to receive Him." She groped for words. "Mother is so—so unique, holy. No one else I know has reached her level of purity. If Jeshua came to any of the rest of us as He becomes one with Mother, I think our bodies could not bear it, that we would die. Remember how the scriptures say, 'Who can look upon the face of God and live?' I think it is something like that."

Mariaerh could not understand all that Ruth had told her, but it did not matter. She simply accepted it, and her reverence for Mary knew no bounds. She basked in the joy and privilege of each day, and at those times when Jeshua's presence among them could almost be seen, she closed her eyes and let the peace of His love flow through her.

# Chapter 10

The day of Naomi's wedding dawned bright and clear. Mariaerh allowed herself the luxury of lying awake in the warmth and comfort of her narrow bed. The servants had refilled the mattress with fresh straw the day before and it was plump and soft, with a faint smell of mint that gave Mariaerh cause to believe they added a few leaves just to please her. There was no reason for her to rush today. The gown was finished. Mariaerh was free to enjoy the day as a guest while others prepared and served the feast.

She stretched and yawned, thinking back over the last few weeks with a sense of deep satisfaction, but also with a nostalgic twinge of regret that those days had come to an end. She rolled to her side and saw her own new dress that she would wear and was suddenly eager to be wearing it. She jumped up from the mat and unfolded the dress with loving care, marveling anew over the fine weave in the linen and the skill of whoever wove such a creation of graduating color. It began as nearly white at the throat, then blushed to the palest pink and continued to deepen in hue until at the hem it ended in vivid magenta. The dress was a gift from Naomi, and Mariaerh had never owned one like it and thought she probably never would again. It was simply cut, straight across at the throat with narrow but loose-fitting sleeves that came to a point at the back of her hand, the sleeves growing in color as did the body of the dress. There were no adornments to distract from the unusual blend of color except for a satin magenta sash and a cluster of magenta roses embroidered at each

113

shoulder. She caressed the roses, valuing them above all, for the Blessed Mother had sewn them herself.

Mariaerh pulled her sleeping shift over her head and poured tepid water from an urn to a bowl so she could bathe. She had the tiny room to herself. Nimmuo and the other unwed girls who were chosen by Naomi as bridesmaids had all spent the night at Zebedee's in the traditional wait for the bridegroom. Mariaerh bathed with leisure. She washed her hair with a sweet smelling soap then brushed it dry until it shone and lay in soft waves about her shoulders. She slipped her undergarments over her head, flipping her long hair free from beneath them, then put on the dress, wishing for once she had one of those full length polished sheets of copper that she had heard the Greek women used to see their own image. She did not roll her hair into a bun at the nape of her neck as she thought Lucius wanted her to do, but let it hang free, brushing it straight back from her brow and caught it with a ribbon the color of her sash just at the crown of her head. She tied the sash at the front of her waist in the smallest bow she could manage, then slipped her feet into white kid slippers, a gift from Salome.

The house was quiet. Everyone who would help with the wedding had already left for Zebedee's. Even Lucius was not there, for Cephas had asked him to serve as a groomsman and he had spent the night in the Lower City. Mariaerh left the house and walked to Thelda's where she would go to Zebedee's with her parents and relatives. Marh wept when she saw her and Jochim cleared his throat and approached her shyly, a bit overwhelmed by seeing his daughter so finely arrayed.

When they arrived at Zebedee's they found the gate wide open and music resounding through the air. The garden was a festive riot of color. Early spring flowers bloomed in profusion and adorned the gaily draped tables in lavishly filled Grecian urns, while multicolored, striped canvas booths were scattered throughout the lawns for children's games and wine and exotic delicacies, and every ancient, gnarled fig tree was festooned with lanterns and streamers of left-over satin and silk. Only a few guests lingered about, for word had just been received that the groom was on his way and most of the guests had gone out to meet him. They heard the high-pitched notes of reed pipes and the clash of cymbals and then the procession appeared at the gate, a long undulating ribbon of revelers, singing and weaving and shouting, "The groom has come."

Once inside the gate the men separated from the women and formed a circle around Cephas, clasping hands to shoulders and dancing around and around while the women clapped their hands and stamped their feet to the rhythm. Someone began a chant for the bride and all joined in, the chant growing in volume until the ground reverberated with their demanding cry.

A great clash of cymbals crashed over the shouts and the garden was suddenly still. Female voices, heart-rendingly sweet and poignantly melancholy were heard in the house, then the doors opened and the bridesmaids appeared, all dressed alike in pale blue silk with ringlets of flowers set like crowns in their hair. Each bore a wreath of tiny buds encircling a burning candle that twinkled like stars aligned in the sky. The bridesmaids walked in two lines, forming an aisle from the house to the groom, and when the last took her place just outside the door, their song ceased and Cephas, his voice deep, strong, vibrant with emotion, chanted the haunting strains of the Song of Solomon.

The canopy emerged from the great double doors, borne aloft on long poles by four young lads resplendent in short, embroidered white tunics. Naomi walked slowly beneath it, and a sigh went up from the onlookers. She was breathtakingly beautiful. Her gown floated and moved with each step, giving the illusion of a gentle sea awash in the morning sun. The undermost garment was of vivid blue satin, while the second garment was of the same pale blue worn by her brides-maids. The outer gown was a gossamer silk of purest white, embroidered with threads of gold that caught and reflected the morning sun. She moved slowly toward Cephas until she reached Lia who stood just behind the bridesmaids' line. Lia's face was drained of color. Her hands were clenched into fists and tears flowed freely down her cheeks. Naomi paused only long enough to exchange a look of profound understanding and love with her sister-in-law, then continued on.

Women wiped at their eyes and men cleared their throats in embarrassed emotion. Mariaerh was puzzled until Thelda whispered in her ear, "Roael sang thus to Lia on the day they were wed. It's a gift from Naomi, given to Lia in Roael's memory," and Mariaerh's own eyes blurred.

The ceremony continued in the traditional manner. James ben Zebedee read from the scriptures and led them in prayer, then gave his blessing to the bride and groom while they exchanged rings as a symbol of eternal pledge. They shared a token sip of wine from a common cup then smashed the goblet underfoot. They were one.

A great shout went up. The musicians began to play and the orderly guests dissolved into a milling babbling mass. Naomi was lost in a crush of embraces and Cephas was carried away to the wine tables. Mariaerh did not try to get near Naomi, but hung back, deciding to offer her blessing later when there was less danger of being trampled underfoot. She saw Lucius making his way through the crush toward her and steeled herself for his reproach over the arrangement of her hair. She thought how handsome he looked in his groomsman's finery, by far the best looking of all the men, and for a fleeting moment wished she had not deliberately displeased him, but quickly banished the thought and renewed her resolve to be a person unto herself. She could not read the expression on his face when he was near, for she had never seen it before, but he did not seem angry. He stopped a few feet away and smiled at her, looking at her from head to foot until Mariaerh blushed with embarrassment.

"You look quite lovely, Mariaerh," Lucius said gently with a note of surprise in his voice. "The way you've arranged your hair suits you well, and your gown is like the heavens at sunrise."

Mariaerh was stunned to speechlessness. Could this be Lucius who spoke like a poet?

He took her arm and said, "Come. I want you to meet Barnabas and Marcia. I've told them of you and they are anxious to know you."

Mariaerh nodded dumbly and allowed him to lead her into the crowd, wondering at the tender, possessive way he guided her through the throng.

Throughout the three-day celebration Lucius rarely left Mariaerh's side. He was affectionate, attentive, and his manner seemed genuine and not a pretense to influence others. He introduced her to all his new friends and made it a point to include her in their conversations.

Mariaerh was confused. If Lucius had boasted over the part she had played in the wedding preparations or over her intimacy with the Holy Women, she would not have been surprised, but he did not. In fact he never mentioned it and if others did, he held his tongue and allowed Mariaerh to answer for herself. Even when her name was mentioned as one of the Holy Women, which much to her surprise it often was, Lucius did not preen and puff himself up as if it were due to his importance, but kept silent and looked at her with husbandly pride.

This new Lucius was disturbing. Mariaerh felt herself being drawn to him and her old feelings of longing and need began to arise again. It frightened her and she fought against it, struggling to remain cool and aloof, insulated against the pain he could inflict, but as the days wore on her wall of defense crumbled. She basked in the warmth of his obvious approval. She laughed at his wit, and applauded when he joined in a dance. She accepted his offerings of food and drink with a grateful smile, marveling that now he waited upon her instead of waiting to be served. Her body responded to his touch, leaving her weak with a melting sensation that flowed from her heart through her veins until she wondered if perhaps she loved him after all. She feared the intensity of her own emotions, yet reveled in the glory of them. She felt as if she were on the threshold of a new life, but feared that first fateful step through the door.

Each day the merry-making began before dawn and continued late into night. All aches and pains and problems and petty differences were set aside and forgotten in the joy of celebration. By the last afternoon Mariaerh was exhausted from all the singing and laughing and the incessant talk, and she sought refuge on a stone bench in the rear of the garden, glad that the long celebration was coming to a close. Her throat ached, her ears rang and her eyes burned from lack of sleep. Her emotions were in turmoil. She had been praised and applauded and complimented throughout the entire three days, an intoxicating sensation she had never had to cope with before. She was suddenly known by everyone. They sought her out, enjoined her to participate in all the activities, and listened intently to all she had to say. For a girl who had always played the part of a quiet observer, her sudden success was overwhelming. She felt the need to be alone, to think and sort out the meaning of it all.

She hardly had time to relax when she saw Lucius appear from the corner of the house and walk toward her. Her heart leapt as she wondered if he had been looking for her. He was smiling as though happy to have found her and again she marveled at how handsome he was. The sun was hot and he shed his mantle, exposing his muscled forearms and the breadth of his shoulders. His tunic came just to his knees and Mariaerh admired the bulge of his calf and his straight, firm legs. She blushed at her thoughts and her flesh tingled when Lucius took her hand and sat down beside her, starkly aware of his thigh that gently brushed her own.

"I've been looking for you. Are you hiding out here alone?"

Mariaerh smiled nervously and admitted, "I did need to get away from the noise for a few moments."

They were silent, shy at being alone in one another's company, each struggling to find a neutral topic of conversation and unable to speak the thoughts that lay deep in their minds. A slight breeze loosened a tendril from the ribbon in Mariaerh's hair and it fell across her face. Lucius tucked it away, a gesture sensual and intimate that made Mariaerh suck in her breath and stiffen a bit at his touch.

Lucius' voice was low and thick in his throat. "I hope you take my advice and wear your hair down all of the time. It's lovely and shouldn't be hidden in a roll at the back of your neck."

Mariaerh felt the heat of a flush creep up her throat to her face. She lowered her head and found it difficult to breathe. She was about to agree to his wish when someone called his name in a high pitched cry of delight and she looked up to see Celicia skipping towards them with arms outstretched.

Lucius groaned and Mariaerh smiled, partially relieved and partially disappointed to be interrupted at such a time. Celicia was a member of the Synagogue of the Freedmen. Her father was a business friend of Zebedee's and the family had been invited even though they were not believers in The Way. Celicia was blond, pretty, and bubbled over with friendliness. She was one of the Greek-speaking youngsters whom the Elders deplored for their lack of sexual restraint, but Mariaerh liked her. Everyone did, for she was like an overly exuberant puppy, who loved everyone she met and cared not a whit for religious or political differences. She dropped down beside Lucius and leaned across him to Mariaerh, carelessly exposing her breasts in her low-cut, clinging gown.

"Mariaerh! What are you doing out here alone with this lady's man! Lucius will gobble up an innocent like you like a ravening wolf." Her hand rested on Lucius' knee and she looked down at it in mock surprise.

"Why Lucius! What pretty legs you have. I've never seen them in the full light of day before."

Lucius stiffened and quickly removed her hand. His face turned nearly purple and Celicia squealed with glee.

Mariaerh was sick with dismay. She knew at once that Lucius was one of the men who took advantage of Celicia's generous nature. Her mind spun. She knew Celicia would never deliberately hurt anyone. She might be silly and naive, even careless at times with her tongue, but she never would have spoken so freely if she had known that Lucius was her betrothed. Mariaerh had always known that Lucius did not live a life of celibacy, but the realization that after two years of regular attendance to the Synagogue of the Freedmen, Lucius had never seen fit to admit his betrothal, or by his actions toward her to lead anyone even to suspect that they were betrothed was unbearably devastating.

For a moment she could not speak. She fought for control, swallowing her outrage and anguish that again she had been duped, that again she had allowed her emotions to sway her good sense. She was trembling and her eyes blurred, but she refused to allow the tears to flow and expose her humiliation.

She drew on her anger for strength to stand, and, though her voice shook with controlled rage, managed to say quietly to Celicia. "You're right. I am an innocent. I'll leave him to your more expert hands," then quickly walked away before she would cry and make an even greater fool of herself.

Lucius called after her and attempted to follow but Celicia grabbed his arm and held him back.

"Leave her alone, Lucius. Mariaerh is sweet and gentle and could easily be hurt by someone like you."

Lucius yanked his arm free and swung on Celicia as if to strike her. He was incoherent with fury and Celicia cringed away from his rage.

"Curse you, Celicia!" he spat. "Mariaerh is my betrothed!"

Celicia's face drained of all color. Her hand flew to her mouth and she gasped, "My God! Lucius! I'm sorry! I didn't know.

Lucius made a sound of disgust and spun away. He stalked off, then broke into a trot, damning Celicia and himself and tried to find Mariaerh.

Mariaerh walked quickly toward the raucous sound of merriment. All she wanted to do was to flee, to escape and never see anyone again. The party was in full swing, the hilarity at a fevered pitch as it entered its last hour. When she approached the merry-makers she put a smile on her face and threaded her way through them, answering gaily when anyone called out to her but not stopping. She reached the gate and paused to see if anyone were looking her way then fled down the path to the road that led to Bethany.

Lucius searched everywhere for her, the grounds, the house, asking everyone he saw if they had seen her and growing more anxious by the moment. She was nowhere, and he decided she must have gone back to Bethany. He wanted to go after her, to explain, but as a groomsman he was compelled to stay until the end. He was filled with guilt. Celicia had been right about one thing, Mariaerh was sweet and gentle and he had hurt her abominably. Somehow he had to make her realize that a brief encounter with a woman like Celicia meant nothing, only a physical release to satisfy bodily passion and made no difference to the affection he felt for her. He inwardly groaned, not realizing until this moment how much he truly did care for her. He heard Cephas calling for him and gave up his search, reluctantly returning to the wedding party.

It was twilight before the festivities finally ended. Marh and Nimmuo asked where Mariaerh was and Lucius told them that she had become weary and so had left early, hoping against hope that it was true. As soon as they reached Martha's house he sent Nimmuo to her room to see if Mariaerh were sleeping, praying that she was, and was weak with relief when Nimmuo returned and said, "She's sleeping like a babe."

Lucius lay awake until dawn, tossing and turning and going over and over in his mind what he would say to Mariaerh. He would marry her, take her to wife as every other man would. Jeshua obviously delayed His coming for a time and chances were he would never see Vesta or his sons again and he wanted Mariaerh! He had been a fool not to see her beauty before. The memory of her in that colorful gown with her hair flowing loose on her shoulders made his loins ache with desire. He yearned for her small, warm body, willing and yielding beneath his own, and thought that morning would never come.

He rose at the first light of dawn and loitered about the house until Mariaerh appeared. She was pale and drawn, her eyes dull and lifeless but were not red and swollen from weeping. Lucius took heart and laid his hand on her arm, saying, "Come walk with me, Mariaerh. I wish to speak with you in private."

Mariaerh pulled her arm away and said without emotion, "There is nothing to say, Lucius."

"There is a great deal that must be said. I must explain my past actions to you."

Mariaerh looked steadily into his eyes and shook her head. "Your past actions have explained themselves from the first day that we met. I apologize for being so ignorant that I did not understand you. I'll not embarrass you with my foolishness again."

She walked away, leaving Lucius feeling forlorn and lost. He left the house and went into the city, hoping that time would heal the damage he had caused and vowing never again to cause hurt to that girl.

For the next few weeks Lucius tried everything he could to make amends, but Mariaerh was unapproachable. She made sure she was always surrounded by others whenever Lucius was near, making it impossible for him to speak to her in intimate terms. She stopped attending classes at Martha of Nicodemus' house, seldom went into the city, to avoid the necessity of walking with him. Marh was not well, and Mariaerh spent most of her days at Thelda's house and gradually came to sleep there more often than not.

Lucius was miserable. The more aloof Mariaerh became the more he wanted her. He began to listen, to really hear, the high opinion others held of her, and to realize that all the time he had thought of her as simply a shy young girl with little or nothing to offer, others knew her to be a wise, compassionate young woman. He marveled to see how often others came to her for comfort and advice. He paid attention when they repeated what she had counseled and was moved by her depth of understanding and insight into the problems people encountered in their relationships with one another. She never criticized, never condemned. Never did she pass judgment as to who was right and who was wrong, but quietly suggested a better way.

After a time he became angry that she would show such compassionate understanding where others were concerned, but turned a cold, unrelenting heart toward him. She counseled non-judgment and forgiveness to others, but judged and withheld forgiveness from him. He was jealous of her friendship with John Mark and Stephen, infuriated when they so easily evoked her laughter while all he could earn was a cool, stiff smile. Even Philas won more approval from Mariaerh than he did, and God knew Philas' sins far exceeded his own. When he saw that she remained as friendly as ever with Celicia, he threw up his hands in defeat and vowed he would no longer try to win her affection. He avoided her as she avoided him until they became as strangers.

# Chapter 11

The Feast of Pentecost arrived and again pilgrims from Laodicea brought letters from Lucius' family. Lucia was expecting another child, Philippi and Merceden pleaded for Lucius and Nimmuo to come back home, their loneliness and bewilderment evident in every line. Jesua wrote that he met regularly with a small group of believers who attempted in their own inadequate way to prepare for the Lord's return, but made no mention of Vesta or her sons.

The Twelve preached the Messiah at every opportunity. Many who came from the lands of exile had heard from their relatives and neighbors of the Nazarene and the healing works performed in His *name*. They converged on The Twelve bringing their sick and lame and possessed, avid for words of hope, salvation.

From the beginning of Man's advent into the realm of earth he had been obsessed with seeing what lay in the future. The prophets of old had fascinated their listeners with perplexing accounts of what was to come, speaking in the veiled language of allegory whose meaning produced a host of varied interpretations. The Twelve spoke clearly. They interpreted the prophets in light of the life of Jeshua, convincing with simple, persuasive eloquence anyone with ears willing to hear that Jeshua's life, death on the cross and resurrection of His body fulfilled the scriptures they had heard all their lives. Leaving little to the imagination, they recounted the Master's words of the tribulations to come and the way of His own return.

Again many pilgrims remained in Jerusalem, relinquishing shops and farms and cattle, sometimes family and friends, that they too might be on hand to greet Him when He returned and be numbered among the Elect.

All of this activity was not lost on the Temple authorities. They watched the burgeoning numbers of Nazarenes with increasing alarm. Every day they saw the simple-minded accept the blasphemy of a man-God, of belief in a man come back from the dead. The priests could feel the power they held over the masses slipping. The peasants' questions became bold, more pointed, and they were no longer satisfied with the traditional answers but shook their heads as though disappointed and wandered away to ask the Nazarenes.

The Pharisees were concerned and bewildered. Why, they asked, were the people turning away from the faith of their fathers? What prompted them to pose questions on life and death and challenge the traditional beliefs? A few Pharisees began to question their own answers and to pose new questions to themselves. Some even furtively sought out a lone Nazarene and after a lively discussion came away wondering if perhaps the sect did have some new insights into the age-old dilemma of life.

The Sadducees reacted with jealous fury. They were losing face, prestige and, with it, their power. The peasants now presumed to approach the Sadducees with confidence, as though they in their rags were as fine as a prince, flaunting their ignorance without shame. The Sadducees blamed the Nazarenes for the rebellion among the masses, and convinced the Pharisees that the evil preached by the Nazarenes must be stamped out or God would punish the whole nation for the sins of a few as He had done in the days of Moses.

The leading Pharisees reluctantly agreed, but cautioned Caiaphas to wait until after the Feast before bringing The Twelve to trial for fear of riot.

Caiaphas agreed. He sent spies to gather evidence against The Way, to question unsuspecting witnesses until he felt he had an incontrovertible case against The Twelve. He bided his time until the Feast had ended and most of the pilgrims returned to their native lands, then sent the Temple guard to intercept

The Twelve before they reached the Temple precincts and threw them all into the public jail. Again The Way waited in prayerful vigil to see what the morrow would bring.

The arrest had not come as a surprise. All through the week of Pentecost the Elders had received reports of Caiaphas' investigation, and The Twelve had noted for themselves the spies who listened as they preached. Each day they expected the Temple police to reveal their surreptitious plan, and their tension grew as each day passed leaving them free and in peace. When the Feast ended they watched the exodus of pilgrims from Jerusalem with some sense of dread, guessing that once the city returned to normal their fate was sealed. It was almost a relief when the waiting was over and Caiaphas made clear his intent.

This time The Twelve were better prepared. They waited at Zebedee's outside the city walls where the women and children would be safe in case of a major disturbance. Too many people had received the benefits of The Disciples' power for their arrest to go unheeded, and knowing the volatile nature of their countrymen, a public outcry against the Temple authorities would not be surprising and could easily erupt into riot.

Nicodemus, Marcus, Cleopas, and the other members who were in the Sanhedrin waited in the city, their own network of informers keeping them apprised of what occurred in the High Priest's palace.

The Saints were anxious but not filled with fear as they had been when Peter and John had been brought to trial. The Lord through the Holy Spirit had saved them then and their faith was great that He would do so again. They waited in Zebedee's great upper room, the doors and windows securely locked and guards stationed at the gate just in case Caiaphas threw caution to the wind and vented his anger against them all.

The house was still. The children slept blissfully, unaware of the potential danger that hung over their heads, while the Holy Women formed a circle of prayer, clasping hand to hand, an unbroken ring of purpose and faith.

It was a long night. The moon was dark, only the stars shed their faint light to break the blackness that covered the earth. The upper room was lit by only a few flickering candles and the rest of the house lay in total darkness.

The midnight hour had passed when suddenly sounds from the garden below intruded upon the silent vigil. The Holy Women stiffened. Prayer stopped, ears strained to hear. They heard the gate creak, then footsteps crunched on the graveled walk. Muted voices approached Zebedee's heavy door and they heard it swing open then close with a muffled thud. No one dared to breathe. Their hearts pounded. Heavy feet ascended the inside stair then the door to the upper room was flung open to reveal an ecstatic Twelve.

For a moment the faithful could only stare in disbelief, then they erupted into a babble of excited exclamations and questions. They surrounded The Twelve, hugging, crying, touching, as if only by touching their solid flesh could their eyes believe what they saw. The Twelve laughed with delight, thoroughly enjoying the furor they caused until Peter called for order and silence.

The Saints obeyed and tooks seats around the room, waiting in avid anticipation to hear how The Twelve came to be free. Salome began to light more candles, but James stopped her. "Let darkness reign yet for awhile. It will soon be dawn and the whole world will be bathed in light."

Salome looked at him fearfully and whispered, "Not all is well then. You are not safe?"

"All is well, but not quite safe. Peter will tell what has happened."

Peter stood at a table in the center of the room. James placed a candle in front of him so all could see his face as he spoke, and its flame was mirrored in his eyes. He spoke quietly, his voice filled with awe as if even he found it hard to believe what he told.

"We were not released. We escaped and the Temple police even now do not know that we are gone."

A murmur arose in the room. Jude ben Joseph asked,

"No one escapes from the public jail. How did you do it?"

Peter grinned. "You of all people should not need to ask that question. Are you not the Lord's own brother?"

Again the murmuring until Peter raised his hand. "We had spent the night deep in prayer, asking that strength be given to us to endure in faith whatever our enemies might bring upon us, when we saw a light advancing down the jail's corridor. We thought it was the guards, come to take us to a secret trial in the night as the cowards had done with Jeshua. The light grew steadily brighter and we were filled with fear, thinking so many guards meant they intended to kill us. The light was so bright we could not look upon it, but turned our eyes away, hiding our faces behind our hands. We heard the iron gate to our cell open, though we did not hear the turning of the key nor a human voice. The whole cell was awash in the light, and then it faded, as if a wick were trimmed on a lamp, and we dared to take our hands from our eyes and look."

Peter paused. His face was suffused with wonder. Tiny jets of flame danced in his eyes. His voice lowered to a timbre of awe and reverence as though even now his mind had not yet absorbed what had happened. The Saints leaned forward in their seats, already guessing what they were about to hear.

"A man clothed entirely in white stood in our cell, his garments the source of the light we saw. His face was hidden, not covered, but shielded from sight by the glow of his cloak. We were overcome with fear and we fell to our knees."

Peter's voice cracked with emotion. "He spoke, his voice so, so tender, so knowing, I cannot describe it to you. He said, 'Fear not, the Lord has heard your prayers and has sent me to set you free that His glory might be manifest in the world of men.' He motioned us to follow and led us out of the jail, past all the guards who were soundly sleeping, until we reached the street outside. There he said, 'Go now, then take your place in the Temple precincts and preach to the people all about this new life.' Then he was gone and we were left standing alone in the street. We came here directly and will stay with you for a while and then return to the Temple before dawn."

No one moved nor spoke. Peter wet his fingers and pinched out the light of the candle. He went to his wife and took her hand. "Let us pray now, give thanks to the Lord for our freedom and ask His help in whatever takes place in the morning."

Hands reached for hands, then all was silence until just before dawn when The Twelve left again for the Temple.

The men who waited at Marcus' house were also up before dawn. They had no way of knowing that The Twelve had been set free during the night, so followed their original plan to be among the first to arrive at the council rooms and obtain choice seats where they could easily see and be heard.

They entered the council rooms from the street entrance and saw there were many men there before them, the majority of them Sadducees. A guard stood at the door to the great hall checking off names of all who approached. Marcus and the others exchanged puzzled looks, wondering at this new procedure, then joined the line for entrance.

When their turn came, they gave their names and the guard admitted them, saying gruffly, "Follow that guard. He will take you to your assigned seats."

The Elect were taken aback. Cleopas demanded, "What do you mean, assigned seats? I have been a member of this council for most of my life and I have no memory of ever before being told where I must sit."

The guard sneered. "I only follow orders. Anyone who disobeys is to be ejected. Do you want to go in or not?"

Marcus saw that it would be futile to argue, so took Cleopas by the arm and said, "We'll go in."

The second guard led them to seats at the far end of the hall, while the Sadducees were taken to the front nearest to the High Priest's dais. Cleopas was livid with rage. "How dare he presume to install new rules without the vote of the body! I will formally protest his action. He cannot get away with this."

"Calm yourself, Father," said Marcus. "Caiaphas knows he is out of order and doesn't care if we protest or not. His objective will already be gained, which is to keep us isolated in a far corner for this trial."

The great hall was filling and it became obvious that Caiaphas knew more about The Way than the Elect had suspected. Nearly every Pharisee who had shown any sympathy to The Way was relegated to the back of the room while the most voluble voices against them were led to the choice frontal seats. When the last member was seated, Caiaphas and his father-in-law, old Annas, took their places in the ornate, high-back chairs on the dais and a scribe formally opened the proceedings, reading the names of the accused and the charges brought against them.

Witness after witness was called, mostly rabble who preened in their moment of glory and spewed forth nonsense of how they had nearly been duped to follow The Way but were saved by the Almighty One's intervention. Others were innocents whose testimony in favor of the The Twelve was the most damning, for on the surface it seemed as if they had unwittingly succumbed to the sleek rhetoric that flowed from The Disciples' mouths.

Marcus felt sorry for them. They came to defend The Twelve but the cunning scribes posed their questions in such a way that they seemed like lambs led to the slaughter.

No one who had been healed by The Twelve was called to testify, and when any of those whose sympathies lay with the Essenes tried to tell of miracles personally witnessed, the tales were so twisted that they seemed to be further incidences of sorcery.

Finally the last witness was dismissed and Caiaphas called a short recess while he sent the Temple guard to bring forth the accused. No one left the great hall. They argued among themselves over the testimony they had heard, their voices echoing in the high-ceilinged room with a muted roar. Marcus and the others were filled with anxiety and seethed with impotent rage at Caiaphas' manipulations. They were helpless. Every time they had stood to be recognized and allowed to speak, Caiaphas had overlooked them, pretending not to see them in the far reaches of the hall.

When a number of minutes had passed and the Temple police had failed to return, the members became restive, twisting and turning in their seats while their voices became more and more shrill. Finally the door was flung open and an officer entered and strode quickly to the High Priest's dais. He was obviously upset. His face showed a mixture of fear, bewilderment and anger, and his movements were spasmodic. The hall instantly stilled and the members strained forward to hear.

The officer's voice was strained, fearful. "We found the jail securely locked and the guards at their posts outside the gates, but when we opened it we found no one inside."

The Captain of the guard shot to his feet. "Impossible!"

Caiaphas' face reddened with rage. "Fool!" he spat. "You have let them escape!"

The captain winced at the High Priest's anger. "They could not escape! There is some mistake." He turned to the officer. "I'll see to this myself. If there has been treachery among your men, may the Almighty have mercy on you."

He began to stride toward the door but was interrupted by someone who stood at a window that overlooked the Temple courts. "Look there! Those men you put in jail are standing over there in the Temple, teaching the people."

A rush was made for the windows. Nicodemus clasped Cleopas' shoulder. They exchanged looks of puzzlement and then glee. Caiaphas was calling for order as the Captain of the guard shot through the door. He returned shortly with The Twelve, bringing them in without a show of force for fear of being stoned by the crowd in the courts.

The members quickly resumed their seats and order was restored. The Twelve stood before the dais as Caiaphas, trembling with indignation and his face quivering with unconcealed rage, began his interrogation. He reiterated everything that had been said before, his fury growing by the moment as The Twelve quietly listened and seemed unconcerned.

Finally Caiaphas lost all control and shouted, "We gave you strict orders not to teach about that *name,* yet you have filled Jerusalem with your teaching and are determined to make us responsible for that man's blood!"

Peter stepped forward. He was perfectly calm, not a hint of fear showed in his face and his strong fisherman's voice rang with power.

"Better for us to obey God than men! The God of our fathers has raised up Jeshua whom you put to death, hanging him on a tree. He whom God has exalted at His right hand as ruler and savior is to bring repentance to Israel and forgiveness of sins. We testify to this. So too does the Holy Spirit whom God has given to those that obey Him."

The hall became bedlam. Some screamed, "Death to the blasphemers!" while others shrank back in their seats in fear.

Caiaphas pounded the table for order, but they did not respond until Gamaliel stood with his arms upraised.

Gamaliel was a Pharisee, a teacher of the Law and the most highly respected and revered of all the Rabbis. The hall quieted. Gamaliel ordered the accused out of the court, then faced the assembly and said, "Fellow Israelites, think twice about what you are going to do with these men. Not long ago a certain Theudas came on the scene and tried to pass himself off as someone of importance. About four hundred men joined him. However he was killed, and all those who had been so easily convinced by him were disbanded. In the end it came to nothing. Next came Judas the Galilean at the time of the census. He too built up quite a following but likewise died and all his followers were dispersed. The present case is similar. My advice is that you have nothing to do with these men. Let them alone. If their purpose or activity is human in its origins, it will destroy itself. If, on the other hand, it comes from God,

you will not be able to destroy them without fighting
God Himself.''

Gamaliel persuaded them. In spite of it, the
Sanhedrin called in The Twelve and had them whipped.
They ordered them not to speak again about the *name* of
Jeshua, and then dismissed them.

\*   \*   \*   \*   \*

## Home of Lazarus in Bethany

The Twelve rested in Bethany for a time to allow their stripes to
heal but now openly defy the council's injunction and are preaching
in the Temple as before. They rejoice that they have been found
worthy to suffer as Jeshua had suffered and sing hymns of praise that
a blow has been struck against the forces of darkness. I admire their
courage and depth of faith. Suffering the pain of stripes holds scant
enticement for me.

The talk in the city is of little else beside the trial's outcome.
Many condemn the Council for its action, saying the yoke of Rome
is more than enough to bear without their own leaders adding to the
burden. They ask, if a Jew cannot speak freely in the Temple of God,
where can he? They are amazed that The Twelve continue to
preach despite the Sanhedrin's warning. The joy of conviction with
which the Disciples preach is obvious and the Jews wonder at the
source of such courage.

The people gather around The Twelve in ever increasing
numbers. They hear what their hearts have longed to hear, that the
Messiah they wait for has already come, been crucified and waits to
come again and gather the faithful to Abraham's bosom. Hope stirs.
Even the most timid secretly wonder in their heart if salvation does
not indeed rest with our outcast sect.

We are not without enemies. The rabble laugh and jeer. Fear of
condemnation for their debauched way of life vents itself in wrath
and scorn. Their love of strong drink, narcotics and every kind of
sexual perversion is greater even than their fear of God. We threaten
their depraved way of life and they cheer the Council's reproof.

The controversy also provides release for the common man's
impotence against all forces of authority. Pontius Pilate welcomes

every opportunity to try the Jews to their limit and takes a perverse delight in any scheme that forces them to choose between their loyalty to God or Caesar. Taxes exacted by Rome, added to the Temple's tithe, leave little in a man's purse to ease his miserable poverty. The poor and beleaguered transfer their hate for their oppressors to The Way, which they see as weak and powerless and despised as themselves.

Philoas journeyed to Caesarea to petition Pilate to exert pressure upon the Sadducees that The Way be left in peace, but Pilate sided with Caiaphas and commended his action. He displayed an overt prejudice against The Way, submerging his discomfort over the role he played in condemning an innocent to death. He responded to Philoas' request with fierce hostility and subjected him to a vitriolic diatribe against "those ignorant rebels." A curious reaction, since Jeshua had once healed Pilate's son. Philoas came away sobered, realizing The Way has a dangerous enemy in Pontius Pilate. He resolves to have him recalled.

The Sadducees, as to be expected, applaud the Sanhedrin's sentence. They fear the displeasure of Rome, knowing their tenuous privileges can be revoked without a moment's notice and they struggle to preserve their riches and high positions by pandering to the whims of Rome. Who knows, perhaps their lack of belief in a life after death causes them to cling to luxury and ease and to resist anyone who threatens its loss.

Saul is no less a thorn in the flesh. He is, without a doubt, the most brilliant of Gamaliel's students. His piety and zeal for the Law has earned him the loyalty and admiration of his fellow students and he has become their undisputed leader. I am told that Gamaliel cautioned Saul lest his zeal turn to fanaticism, gently reminding him that the letter of the Law untempered by love and compassion in its execution deprives it of life, and becomes a stumbling block to those it was intended to guide. Saul was stung by the chastisement. He complains to his friends that Gamaliel is blind to the necessity of the exact fulfillment of the Law and accuses his master of showing weakness.

Gamaliel's defense of The Twelve is discussed across the city and has swayed many to share in his point of view. Saul believes he is wrong and voices his complaint among his friends. While they are reluctant to criticize their teacher, Saul's forceful arguments are persuasive.

These young men are exuberant and eager to find a platform on which they may preen their love for knowledge and Torah. They have taken up Saul's cry for adherence to the Law and for the rejection of those who would usurp it.

I see Saul often in the Lower City where he lives and works at his trade as tentmaker. Our meetings invariably result in argument. He sought me out after the arrest of The Twelve to warn me that I tread the path to destruction by following blasphemers. He also warned Barnabas, but we agree that he is no doubt harmless, that he only attempts to make up for his lack of grace and attractiveness by an excessive zeal for the law.

The city is a cauldron of malcontent. The Jews, as is well known, take great pleasure in debating the Law and they debate this issue as well. Passions run high and those who sympathize with The Way have, at times, come to blows with those who do not. The Elders preach love and forgiveness and admonish them to turn the other cheek, to forgive seventy times seven times, but their words often fall upon deaf ears.

Judith and Justin came down from Mount Carmel and met with the Elders in Bethany. After some days of exchanged counsel and of entering the silence, it was decided to follow Jeshua's directive, to take the Word out of Jerusalem, through all of Judea, Samaria and Galilee. We reasoned that the absence of our leaders will remove the affair from the forefront of thought and defuse the situation. By the time they return to the city, the incident will no doubt be forgotten.

The Good News will be taken to Brothers who live in communities scattered throughout Palestine and the lands of exile. James and Matthew ben Alphaeus will preach in their native Galilee and their brother, Simon, and Matthias have chosen to go to the Saints in Damascus. Philip volunteered to brave the hostile Samaria to nurture the seeds of faith which Jeshua planted there, while Andrew and Thomas will journey to the desert lands west of Petros. James ben Zebedee and Nathaniel will venture farther afield, to Persia where Jeshua had gone as a lad to study under the great masters and magi. Peter, as leader of The Way in Jerusalem, deems it wise to stay near to the city and so chose the coastal cities along the Great Sea.

Jude ben Joseph and Thaddeus ben Alphaeus asked to be sent to Edessa. The King of Edessa, Abgarus, had once requested that Jeshua visit his country and heal him of disease. Jeshua promised to send one of his followers and the Elders agreed his promise should be kept. James ben Joseph will carry the Word into Perea and the Arab lands beyond the Jordan.

Only John ben Zebedee will remain in the city. His youth and family name are least likely to attract Caiaphas' attention and he is reluctant to leave the Lord's mother unprotected with the city in a state of turmoil.

*　　*　　*　　*　　*

Excitement ran rampant throughout The Way as initiates speculated over who would be selected to accompany each of The Twelve. Everyone hoped to be chosen, women as well as men, everyone with the exception of Lucius. His previous experience, passed over time and again by The Twelve, gave him little or no hope of selection and he refused to even imagine the possibility. He could not bear to be so disappointed once more and would not discuss it. He thrust the subject from his mind and went ahead with his daily routine appearing totally disinterested. When Peter asked him to be his companion along the coast, Lucius was stunned and could only stammer an incredulous, "Who, me?"

The big Galilean laughed and clapped a mighty hand on Lucius' shoulder. "You've earned the right, lad. You handle yourself well. You've gained an understanding of what we are trying to do, and show talent and fortitude to do it. Besides! I'm told you're accustomed to using your feet and making your way in unknown territory. Get some sturdy sandals and a good walking stick. You'll need both."

Lucius nearly danced with delight and could hardly believe his good fortune. To be chosen at all was more than he had ever dared to hope, and to be chosen by Peter was no less than a miracle. He sped to Bethany and swung Nimmuo high off her feet in sheer glee, then hurried to Thelda's to share his happiness with Mariaerh. He saw her in the garden as he approached and called her name from the gate, so filled with excitement that he did not bother to extend a greeting but blurted his good news even before he reached her side.

"Peter has chosen me for his companion!" he exclaimed triumphantly.

Mariaerh did not answer. Her face was blank and Lucius saw that she did not understand what he was talking about.

Lucius explained, his words tumbling from his mouth in uncontained joy. "He has asked me to go with him to tell the Good News to the Jews along the coast. I never thought I would be chosen, certainly not by Peter."

Comprehension dawned on Mariaerh's face. "Oh, I see," she said quietly. "That's very nice, Lucius. I wish you a safe journey." Mariaerh's lack of interest dashed Lucius' high spirits. He wanted her to share in his joy, to show pleasure and pride in his selection, but Mariaerh seemed indifferent to his news. Everything he had planned to say fled from his mind and he stammered self-consciously, "We leave tomorrow. I don't know yet if anyone else will go with us or when we will return."

Mariaerh only nodded.

Lucius was dismayed. He struggled to find something further to add. "Your Mother. Has she improved?"

"Some days she is better than others. Today she is feeling quite strong."

"I'm . . . I'm happy to hear so. You are a good daughter to her. I'm sure she appreciates your devoted care."

Again Mariaerh did not answer and Lucius found it useless to continue the one-sided conversation. "I should leave you to your duties. Is there anything you need before I leave tomorrow?"

"No. Thank you."

"I'll go then." Lucius turned away, then stopped and said lamely, "Take care, Mariaerh, and may God be with you."

Mariaerh waited until Lucius was through the gate then said softly to the empty garden, "And with you, Lucius, and with you."

# Chapter 12

Lucius and Peter left Bethany at sunrise. Ribbons of pink and lavender and shimmering gold streaked across the azure sky, a rainbow of color heralding the promise of a glorious day.

Lucius was buoyant. He felt freed from the stress and pressures that had dogged The Way and was eager for new adventures. The fact that Peter had asked no one but himself to accompany him on the journey added to his exhilaration and his spirit soared on the wings of euphoria.

Peter was as light-hearted as Lucius, and regaled him with tales of his boyhood on the shores of the Galilee, of carefree days with naught but blue skies overhead, gentle breezes and the comforting sense of a sturdy boat beneath his command. All he had wanted from life was a good wife, a full net, and to be left to live in peace, until one day a golden-haired girl called Judith had visited his father's house and his heart knew his dreams would never be realized.

Lucius listened with intense interest as Peter related the struggle that had taken place within his soul. He had rejected the Essenes' belief that the Messiah was soon to enter the earth. Even when he heard that the child had been born, he had brushed it aside as nonsense, yet an inner disquietude of spirit confirmed that his destiny lay with this child and his life of obscurity was soon to be lost in the wind. When Andrew returned from the Jordan and repeated the baptizer's words, Peter had reacted with anger, afraid to let go of the life he had planned until he had heard the Voice call his name and had seen the face of his Lord.

"Come! Follow me!"

Who could disobey! Who could not hear! The sheep know the voice of their master, and Peter knew the voice of his Lord.

Lucius was amazed, then humbled. He had never thought of Peter in any other light than that of his superior, the leader, the "Rock" on which Jeshua would build The Way. He would never have guessed that Peter, so sure, so forthright, so grounded in faith, could ever have struggled with doubts. Jeshua must have known the state of Peter's mind, yet had chosen him over all. Lucius was encouraged, suffused with hope that if one whom he thought of as a pillar of faith could have one time been shattered by fears, then he too could one day overcome the faults that plagued his own soul. He was touched that Peter would reveal his secrets as if they were intimate friends, and he felt profound affection for the fisherman from Galilee.

They skirted Jersualem, keeping to the path on the floor of the valley and, by mid-morning, began the ascent at the western end of the city. The road through the Judean hills snaked around great menacing boulders and sheer rising cliffs that were scored like the claw marks of a giant cat by the torrential rains that roared in from the distant sea. It was a wilderness of stone, bleak, barren, brown, with only a stray clump of struggling brush to break the monotony of color.

They climbed without speaking. The sun glinted against the rocky terrain and Lucius peered through only a slit of his eye. The hot stone burned through his sandals and scorched the soles of his feet. In less than an hour they were drenched with sweat, their eyes burned and their breath rasped in their throats. They stopped in the shade of an outcropping to eat a meal of cheese and bread, taking long pulls from the skins of water they carried in their packs.

They pushed on. When they reached the crest of the ridge, they gasped, for it seemed they could view the whole world from the place where they stood. They were panting, trembling with fatigue, but grinned at each other as boys who had just run a race and won.

The land sloped gently toward the sea, changing abruptly from the colorless, smooth-worn rock into lush valleys blanketed with multi-hued lilies of the field. They rested only until they caught their breath, then rushed to leave the stark isolation of the Judean hills and enter the verdant promise of life that lay at their feet.

They spent that night at a small settlement of sheep herders, sharing their strong goat cheese and tough black bread, and wine that was fit for a king. They squatted around a campfire with the stars hung low overhead and Peter told them of the night a star hung low over Bethlethem when a child was born in a lowly cave and grew to become the King of kings.

They made their way slowly toward the sea, stopping to speak with the shepherds and farmers they met along the way. Peter was a gifted storyteller. He wove his message of the crucified One through parables that mirrored the people's own lives. He laid his healing hands on the sick and lame and ordered demons to leave the possessed. Word spread throughout the countryside of the big fisherman from Galilee who healed by the very *name* of Jeshua the Nazarene, and soon there were crowds to meet them in every village where they stopped to rest.

At Lydda he healed a paralytic who had been bedridden for eight years, and they tarried there for weeks until messengers arrived with an urgent request that they come at once to Joppa.

Joppa was an ancient, walled seaport some thirty miles south of Caesarea. Few Gentiles lived there, in fact during the reign of Herod, the Great, Joppa was the only Judean town except for Jerusalem that was governed solely by Jewish law. The people of Joppa lived as their forefathers had lived, with strict adherence to the dietary law, keeping all the feasts and festivals faithfully as set down by their law-maker Moses.

A small, secret community of Essenes had been established at Joppa for generations, their proximity to

Mount Carmel along the coast to the north keeping them informed of all that took place within the sect. One of their women was desperately ill. When they heard rumors of the fisherman from Galilee who healed in the Messiah's *name* they knew who was meant and sent for Peter. The woman died before Peter and Lucius arrived, but Peter asked to be taken to her and, after kneeling in prayer for a long time, took her hand and commanded her to stand.

To heal and cast out demons was one thing, but to raise the dead to life was another! Lucius' mind reeled. He knew that Jeshua had raised the dead to life, but Peter? How could it be? What mysterious forces came into play that brought breath back into collapsed lungs and caused congealing blood to flow freely again?

Lucius and Peter stayed at the home of Simon the tanner, the supervisor over the Essenes. The townspeople's reaction to Peter stopped just short of adoration. They flocked to him in droves, bringing their sick and lame and blind and possessed for healing from the one who brought a dead woman back to life.

Peter preached the Messiah at every opportunity. He was welcomed in the synagogue, invited into private homes.

Lucius acted as his secretary and scribe. He set up home altars and prayer circles. He made lists of those who were ready for baptism and of those who were prepared to receive the Holy Spirit by the laying on of hands. He appointed teachers who were secretly Essenes to oversee each organized group and kept records of all who prophesied, to test if their prophecies came to pass. He arranged Peter's appointments and tried to keep Peter on schedule, setting aside time each day for healing, preaching, counseling with the Elders and for the many private audiences requested. He kept track of groups and households who were eager to hear the Word, and set up appointments so none would be inadvertently slighted.

There was a great outpouring of the Holy Spirit among the people of Joppa. Some spoke in unknown tongues, others found they had the ability to interpret what was said. Some received the gift of prophecy, others the gift of wisdom and others could heal. A network of messengers flowed to and from all The Twelve who labored in the field, and they all reported successes but also many trials and some discouragement.

Jude and Thaddeus had healed the King of Edessa and in gratitude Abgarus had ordered his entire court to adopt the faith of the Nazarenes. The Essenes of Damascus had welcomed Simon and Matthias with open arms, eager for the Word of the risen Lord, even though their orthodox neighbors condemned them for heresy and murmured against them in open hostility.

James ben Zebedee and Nathaniel found many in Persia who remembered Jeshua as a young man who studied there under the masters and quickly accepted baptism in water and then in the Holy Spirit. Philip also found that the seeds of faith that Jeshua had planted while still in the earth had taken root and grown in Samaria, and his reports reflected his joy.

Lucius was happy in Joppa. He was proud to be Peter's right hand and enjoyed the respect and prestige the office gained him. The city was clean and uncrowded. The fresh sea air was invigorating and cleansed his lungs of Jerusalem's stench. He felt free and unburdened. No Roman soldiers patrolled the streets and Caiaphas and his cohorts were far away. He missed Nimmuo, but was relieved to be away from Mariaerh for a time. He knew the day would come when he would have to resolve the state of their relationship, but the longer he could put it off, the better.

Lucius' hope for a prolonged stay in Joppa was not to come to pass. One morning Peter was praying on the roof when he slipped into a trance and saw a vision of a canvas lowered from the sky. It was filled with wild beasts and snakes and birds of the sky and he heard a voice say, "Get up, Peter! Slaughter, then eat." Peter refused to eat anything unclean, but the voice said, "What God has purified you are not to call unclean." Then he was told that two men were looking for him and he was to go with them.

When two Roman soldiers appeared at Simon's door,

Peter was not surprised. They served under the command of a centurion named Cornelius, a man of wealth and influence and second in command over all the Roman forces in Judea. Only Pontius Pilate held more authority than he. The soldiers reported Cornelius' request that Peter come to Caesarea and, though Lucius was wary and cautioned Peter to resist acting in haste, Peter was determined to obey the command in his vision.

They left at once—an easy journey only thirty miles up the coast from Joppa. When they arrived at the centurion's palace, they found not only Cornelius, but his entire family, servants and friends had gathered to hear what Peter had to say. Cornelius was a God-fearer, a Gentile who had studied the Law and the Prophets and believed in the One God of the Jews. He told them that he had experienced a vision. While he was praying, a man in dazzling robes suddenly appeared before him. "Cornelius," he said, "your prayer has been heard and your generosity remembered in God's presence. Send someone to Joppa to invite Simon, known as Peter, to come here."

Peter believed him. He began to tell them of the Nazarene when Cornelius suddenly began to speak by the Holy Spirit. Then the others also joined their voices until they sang a song, blending, rising, fading, growing, a song of praise and glory to God. Peter was amazed. He turned to Lucius and said, in a voice thick with emotion, "What can stop these people who have received the Holy Spirit, even as we have, from being baptized with water?" They baptized all of Cornelius' household that day.

Lucius was more shaken by what he witnessed than at any other time in his life. Merceden had insisted that her children be schooled in her faith and, all of his life, Lucius had been taught that only those who bore the mark of Abraham could inherit the Kingdom. But if Cornelius could reap the fruits of the Kingdom, then the doors were open to all. Lucius thought of Philippi and Vesta and of all his kinsmen and friends of his father's race. There were many God-fearers, people who sought an understanding of life that went beyond the belief in many gods. There was a hunger in their souls, a need to know who they were and how they came to be and, perhaps the most urgent question of all, where would they go from here?

Lucius remembered that Jeshua had known of his Roman blood, yet chose him as one of the seventy-two. He thought of the Gentiles Jeshua had healed, the centurion's servant, the Samaritan lepers. Did Jeshua intend Gentile and Jew to share the truth and live together in peace? Is this what the Prophet Isaiah saw when he said, "Then the wolf shall be a guest of the lamb, and the leopard shall lie down with the kid"?

A mixture of excitement and dread began to grow in Lucius' heart. He asked himself, why had Peter chosen him as his companion? Why was he the one to witness the Holy Spirit poured forth on a Gentile? The mingling of Roman and Jewish blood in his body had forever been a plague, but did it course through his veins for some unknown, specified purpose?

The question plagued Lucius' mind for all the months they stayed in Caesarea. He carried out his work for Peter as usual, but always the sense that he should be doing something else shadowed everything he did. He did not know what it was that he was expected to do. Bring the Good News to the Gentiles? He knew he was ill prepared to bring the Gospel to an unbelieving race and even if he were capable, where would he begin? His thoughts went round and round. His appetite waned; his nights became sleepless.

One day he was walking through the streets alone. A cold rain fell and his thoughts were as dark as the sky overhead. He walked with his head lowered, the hood of his mantle pulled far down his brow. He was miserable and dispirited. His work with Peter had lost its flavor. He was restless and weighted by a sense of biding his time. He felt close to despair and had nowhere to turn. He sighed into his mantle and uttered a half-hearted prayer. "Oh, Lord. What is it you would have me do? Where is it you would have me go?"

A sudden break occurred in the clouds and the

warmth of the unexpected sun caused Lucius to raise his head. He was on the causeway by the sea facing north and gazing directly at Mount Carmel. It was aglow in brilliant sun, rising in the distance above the sea like a beacon among the lowering clouds. Lucius stared in wonder. His heart was thudding against his breast. Then the clouds closed as suddenly as they had opened and the driving rain resumed.

Tears joined the rain coursing down Lucius' cheeks. His prayer had been heard and answered.

That night when he joined Peter for their evening meal, he was not surprised when Peter said, "I received a letter from Judith today. Luke is at Mount Carmel studying the records Judith kept regarding the Master's life. You deserve a rest; why don't you join him for a week or so? There are many things there you would find of interest." He might have known that there were no secrets withheld from this man.

Peter saw that Lucius understood, and laughed. "When the Lord wants something done, He opens all doors. We only have to choose to do it."

Mount Carmel had been known by sages throughout antiquity as a spiritual center in the earth. During the reign of King Saul, Samuel had begun a school for prophets on the isolated Mount where any children of Israel who demonstrated the gifts of the Spirit were brought to develop those gifts for use in the service of God. The Sons of Darkness had many times tried to expel the Elect from their holy place, and the Mount had known many battles with the forces of Belial, but God protected His Saints, and Carmel had flourished throughout the generations.

It was to Mount Carmel that Judith had come as a child, tutored and nurtured by the gentle monks until she arose to become the first female to hold the office of Prefect. It was at Mount Carmel that Mary, the mother of the Lord, was chosen by the Divine, kept and protected until the fruit of her womb could enter the world of men. It was here that the young Jeshua learned his lessons from Judith until there was no more she could teach him, and she sent him from the Mount to

Egypt, Persia, India, to continue his preparation as the Savior of the world.

Those were years of accelerated activity within the sect. Brothers from all over the world convened at the Mount as they looked for the coming Messiah. It was during that time that the old City of Salt had been re-established above the shores of the Dead Sea as a school, a scriptorium, a refuge for those who prepared for the Day of the Lord.

Throughout the generations the main purpose of the Elect had been to keep alive the true meaning of the Law in a world of forgetfulness and indifference, and to prepare the way for the entry of the Anointed One. That purpose accomplished, they now prepared for His coming again, to gather His own and establish His kingdom on earth.

Today the Mount was a haven of peace. Few members attended the feasts in the small temple on the Mount, and few made the annual summer journey to aid the monks in maintaining the compound. With Jeshua's ministry and subsequent death and resurrection, the focal point of the sect had shifted to Jerusalem. The Twelve were now the voice of authority, and the Saints gathered in the city to be near the new leaders.

The work of copying and preserving the scriptures and of compiling the records of Jeshua's birth, ministry, and death was still carried on at Mount Carmel and the City of Salt. Each maintained a school and an infirmary and lodgment for the old, but the numbers had dwindled. With classes now being held in private homes it was no longer necessary for the Saints to send their children away for instruction, and the communal treasury saw to the welfare of those whom age prevented from earning their own livelihood.

Lucius had entered the forest at the foot of the Mount. The earth was spongy underfoot and the sun danced in and out through the leafless branches, dappling the ground with moving patterns of light. The air was perfumed with tree sap and rotted foliage, a fertile, sensual odor that promised the advent of life. A narrow path was cut through the trees, scarred by gullies

washed by the winter rains that forced Lucius to
concentrate upon where he put his feet and to abandon
his thoughts about the Mount. It was cool in the forest,
but even so, droplets of sweat clung to his brow, the
effects of exertion from his upward climb. He was free of
the forest without warning. A red brick walk lay at his
feet and it drew his eyes upward, following it past low,
rectangular buildings, some large, some small, until
they came to the crest of the Mount and rested upon the
temple.

Lucius was out of breath, but still he gasped. He had
seen some of the most renowned architecture in all of
the world, but none could compare with the simple lines
and symmetrical beauty before him.

The temple itself was two stories high, nestled in the
midst of a large, walled court. The gate leading into the
court was huge, as high as the walls and wide enough
for two chariots to enter abreast. Both temple and court
were built of white limestone, sparkling in the sun like
glorious gems cut to size for the gods. Arched windows
overlooked the court and beyond, outlined with red clay
bricks that had faded with age to a soft, dusty rose. A
tower ascended at one corner of the temple with the
same arched windows all around and a wonderfully
carved stone railing that encircled a platform on top. A
porch extended from the upper story. It too was railed,
but with exquisitely carved wood, and Lucius could just
see the beginning of a gracefully curved double stair.
Rows of giant, soaring pines stood back from the court
along either side like a regiment standing guard and
restraining the advancing forest.

But it was the aura of peace that emanated from the
temple that filled Lucius with awe. He could sense its
holiness surround him with warmth. He felt he should
pray, or weep, or fall to his knees. He could not name his
emotions for he had never experienced such feelings
before. He only knew he had never been in such a holy
place.

"It is even more beautiful in the summer when the
flowers are in bloom and the grass green and the trees
fully leafed."

Lucius was so startled by the voice at his side that he jumped and cried out.

A white-robed monk smiled sympathetically and said, "Peace be with you, and welcome to Mount Carmel."

Lucius was embarrassed by his outcry. "Peace be with you," he stammered. "I'm sorry. I was lost in thought and did not hear you approach."

"You are Lucius. We've been expecting you."

"How did you know? Did Peter send a messenger to you?"

The monk shook his head. "Our Judith knows many things. She said you would come today. Your uncle awaits. Come."

Lucius followed him up the path and through the double gate into the court, bewildered by his enigmatic answer. Trees grew in the court, some encircled by stone benches. Other benches of stone and wrought iron were scattered about. A fountain played in the center and monks walked about or pored over scrolls, or worked among the flower beds. The court was hushed, the peace even more profound than when Lucius surveyed it from the base of the slope. He saw there were other gates, four along each side, though only half as wide as the one they had entered. They skirted the stair and entered a door beneath the porch that opened into a wide hall that seemed to run the length of the temple. They stopped at a door midway down the hall that the monk opened, then stepped aside for Lucius to enter.

Judith was sitting behind a magnificent, carved teak desk. She looked up and smiled, then came around the desk and clasped Lucius' hand in a surprisingly strong grip. "Peace be with you, Lucius. So you are finally here! That short walk from Caesarea took you long enough."

Lucius felt like a chastised schoolboy. "Peace be with you. I didn't realize you were expecting me. It's such a fine day, I took my time. I'm sorry if I kept you waiting."

Judith waved aside his apology. "Never mind. Young people are prone to wander these days. Are you thirsty? I'd offer you food but the *Agape* will soon be served and I don't want to spoil your appetite."

Lucius thought ruefully that his appetite had never been spoiled in all of his life. He was famished, having had nothing but a bit of cheese since he left Caesarea at dawn, but wine was better than nothing. He accepted the goblet Judith offered and found to his dismay that it was water, but he drank thirstily, grateful that at least it was cool.

Judith motioned to a divan behind Lucius. "Sit," she commanded, then resumed her seat behind the desk.

Lucius did as he was told and looked around the room. It had been an elegant room in its time. The furnishings were Roman, faded with age, but of high quality and discerning taste. A wonderful Persian rug graced the floor and the lamps were surely wrought from precious Corinthian copper. Exquisite marble tables held beautifully molded alabaster vases that would excite the most meticulous collector. Lucius' face showed his surprise. He had hardly expected to find such a room at Mount Carmel.

Judith watched his inspection in silence, then said, "It meets your approval?"

Lucius was somewhat at a loss for words. He was not sure if Judith wanted him to approve or not, and the sun shining through the window behind her head made it impossible for him to see her face and find a clue. He hoped his answer was neutral.

"It's a lovely room, though it seems a bit out of place on Mount Carmel."

Judith studied him for a moment, then said, "The answer of a diplomat."

Lucius flushed. Judith moved to a seat opposite him where he could see her face. "This room was the invention of Aristotle. He designed it to confuse our Roman persecutors and bemuse them into thinking we were a harmless bunch. He succeeded very well."

Lucius squirmed at Judith's derisive tone when she said "Roman" and at the term persecutors, aware that Judith knew full well that he was also of Roman blood.

"Who is Aristotle?" he asked in an attempt to steer the conversation away from his countrymen.

Judith's face softened. She relaxed, and her tone

became more friendly, less authoritative. "He was our Prefect prior to Jeshua's birth and during the time he studied here at Mount Carmel. I succeeded him and he went to the City of Salt to oversee our work there. He died there and is buried among the Saints."

She paused, remembering, then went on, her features pensive and her voice breaking a bit with emotion.

"He was a dear soul, beloved by all. A man to be reckoned with in all circumstances. He led us through the worst of times and never faltered."

She was quiet a moment, then brightened, and leaned toward Lucius as if to share a secret and her eyes danced with merriment. "He and I once fought like two cats over the propriety of this room."

She laughed aloud, a full, joyous, infectious laugh that compelled Lucius to laugh with her. "He put me in my place all right. He knocked me right off my arrogant, self-righteous stance and made a woman of me with one good blast of his tongue."

She wiped her eyes and settled back in the chair, again somewhat pensive. "There are few Aristotles in this world. He was Jewish, but raised in Rome of a wealthy family. Like you, I'd say."

Lucius recognized that he had been given a compliment and ducked his head to hide his pleasure as he guessed that she did not dispense them freely. Her hint of approval gave him courage to ask, "Are you still plagued by Roman authorities?"

Judith shook her head. "Not in the last years. Not since Cornelius commands the Caesarean regiment. He makes his yearly report on the activities of the Jews, but they are always in our favor. He's a good friend, a valuable ally, as you now know."

So, Lucius thought, she also knows about Cornelius. What more did she know? Her next remark sent Lucius' mind reeling and confirmed his suspicion that she was no ordinary mortal. She had leaned back in her chair and was again scrutinizing him with her disconcerting, steady gaze. Lucius was at the point of squirming with self-consciousness when she bolted upright as if she had come to some decision and said, "Well! Tell me what happened that day in the storm."

Lucius was so aghast that for a moment he could not answer, then he was angry. Blast the woman! She could read his mind! "How did you know that?" he demanded.

Judith ignored his anger and, with a click of her tongue, said, "How does anyone know anything worth knowing? By the Spirit! Everything we learn by any other way is so much trash. They tell me you're a traveler, an adventurer, full of worldly knowledge. Useless! I've stalked the earth a bit myself in my younger years and I can tell you that all knowledge that has any worth at all is to be found within. We are all ancient souls, after all, and we all know everything there is to know. Just too lazy to exercise the discipline it takes to bring it to our remembrance. Now! Will you tell me or not?"

"I might as well, you'll learn it anyway," Lucius said testily.

Judith laughed uproariously. "Now you're provoked! I've bruised the poor lad's selfhood!" she chortled.

Lucius grinned in spite of himself, suddenly liking her enormously. She was as changeable as the weather, first stern and authoritative, then soft as a kitten curled at the hearth, then unbearably domineering, and just as quickly as raucous and comical as his comrades in the Lower City. He sprawled on the divan and said affectionately, "I wish I had your Aristotle's tongue."

Again she laughed, that wonderful, marvelous laugh that he had never before heard come from a woman.

He told her then, eagerly, happy to do so, trusting that she would understand. He left nothing out. He told of his thoughts and his vision of what the world could be and of his desire to aid that vision in coming to pass. His voice lowered with emotion and reverence as he told of the sudden ray of sun that appeared in the storm.

Judith listened without interrupting. She was sobered and intent, hearing every word. When Lucius had finished, she stood and walked to the window.

"He calls you again, then. I thought He would. I've waited to see what He had in store for you."

She turned. The sun had moved far to the west and no

longer blinded her face. Her eyes were tender, her voice nearly crooning, "He knows His own, my son. You'll do well. We'll help you all we can."

A lump formed in Lucius' throat, but before he could answer, a monk summoned them to the *Agape*.

# Chapter 13

It took Lucius a few days to become accustomed to the routine on Mount Carmel. The Carmelites followed a strict Rule of Order that covered in detail nearly every aspect of daily life. Ritual washings were prescribed for set times during the day. A rule of silence was observed at all meals and, at appointed times, all activity stopped for prayer. There was an order in which they were seated, an order in which they spoke and an order in which they advanced in rank.

At first glance, the Rule seemed limiting to the extreme and prohibited all freedom of thought and action, but Lucius came to realize that the Rule conformed to a sort of rhythm, a rhythm in harmony with nature and man. Each monk became the Rule in the same sense that Jeshua became the Law, and by becoming the Rule, was liberated from all worldly cares and was free to pursue the loftier activity of mind and spirit. Lucius admired their dedication and fortitude, but knew he would never be able to conform to such restrictions over a long period of time.

Most of Lucius' time was spent in the library poring over the records of Jeshua's life and death. Much of the story he had heard before, but to read it in the form of day to day accounts, transported him back to those days and he felt as if he lived and shared them with the Saints. The documents of events and endeavors of the sect before Jeshua's birth filled him with a profound respect for the Carmelites' faith and unflagging sense of purpose.

There were other Hebrew texts that Lucius was

allowed to study, and one caused icy fingers of dread to squeeze his heart. It was a plan of war, a detailed battle plan in which the Sons of Light would engage the Sons of Darkness in an all-out bloody confrontation for supremacy over the world. The Lord himself with His legions of angels would fight at the side of the Saints, but for forty years the Elect would writhe in the pain and misery of war until the Era of Peace was ushered in.

It did not take much imagination for Lucius to recognize that the veiled word used for the enemy, the *kittians,* referred to the hated forces of Rome. He recoiled at the thought of his two strains of blood at war with one another. The only way he could see to forestall such a calamity was to reconcile Jew and Gentile in the tenets and creed of The Way, and his newly-found mission became vitally urgent.

Lucius studied the documents that outlined the rules for organization, paying particular heed to the Code for Urban Communities. He carefully read all the material regarding the coming age, filling his own journal entries with notes in preparation for the day when the responsibility for leading a community of Saints might lie upon his shoulders. His vision of the role he would play in preserving the Saints through their forty-year trial in the desert of war was still blurred outlines and fragments of disjointed ideas, but his experience during the storm in the streets of Caesarea fortified his faith that the vision would take shape and direction in the Lord's own time. Meanwhile he would go where he was led, do what was set before him to do, and watch for Jeshua's next command.

The network of messengers brought news from Jerusalem. Love matches and births seemed to be occurring with increasing rapidity among the Saints. James ben Joseph returned from the Arab lands to wed Suphor who conceived without delay. Martha bore a son to Nicodemus. Sylvia and Jeseuha had a second child before the first was weaned. Marcia and Barnabas had a daughter; Jehul and Rhea were about to announce a birth. John ben Zebedee and Mary of Syrus had recently wed and Lucius thought, ruefully, that no doubt they too would soon be the objects of female whispers.

With The Twelve removed from the city and no longer preaching Jeshua's *name* in the Temple courts or healing cripples in the streets, Caiaphas seemed to have forgotten The Way and the Saints were allowed to live in peace. But a letter from Nimmuo hinted that all was not as well as it seemed.

Saul had begun visiting the Synagogue of the Freedmen and was proving to be a popular speaker, particularly among the youth. He thundered a strident call to righteousness under the Law and for the abolishment of all heretical thought. He denounced all gods excepting the One and condemned any search for a new interpretation of the Law. Anyone who deviated one iota from the original faith of the fathers did so under the influence of Satan and would burn for eternity in the bowels of Gehenna, cast out, forever cut off from the tree of life.

The young people became enamored with Saul's charisma. His eyes, aflame with the ardor he felt for his cause, were entrancing, and his forceful gestures and resounding voice were even more fascinating than the words he spoke. His rhetoric was skillful. He often alluded to the warriors of old and his allegorical use of armor and weapons of war incited them into taking some action. He cunningly refrained from naming any particular sect or school of thought whose philosophy differed from his own, thus exonerating himself from any violence that might result from his oratory, but the youth in the synagogue took his denunciations to be directed at those of The Way, and Saul did not attempt to correct them.

Stephen debated Saul's bombast with logic and reason, using the Law and the Prophets as text-proofs for his faith, but the gentleness and consummate love with which he delivered his homilies were no match for Saul's fiery exhortations. Each time Saul appeared in the synagogue the harassment and verbal abuse heaped upon The Way increased, but the Saints held their ground and refused to be intimidated by hatred and spite.

Lucius was disturbed and spoke to Luke regarding his fears, but Luke did not think there was anything to become unduly alarmed about. No physical acts of violence had occurred, and while jeers and ridicule were difficult to endure, he could not see that any real harm was being done. He advised Lucius to write to Stephen and caution him to ignore the abuse and refrain from debating Saul. Lucius did so, but felt uneasy and wrote Nimmuo to take extra care.

There were no letters from Mariaerh, though Lucius, out of obligation, occasionally wrote to her. Nimmuo's letters informed him that Mariaerh had moved back to Thelda's house to care for her mother and, when Marh's health was restored, remained there. Nimmuo seldom saw her. She had not resumed her work with the Saints in the city, nor did she join the group who met at Stephen's house and attended the synagogue. She had begun teaching a few village children the tenets of The Way and had become so popular with the youngsters that her number of students had increased twofold.

The peace and silence and leisurely pace on Mount Carmel induced Lucius to give a good deal of thought to Mariaerh. His excuse of not making her a true wife because of Jeshua's imminent return was no longer valid. If his mission to bring the Good News to the Gentiles was to be successful, he must have the appearance of stable dependability like that of a family man, for a home and family were as important to Gentiles as they were to Jews.

Vesta could never bring him that image. She was uncontrollable and willful. She ignored his attempts to exert authority with a merry laugh and did as she pleased despite his angry commands. Intolerable behavior in one who would be a wife. She was irreverent, even in regard to the Greek gods, and she dismissed the Nazarene, labeling His teachings as a new superstition. He also knew that she had many lovers, that her fidelity lasted only while he was with her and that fact alone made even the thought of marriage with her impossible.

Mariaerh, on the other hand, was obedient and malleable. She knew the proper role for a wife. Marh had seen to it that she was skilled in all the wifely duties and there was no doubt that she would make a wonderful mother, and he wanted children. He longed for Pebilus. Hardly a day went by that he did not remember his son's bright, curly head or wonder how his brother had grown and what the boy looked like. It could be a delight to create a child with Mariaerh. She had proven at Naomi's wedding how beautiful and enticing she could be, and willing. Only the unfortunate intrusion of Celicia had prevented his taking her to his bed at that time. To have his wife regarded as one of the Holy Women would be a definite advantage for his purpose. She was devoted to The Way and was nearly as knowledgeable and experienced as himself in the teachings.

By the time Peter sent word to Lucius that he intended to return to Jerusalem for Passover, Lucius had resolved to heal the breach with Mariaerh and, with her at his side, begin in earnest his ministry for the Messiah.

Lucius went home to Jerusalem with Peter. After searching out Nimmuo and receiving an exuberant welcome, he went on to Bethany to find Mariaerh.

He approached Thelda's gate and hestitated. He rehearsed once more the speech he had prepared and gone over a thousand times during the journey back to Jerusalem, and wondered what he should say in case Mariaerh rejected him. He knew it was a possibility. She had shown how unrelenting she could be over the incident with Celicia, but then he had been weak and unassertive, allowing his guilt to override his authority. This time he would be firm and insist upon his rights as a husband. He gathered his faltering courage by taking a deep breath, then pulled the latch and swung the gate open.

Before he had time to close the gate behind him, Mariaerh emerged from the door of the house and stopped short as she saw him. She stretched her mouth into a thin line and formed her hands into tightly clenched fists that hung rigidly at her sides. She was stunned to see him. She had known he was expected to return with Peter, but thought she would have warning of his arrival.

Mariaerh had been painfully lonely while Lucius was gone. She had cut herself off from the other young people when she stopped going to the city and attending class, and with the leaders of The Way gone from Jerusalem, the Saints no longer gathered nightly at Martha's house so even that contact had come to an end. There had been little for her to do except care for her mother. Thelda and Elizabeth handled most of the household chores, and as Marh's health had gradually improved, Mariaerh found even less to occupy her time.

There was no one for companionship. The older women, more often than not, spoke of people and events long past, tales Mariaerh had heard many times and no longer held her interest. Her move back to Thelda's had put an end to the nightly, whispered confidences she had shared with Nimmuo as they lay in the dark on their pallet, and she longed for the harmless gossip about flirtations and petty quarrels that were common among the younger Saints.

She missed her friends. She missed Nimmuo and John Mark and Stephen and Jeseuha. She even missed Philas who, once he had learned she was betrothed, continued to tease and banter but without the sexual overtures that made her face burn with shame. And, as much as she hated to admit it, she missed Lucius.

With little to do and less to occupy her thoughts, Mariaerh had fallen into her old habit of day dreaming about the way she wished Lucius to be. In her imagination he was steadfast and faithful like her father; attentive and loving like Sylvia; teasing and affectionate like John Mark and as pious and good as Stephen. She created an image in her mind of Lucius coming home unexpectedly, calling her name from Thelda's gate and crushing her in his arms as she flew with ardor to meet him. No matter how often she tried to banish such thoughts from her mind, the day dreams had continued and the betrothals and weddings and births that occurred had only fueled her imagination.

Now he was back. Her heart raced with happiness as all her past fantasies flashed through her mind, but fear of rejection made her cautious and defensive and she waited for him to make the first move.

They stared at one another without speaking for a long moment. Mariaerh had changed during their long separation. Her breasts had become more full and strained against the bodice of her dress that had grown too small. Her arms were round and her hips had become womanly. Lucius saw that her thick, dark hair hung loose down her back instead of the usual severe roll at the nape of her neck. The long weeks of enforced celibacy made themselves known and Lucius set his face to guard against revealing the rush of desire that warmed his loins.

Mariaerh was dismayed. She mistook his stern look to indicate disapproval and wondered what she had now done to deserve his censure. There was no question of her running with ardor into his arms, for he obviously was not pleased to see her. She lifted her chin and walked toward him, speaking politely, as she would to any other guest.

"We have expected you. We knew that Peter was returning to Jerusalem and thought you would no doubt be with him. Do you wish to come in? I will fix you something to eat."

Her tone and formality angered Lucius. He did not want a quarrel so answered her evenly, trying to keep his irritation out of his voice. "I'm not hungry. I want to talk to you, Mariaerh. These many months apart have given me much time to think over our situation. It is time we resolved our differences and came to an understanding."

He also did not want their conversation overheard and commented upon by her family, so added, "Come and walk with me on the Mount where we can be alone and speak our hearts in peace."

Mariaerh hesitated, remembering the last time she had walked with him on the Mount when he had sent her to share a pallet with Nimmuo. She dreaded what he might have in mind this time, but her training in obedience overrode her impulse to refuse. She dropped her chin and nodded her compliance. She allowed Lucius to open the gate for her but carefully kept her distance lest their bodies should accidentally touch.

Lucius led the way up the same wide, sloping path they had taken before. It was late afternoon. The sun had lost the force of its midday heat and hung low in the cloudless sky. A gentle breeze stirred the olive trees and the air was redolent with field blossoms. The fine day and the beauty of the Mount lifted Lucius' spirits and restored his optimism. He stopped at a grassy knoll beneath a tree and said, cheerfully. "Sit here in the shade."

Mariaerh did as he bid and Lucius sat beside her with his back resting against the tree trunk. He put his head back and closed his eyes, saying, "It is good to be home. I've missed the Mount. I've missed the city and our friends here." He opened his eyes and looked at Mariaerh. "I've missed you."

Mariaerh ducked her head and avoided his eyes.

"I know you have reason to doubt it," Lucius said. "But it is true. I do have affection for you, Mariaerh, even if my past actions have seemed to deny it. You were very young when we first met. You seemed hardly more than a child to me and to take you as a wife seemed indecent. I did not lie when I told you that I did not wish you to be with child when Jeshua returned. He warned against it, but things have now changed. We now know He delays His coming."

Mariaerh picked a blade of grass and began to shred it. She offered no comment, too embarrassed to speak on such an intimate level. Lucius went on.

"There are many areas of misunderstanding between us, all, or at least most, created by our different upbringings. Such as the matter of Celicia."

Mariaerh stiffened. Lucius groped for words that she would not find offensive.

"Such casual liaisons are commonplace in Laodicea and no one thinks anything of them. They are taken as a matter of course. My father adores my mother. He would die for her without hesitation and yet he has known many such unencumbered involvements. My mother is not unaware of them and while she enjoys using her knowledge to prick my father's conscience, say during a quarrel, she knows they pose no threat to the place she holds in my father's heart."

Mariaerh could not hide her shock of this disclosure. Lucius took her hand and said, gently, "I know this seems reprehensible to you, but that is how it is. It never occurred to me that my indiscretions would cause you any disturbance at all, let alone the anguish I saw in your eyes when Celicia unwittingly told you of our casual former relationship."

Mariaerh was trembling. Lucius' hand tightly grasping her own sent shivers racing down her back. The subject he chose to speak of was shocking to hear from the mouth of a man. She burned with embarrassment and tried to dissuade him from speaking further. "Please, Lucius. This is not a seemly topic for discussion."

Lucius groaned. "You are wrong, Mariaerh! We must be able to speak freely to one another. We are strangers, though man and wife! If we do not speak freely, if we are not honest with one another, we will continue to guess at the motives behind our actions, at what our thoughts and feelings are, and create insurmountable barriers between us until we are both miserable and angry. Tell me your thoughts that day at Naomi's wedding."

Mariaerh was horrified. She could not possibly tell him that! She started to rise, saying, "We should go back, Lucius. No one knows where I am and Mother will worry."

Lucius pulled her back and said, "No! We are not going back until we understand one another."

Mariaerh was near tears. "Please, Lucius," she whispered, "I cannot."

"You can and will," Lucius said, firmly. "Tell me."

Mariaerh had no choice but to obey. She could not look at him, and Lucius had to strain to hear as she falteringly did his bidding.

"I—I thought you didn't want me, that you found me plain and dull and foolish. I thought you were ashamed of me and that the only reason you paid so much attention to me then was because Mary asked me to help with Naomi's dress and that you thought the only reason she asked me was because of you and that I couldn't possibly sew well enough and, and . . ."

Mariaerh could go no further. She began to sob and Lucius took her into his arms. He rocked her like a child and tried to comfort her.

"Hush, Mariaerh. There is no need for such anguish. You see what we have done to one another. You believed that I thought you unattractive when in truth I found you beautiful. You believed that I did not desire you when I ached at the very sight of you. And I! I thought you were totally unreasonable, using a harmless flirtation, for that is all I considered it to be, as an excuse to keep me at arm's length. I believed that you were perfectly content with this marriage that was not a marriage and used the incident of Celicia to keep it that way."

"Oh, Lucius! That's not true!" Mariaerh wailed.

"I know that now, but not until you told me. Do you see how vital it is that we speak our minds to one another?"

Mariaerh nodded. Her sobs had subsided. Her head had come to lie against Lucius' chest and her arms had somehow come to encircle his waist. She relaxed against him, unaware that she held him in embrace.

Her position was not lost upon Lucius, or its effect upon his senses. He ran his fingers through her hair and brought it to his face and inhaled its freshly-washed fragrance. He stroked her shoulders and down her back. He laid his cheek next to hers, kissed her ear and then her hair and let his hand explore her thigh, then hip, until it crept to her breast.

Mariaerh was lost in the confusion of her thoughts and in the contentment of being caressed and held. She did not realize what Lucius was doing until she felt the gentle pressure on her breast and heard his heaving breath. Fear washed over her. Fear of the unknown, of her vulnerability and of her lack of experience that could humiliate and degrade her.

Lucius' hand was pushing aside the front of her dress, searching for the warm, soft flesh he would find. Mariaerh panicked and tried to push free, but Lucius' arm and knees held her captive. His voice was hoarse with desire. "Don't go, Mariaerh," he groaned, "stay still. Let me have my way."

His hand found what it sought and Mariaerh gasped. He rolled her onto her back, his mouth locked against hers and his hands explored her body—tender, gentle, expert—moved across her bared flesh, probing, discovering her most intimate places until she burned with both shame and intense desire.

Mariaerh struggled to retain control over her body, terrified by the rising tide of physical sensations that washed in ever-increasing intensity throughout her being, but her body responded against her will. She was conscious of Lucius' rasping hot breath against her ear, and of a sudden, stabbing pain and the compulsive thrust of his body as he violated her own. Then her own body shuddered and seemed to explode and she cried out in both fear and ecstasy.

They were still. Lucius lay panting, heavy upon her. Mariaerh blinked back tears born of a multitude of emotions she could not identify. Tears of pain, remorse, humiliation, tenderness, wonder, fear, victory, love and an unfathomable sense of loss.

Lucius lifted himself from her and Mariaerh rolled to her side, turning her face away. He pulled her skirts down and curled himself around her back, cradling her in his arms. They lay quietly until Lucius asked, "Are you all right? Did I hurt you?"

Mariaerh could not look at him. She shook her head.

Lucius moved away a bit and rolled her to her back so she was forced to look at him. He grinned at her and teased, "You may not be the first woman I have known, but you are the first virgin. That should be of some consolation."

Mariaerh thought she would never understand how he could speak so freely of such things, even joke about them. She cried, "Oh, Lucius! How can you say such things!"

Lucius had been rearranging her clothing, and he laughed and pulled her to her feet and hugged her playfully. "Prudish, Jewish wife! Will you come with me to Martha's or shall I come to stay at your aunt's?"

Mariaerh was stunned. Was he saying that they would now, at last, live as husband and wife? She stammered, "What, whatever you wish, Lucius."

Again Lucius laughed. "My good, obedient little wife. Very well. There is hardly room for me at Thelda's so we will live at Martha's." He suddenly realized that Mariaerh needed an explanation to offer her family. "Tell your mother that I have decided since Jeshua delays His return, my reason for not bringing a child into the world seems to have become non-existent. It is the truth, though not the entire truth, as you have learned. It will suffice."

It did suffice. No one commented or seemed to find anything at all unusual. Marh and Thelda and Elizabeth helped her to gather her few belongings together, and Nimmuo and Martha welcomed her back with enthusiastic embraces and even Lazarus gave her a timid kiss on the cheek. She was at last a true wife and knew that soon she would also be a mother.

# Chapter 14

## Home of Lazarus in Bethany

Peter's baptism of Cornelius and his household shocked and outraged the Elders and they called him to account for his actions. They accused him of consorting with Gentiles, of entering their houses and eating with them which, to them, is clearly a breach of the Law. They say that the gift of baptism is a privilege reserved only to the Sons of the Circumcision. I and the men from Joppa bore witness to the truth of Peter's vision and, after much heated debate, the Elders conceded that it was the will of God.

The Way is divided over the Elders' decision. They cannot forget the long, bitter history of animosity between Jew and Gentile. It is understandable. The Gentiles have ever been the conqueror of the Hebrews and few times have Hebrews been free from Gentile domination.

Generations of political supremacy bred an attitude of superiority in the Gentile for the Jew and a distrust and resentment in the Jew for the Gentile. Many Brothers fear their old enemy will one day assert that attitude and subtly assume leadership of The Way and the pure teachings of Jeshua will become diluted, tainted by pagan thought and custom. They recite the warnings of the Prophets of old that the Elect avoid all intercourse with pagans. But others whose wisdom and awareness go beyond the literal sense of the scriptures disregard that argument and rely on the deeper, spiritual meaning where the pagan nations are but a symbol of the adverse emotions of man.

Jeshua is quoted by both sides. "Do not throw pearls to the swine. Do not visit pagan territory, go instead after the lost sheep of the House of Israel." Others remember the centurion's son, the woman from Tyre and even the son of Pontius Pilate, believing them as proof Jeshua extended salvation beyond the borders of Israel.

Events taking place in Rome strengthen the argument against admitting Gentiles. A rich and prominent Roman woman had embraced the Hebrew faith and, under the persuasion of four unscrupulous Jews, had given a gift of great wealth for the Temple in Jerusalem which the four had then cleverly taken for themselves. When her husband had complained, and rightly, of the fraud to Tiberius, the Emperor had been incensed and expelled all Jews from Rome. Those in The Way who disagree with the Elders are quick to point out the vagaries of Gentile thought that would punish thousands for the sins of a few.

All those who knew Jeshua in the flesh uphold the Elders' ruling, but the majority do not. Even Mariaerh is disturbed! She lacks faith, even in me, and is not convinced that my own vision is true! The season's intolerable heat dissuades further debate.

I write this account by the light of a candle in order to avoid the heat of the day, but even so I perspire. My tunic clings to my back. The reed slides in my fingers and my palm smudges the ink. What little breeze there is does not penetrate this abominable city and the yellow dust hangs in the air like a miasmic cloud.

Only James ben Joseph, John, Peter and I remain in the city. John bought a summer house in Capernaum for the Lord's mother. Josie, Mary's handmaid, Elizabeth and Mary of John are with her, hopefully enjoying the breeze from the Galilee. Naomi and Cephas have also removed to Capernaum where they aid Matthew in The Way there. Lia has gone to the City of Salt and Philoas and Ruth sailed for Rome as soon as the winter storms had abated. Philoas intends to meet with Tiberius and persuade him to recall Pilate. He has enough evidence of Pilate's cunning and malice to depose ten such men, and took with him witnesses willing to testify against Pilate.

I aid Susane and Jonas in the Lower City. Disease caused by this intolerable climate is rampant. Heat prostration, heart failure, sunstrokes, every malady is on the rise. Tempers are short fused. Children are quarrelsome and whining underfoot. The wealthy have quit the city in disgust and have moved to a more compatible climate, leaving the small shops and booths bereft of their coins. The loss of earnings augmented by the unbearable heat is responsible for outbreaks of violence within once close-knit families.

Even I become short tempered. I leave Bethany before dawn and sometimes do not return until long after sundown. This season is like the harsh winter two years ago when I stayed with Barnabas, but now, with a wife, I am obligated to return to Bethany each night. I resent the hour's walk each way and feel deprived that much more of my wife's company. We have so little privacy, even the *Agape* we share with others. A solution must be found to make this existence more bearable.

*    *    *    *    *

Even though he had resolved never to do so, Lucius drew against his father's wealth and purchased a home for himself and Mariaerh in Jerusalem. It was a modest home, particularly when compared to Philippi's, but hardly the hovel in which so many in the Lower City were forced to live. It contained three rooms, one quite large, and two smaller chambers across the back. An inside stairway afforded private access to a flat-topped roof where Mariaerh could spin during warm afternoons.

Lucius planned to use the two smaller rooms as sleeping alcoves, one for himself and Mariaerh and one for Nimmuo who would, of course, live with them. The larger room he intended for a meeting place. The *Agape* could be held there, as well as group study, home altars and prayer circles.

The location was convenient, midway between the Upper and Lower cities and near to the Synagogue of the Freedmen. Now Lucius would no longer be forced to endure the arduous walk from Bethany and back.

Lucius bought the house without consulting Mariaerh. He intended to surprise her and anticipated the look of delight on her face when he told her. He elicited his desired reaction from Nimmuo, but not from Mariaerh.

Mariaerh was shocked when Lucius threw open the door of the house and announced it was theirs. The school where she worked seemed to evaporate before her eyes. She did not want to live in the city. The city frightened her. Beggars reached for her skirts and the rabble leered as she hurried past them. The marketplace was crowded and filthy and impatient buyers were rude, jostling and pushing for a place in line. In Bethany she knew everyone and Jerusalem was filled with strangers. She tried to hide her distress as Lucius pulled her into the house and ushered her from room to room, all the time expounding upon its wonders. He obviously thought he was giving her a marvelous gift so she forced a smile and nodded her head in half-hearted agreement.

Lucius could not help but notice Mariaerh's lack of enthusiasm. He cut short his elaboration of the house's virtues and said, in a tone of exasperation, "You do not like it! What is wrong with it, Mariaerh? I thought you would be pleased to have a home of your own!"

Mariaerh felt she would be selfish to reveal her true feelings and tried to express her objections as gently as she could. "It—it's not the house, Lucius," she stammered, "I do like it. It's a lovely house. It's just that you took me so by surprise and I had not given any thought to leaving Bethany. Mother needs me to be close by, and it will be very difficult for me to continue my work at the school if we live here in the city."

Lucius was relieved. "Is that all!" he exclaimed. "Your mother will be delighted to have you established in your own home. Is not that every mother's desire for her daughter? Martha and Thelda will gladly see to her care. You need not worry over her. As for the school, there are any number of women who can perform that task. You will not even be missed. Here you will be able to perform a real service to The Way, as my aide and helpmate in providing a meeting place for the Saints."

For a moment Mariaerh could only stare at him, stunned, speechless, then she spun away so Lucius would not see the fury that flooded her face.

Again he belittled her accomplishments! He considered her school to be no more than a diversion to pass her time while he was off in Caesarea! She choked back tears of rage, frustration. First he wanted her to express her opinions freely, then made a major change in their life without even discussing it with her. He only wanted her opinions voiced when they were in harmony with his own. She knew if she spoke he would hear the anger in her voice and respond in kind, resulting in days of stony silence and tension between them, so she clenched her teeth and remained silent.

Lucius saw the tension in her back and thought she had turned away to hide embarrassment, that she felt foolish at not recognizing the advantages to the move. He approached her and put his arms around her, laying his cheek against her hair.

"You worry over-much about inconsequential things, a trait I find endearing," he said to reassure her. "Think of the pleasure you and Nimmuo will have in choosing the proper furnishings from the storehouse. This house can be as much a haven and refuge for our people here as Martha's home is in Bethany. What better way to manifest the Master's love?"

There was nothing Mariaerh could do but resign herself to Lucius' will. He was her husband and she was duty bound to follow his direction. She consoled herself by thinking he was right. She could make the house into a haven for those in The Way. She swallowed her sorrow at leaving Bethany and the school she had worked so hard to establish and refused to consider her fears.

She turned to Lucius and said, submissively, "Nimmuo and I could begin tomorrow, if you wish."

"I do!" Lucius cried, joyfully. He picked her up and swung her around. "I am a fortunate man to have such a sensible wife!"

Mariaerh refused to dwell upon her sense of injustice and loss. She threw herself wholeheartedly into making the house a home and the haven that Lucius envisioned. Nimmuo had a natural talent for arranging color, shape and size to give a room balance and sense of harmony. She and Mariaerh drew on the teachings of the Essenes regarding the effect of color and chose those colors which would be conducive to prayer, meditation and healing and would not intrude upon contemplative thought. While Nimmuo looked for aesthetic value, Mariaerh chose ease and practicality. Together they created a setting that encouraged intellectual and spiritual pursuit, but also provided comfort that answered the needs of Lucius' diverse groups of friends.

The house offered the privacy that Mariaerh and Lucius had never known in Martha's home. They no longer had to climb the Mount for personal conversation and, as Nimmuo was part of the family, both felt free to speak in her presence.

They were at last beginning to know and understand one another but their past misunderstandings made them fearful of starting a quarrel. They strove to please and took great care to guard their words to avoid giving offense. They approached one another with caution and treated one another with an unnatural courtesy and concern, often creating an atmosphere of tension and strain.

Nimmuo's incessant chatter filled the awkward silences that arose between them when they found themselves at a loss for what to say or do. Her boundless energy brought her into contact with many in The Way and she was an inexhaustible font of information and gossip, which often unknowingly eased the strain and defused a possible quarrel.

Entertaining guests was also difficult for Mariaerh. She could not dispel her sense of being a country peasant among Lucius' sophisticated friends and, for the first few meetings, she retreated into bashful silence, a timid observer of events taking place within her own home. Nimmuo understood and gently drew Mariaerh into conversations, asked her opinion and publicly acted upon her advice.

After a few weeks, a comfortable routine evolved and the tension eased. Mariaerh became more confident in her new position and, much to her own surprise, she slowly emerged as one of the leaders. Her initial fear of the city had proven to be without foundation and, while she missed her school, she found fulfillment in her new activities. Lucius' friends were now hers. Nimmuo was like a sister to her and Lucius seemed well pleased. She felt that she had at last successfully become the wife Lucius sought, except in one area and, there, even Nimmuo could be of no help.

Mariaerh's painful shyness would not allow her to respond to Lucius' passion. She could not discuss subjects of intimacy without stammering and feeling a hateful flush creep into her face. Any spoken word of intimacy sent her into a fluster of embarrassment. She could not bear to have him see her unclothed body, but bathed behind a curtain and allowed him to touch her only under the cloak of darkness.

Mariaerh was aware that her crippling sense of modesty reflected her stringent upbringing in matters of virtue and morals, but she also knew that her inability to give herself freely to Lucius stemmed from her lack of trust in his inner voices.

The scars left by Lucius' past conduct ran deep. Each time his hands and mouth tempted her to abandon her rigidly held control, her fear of being used only as an instrument for lust quickly cooled her desire and she frantically put a stop to his caresses. She feared if she once acquiesced to his demands and then one day he left her, she would not be able to bear it. The humiliation and degradation of nakedly revealing herself to one who did not love her would be beyond her capability to endure.

She wished it were different. She wished she could freely do anything Lucius wanted in order to please him, for she loved him to a degree she had not known was possible, but her fears overruled her love.

She was also jealous. Lucius was popular among the younger members in The Way, especially among the girls who were drawn to his unusual appearance, the combination of Roman and Jewish blood. He had the height, curly hair and facial features of a Roman, and the olive skin and dark, brooding eyes of a Jew. He followed the example set by Philippi and treated all women as precious jewels who must be protected and sheltered from the harsh world of men, and the young women found him irresistible. They were, for the most part, Hellenists, raised in the midst of the Gentile world where the interchange between men and women was much more free and open than in Judea.

Mariaerh was shocked when Jeseuha confided to Lucius her acute discomfort during her last confinement. Mariaerh would never speak of such things to a member of the opposite sex. She seethed with jealousy when one of the unwed maids would take Lucius' arm and draw him into a harmless flirtation, and burned with shame when she and Lucius were the brunt of sexually implied teasing.

Lucius was blind to Mariaerh's distress. When she suddenly paled and withdrew into silence, he accepted her feeble excuse of weariness and urged her to retire to their rooms to rest, which Mariaerh understood as his way of politely dismissing her.

Except in the area of intimacy, Lucius thought his marriage was nearly perfect. Mariaerh was uncommonly agreeable. She recognized that his advanced years and experience made him more capable of making decisions, and wisely deferred to his wishes. He thought her an excellent cook and well-versed in the dietary teachings of the Essenes. Her table was abundant with fresh fruits and vegetables, while fowl, lamb or fish were served only once a day and then in a meager amount. She urged him to drink a goodly quantity of fresh, clear water and, while he was accustomed to taking wine with his meals, he had to admit that he had never felt more fit.

He was proud of Mariaerh. He did not tell her so for he thought that she knew by the ardor he displayed. Marriage had added a glow to her already blooming beauty. Her dark eyes had become even darker, her olive complexion was clear and luminous with a rosy hue. Even her dark, shining locks seemed to have an added sheen and her girlish body had ripened into full womanhood. He desired her greatly and expressed his desire each night in the privacy of their room. When she reacted with shock and repulsion when he tried to arouse her, he simply satisfied his own need and fell quickly asleep, secretly pleased that she displayed modesty.

Lucius was also pleased with Mariaerh's popularity among his friends. He had thought her initial shyness was caused by youth and inexperience and had given it scant attention, thinking that time would be the cure. He had never noticed the effort Nimmuo made to assist Mariaerh through those difficult first weeks and, now that she seemed confident and at ease in her position as his wife, he believed he had been right.

With his marriage established on a firm foundation, Lucius felt he could turn his thoughts and energies to more important pursuits and leave his home in Mariaerh's capable hands.

\* \* \* \* \*

The young people in Martha's class were emerging as leaders of a new generation of believers in The Way. Five of the seven deacons appointed by Peter were from that group and all seemed to be endowed with gifts of the Spirit. They progressed from the foundation of faith laid by Martha, became initiates into the mysteries of God and relied upon the Holy Spirit to further instruct them.

They drifted away from participation in Temple life. The majority had been raised in the Gentile world away from the looming presence of the Temple and had little or no emotional attachment to Herod's great structure of stone. They came to view the Temple as a symbol of the self-aggrandizement to which man had fallen, deplored the hypocrisy they found in some priests and condemned the greed for power and prestige exhibited by the rulers. They were incensed at the injustices wrought upon the poor and believed that the sacrificial rites had become no more than an ingenious way to enrich the Sadducees and keep the people in bondage.

That attitude had long been held by the Essenes. Generations ago they had broken away from the Temple and had built their own center of worship and study on Mount Carmel. They believed in a coming Age of the Spirit, when God would once again speak directly to men. It was now understood that Jeshua's resurrection heralded the beginning of this new age and the outpouring of Spirit upon those of The Way was further justification for their faith.

The young debated Jewish text and law point by point. The body of man was the true temple of God, not a building of stone erected by the hands of men. The transcendent, Almighty God had no need for sacrifices of blood or grain but longed for the love of His children. God would heed the prayer of each soul who trod the earth, and those souls had no need for the rites of intercession overseen by the priesthood. Jeshua, the Messiah, was now the only advocate, they said, for His death had rent the veil between heaven and earth and God now communed directly through the Spirit. The Synagogue of the Freedmen became the stage for those debates, with Saul expounding the faith of the Jews and Stephen the faith of The Way.

Stephen's gift for preaching was extraordinary. He debated Saul with the eloquent tongue of an angel. He was fearless in his condemnation of the corrupt Temple leaders and openly accused them of polluting the Law. He affirmed that Jeshua was the longed-for Messiah and that His coming had sounded the death-knell for both the Temple and the Law.

Stephen and Saul flung the words of the Prophets back and forth like the handball used in games of sport. Both young men were inordinately agile and learned in the Law, but Stephen's understanding of the mysteries therein was far greater than Saul's and he usually emerged the winner.

If it had not been for the seriousness of the matter, those debates between two brilliant, pious young men would have been thrilling to hear. Bandy-legged, balding, Saul was the epitome of the impassioned prophet, aflame with zeal for the Lord, while Stephen, with his golden locks and sweet, loving face and the body of a young Adonis, reminded one of young David playing his harp in the fields.

The people were drawn to Stephen's oratory. He spoke with the passion of love, yet his message threatened the Jewish people's very foundation. The faith of the fathers that had sustained them through famine and war and exile, Stephen swore, was on the verge of collapse, and fear overcame their affection.

Saul could sense that while the people agreed with what he had to say, they loved Stephen. He was jealous of Stephen, jealous of his beauty and health and of his gentle, loving ways that drew people to be in his presence. He believed Stephen to be a tool of Satan, cunningly arrayed to lead the people astray, for his words were the words of blasphemy no matter if spoken from the face of an angel. Saul voiced that belief among his followers and the rumor soon spread.

News of the debates reached the ears of the Temple rulers. Caiaphas groaned and rent his robes in frustration and despair. He thought he had rid the land of that scourge when he had turned over the Nazarene and frightened his main followers out of the city. Now it arose again.

Some of the priests cautioned him against taking action, citing the youth of the two lads involved and reminding Caiaphas that the Synagogue was mostly Greek-speakers and that no truly devoted Jew would take it seriously. Caiaphas was appeased for the moment but he remembered that twice before such heresy had captured the minds of the faithful and he sent his spies to keep an ear to the ground.

There were other events taking place that occupied Caiaphas' thoughts and time. A self-proclaimed prophet had arisen in Samaria and was drawing frenzied crowds of believers. He claimed to know the hiding place on Mount Gerizzim where Moses had hidden the sacred vessels used in the tabernacle and promised to lead them to it. The Samaritans gathered around him in droves, disrupting commerce by abandoning their shops and places of business to follow the charlatan's heels.

Pilate was furious over the uproar. He wanted no disturbance to reach the ears of Rome and cause him embarrassment with Tiberius. He was putting pressure on the Temple authorities to put a stop to the nonsense and refused to acknowledge the difference between Jew and Samaritan.

Nor was that all. Herod Antipas was threatening war with King Aretas of Arabia. It was Aretas' daughter whom Antipas had divorced in favor of Herodias and Aretas had never forgiven him. When a boundary dispute arose between the two rulers, war was inevitable.

Herod's war was unpopular with the Jews for they had never approved of his marriage to his brother's wife, nor had they ever forgiven him for John the Baptiser's death. When he tried to muster additional troops from among the Jews, he was met with stubborn opposition and he pressured Caiaphas to aid him by ordering the Jews to comply.

The land was a hotbed of unrest. Tax revenues were down as the heat and lack of rain diminished the yield of crops and the cattle died of prostration. Even the Temple treasury had shrunk as few pilgrims came to the city and those who were already there had little to spare for sacrifices. The scramble for any loose coins was on and the Jews vied with the Romans for funds. The priests were hard-pressed to appease Pilate's wrath and the businessmen quarreled with each other. The debates at the Synagogue were temporarily discontinued.

# Chapter 15

After weeks of agonizing, scorching heat, the weather broke and a cooling breeze blew in from over the Great Sea. The colorless sky became blue again and the angry, white-hot sun softened to a friendly golden glow. Tempers cooled with the air, children could play in the streets again instead of complaining underfoot while confined to the shade of the house, and their mothers once more could take their work to the roofs.

Business resumed. The wealthy returned and foreign merchants who had avoided Jerusalem's suffocating heat now flooded the city to buy and sell, frantic to make up for precious time lost. The clink of coins exchanging hands was music to the ears of rich and poor alike, and the city heaved a sigh of relief and gave thanks to a merciful God.

The epidemic of ailments waned. Jonas and Susane released Lucius from his assistance in caring for the ill and he turned his energies to making his home a refuge for the Hellenists who followed The Way.

His work in the Lower City had left little time for Lucius to give any thought to events taking place elsewhere. Nimmuo and Mariaerh had attended the Synagogue of the Freedmen regularly and told him of the heated debates between Saul and Stephen, but Lucius had been too exhausted to hear. Nimmuo thought the debates were thrilling, and regaled Lucius with Stephen's expertise and hooted with triumphant laughter whenever Saul was outwitted. Mariaerh was less jubilant. She expressed her admiration for Stephen's gifts, but also her concern that the matter was going too far.

178

Mariaerh had lived in Judea all of her life. She was fully aware of her countrymen's zeal in protecting the Law and her childhood was steeped in stories of her people voluntarily sacrificing their lives to preserve the teaching of Yahweh.

Nothing inflamed the passion of a Jew more than an attack on his faith. He would willingly die in battle to protect the Law.

Although the majority in the synagogue were Hellenists and less constrained by issues of pious devotions, Saul's mania for the Law was infectious. The fact that Saul's father had been named a citizen of Rome, a privilege handed down to one's son, carried great influence with the Hellenists and swayed many to his point of view, otherwise he might easily have been regarded as simply another Hebrew fanatic.

From her place in the women's section, Mariaerh observed the expressions of hate and fear on the faces of those who heard Stephen, and felt the tensions that pervaded the hall. She sensed a growing undercurrent of deep-seated hostility toward Stephen that extended to everyone connected with The Way. She remembered that it was a mob that incited the riot that caused the death of the Baptiser's father when he proclaimed his faith in the Essenes, and she feared another such outbreak of violence. She expressed her fear again and again to Lucius, until he finally went to see for himself.

It was a warm, humid evening. The synagogue was filled to overflowing with visitors—an influx of Jewish merchants trying to cram a whole season's business into the few short weeks left before winter set in. Women were bustling about and chattering in high excitable voices as they renewed social ties and tried to arrange betrothals and marriages that would bring an increase to the wealth and prestige of their families. The regular, year-round members were more concerned over whether or not Saul and Stephen would appear that night and listened half-heartedly to the visitors' business propositions and the virtues of virginal daughters, while their eyes scanned the hall for a glimpse of the two antagonists.

Lucius left Mariaerh and Nimmuo in the women's section and joined Philas, Philip, Sylvia and the other young men of The Way. They found seats close to the front where they could come to Stephen's support if necessary, and settled back in tense anticipation.

Stephen did not need their support. At first Lucius was amused and delighted by Stephen's adroit handling of his fanatical kinsman. He applauded enthusiastically and cried out "Amen!" as loudly as any when Stephen cleverly drove a point home, but after a while he realized that the "Amens" for Saul far outnumbered those for Stephen, and the shouts against him were ugly and slanderous, and rang with hate.

The visitors cared nothing for the issues being debated. Indeed, if someone had questioned them later as to the topic of the debate, they would have been at a loss to answer. They only grasped that Saul expounded the traditional creed of the Jews and that Stephen taught some vague deviation of the Law. They automatically chose the side of Saul, and in Stephen found a scapegoat for their frustrations and ire. They stomped their feet when he spoke to keep his arguments from being heard, hissed and cried out against him with ridicule and scorn. Their crude behavior incited others to do the same and the great hall resounded with outraged malice.

Lucius became alarmed. Saul had spotted him early in the debate, and Lucius' presence seemed to fan the fires of his zeal. Each time Lucius applauded or called out "Amen!" Saul's eyes would flash with renewed fervor and his rhetoric would become even more vitriolic which in turn gave license to his champions to do the same. When Lucius realized what was happening, he stopped showing public support for Stephen and sat quietly without reacting, even though it galled him that Saul could dictate his actions.

Saul took Lucius' non-participation as a triumph and increased his venomous stream against Stephen until the mood in the hall became volcanic and teetered on the brink of hysteria. Lucius frantically signaled to Stephen to give way, to call a halt to the growing

madness. He went weak with relief when Stephen saw
his signal and complied, though with obvious reluctance, and conceded the evening's debate to Saul.

Lucius was shaken. He whispered hoarsely to Philas.
"All of you stay with Stephen and escort him out of the
synagogue lest someone begins an argument that could
easily come to blows." He left before he could chance to
meet Saul, knowing his anger with Saul was so great
that he himself could start a riot. He pushed his way
through the crowd toward the women's section where
he found Nimmuo and Mariaerh and without explanation, grabbed them by the arm and hurried them out
of the synagogue.

Nimmuo was breathless with excitement. "Isn't he
wonderful!" she exclaimed. "Poor old Saul hasn't a
chance against our Stephen!"

Lucius did not reply. He glanced at Mariaerh and saw
that her face was pale and her eyes wide with trepida-
tion. He put his arm across her shoulders and drew her
close to comfort her. "You were right, Mariaerh. These
debates have become dangerous. I must speak to
Stephen, try to convince him to stay away from here, at
least until winter when all the foreigners have returned
to their homes."

Nimmuo was shocked. "Lucius! You can't mean that
Stephen should bow to Saul!"

Lucius sighed. "You make the same mistake I made.
You see Saul as your laughable, eccentric cousin, a bit
mad and full of insecurities that he hides beneath a
cloak of religious zeal. I saw tonight that he is more
than that. His zeal is real, his love for God all
consuming. In his mind an attack on the Law is an
attack upon God. He will go to any lengths to defend
what he believes is an attempt to destroy the Law."

Nimmuo was not convinced. "He spouts fanatical
nonsense. What intellegent person pays heed to that?"

"Did you not see what happened tonight? Intelligence
and knowledge have little play when it comes to
religion. Emotion! When it comes to God a man thinks
with his heart and not with his head. Fear! Fear of the
loss of his soul to everlasting damnation. Even those

who dare to publicly proclaim the non-existence of the soul feel this fear, for somewhere in the depths of their mind looms the nagging sense that in truth they do possess a soul. To entertain a notion that deviates from the teaching heard at their mothers' knee is to court annihilation and risk losing their membership as one of God's chosen people."

"Then they are fools," Nimmuo retorted.

"Saul is not a fool," Lucius warned. "He is brilliant, dedicated, unwavering in his conviction. Listen to his words! He believes he is the mighty arm of the Lord, slaying his enemies with the sword of his tongue. He believes that sword is weapon enough, at least for now, but he begins to be carried away by his own rhetoric, and words will one day be not enough and he'll search for a more powerful weapon to use."

Nimmuo was aghast. "Surely you can't believe Saul would come against us in violence!"

Lucius did not answer. He would never have thought so before tonight, but now he felt Saul was capable of anything if he thought it were the will of God. He was sobered, and filled with apprehension. A shiver raced down his back and he was suddenly enveloped in a sense of impending doom.

"I want you and Mariaerh to stay away from the synagogue for a time."

Nimmuo started to protest, but Lucius cut her off. "That's an order, Nimmuo, and I will not be disobeyed in this matter."

Nimmuo sulked all the way home, but knew it was useless to argue and that she had no choice but to do as Lucius commanded. As soon as they reached the house, she went directly to her bed, thinking that Lucius had exaggerated the whole matter and that the Saints were in no danger from one of the likes of Saul.

During the next few days Lucius used all of his powers of persuasion to try to convince Stephen and the others of the threat Saul imposed, but they held the same attitude as Nimmuo. Stephen enjoyed pitting his gifts against an adversary as capable as Saul, and refused to back down. Sylvia, Philas, and Philip agreed, accusing Lucius of a lack of faith that Jeshua was with them and thus they could come to no harm.

Lucius gave up his efforts, but his sense of doom did not abate and he held Nimmuo and Mariaerh to his order that they stay away. He too did not go to the synagogue. At least the others agreed with him that his presence only served to incite Saul's fury and that his absence would help to keep the debates to the issues instead of dissolving into an emotional tirade.

A few of the young adults in the synagogue wondered if Stephen's proclamation that Jeshua was the longed-for Messiah and that His death ushered a new age into the world of men was true. They were idealistic youth who viewed the hypocrisy and shallow faith of their elders with contempt and disgust and abhorred the pomp and glory of the Temple feastdays, thinking that the money would be better spent to alleviate the misery of the poor. They were ashamed of their fathers who paid little heed to how their fortunes were made, and felt their concessions to Rome were traitorous to the people of God. The thought of a just and holy leader who would restore Israel to its former glory as a nation ruled by God was exciting to the extreme, and the more daring quietly sought out Stephen to hear more of the One who was soon to return in glory from the clouds on high.

They were courageous, for they risked ostracism by their peers and condemnation from their elders, yet their impatience and hunger for their people's long-promised redemption made the perils negligible. Lucius invited them to attend the meetings for prayer that were held in his home, then began a class to initiate them into The Way. The class began with only a few, but as summer waned and autumn began, their number steadily increased.

At first they came in secret, telling no one where they spent each afternoon, but as the class grew, word began to leak out and the synagogue became incensed that the followers of Stephen were leading the youngsters astray. Harassment of The Way increased. They were accosted in the streets by teenagers shouting ridicule and abuse. Mothers drew their children close to their skirts as if even a glance in their direction would contaminate their little ones' souls. The synagogue leaders met to find a way to prevent Stephen from speaking. When Celicia began to attend the classes, a general outcry against The Way was raised, for if one from the family piety of Celicia could be so seduced, then every family was threatened.

Celicia's attraction for The Way raised comments even from followers. Her morals were highly suspect, and many believed she joined their group simply because of her infatuation with Philas. They questioned her sincerity. It was well known that Celicia had in the past freely dispensed her favors among the young men in the synagogue. They considered her latest dalliance with Philas to be merely temporary and as soon as someone else caught her fancy, her interest in The Way would vanish. In the meantime, her attendance fanned the flames of bias and fear, and some thought it might be prudent to ask her to stay away. Surprisingly it was Mariaerh who prevented Celicia's rejection.

Barnabas and Marcia, Jehul and Rhea, Jonas and Susane, and others from the Lower City were at Lucius' house to share in the evening *Agape* with the young Hellenists from Martha's original class. The air was cool and smelled of rain. A full moon shone outside the open door, adding its light to flickering candles and creating an aura of cozy intimacy. Sylvesta and Celia led them in hymns and Philip in prayer. They joined their hands and entered the silence.

A sense of oneness pervaded the room. Their hearts were filled with love for one another. The abuse they shared had served to make them all more aware of the value of trusted friends. They felt content, joyful, safe in the company of others of like mind and spirit. They laughed together, offered encouragement and counsel, revealed their innermost thoughts and feelings with the freedom of total trust. Then someone asked where Philas was and Jacobean answered in a tone of disgust, "No doubt he lies with Celicia!" and the mood of love was shattered.

The Saints withdrew into an embarrassed silence

until Rhea asked, "Who is Celicia?"

"She's a girl from the Synagogue of the Freedmen who has joined our class for initiates," Nimmuo answered.

"A troublemaker and a little tart!" Jacobean spat.

John Mark came to Celicia's defense. "Be fair, Jacobean. It's not Celicia's fault that coming to our classes has caused such an uproar." He turned to Rhea and explained. "Celicia's father is very rich and is one of the leaders in the Synagogue. He's a friend and has commerce with Zebedee and is tolerant of our beliefs, but his friends take Celicia's interest in The Way as a desertion of the faith of the fathers. They can't risk angering her father by blaming Celicia, so they accuse us of exerting evil influence over her and luring her into The Way by means of magic or sorcery."

"There's nothing new in that accusation," Marcia said dryly.

"John Mark tells only half," Jacobean snorted.

The men in the room shifted uncomfortably on their mats and recoiled from entering the discussion. More than one of them had taken advantage of Celicia's charms, and they kept their eyes lowered to the floor lest they meet an accusing stare from a wife or a girl they pursued.

Archar tried to be tactful. "Celicia is . . . well, to say the least . . . overly affectionate. Unfortunately she craves male attention and since she has joined The Way, the men in the synagogue have been deprived of her company."

"Their loss is Philas' gain," Jeseuha interjected archly.

Archar continued, "It's a blow to the men that Celicia would prefer one of us to them. They all covet Celicia's wealth and social standing, let alone her cheery nature and beauty. Their jealousy is expressed in persecution of The Way."

Mariaerh listened to the exchange with dismay. When Celicia had first asked to participate in The Way Mariaerh's impulse had been to flatly refuse her entrance into her house. The memory of Celicia's hand resting on Lucius' knee still burned as brightly as ever, and she did not want Lucius anywhere near the girl. Only Jeshua's teaching of forgiveness had forced her to swallow her pride and subdue her jealousy, but it had not been easy. She sensed that nearly everyone in the room knew of Lucius' indiscretion. They tactfully omitted his name as they counted off Celicia's lovers and Mariaerh's face burned with shame. As the discussion went on and the evidence against Celicia grew suggesting that she should be barred from The Way, Mariaerh suddenly found herself angry. She stood and faced them all, carefully avoiding Lucius' gaze.

"I think we do Celicia an injustice. If she is guilty of sin then so are all the men who take advantage of her. If Celicia is to be rejected, then so should Philas and others whom we so carefully refrain from naming."

A thick silence fell over the room. Mariaerh continued, determined to bring the discussion to an end and never have it surface again.

"Why must a woman carry the full burden of this sin? Are not men equally guilty?" Mariaerh's anger vanished as suddenly as it had risen. Her voice softened and her face became almost luminous. "I am thinking of Mary of Syrus, now of John ben Zebedee. Jeshua did not expel her from communion with the Saints. What was it our Lord said? 'He who is without sin cast the first stone.' Are any here prepared to throw that first stone?"

She paused, and when no one answered, said gently, "There is no one in The Way who is more loved and respected than Mary of John. With our love and example, Celicia could be the same."

No one moved. Lucius was astounded. For a moment he thought Mariaerh was accusing him directly in front of everyone, but then he wondered if she were not actually telling him that by publicly defending Celicia, she had totally forgiven him once and for all. He raised his head and met Mariaerh's eyes. She was smiling at him, timorously, pleadingly. A tide of love and pride washed over him and he arose and went to stand at her side. He put his arm about her shoulders and cleared his throat.

"Mariaerh reminds us all of the One we follow. Surely the Lord speaks through her words."

The matter was settled. Celicia was welcomed into The Way without restraint. The synagogue seethed with fury and employed every means to discredit The Way, but the Saints held fast, for Celicia was one of their own.

\* \* \* \* \*

At the close of autumn Herod suffered a crushing defeat at the hands of King Aretas. The Temple authorities had forestalled his attempt to recruit Judeans into his army, and Herod had turned to his brother Philip for aid. Philip was a peace-loving man and made only feeble objections when Herod forced his unwilling subjects to join his campaign, but the wily Judeans in the end had their vengeance. Once battle was engaged, they deserted Herod and fought on the side of Aretas, revealing vital secrets of Herod's numbers and arms, and Herod's army was utterly destroyed.

When word of the rout reached Herod in his haven of safety in Tiberias, he shot off a letter to Rome, accusing Aretas of treachery against the Empire and viciously condemned the fugitives who chose the role of turncoat. The Jews secretly rejoiced, thinking it just recompense for Herod's sins and for the murder of John the Baptist, but their joy was short-lived.

The prophet in Samaria had succeeded in convincing the people that he could lead them to the vessels of the ark, and a multitude of armed men gathered at a village called Terathaba to follow him to Mt. Gerizzim. When Pilate was informed of the mass congregation, he ignored the reason for their assembling and sent a regiment to disperse them. Hundreds were slain, more put to flight, and many of the principal leaders of Samaria were arrested and executed.

Samaria was outraged. The senate sent an emissary to Vitellius, the proconsul of Syria, demanding he take action against Pontius Pilate. While the Jews had no love for Samaria, they hated the forces of Rome more and they added their voice to the outcry against the massacre.

The ease by which innocent lives could be lost on the order of one unreasonable official struck terror into every Jewish heart. Even if Pilate were punished by Vitellius, what recourse did anyone have in preventing such disasters in the future? A Jew's very life and livelihood depended on the mood of his Roman master. They were but helpless victims in a deadly game for power, and their only defense seemed to be total submission to the whims of their oppressors.

The attitude of life at any cost to personal freedom pervaded throughout the Jewish leadership. The Elders in the Synagogue of the Freedmen were terrified that if the debates between Stephen and Saul should erupt into any form of violence, Pilate might move against them as swiftly and deadly as he had against the Samaritans. They filed a formal complaint against Stephen in the Sanhedrin, accusing him of blasphemy and of being a potential threat to peace.

Caiaphas read the complaint then flung the indictment across the room and screamed, "Have I not enough to contend with without constantly being plagued by these heretics? The Nazarenes are like an ulcer! They heal over with a disgusting scab only to erupt again at a time most inopportune! Arrest the malcontent! Bring him to trial, anything to settle this question once and for all!"

His terrified underlings rushed to do his bidding. Caiaphas' mood of late had been fearful. He was beleaguered from every side. Herod was furious that he had dragged his feet in helping him to raise an army. Who could guess what revenge Pilate would take when he learned the Sanhedrin supported Samaria? And what of Vitellius? All Palestine lay under his authority. If he ruled in favor of Pilate, what havoc would then be unleashed?

Caiaphas' struggle to keep his nation alive until God saw fit to intervene stretched his patience and objectivity to the breaking point. He saw the People of

God engaged in mortal combat for survival, and any disturbance or rebellion from within their own ranks as treasonous. He needed every support he could find, and the Synagogue of the Freedmen contained men of influence and prestige with Rome. They were invaluable allies. He sent his aides to exert whatever pressure necessary to insure a verdict of guilt over Stephen.

Stephen's arrest struck a mortal blow to the hearts and minds of the young Hellenists. Their experience in the Gentile world had never prepared them for charges of religious crimes and they could not believe that one could be brought to trial for proclaiming religious beliefs. They did not know what to do. Peter was in Samaria with Philip, and John had gone to Capernaum to bring the women back to Jerusalem for the winter. None of The Twelve was in the city.

Lucius sent messengers to Peter and John, but Caiaphas moved with lightning speed and the trial was underway before they had barely left the city gates. Lucius even swallowed his pride and appealed to Saul, but Saul only leered in triumph.

"I warned you, cousin. This is only the beginning. If I were you I would repent and return to the arms of the Law. The Almighty One is a jealous God and will countenance no other. You have either forgotten or have chosen to disregard the first of the Laws handed down to Moses. 'You shall have no other gods before Me!' You people set this Jeshua of Nazareth up as a god! Blasphemy!"

Lucius knew there was nothing to gain by arguing with Saul. When he felt his temper rise and the impulse to strike him down, Lucius turned on his heel and left Saul laughing gleefully in the street.

Marcus, Cleopas, Nicodemus, all did what they could. They spoke to every member of the Sanhedrin who had shown any interest in The Way, but a mass mood of fear held the Sanhedrin in its grip and the sacrifice of one young rebel seemed little price to pay for peace. The only comfort they gained was the assurance that Caiaphas would not appeal to Pilate for permission to use the death penalty, for Pilate's displeasure with the Jews was at an all-time high and Caiaphas would not risk angering him further. The most severe sentence would no doubt be a lashing and a long-term jail sentence.

On the morning of the trial, Mariaerh and Nimmuo arose at dawn and went to Veronica's house to wait with her until Lucius came to tell them of Stephen's fate. Dorochen, Archar, Jeseuha, Duors, and other young women in their group joined them, forming a circle of prayer to plea for Stephen's deliverance.

It was a bleak morning. A solid cover of gray, foreboding clouds hung just at the tip of the towers on the Fortress Antonia, and a penetrating wind whipped around every corner. Lucius and John Mark pulled their mantles close and ducked their heads to the biting wind that brought jets of tears to their eyes. They found Sylvia, Philas, and Philip waiting for them on the Temple steps. Philas was holding tightly to Celicia's hand, while Helene, Lydia, and a girl from the synagogue whom Celicia introduced as her friend Judith, stood nervously about, unsure of where they should wait since only men were allowed in the council rooms.

Lucius frowned as he noticed Louie and Silas. Sixteen was too impressionable an age to witness the degradation of one they loved. Before he could voice his objection, he heard his name called and looked up to see Sara hurrying toward them.

"Sara!" he exclaimed. "You shouldn't be here. Why didn't you wait at Veronica's?"

Sara snorted. "There are enough women there to give Veronica support. I wanted to see for myself what kind of justice our good leaders hand down."

They all laughed. Things did not seem quite so dire with Sara along. She took charge of the girls and led them to the women's court while the men went on to the council rooms.

Unlike the trial of The Twelve, no guard checked off names at the door and no seats were pre-assigned.

"I don't know if it's a good omen or bad," Philip growled. "Obviously Caiaphas does not regard Stephen as anyone of importance."

"That might weigh in his favor," said Lucius.

"Or make it easier to condemn him more severely since there is no one of influence to come to his defense," Philas added gloomily.

Lucius spied Barnabas sitting in the spectators' section and led the others to take seats beside him. The council rooms were sparsely filled. The mood was quiet, almost one of boredom. It seemed an unknown youngster from Antioch drew little interest from the natives of Jerusalem.

Philas nudged Lucius and tilted his head toward the opposite end of the section. Lucius looked and saw that it was filled with men from the synagogue. Saul and his rabid followers were there, ringed by the young Hellenists who spoke in excited whispers and vied for Saul's attention by jostling one another and barely muffling their laughter at what Lucius guessed were ribald jokes.

Lucius watched them with disgust. He thought their behavior was infantile and wholly out of place in a court of law. He caught Saul's attention and quickly looked away, sickened by Saul's smug expression. He looked toward the witness box and saw a number of mature men from the synagogue, all who boasted of generous gifts to the Temple treasury, and his heart sank. The opposition was overwhelming, while there was no one to speak for Stephen except himself.

The members of the Sanhedrin who would hear the testimony and judge Stephen's innocence or guilt were filing in and taking seats on wide, semi-circular benches behind the High Priest's throne. Lucius was somewhat heartened to see Cleopas, Marcus, and Nicodemus among them. He mentally took a count of the Elders who were sympathetic toward The Way. They were few, too few perhaps to sway their colleagues to leniency, but a few were better than none.

A clash of cymbals made Lucius start. Two guards on either side of a single door snapped smartly to attention.

The great hall hushed. Every eye turned toward the

door. It opened, and Caiaphas entered, pausing a moment to let everyone absorb the dignity and grandeur of the office he held, then walked with slow, measured strides toward the dais. He lifted his heavy, lavishly ornate robes and ascended the steps, his head held erect, his eyes focused straight ahead. He stopped in front of the judgment seat then turned and faced the hall. He raised his hand in a prolonged blessing, then lowered himself majestically to the High Priest's throne.

Caiaphas' face was inscrutable, his eyes hooded. He gave an almost imperceptible movement of one heavily ringed hand, and the proceedings began.

# Chapter 16

An armed guard opened a small door to the right of the priests' dais and Stephen was ushered in to an audible intake of breath. As always, Stephen had a profound impact on all who looked upon him. He seemed terribly young and vulnerable. His hands were shackled behind his back and a burly guard flanked either side. The guards looked incongruous, like two thugs guarding an innocent babe. Stephen's angelic face shone with innocence and purity. His golden curls needed no light to set them aglow, and his straight, slim, athletic body moved with the easy grace and confidence of one who has never committed a wrong.

Lucius' heart went out to Stephen. How Jeshua would have loved him, he thought. He turned his attention to the scribe who was reading the charges in a loud, sonorous monotone.

The charges were brief and to the point. Blasphemy, both against God and Moses. Blasphemy was the most dread charge of all, yet when charged against Stephen, seemed utterly ridiculous. How could blasphemy be spoken from a face so obviously created by God? Lucius settled back in his seat and exchanged encouraging glances with Barnabas and Philip.

The first witness was called, and while his testimony was damning, his voice lacked conviction and his eyes betrayed a confusion. "We have heard him claim that this Jeshua of Nazareth will destroy this place and change the customs which Moses delivered to us."

One by one witnesses were called, each repeating more or less what the first had said. Jeshua would destroy the Temple, the place of God's indwelling with His people Israel, and the destruction of the abode of God would bring an end to the feast days, the blood sacrifices, all the laws prescribed in the Torah.

Caiaphas was well aware of what the end result of such a disaster would be. Throughout the proceedings he remained immobile. His fingertips were pressed together beneath the point of his chin and his eyes downcast, fixed at some point beyond his feet. His face betrayed not the slightest hint of emotion, but his mind spun and his breast heaved with anger and fear.

Caiaphas became aware of an expectant silence and realized that the last witness had spoken and that the Elders waited for him to respond. He remained unmoving, letting them think he was deep in prayer, then lowered his hands and slowly lifted his head. He turned his eyes upon Stephen with a long, penetrating gaze. Finally he said, "You have heard the testimony against you, what have you to say?"

Stephen met the High Priest's gaze unwaveringly. He smiled at Caiaphas, a pitying, forgiving smile that infuriated the Priest though his expression did not change. Then Stephen addressed the entire hall, his voice clear and musical, capturing every ear.

"My Brothers! Fathers! Listen to me."

Stephen recounted the history of Israel, of Abraham's call from the land of Chaldea, of Isaac, and Jacob, and Joseph in Egypt. He told the story of Moses, a babe abandoned who became a friend of God, and of Israel's forty years wandering in the desert of darkness, and of the Law that the Israelites disobeyed. He reminded them of the tent built by Moses and brought by Joshua to the promised land. Then of David, and finally Solomon, who erected a house of the Lord.

Stephen's sweet voice and angelic countenance held the assemblage enthralled. They had heard the story countless times before, but never directly from an angel.

"Yet the Most High does not dwell in buildings made by human hands, for as the prophet says, 'The heavens are my throne, the earth is my footstool; what kind of house can you build me? asks the Lord. What is my resting-place to be like? Did not my hand make all these things?' "

Stephen stopped. His eyes traveled over the entire room. His face was luminous. He leaned forward. His eyes flashed with challenge and his voice rang with righteous anger.

"You stiff-necked people, uncircumcised in heart and ears, you are always opposing the Holy Spirit just as your fathers did before you. Was there ever any prophet whom your fathers did not persecute? In their day, they put to death those who foretold the coming of the Just One; now you in your turn have become his betrayers. You who received the Law through the ministry of angels have not observed it!"

Lucius groaned and buried his face in his hands. The hall erupted in angry denial. The spectators were on their feet, shouting, cursing, shaking their fists with full-fledged rage.

Caiaphas allowed them to vent their fury. He sat back on the throne and closed his eyes, seemingly unperturbed by the chaos around him.

The young fool, Caiaphas thought, he had them eating out of his hand and now he has brought them down on his head.

Caiaphas knew that Stephen was right on many counts. God did not dwell only in the Temple! As High Priest, the only one allowed to enter the Holy of Holies once each year, on the Day of Atonement, he knew that the Holy Place was not God's only dwelling. True, he sometimes felt The Presence there, but he had also felt It elsewhere, walking in his garden as the sun slipped behind the hills, or gazing out over his beloved city from the porch in front of the Holy Place. But the simple, untutored country folk did not know that! They did believe that God resided in the Holy of Holies, and to tear it down would be to evict the Almighty One from Israel!

What the fool boy did not know was that to destroy the Temple was to destroy the very center and spiritual stronghold of the Jewish people, let alone its economy. Twenty thousand priests would be without a function.

Untold numbers of scribes, caretakers, herdsmen, carpenters; all would be displaced. The economy was already precarious. With Rome filching every drop of the cream from the pail, the milk that was left was blue and watery and barely sustained Judea.

Caiaphas sighed. He signaled the guards to bring order, then beckoned to the Elders to confer.

The hall waited in tension-filled silence, their mood still explosive. Lucius was rigid with apprehension. He watched Marcus and the others argue earnestly with their fellow Elders, their faces intense, their hands gesturing widely, then sit back, disgruntled and resigned, but not despairing. Stephen looked unconcerned, musing, as though he listened to voices no one else heard.

The Elders did not confer long. Caiaphas listened to the foreman's whispered verdict, and nodded his head. He turned toward Stephen, again regarding him with that penetrating gaze.

"I commend your knowledge of the Law, and applaud those who have been your teachers. However! You have obviously become intoxicated by this false prophet called Jeshua of Nazareth who was no more than a common criminal crucified under due process of law. Your misplaced infatuation has led you to a blasphemous interpretation of the Law. I order you to henceforth cease from publicly proclaiming your distorted, self-damning views, and encourage you to comply with the order of this court. I sentence you to forty lashes, to be administered immediately upon your removal from these chambers. This hearing is hereby adjourned!"

Lucius slumped weakly in his seat. Forty lashes! Could Stephen survive so many?

Barnabas whispered. "Take heart, Lucius. The Jewish whip is not the instrument of torture that the Romans employ. It is of one lash only, and no bits of bone or rock to chew a man's back to ribbons."

The men of the synagogue were incensed. "Foul!" they cried. "A blasphemer goes free! Unjust! Too lenient!"

Lucius was stunned by their ferocity. He glanced at

Saul and recoiled from the sight of his contorted face, not sure if it was hatred he saw or if Saul was suffering one of his fits.

The guards hustled Stephen out of the council rooms. "Come on, lad, let's get this over with before they turn into a mob with a lust for blood," one growled.

The crowd stampeded for the doors. Barnabas cupped his hands and shouted into Lucius' ear, "Go to Veronica's. Tell the women. We'll bring Stephen home when it's over. Send someone for Jonas. Stephen will need a physician." He glanced at Silas and Louie, both pale and frightened. "Take the boys with you. They shouldn't witness this."

Lucius only nodded, not even attempting to make himself heard over the roar of the crowd. He motioned for Silas and Louie to come with him, but the boys refused. Silas was close to tears. "If Stephen can stand to be flogged, the least we can do is stand by him."

There was no time to argue. Lucius shrugged his shoulders and shook his head in exasperation, but let them do as they felt they must.

They melted into the crowd and surged through the door, across the priests' and women's courts and out to the Court of the Gentiles where Lucius turned against the crush and fought his way to one of the side gates. He descended the steps to the street, his heart aching for Stephen, and filled with dread to tell Veronica that her son was being flogged. At least he could reassure her that Stephen would not be jailed. It would be some comfort for her to know that she could nurse his wounds herself and that Stephen would not languish in some filthy cell deprived of aid and comfort.

The Elders left through a door reserved for officials which led to a private exit at the rear of the Temple complex. Marcus and Cleopas waited for Nicodemus to catch up with them on a small, roofed porch at the top of the steps that led to the street.

Cleopas looked dejected. Marcus put his hand on his arm and said, "We did the best we could, Father, better even than I had hoped."

Cleopas nodded, but sighed. "I haven't the influence I

once had. In the old days I might have swayed them."

"Nonsense!" Nicodemus' voice boomed from behind them, "The High Priest himself could not have exerted more influence." He shivered. "It's freezing. This rain could turn to snow." He gave Marcus a knowing look. "Let's let the younger men attend to this spectacle and we old men go home and warm our bones with a glass of Martha's mulled wine."

Marcus glanced at Cleopas and suddenly realized that his father was old. His shoulders were bent, his eyes dull with weariness from seeing too much sadness during his lifetime. He seemed frail, worn, and he trembled with chill.

Marcus forced a note of cheerfulness into his voice. "I agree. The lads will take care of Stephen. A glass of wine and a blazing fire is what we need."

Cleopas did not argue. They helped him down the Temple steps and turned toward the Upper City.

Inside the Temple walls, the guards were growing alarmed. The mob was sounding uglier by the moment and they feared they would try to take the law into their own hands.

"We'd better get reinforcements," one growled to another.

The second guard nodded and slipped into a small door in the Temple wall. He ran down the dimly-lit passage, his iron-soled sandals echoing upon the stone until he came to a door that opened into the priest's offices. He was out of breath. A scribe immediately gave him admittance to Caiaphas' office and he entered, panting, and saluted sharply.

"Sire! The mob grows unruly. There are not enough of us to keep them under control."

Caiaphas raised his hooded eyes from some papers upon his desk. "I'm sure you will manage. Don't be too hard on them. They are like children deprived of their sweets."

Caiaphas resumed his perusal of the papers before him. The guard paused a moment, stunned by the realization that the High Priest hoped the mob would kill the lad, then he saluted and left the room. He hurried back down the passageway, sickened, disgusted. He had no stomach for seeing a boy torn apart by wolves.

Sylvia, Philip, and the others were helplessly borne along by the crowd. When they reached the Women's Court, Philas tried to break free to find Celicia, but it was hopeless. They were pushed and buffeted about, barely able to keep to their feet. They tried to stay together, but the wave of crushing bodies forced them apart and each had to fend for himself.

The noise was deafening, ringing in their ears until their heads swam. The mob was like a mindless, maddened beast, screaming for blood. Philas' heart pounded with terror. The coppery taste of fear flooded his mouth. He was in a state of panic, frantic to get away, to flee the scene of madness. There was no escape.

The guard came out onto Solomon's Porch and saw Stephen ringed by three other guards in the midst of a frenzied throng. He used his club and forced his way to them, cracking heads in anger as he went.

He reached them and shouted, "Let them have him if they persist. Put up only a token show of resistance."

The guards obeyed. They left their swords in their scabbards and used only their clubs, and those in a half-hearted manner. They allowed the mob to push them away, striking back with poor aim and little force until they gradually let the swarm come between them and their prisoner.

The crowd roared with triumph. They dragged Stephen across Solomon's Porch and through the majestic golden gate. The rain had turned into cold, stinging sleet. The wind howled with protest and the clouds bent even lower as if to hide man's shame from the heavens.

Once outside the Temple, the full fury of the crowd broke loose, as if outside the House of God they were free to do their worst. Stephen was dragged, fell, pulled to his feet, stumbling, kicked, and struck from all sides. Barnabas found himself shoved near to Louie and Silas, both boys sobbing hysterically. He managed to get to them and used his strong body as a shield to allow the crush to surge by.

Sylvia caught up to Philip and, linking arms, they fought like ones possessed to reach Stephen's side. John Mark had already reached him, and the three formed a circle around their friend, like lionesses protecting their cub. The mob screamed ecstatically to find they had more than one prey.

Then suddenly the wind died. The clouds parted, and a beam of light fell upon Stephen, an eerie, unearthly light. The crowd hushed, stopped in mid-motion.

Stephen looked up at the sky. The light illumined his face, diffused his hair into a halo of gold. His countenance was one of ecstasy, his voice rang out with joy.

"Look!" he cried, "I see an opening in the sky, and the Son of Man standing at God's right hand."

A low growl began in the bowels of the mob and swelled until it became a deafening roar. The clouds rolled shut. The light disappeared. The wind resumed its howl and the heavens began to rain stones.

The first stone landed between Sylvia's shoulders. His back arched against the pain, then a deluge of rock descended upon them. The last words Stephen ever uttered were, "Lord, do not hold this against them," but only John Mark heard.

Celicia was lost in the crowd, crazed with fear and screaming Philas' name. She could not find him. She was separated from Sara and Judith, Lydia and Helene. She was alone, caught up in a nightmare from which she could not awaken. She was borne by the mob through the gate and was close in the crush to where Stephen stood. She saw the shaft of light, and for one brief, desperate moment, thought Jeshua was coming to save him. But the light went away and the stones began to rain.

Celicia watched in horror. She did not even realize that her mouth was wide open in one, never-ending scream until she locked eyes with one of the youths from the synagogue, a youth that once she had loved. The scream caught in her throat.

The boy stared at Celicia. Then a look of satanic lust

spread over his face. He nudged a companion and pointed Celicia's way. The youths turned their backs on the stoning and started toward Celicia, picking their way carefully through the mob, their eyes aglow with gleeful malice.

Panic surged through Celicia. She spun and fled, turning away from the Temple that seemed now to be the doorway to hell, running away, down the steep bank to the Kidron Valley, slipping, falling, scrambling up again and again to flee in absolute terror. She saw a tumbledown stable with its door hanging askew on its hinges and fell headlong inside, anywhere to hide from her pursuers.

The stable was airless, filled with dust and stank of rotted feces and filth. Celicia did not notice. She saw a pile of chaff-filled, ancient straw in one corner and flung herself into it, clawing the fifthy stuff over her body to hide it. She heard the pound of running feet and froze, clenching her hands and holding her breath, cringing as far into the straw as she could get. She heard a voice call, "Hey! Look here!" Then soft snickers and muffled laughter.

"Well lads, I guess little Celicia has given us the slip. Let's go in here and catch our breath out of the rain."

Celicia did not move. Her heart pounded so loudly she feared they would hear it. The boys moved about making coarse jokes and cursing the rain. One came close to the pile of straw and began casually kicking it about. The toe of his boot struck Celicia's hip and she involuntarily jerked.

At once the lad was upon her, flinging away the rotting straw until she lay exposed before him.

"Well, well! See what we have here, men," he sneered.

Eight faces leered down at Celicia. She whimpered and pushed herself back against the wall.

"So," one of the youths said softly. "This filthy hole might provide some entertainment after all." He reached down and grasped Celicia's bodice and tore it away.

Celicia's hands automatically flew to cover her nakedness. "Please," she whispered.

"Hear that? She says 'please.' Please what, Celicia? Are you hungry for love as always?"

The boys laughed uproariously. Then one struck Celicia across her face with his open palm.

"Slut!" he snarled. "Whore! You prefer those scum in The Way to us, eh? Well, we'll see who gives you the most satisfaction!"

He jerked his belt loose and flung open his clothes. Celicia closed her eyes and another slap stung her cheek.

"Open your eyes, harlot! Look upon the instrument of your pleasure!"

They fell upon her then, pinning her arms and legs and muffling her screams as they used her. They were cruel, rough, intending to hurt and maim. Celicia endured it as long as she could, then fainted to blessed oblivion.

Lucius paced the floor in Veronica's house. Veronica was weeping softly, a sorrowful, keening sound, so filled with grief it tore at Lucius' heart. She was on her knees, her body bent almost to the floor, rocking back and forth in rhythmical, swaying motions. Mariaerh knelt at her side, her arm around the beloved old woman, swaying with her, whispering words of comfort in her ear. The other girls were silent, waiting.

Back and forth Lucius paced, unable to be still. The house was cold, dark. The rain pelted upon the roof, drumming a dirge to the screaming wind and threatened to drive Lucius mad. He tried not to hear it, to think, to keep himself occupied with thoughts while he endured the interminable waiting.

Where were they? Why was it taking so long? Why did Jonas not arrive? Dorochen had gone for him as soon as Lucius had returned. They should have come by now.

He looked at Veronica. She had taken the news well. No hysteria or uncontrollable behavior, only that terrible keening. He walked to the door. It was as black as night out there. A flash of lightning split the sky and Lucius saw three figures racing toward the house. When they reached the door, Lucius flung it wide and Jonas, Susane, and Dorochen stumbled inside.

They were soaked to the skin, windblown, freezing. The girls catapulted into action to get them dry clothes and blankets, but Jonas shrugged them off and knelt by Veronica.

"She's all right, Jonas. Only grieving," said Mariaerh.

"Have you given her a bit of wine? It will strengthen her."

Mariaerh shook her head. "She didn't want it. We tried."

Jonas stood and allowed the women to remove his sopping coat and wrap a blanket around him. He drew Lucius to one side. "What happened?"

"Caiaphas sentenced him to forty lashes. The men in the synagogue thought he got off too easily. They were like a crazed mob. Thank God for the storm. It will send them fleeing for cover. Can Stephen live through forty lashes?"

"Of course!" Jonas answered curtly. "He's young and strong and healthy. We'll have him back on his feet in no time at all. The Twelve were also flogged, remember."

"They should have brought him home by now! Where are they? Why aren't they here!" Lucius cried in a hoarse whisper.

"Take it easy. The lads will be taking great care with Stephen. The wind makes it nigh impossible for someone unburdened to walk and they will be carrying an injured man. They'll come as soon as they can."

Nimmuo was ladling bowls full of broth and urged Jonas to come and eat. He and Lucius started toward the table when Veronica suddenly stopped keening. Her head came up, listening. Her back straightened until she was upright on her knees. Her eyes gazed at a point near the ceiling across the room, her face was alight with joy and her arms outstretched as though to embrace a loved one.

"Stephen? Son?" she asked in wonder.

Then her face changed to horror. A long, piercing scream tore from her throat. She clutched at her breast and pitched headling onto the floor.

They all rushed toward her. Jonas shoved Mariaerh aside and rolled Veronica onto her back, grabbing her wrist to feel for her pulse.

No one moved, did not even breathe. Jonas looked up into the shocked faces around him and said in stunned disbelief, "She's dead."

The door crashed open. John Mark burst into the house. One eye was swollen shut. Blood streamed from a gash in his forehead. He was filthy, mud-spattered, sodden, his coat torn. One hand dripped blood from a tattered sleeve.

"The dirty, lousy, filthy, whore-mongering bastards! May their stinking souls rot in Hell! Sons of Satan!" he screamed through sobs. "They killed them! Rotten bastards straight from hell! They've killed them all!"

The Saints were frozen, stupefied. They stared at John Mark as if he were a spectre, a ghost. Never had they heard him curse! They were so astounded by the filth that streamed from his mouth that no one realized what he was telling them. No one but Jeseuha.

Jeseuha walked toward John Mark with a jerking, stiff-legged gait. Her face was bloodless, her eyes cold as stone. Her voice was hard and deadly quiet. "Who have they killed, John Mark?"

John Mark did not even see her. He sobbed uncontrollably, still spewing curses. Jeseuha drew her arm back and brought the palm of her hand across his face with all the strength she could gather. John Mark staggered back against the wall. He began to whimper, holding his cheek where the blow had landed.

Jeseuha spoke through clenched teeth, slowly, distinctly, "Who did they kill, John Mark!" she hissed, "Tell me or I will strike you again!"

"Stephen." John Mark whimpered.

"Who else?"

"Philip." He looked at Jeseuha and his head lolled from side to side. Pain, pity, despair, unfathomable sorrow, all registered in his eyes. "Sylvia," he whispered finally.

Jeseuha screamed and screamed and screamed. She bolted for the door and flew out into the storm. Lucius went after her and tried to drag her back into the house, but she fought him with the might of ten. Nimmuo rushed to help him. The wind whipped the rain in their eyes, blinding them, freezing their hands to near uselessness, exhausting them, until Jeseuha's strength suddenly evaporated and she slumped into Lucius' arms and he carried her back into the house.

Celicia opened her eyes. It was dark. Rain drummed a song upon the roof. Thunder grumbled afar off. She smiled, for a moment thinking she was home in her bed, safe and warm while the rain sang a lullaby to soothe her to sleep.

Dust filled her lungs and she coughed. A searing pain tore through her body and blood filled her mouth. She spat, and memory flooded her mind. She moaned and tried to move, but again the torturous pain. Tears wet her cheeks. The acrid stench of age and decay assailed her senses and she retched, fainting from the pain it caused.

She awoke again, hot, her body on fire and a heaviness pressing her groin. She had to move, to get up and relieve herself. She tried to roll over but tongues of fire licked at her belly and she lay back, panting. A wetness seeped down her thighs and she whimpered, shamed that she had soiled herself. Her hand stole across her body and found her skirts flung up to her waist. She tried to push them down, to cover her nakedness, but every movement made her cry out in agony. Her hand came away wet, sticky. The odor of sex and blood overrode the other stench and she recoiled in disgust.

She wept, mortified, humiliated, dirtied, used. Weeping made her cough blood again and then to vomit. She had to get up. She could not let anyone find her like this. She rested a bit then heaved her body with all her remaining strength. Blood gushed from between her legs. Razor-like blades of pain slashed through her body and she whirled downwards, tumbling, falling, in a void of darkness.

Then the sun suddenly shone. Stephen and Philip were laughingly helping her to her feet. She looked

shamefacedly down at herself, expecting to see the filth
and dirt with which she was covered, and her eyes
widened in wonder when she saw that she was clean.
How could that be? Was it all a dream? She saw Sylvia
who was smiling and pointing downward. She looked
and saw her body lying in a tangled heap on the stable
floor. Poor thing, she thought, poor, broken, bloodied,
abused thing.

Then Stephen turned her toward the Light that was
not the sun after all, but a wonderful, marvelous Light
that emitted sheets and rays of pure, golden bliss, and
she laughed with uninhibited joy. She grasped
Stephen's hand and they raced toward the Light,
leaving her crumpled body behind.

# Chapter 17

The storm had ended. A dense blanket of cold gray clouds hung over the city, throwing its dismal shadow over all of Jerusalem and thwarting any attempt of the sun to shine through. The howling gale had died to woeful, biting gusts that kicked at fallen branches and other debris that littered the deserted streets.

A thin layer of ice covered most of the Upper City, gilding the trees and wrought-iron fences until it seemed as if the entire landscape had been plunged into the colorless, lifeless depths of the nether world. The wind groaned as it labored to free the city from its icy tomb, buffeting bushes and branches until the ice lost its grip, snapping and crackling, then hitting the brick-paved streets with the tinkle of shattering glass.

Lucius, Jonas, Marcus, and Nicodemus picked their way through the litter, slipping and skidding on hidden patches of ice and shielding their faces from the tiny shards that stung against their flesh. They did not speak except for an occasional curse when one nearly lost his footing, their minds numbed by shock and filled with dread at the task that lay before them.

They found the Lower City a carnage of destruction. The personal belongings of the poor lay strewn in the streets. Thatched roofs gaped with ugly holes, shutters hung at crazy angles, torn loose by the force of the storm. Booths and market stalls were a shambles of ruin. No life stirred. The poor huddled behind their broken doors in despair, wondering where the money would come from to repair the wreckage and replace the precious goods they had lost.

A ghostly silence hung over the Temple. Lucius and the others climbed the steps to Solomon's Porch and gaped at the mutilation they witnessed. Here too, booths and market stalls were overturned and smashed, their contents scattered in a jumble of refuse across the court. Canopies were ripped into shreds that fluttered desolately in the wind, their brilliant colors faded and bled together into ugly hues by the rain. The Temple was abandoned, as if some invisible enemy had put all the priests and scribes and worshippers to flight and only the wind was left to sough and moan with grief at the destruction wrought in the House of God.

Lucius shivered and his skin crawled. Jonas nodded his head toward the Golden Gate and they slowly made their way toward it, skirting puddles and heaps of debris, keeping close together as though they expected a spectre to appear before them and carry them off to Gehenna. Their footsteps echoed throughout the court, a harsh, grating intrusion upon the deathlike silence. The great gate hung ajar and the four slipped through, heaving a sigh of relief to quit the ominous devastation on Solomon's Porch.

The Kidron Valley had fared no better than Jerusalem. It was a tangle of broken branches and wind-whipped grass. The wide road leading to the floor of the valley was nearly washed away, and sticky, yellow mud oozed everywhere.

Someone hailed them and they each gave a start at the first human voice they had heard since leaving Marcus' house. They whirled toward the voice and recognized Zebedee waving his arm to attract their attention. They ran, slipping and sliding in the viscous mud that sucked at their feet, their hearts pounding with dread for they knew what they would find.

James ben Joseph and Barnabas were with Zebedee. Three blanket-wrapped bundles lay at their feet, and not far away a cairn of heaped and scattered stones. Lucius' eyes slid over the stones, unable to rest on that instrument of death. He gave Barnabas a fierce embrace, weak with relief to see him alive. He dropped to his knees, mindless of the mud that ruined his robes, and pulled one blanket back to see the face. He grimaced and closed his eyes against the sight, then quickly covered it again and did the same with the other two. He knelt there, bowed by grief.

Barnabas gripped Lucius' shoulder to steady him and tried to ease his sense of loss by telling him, "Louie and Silas are safe. I took them to Zebedee's before the first stones were thrown. We came back as soon as the storm let up. Do the women know?"

Lucius could only nod. He could not trust himself to speak or even to raise his eyes and look at Barnabas lest the lump in his throat dissolve and his pent up grief break loose.

Marcus answered for him. "Veronica is dead," he said gently. "John Mark escaped and brought the news. He's injured and in great shock, but he will be all right. Jonas and Lucius brought him home and told us what had happened."

Marcus looked down at the bodies at his feet, then at Nicodemus. "If only we had stayed," he cried. "We might have prevented this tragedy!"

Nicodemus shook his head. "Only God knows. It was a mob riot, Marcus. I think there was nothing we could have done."

Zebedee stood with his head bowed and his shoulders slumped. So much death. It seemed his life had been filled with death. He rubbed his hand over his face. "Poor Veronica," he moaned. "May the Almighty One embrace her soul. She was a good and loyal friend."

James reached out a hand toward Zebedee, but drew it back before touching him, too shy to demonstrate physical intimacy. "Better that she is with God than here grieving for her son." He scanned the skies, trying to determine the time of day without the sun to aid him and guessed it was mid-afternoon. "Night will fall before we can bury our friends if we do not hurry. We'll carry them back to Zebedee's so the women can prepare them for burial."

Lucius got to his feet and asked Barnabas, "What about Philas? And Sara and the girls?"

Barnabas made a helpless gesture with his hands. "I

never saw the women, and was separated from Philas by the crowd."

They lifted the bodies from the mud, two men to a bundle, and carefully picked their way down the bank to the valley floor. Lucius led the way, trying to find the least treacherous track down the slippery hillside. He had not gone far when he heard a sound that at first he thought was the keening wind. He heard it again and stopped and cocked his head to listen, this time wondering if it were not a crying child he heard. He shouted to the others and ran toward the sound, flinging tangled branches aside until he found the source of the voice and cried out aloud in dismay.

It was Philas, sitting on the ground with Sara's head in his lap, weeping, pleading with Sara to speak to him.

"Sara. Please wake up. Please Sara, tell me where Celicia is. I can't find her, Sara."

One look at Sara's lifeless face and Lucius knew she would never answer. He turned his attention to Philas who had not even looked up when Lucius appeared, and his heart constricted with fear.

Philas seemed to have lost all sense of reality. His face was haggard and deathly pale, his eyes glassy and unseeing. He kept whimpering to Sara and petting her cheek, totally unaware of Lucius' presence.

Lucius' hands trembled and his blood pounded in his ears. He dropped to his knees and grasped Philas' arms and shook him. "She can't hear you, Philas. Sara is gone."

Philas' head flopped back and forth like a rag doll's. He looked at Lucius as if he were a stranger, then said in a forlorn, childlike voice, "I can't find Celicia. I've looked and looked but I can't find her."

Lucius took a deep breath and tried to inject a tone of confidence and authority into his voice, though with Sara dead on the ground, he did not truly believe what he said himself. "She's no doubt home safe and well. You know Sara. She would have seen the girls safely on their way and then come back, having to see for herself what was happening."

A gleam of hope flashed in Philas' eyes. Lucius gently

removed Sara from Philas' knees and he allowed Lucius to help him to his feet. By the time the others reached them, Lucius had wrapped Sara in his coat. Philas was still dazed, but obediently followed Lucius' directions and helped him carry Sara back to Zebedee's.

News of the riot spread throughout The Way and the followers were drawn to Zebedee's. The women brought ointments and spices and burial cloths and food, weeping and wailing and beating their breasts while the men stood idly by, hanging their heads and shuffling their feet, embarrassed to let their grief show and uncomfortable lacking anything to do. Burying the dead was women's work.

Lydia and Helene were among those who filtered in from the Lower City and the Saints rejoiced that at least their lives had been spared. Lucius had guessed rightly about Sara's actions, she had seen the girls on their way, but Celicia had turned back to search for Philas and the girls never saw her again.

Zebedee sent a servant to the Upper City to try to learn anything of Celicia, cautioning him to use only his ears and not his tongue lest the wrath of the synagogue men be rekindled. By the time he returned with the news that Celicia had not returned home and that her father was organizing a search, it was too late in the day for The Way to search for her themselves, and they decided they must wait until morning. They said nothing to Philas, not even that the servant was sent. Salome put him to bed with the compassionate lie that surely he would see Celicia tomorrow.

Veronica was brought to lie with the others in a tomb on Zebdee's estate, their bodies hastily prepared for burial and quickly entombed before the hidden sun could set on that infamous day. Mariaerh and the Holy Women remembered how once before they had been forced to bury a loved one with the same irreverent speed, and the memory of Jeshua's death added increase to their grief.

Jeseuha washed Sylvia's body herself, performing the last service she would ever do for him. Like the fury of the storm, the fury of her grief had passed quickly, leaving her emotions as frozen in ice as the trees in the Upper City. She stood by the tomb with her babe in her arms and her firstborn clinging to her skirts, dry-eyed and stoic, and wrenched the hearts of the Saints who stood by her side.

The Saints gathered that night in Zebedee's upper room to pray for the souls of their dead. They were exhausted and numbed. Less than forty-eight hours before they had been safe and secure, following the way of the Lord in peace, then hate and violence had struck as a flash-flood without warning, leaving death and destruction in its wake. It seemed like a dream, a nightmare from which they could not awaken. They intoned the prayers in a monotone, chanting the words by rote without comprehension or feeling, for they were drained of emotion and mentally dazed.

The *Agape* was served. James blessed the bread and wine and the Saints ate and drank with added devotion, for it was not only Jeshua's memory they honored, but those who had died for His *name*. Salome and Martha had prepared a lavish feast, hoping the odor and taste of good food would lift their spirits and ease their grief, but few could eat. Lucius stared at his plate and realized it was the first meal he had seen since dawn, but his stomach rebelled and he pushed it away in distaste.

When the half-eaten meal was cleared away, the Saints drifted into small groups where they spoke in whispers or quietly wept. The older followers, conditioned by years of discipline in the teachings of the Essenes, formed a circle of prayer and united their hearts and minds to the precept of "Thy will, O Lord, not ours be done." How many times in the past had they feared that God had turned His face away from the Elect and left them in the hands of Belial, only later to realize that the hand of God moved inexorably through the affairs of men, bringing Light to a world of darkness?

They drew comfort from the belief that all that occurred was according to some Divine Plan, that there were no accidents, that man himself set the stage for future events and eventually reaped what he sowed. They believed they were instruments used by God, willing channels through which He worked to evolve the souls of men and return them to the Unity they had once enjoyed. They saw the deaths of their friends not only as possible retribution for some past debt incurred, but also as a voluntary, willing sacrifice to further the Kingdom of God. How would this be? They did not know, but rested content in their faith that one day all would be revealed.

The younger believers, the newly-initiated, did not have the knowledge of past experience to draw upon. Most of them had not yet been introduced to the hidden, spiritual truths contained in the teachings, and they found themselves locked in the grip of doubt and despair. They asked themselves over and over again, why? Why did this happen? Why especially to Stephen, and Philip, and saintly Veronica, all of the fallen who were such sources of light and inspiration to all? Why did Jeshua allow it to happen? Some even questioned their belief in the new teaching. If The Way were truly the Elect of God, then why did He withhold His protection? Perhaps they followed a false, heretical teaching as Caiaphas had said and God punished them to show them their error.

Lucius was one who doubted. He withdrew into silence and watched the others with the cold, hard stare of distrust. The only word his mind could register was "waste!" Stephen had been his friend, his closest friend since coming to Jerusalem. He had loved him more than any friend he had ever known. He loved his intelligent, questioning mind, his cheerfulness, his childlike wonder of all the world. He loved his compassion, his concern for all men, and yes, most of all he loved Stephen's total commitment to The Way.

But what did it benefit him? A violent, untimely death at the hands of a vicious mob! A waste! A waste of all that was good in the world! Lucius' heart was more torn over Stephen's death than it had been over his own brother's. Death by disease he could understand, but murdered because of a difference in faith was incomprehensible. A waste!

Lucius was sullen. He wondered why he had ever come to this place. All he had ever known in Jerusalem was misery. He had been rejected, distrusted, forced into a marriage that was not of his choosing, admonished for following his natural urges, and impelled to exercise a rigid schedule of prayer and diet. Following The Way had required him to give up a life of ease and luxury and to throw in his lot with the poor. He had even relinquished his claim to his sons and deprived himself of the joy of their mother! Now he wondered if it were worth it. What advantage had he gained? Would his reward also be violent death?

James ben Joseph was aware of the doubt and fear that raged through the initiates. He drew them together at a far end of the room and tried to console them.

"I know what you are feeling. I know the doubts that fill your minds. No one knows better than I. For years I doubted. Jeshua was my Mother's son, my brother according to flesh, yet He commanded my unwavering faith as He did from everyone. No man likes to admit his brother is wiser and greater than he, and I was no exception.

"I questioned Jeshua's teaching, for his words were often at variance with even The Poor. I could not understand when he broke the Law, when he healed on the Sabbath, consorted with sinners, and ate what I thought was unclean. If he were indeed the Son of Man as he claimed, then why did he bait the authorities until they sought to destroy his life, and why did he not save himself? When Jeshua lay in the tomb my mind could only ask why? What did his death gain us? Were all those years of misery and strife for naught? If he were truly the Promised One then how could he die?

"But He did not die! He lives, as Stephen and Philip and Sylvia and all who die in the flesh live. I saw Him myself. He came to me and spoke to me and I know!"

Dorochen voiced the thought of all the initiates. "It's easy for you, James, you saw! But what of us who did not see?"

"Our Lord answered that question Himself when

Thomas doubted, then saw and believed. Jeshua said, 'You became a believer because you saw me. Blest are they who have not seen and have believed.' "

"But it hurts so!" Nimmuo cried. "Why must we suffer so? Why must we mourn!"

"Man has mourned from the time he first separated himself from The One, through his own willfulness. Times of adversity and suffering are a gift and we should give thanks for that gift. What man remembers the Lord when his belly and coffers are full and his life abundant with the pleasures of earth? Does he then reflect on his soul's journey or ponder the mysteries of life? Does he then hunger for wisdom and truth that will bring him life everlasting? Or is he content and grown fat on the world and pays no mind to that which comes after?

" 'Blessed are they who mourn, for they shall be comforted.' To have the capacity to mourn is to be greatly blest, for by your grief you know you stand before the Holy Place."

Lucius was discomfited by the truth he intuitively felt were in James' words, but he was not yet willing to relinquish his anger. "Why Stephen?" he asked. "Why one that had so much to give to the world?"

James smiled, an awkward, crooked smile that seldom appeared on his solemn face. "Why Jeshua? You came to hear a great teacher, to see miracles performed. You found a man tried and condemned and hung from a tree. Why did you stay? If yet He lived and trod the world would you be here still, or would you have listened and watched for awhile then returned to your homes unchanged? His death yes, but more His rising again is what sustains you. 'Follow Me!' Does that mean only through joyous times and not through suffering and trial? You say, 'I believe,' but only your works will give proof to your words."

No one could argue. James left them to ponder what had been said and they were comforted, not wholly understanding it all, but their spirits bore witness that all he had said was true.

The next morning the city began to clear away the

destruction left by the storm. The poor dejectedly
searched the debris, retrieving anything salvageable
and kicking forlornly at that which was not. The sun
shown. The ice had melted away and a temperate breeze
blew in from the sea, but no one rejoiced. An aura of
solemnity enveloped the city and, despite the activity of
clearing the streets, it seemed unusually quiet.

The Jews were stunned by the violence of the day
before. Even Caiaphas was disturbed. He was deluged
with complaints from the Pharisees who expressed
their disapproval in no uncertain terms and demanded
that such outrages be prevented in the future. He
worried over Pilate's reaction, and mentally rehearsed
a plausible excuse for his failure to control the crowd.
When a courier brought a notice from Vitellius in
Antioch stating Pilate had been relieved of his post and
a new procurator would be forthcoming, Caiaphas
breathed a sigh of relief and rubbed his hands together
in self-satisfaction. He absolved himself of all guilt,
convinced that Pilate's recall was a sign from God that
he had been right in letting the boy serve as an example
to that heretical sect! He believed that God intended
him to cleanse the entire city of all that scourge before
the new procurator arrived in Caesarea. The first thing
he decided needed to be done was to convince the
Pharisees and Elders that such action was necessary,
then find a dupe to carry it through. By late afternoon
both problems were solved—again, Caiaphas thought,
through Providence.

Celicia's father and his search party found her body a
little after noon, and as reports of her condition and
cause of death flew through the city, the lurid details
became embellished with every recount. The city was
appalled, incensed that a child of a leading family
should be so basely used. Who could perform such a
dastardly act? Blasphemers, ungodly men, surely not
someone who followed the Law! The finger of blame
pointed to The Way.

The possibility that the abuse and murder of Celicia
had been committed by young men in her own social
circle never occurred to Saul. He, like most of Jerusalem,

assumed it was done out of revenge against her father and the men of the synagogue for bringing Stephen to trial. He applied for an audience with Caiaphas and petitioned the High Priest for his blessing in routing The Way.

Caiaphas welcomed Saul with delight, though his face remained closed and unreadable. He listened to Saul's impassioned plea with downcast eyes, heaving sorrowful sighs and mouthing pious platitudes of mercy and forgiveness. But in the end he let himself be swayed by the ugly, fanatical youth who stood before him and, with feigned grief and reluctance, admitted the deed must be done. Caiaphas had found his dupe.

The blood of Saul's youthful band ran hot with righteous intent, unaware that the underlying cause for their zeal was their own sense of guilt over the deeds committed the day before, and their need for absolution. The High Priest's consent to destroy The Way was the only sign they needed to convince them that they had performed the will of God, and they set out to complete the task with the exhilarating fervor of avenging angels.

The vigilantes swept through the Lower City without warning. Market booths and stalls were pulled down, their contents smashed and trampled underfoot. Jehul's weavers' shop was raided, his vats overturned, looms and spindles broken to bits, and oil and honey poured over his wool. The carpet shop left to the Saints by Naomi and Cephas was razed to the ground and the carpets burned. Metalworks were twisted into useless shapes, forges demolished. The potters' kilns were kicked in, even the clay destroyed, while the finished product was thrown against limestone walls until heaps of shards were all that was left. Cheeses and baked goods were flung into the streets to the joy of scavenging dogs. Everything of value was confiscated, later conferred to the Temple authorities as a donation to the poor.

Only the Greek-speaking Jews were molested. Their doors were kicked in and anyone found inside was arrested. They were bludgeoned, beaten, heaped with verbal abuse, then shackled and marched off to jail. Families were separated. Little ones screamed in terror as they watched parents carried away. Everywhere was mayhem and chaos. Fires blazed which the Hebrew-speaking Jews fought desperately to put out lest the whole Lower City go up in flames. Screams of the injured and lost rose over the crackle of fire, and the stampede of fleeing victims left many trampled in the streets.

Saul's vengeance was swift and without mercy. By nightfall many lay dead, many more injured, and many languished in the Temple cells.

The Hebrew-speaking Jews who had fled from the scene lest they be mistaken as one in The Way, came back as soon as Saul's band had exhausted themselves for the day and left with the promise that they would return. They were appalled by the destruction they found, their hearts wrung with pity at the plight of their neighbors. They remembered the charity received from The Way and rushed to their aid, gathering the maimed from the streets, taking the aged and orphaned into their own homes to hide them, and furtively helping the able-bodied out of the area to the safety of their friends.

The houses of Zebedee, Marcus, and Nicodemus resounded with the wail of suffering and grief. Peter and Philip arrived from Samaria minutes before the first refugees straggled dazed and terrorized through Bethany's gates. Peter roared with outrage. He cursed the Sons of Belial who posed as Children of Israel then tortured their fellow Jews. He left Martha and Ulai and Pathos in charge, then he and Philip ran to Zebedee's.

Zebedee's estate was a scene of chaos. Peter and Philip forced their way through the panic-stricken Saints in search of Alphaeus and Zebedee. The sight of their leaders was like sighting a ship when their boat was foundering in a storm. They clung to their cherished comrades, pulling and tugging at their arms and entwining their fingers in their cloaks. They needed to touch, to hear their voices give reassurance, to know that all would be well.

They broke Peter's heart. He wanted to gather them

all in his arms and comfort them as a father his children. There was no time. He gently pushed them away and pulled his coat from their grasp. "Later, my children, later. First we must end this atrocity."

They found Zebedee and Alphaeus and after a hasty discussion decided there was little Peter could do. None of them carried any influence with the Temple authorities, and only they could stop Saul. Since the uproar caused by the Samaritan revolt, the Roman contingent had been recalled to Caesarea and the few soldiers left would not go against the High Priest unless ordered to act by the procurator.

"Pilate's in Antioch. So are Cornelius and Barrian. We have no friends among the Romans," said Peter. "We'll have to rely on Marcus and Nicodemus to sway the Sanhedrin."

Marcus and Nicodemus had already tried and met with failure. Caiaphas had retired to his palace and would see no one. Their supporters among the Pharisees advised them to get the Hellenists out of Jerusalem for they knew Saul had authority to search any house known to be in sympathy with the Nazarenes, and every Greek-speaking member of The Way was to be arrested on sight.

The Hellenists fled in the night. The Saints raided the communal storehouses and provided them as well as they could, but there was so little time. The injured who were able to walk were shepherded away from the city to Bethany, while those who could not be moved were left in Jonas and Susane's care, hidden in Zebedee's upper room, but the vast majority slipped through the gates and were lost in the cloak of darkness.

Lucius and Barnabas refused to flee. Saul was their kinsman. His blood ran in their veins and they felt as if by sharing his blood they also shared his guilt. They would not run from him. If he shed the blood of his kinsmen, then he shed a part of his own, and so be it.

It was long past the midnight hour when Barnabas and his family, Lucius, Nimmuo, and Mariaerh trudged wearily through the dark, sleeping city to Lucius' house. Marcia put her little ones to bed while Mariaerh and

Nimmuo set out wine and cheese and some dry dark bread. It was a meager meal, but the first they had eaten since early morning. Even the *Agape* had been forgotten in the panic to save the initiates. They were famished and ate hungrily, dipping the days-old, crusty bread into their wine to soften it.

The simple fare somewhat restored their spirits and eased their exhaustion. They sat around Lucius' table in the light of a single candle and spoke of the last few days in hushed, subdued tones. When Saul's name arose, Nimmuo's reaction was so filled with hatred and acrimony that the others were stunned.

"Saul!" Nimmuo hissed. "Would that he had died in his mother's womb! A viper, spawned by the devil himself! I swear if the opportunity were to arise I would kill him myself!"

"Nimmuo!" Mariaerh gasped.

"It's true!" Nimmuo cried. "I hate him! I hate him!"

Barnabas reached across the table and took Nimmuo's hand. "Do not hate, Nimmuo. Your hatred will only destroy you and will not harm Saul at all. Better to do as Jeshua, forgive him and pray for him. Try to bring him into the kingdom."

Nimmuo snatched her hand away. Her eyes blazed. "Are you out of your mind? You are mad! I will never forgive him!"

Nimmuo burst into tears. Her nerves were stretched to their limits, her emotions too jumbled and raw to contain. Mariaerh threw her arms around her and looked at Lucius, her eyes pleading with him to do something.

Lucius remained immobile. He knew Nimmuo's outburst was born of fatigue and shock and crushing grief. She would be all right. It was not in Nimmuo's nature to hate. She might rail and scream and say terrible things, but it would pass. Her own good sense and innate cheerfulness would see to it. He let her cry, knowing her tears were a release, a cleansing. He was more concerned with his own feelings about Saul.

Lucius did not hate Saul. He was not even angry with him. In fact, he had felt much more anger toward him during all the years before these last horrendous days than he did now. He did not understand himself. He examined his feelings and decided that what he felt was pity! He got up and walked to a window and opened the shutter and stared out into the cold, black night, lost among his churning thoughts.

Why should he feel sorry for Saul? Was it because he created a future for himself that would be filled with persecution and violence? "He who lives by the sword, dies by the sword," whether in this life or some future one. Lucius shook his head. No, that was not it. Saul would only meet the results of his own undoing like every other soul who entered the world, and the depth of his pity for Saul went beyond what he felt for souls in general. When had he first felt this overwhelming sense of compassion for Saul?

Lucius' mind drifted back over the events of recent weeks. He remembered the heated debates, the accelerating tensions in the Greek-speaking synagogue. He remembered his anger at Stephen's arrest and the image of Saul's face at the trial. He hated Saul then as much as Nimmuo hated him now! What changed that hatred to pity?

Lucius sighed. He turned away from the window and watched Mariaerh drape his coat over Nimmuo's shaking shoulders.

The coat! When Lucius and Jonas took John Mark home, John Mark had told them that Saul did not throw any stones himself, but only held the coats of those who did. Now Lucius remembered how his heart had sunk and that his thought then had been, "poor Saul."

Why! Lucius turned back to the window. He rubbed his hand over his face as if to clear his head and tried to think. If Saul had truly believed that Stephen's death was just, and that he himself was doing the will of God, he should have been the first to throw a stone. What had stayed his hand? Fear? No! Lucius rejected that idea immediately. Saul was afraid of nothing or no one. Had he not even dared to publicly criticize the revered Gamaliel?

Doubt! It could only be doubt! But what could so

suddenly instigate that doubt? Surely not squeamishness at causing another's death. He knew Saul would never flinch in executing righteous justice. An idea occurred to Lucius and his thoughts took wing. Excitement bubbled in his breast and his mind touched upon all the teachings of the Essenes that Martha had so patiently put before him.

The Law is the totality of all laws that govern the universe and all creation. The Law creates life. The greatest law of all is love. God is love. God is life. God is the Law.

When man lives within the Law, he lives in harmony with his fellow man, nature, and all that is contained in the cosmos. Once man, through his own free will, deviates from the Law by negative emotions, thoughts, and deeds, he creates disharmony between himself and all that is. This disharmony results in disease, madness, strife and despair. The spirit that lives and moves within each man is part of the Spirit of the Law, God, that lives and moves within all creation—one voice in constant communication. Could it be that the Holy Spirit bore witness against Saul's spirit, convicting him of wrongdoing?

The seed of this astonishing idea took root and began to grow. Lucius' brow knit as he struggled to bring it to full bloom. He clenched his teeth in concentration and a muscle in his cheek twitched with his effort.

Would . . . could . . . Saul hear that small still voice that spoke to any man willing to hear? With an ever increasing excitement, Lucius knew the answer was "yes." Saul had spent his entire life in the study of the Law. True, as yet he understood only the outward, apparent meaning of the Law, but some students must learn that level first before their minds and souls can grasp the deeper, hidden meaning. God knew when any soul was ready to be taught from within by the Holy Spirit. Did He know this of Saul?

The implications of what that could mean were overwhelming. Lucius took a deep breath to calm himself. He must not let himself be carried away by wishful thinking. He had to examine this from every side.

If it were true, why then would Saul launch upon a full-blown persecution of The Way with such ferocity? If the Holy Spirit spoke through Saul's conscience and restrained him from stoning Stephen, then why did his conscience allow him to maim and kill and destroy as he had done today? The answer only served to convince Lucius that it was indeed the Holy Spirit moving within Saul's soul.

The Essenes believed that two spirits were contained in man, the spirit of truth, or Light, and the spirit of perversity, or Darkness. When a soul, by practicing righteousness, began to grow more and more toward the Light, the spirit of darkness within him grew fearful of extinction and rebelled and a battle for supremacy was waged within the soul.

With a flash of insight, Lucius realized this could be happening to Saul. Saul had to prove to himself and to his followers that he was right in his actions and beliefs, and that the Spirit that spoke was wrong. To obey the Spirit was to deny the entire world of thought, attitude and belief he had created for himself, to publicly admit his error and relinquish his will to God. Few men who walked in the world of flesh had the strength of faith to do this, for they feared to lose their selfhood in the process. The prophets of old who had done so were persecuted or killed for their faith. Jeshua the man had brought his body, mind, and soul into such perfect accord and oneness with God that God said, "You are my beloved Son," yet even the Son had suffered and died by the hand of the spirit of darkness.

Lucius knew Saul. He did not lack in courage or in faith. Sooner or later he would heed the spirit of light and yield to the will of God. Lucius was on fire with enthusiasm over what it would mean if a man like Saul would champion The Way and help to spread the Good News. He spun from the window to tell Barnabas and the women of his revelation, but they were asleep. Marcia had lain down beside her tots. Barnabas slept with his head in his arms on the table, and Nimmuo and Mariaerh were asleep upon mats on the floor. Nimmuo was still wrapped in his coat, but Mariaerh lay curled in a ball, huddling against the cold.

Lucius found a blanket and tucked it around Mariaerh, thinking how small and vulnerable she looked in sleep. He was suddenly overwhelmed with tenderness for her. He hardly had time to even speak to her these past days. He wondered if she were afraid, waiting here for whatever turn Saul's vengeance would take, and he wished he had taken time to reassure her. He did not believe Saul would vent his spleen on those of his own mother's blood, and Saul was cousin to Mariaerh as well as to Barnabas and himself. He wanted to wake her, to lie at her side beneath the blanket and cradle her in his arms as they whispered to each other in the dark. But he could not. It was the first real sleep any of them had known for hours. He kissed her softly on the brow and returned to the window to wait for dawn.

# Chapter 18

Saul's vigilantes met in the morning at the Synagogue of the Freedmen then marched to the Lower City. His route took him close to Lucius' house, but he passed it by as if he did not know who lived there. Lucius and Barnabas and the girls stood in the doorway and watched him pass with a mixture of relief and contempt, relief that he had granted them a reprieve, and contempt that he should spare them. If he truly acted in such righteousness as he proclaimed, then even those of his own blood should fall before his sword. Nimmuo slammed the door shut before the last of the band had passed, not caring if Saul heard it or not.

"Devil's spawn!" she cried. "He hasn't the courage to take on anyone who might defy him. He only picks on the weak and terrified. I'd like to see his face when he finds there is no one left for him to bully!"

Nimmuo was right. Saul's face contorted with fury when he found the Hellenists had fled. He made a house to house search of the area and his anger and frustration grew when he found the Hebrews uncooperative and some even openly hostile.

A number of the city's rabble had gathered to watch the fun. They were the drunkards, the opium-eaters, the degenerates who embraced any event that brought a passing excitement into their otherwise dull and despairing lives. They jeered and taunted Saul each time he came up empty-handed, and applauded whenever a Hebrew cursed and refused Saul entry into his house. Saul became so enraged that he feared the onset of one of his fits. He ordered his men to disperse the rabble. They brandished their swords and clubs and threatened to kill them all, but the rabble only laughed and scampered out of their reach, then returned as soon as the threat abated.

Saul finally gave up and left them alone, roaring, "May that lot join the cursed Greek-speakers in the bowels of Gehenna!" He turned to his followers, "There is only one place the Greek-speakers would flee for safety. That one called Lazarus who claims to be risen from the grave would take them in. We go to Bethany!"

They left Jerusalem through the Dung Gate at the southern tip of the Lower City and took a shortcut over the hills to Bethany. The rabble followed but kept their distance, gleefully anticipating the prospect that someone other than themselves would receive the heavy end of a club and the sole of authority's foot. They gathered their own weapons along the way, thick branches for clubs, stones, even vines to be used as ropes, hoping for a chance to take part in the melee.

On the outskirts of Bethany, the vigilantes drew their swords and gripped their clubs then crashed through the gates with a hair-raising, warlike cry. The rabble followed, screaming with joy and the lust for blood, crazed by their fervor to avenge themselves against a society that kept them on the fringes of life.

It was a replay of the day before. They burned, looted, raided and destroyed. They began at the village gate and swept through the streets like the angel of death. By the time they reached Martha's house at the foot of the Mount, any restraint they had used at the start had long disappeared. They descended on the house like a horde of demons seeking the prize of the day, jabbing their swords, smashing everything breakable in sight, overturning tables and cupboards and couches, and ripping Lazarus' precious scrolls into shreds. One battle-crazed youth ran Lazarus through with his sword without even knowing who he was, while his comrade clubbed Martha down as she tried to intervene.

Marh, Jochim, and Thelda were overcome by smoke and failed to escape from Thelda's burning house. Sara's old friend, Bartimaeus, whose sight Jeshua had restored with a word, was cut down in a trice and with him his mother, Cleopas. No one was spared. The Bethanyites fled to the Mount of Olives and watched their village become a funeral pyre.

The Hellenists who had fled from Saul the day before had only prolonged their fate. They died of the added maltreatment, smoke inhalation and exposure to the winter air. Those who survived were taken prisoner, their wounds ignored as they were shackled and led away while the rabble screamed in ecstacy.

Bethany was leveled. Saul gazed on the results of his day's work and relished the sight. At last! After years as a haven for blasphemers and criminals, Bethany was no more.

John stood on the mountainous ridge that separated Jerusalem from the Jordan Valley and watched as Bethany burned. It could only be Bethany. No isolated house or inn could make the huge, black, billowing cloud that spread across the bright, sunfilled afternoon sky. Only an entire village, torched by human hands to burn all at once, could raise such an ominous witness to the virulence of man.

John held the reins of his rented horse with one hand and clutched at his churning stomach with the other. He was sick with dread. His knees were weak and threatened to give way. His throat ached. He felt as though he had been run through with a jagged, rusty sword. He buried his face in the horse's withers and wept.

Another watched Bethany burn. Caiaphas stood on the porch in front of the Holy Place and gave thanks to God for the ways and means of cleansing His people from the taint of idolatry. Never again would anyone dare claim to be the "Son of God."

Not since the day when Herod had slaughtered the innocent babes had the Saints known such despair. Six years had passed since that Feast of Pentecost when the Holy Spirit descended and blessed The Way with over three thousand souls. Six years had seen that number doubled and more. Thousands had turned their lives upside down, abandoned homes and friends and families, relinquished all they owned to be counted among The Way. Now they were lost, wandering cold and hungry, homeless in a hostile world. It seemed The Way stood on the brink of extinction.

The dead were buried. The mourners mourned. The weeks passed. Lucius trudged home in the twilight with his shoulders hunched against the cold. It was a clear, frosty night. A few stars twinkled brilliantly overhead and a full moon had just begun to peer over the distant Mount of Olives. The radiance seemed disrespectful, the deserted streets more in keeping with his despondent mood.

Lucius was weary to the bone. He had spent the day with the Elders assessing what was left after the devastation and trying to reunite their depleted number of followers. He was drained by the effort to comfort and raise the spirits of the Elect when his own spirits were grieving, and he resented having to pretend optimism when his own heart was near despair.

He dreaded going home. Mariaerh was prostrate with grief over Jochim and Marh. She lay on her bed with her face to the wall and rebuffed all Lucius' attempts to console her. He had declined Josie's invitation to share in the *Agape* out of duty to his distraught wife, but he knew it would be useless even to try to penetrate the wall of isolation she had raised around herself. He understood the depth of her grief for her parents, but could not understand her withdrawal. He thought a wife should seek solace in her husband's arms, to weep on his shoulder and pour out her heart to his comforting ear, but Mariaerh recoiled from his touch and refused even to look at him.

Lucius took Mariaerh's rejection of his loving concern to be a silent accusation, that if he had not insisted they move to the city, she might have been able to save her parents from Thelda's burning house. Lucius thought it was nonsense. It was more likely that Mariaerh would have died in the fire also and should be grateful that he had inadvertently saved her life. He was stung by her lack of gratitude, and resented being unjustly accused. He tried to tell himself that he was wrong in surmising

Mariaerh's accusation, but when she refused to give him a better explanation for repelling his advances, he became more and more convinced that he was right. He reached his door and heaved a sigh of resignation, then reluctantly went in.

Nimmuo was preparing their evening meal. Bread, cheese, olives, and warm honey cakes were set on one end of the long plank table, and the aroma of hearty stew filled the room from a brazier at the far end. She looked up with a smile as Lucius entered and welcomed him home with a kiss on the cheek. She closed the door behind him and latched it, then helped him off with his cloak.

"You must be freezing! Your feet are soaked. Sit down and let me take off those foot-coverings."

Lucius wearily lowered himself to a bench and stretched out his legs, averting his eyes from the table. Barnabas and Marcia had moved back to their own house and the table seemed incongruously oversized for three. The whole house was depressingly silent. His eager-faced students were gone. The table, once groaning with dishes and lined with friends who shared the evening *Agape* in such companionable love, now stretched in sullen emptiness.

Lucius sighed and closed his eyes. He let his head drop back to ease the tension across his shoulders. Nimmuo removed his sandals and unwound the woolen cloths, then massaged some warmth back into his feet. Lucius groaned with pleasure. His heart warmed with gratitude for Nimmuo's sisterly concern. He thought his mother had done exceptionally well in teaching her daughters the proper care of a man. He could not imagine either Nimmuo or Lucia sulking in self-pity while ignoring their duty to the man of the house. The rhythmical movement of Nimmuo's hands and the silence in the house lulled Lucius into a reverie and his mind drifted. The room seemed haunted by ghostly faces, Jehul and Rhea, Agnosta, Sachet, Lydia, Archar, Duors, Josida, Jeseuha and her babes, and so many more. Where were they? Were they alive, well, injured, hungry? Even Philas was gone. He blamed The Way for

Celicia's death. His tortured mind denounced his beliefs, Jeshua and even God Himself, and he fled from the place where all his hopes and dreams had died with the one he loved. Where had he gone? What would he do? Would he allow bitterness and hate to forever rule his life and come to destroy him?

Nimmuo's voice shattered Lucius' thoughts. "What happened today?"

"We sent messengers to the rest of The Twelve telling them to come back to Jerusalem before there are no believers to come back to. John went to Capernaum to tell Mary about Lazarus and Martha."

Nimmuo rocked back on her heels and looked up at Lucius. "That's so terrible. All those years when she ran away and no one knew where she was, and Martha and Lazarus suffered so over her and now to learn they died so horribly! How will she bear it?"

Lucius brought his head up and looked at Nimmuo. The last weeks had taken their toll. Her face was lined with sorrow and her eyes had lost their merry luster and now brimmed with tears. He took her hands and noticed they were rough and chapped. Where was the little sister who had been carefree and gay and dressed in silks and plagued him to distraction? He impulsively drew her into his arms and held her tightly to his breast.

"Ah, Nimmuo. I should never have brought you here. You shouldn't have had to endure all of this."

Nimmuo pushed herself out of his arms and pulled at his beard with both hands. "Don't be silly. I'm here because I want to be here. Since when have you had any command over me? I do as I please! Your beard needs trimming."

Lucius laughed. "That will be another task for you after you feed me." How independent she is, he mused, how consistently independent! He glanced at the curtain that hung in the doorway to his sleeping room. "I'll see if I can persuade Mariaerh to come out and eat."

Nimmuo opened her mouth to advise against it, but closed it again without saying anything, deciding it was wiser to hold her counsel.

Mariaerh did not move when Lucius entered. He knelt

by the mat and stroked her back. "Are you awake, Mariaerh?"

She did not answer. He slid his hand beneath her cheek and turned her face toward him. She kept her eyes closed, but he knew she was not sleeping.

"Come out and eat. Nimmuo has fixed a wonderful stew. Can't you smell it?"

Mariaerh turned her face away. Lucius tried again, this time with more authority. "Come, Mariaerh! You can't lie here forever. Despair will not bring your parents back to life. You must go on. Your mother would scold you for not eating."

"Leave me alone," Mariaerh said dully.

Lucius sighed in exasperation. "What do you want, Mariaerh? How can I help you? Tell me what to do and I will do it, but at least talk to me!"

She remained unmoving. Lucius threw up his hands in disgust. He stood up and, looking down at her, said coldly, "Very well. Remember that I tried to help you. You'll have to resolve your grief by yourself, since that is what you obviously choose. I'll not bother you again!" He turned on his heel and left the room in anger.

Full winter set in. The Way strove to restore their unity, determined to survive no matter what defeats were forced upon them. The *Agape* was shared, the circles of prayer and the home altars were resumed. Suphor gave birth to a son whom James named Clement, the only ray of happiness in all those frightful weeks. The people of Bethany came down from the Mount and started to rebuild their village despite the bitter winter wind and frequent freezing rains that numbed their hands to uselessness. If Saul had hoped to break the back and spirit of The Way, he had hoped in vain, for his persecution only strengthened their belief that the end times had truly begun. "Lord, Come!" became the standard cry at the end of every prayer.

The enemies of The Way regarded Lazarus' death as a stunning victory. For years Lazarus had been living proof of the power of the Nazarene. It was even rumored among the poor and ignorant that Lazarus would never die, that the life restored by Divine Power would never leave his body, and many joined The Way on the strength of that belief. While Saul had not ordered Lazarus killed, he rejoiced when told he was dead, and believed the Almighty One directed the hand of the one who ran him through.

Saul thought Lazarus' death would prove that his so-called "resurrection" had been no more than a cunning plot to dupe the superstitious. He thought that if the physician who testified that Lazarus had truly died of the fever could also be destroyed, then that heresy would end once and for all.

The Saints were warned by a sympathetic Pharisee that Jonas was sought by Saul, and they devised a plan that let Jonas and Susane escape right under Saul's nose.

Jonas and Susane, along with Ulai and Pathos, had been at Zebedee's on the day of the holocaust, and had thus escaped the fate that befell the Bethanyites. No one could ever doubt that Pathos was of Roman blood. He had the classical, broad-shouldered, sturdy build of his race, the aquiline nose, black curly hair, although beginning to gray, and small, piercing dark eyes that could intimidate anyone who dared to confront him. He borrowed a uniform from a friend in Caesar's legion, and Salome and Mary of Alphaeus quickly created a fashionable Roman dress for Ulai. Jonas and Susane posed as their servants and they left Jerusalem in broad daylight without blinking an eye. It was a small victory for the Saints, but one they would retell for years to come.

Word of the refugees and reports of Saul's persecution spread throughout Palestine. The people remembered the compassionate love of the Nazarene and opened their doors to His followers. They hid them in their homes, fed them, clothed them, then smuggled them on to the next courageous soul who risked the wrath of authority to aid the Nazarenes. An underground of aid had spontaneously formed and hundreds of Saints were saved from freezing and starvation by the helping hands extended in sympathy. Many died from exposure, disease, and extreme hardship, but many more were saved. They settled in small groups wherever they found a community of Essenes. Some in Samaria with Jodi, the woman Jeshua spoke to at the well, in Cana, Capernaum, Bethsaida, Caesarea, and all the towns of Judea where Lucius and Peter had gone. Some went as far as Sidon and Tyre and on to Antioch of Syria, while a great many went to Damascus, the ancient haven for the sect of the Essenes. Some who sought refuge at the City of Salt and at Mount Carmel were so traumatized by Saul's brutality that they spent the remainder of their lives there, terrified to ever face the outside world again.

It was a lonely, sorrowful winter. Lucius' house echoed with silence. Mariaerh eventually left her bed and took up her household duties and resumed her work in The Way, but she was pinched and drawn and spoke only when necessary. Her slender body had grown emaciated. Tiny lines furrowed her brow and formed a network around her mouth. Her hair was dull and lifeless and she pulled it back into the severe, uncomely bun she had worn in the past. She was distant and aloof, often lapsing into an almost trance-like state, her body rigid and her eyes glazed, as if staring into a happier past.

Lucius did not know how to help her or what she thought or felt since she would not say. Not even Nimmuo's inane chatter could bring a smile to Mariaerh's face. She refused to sleep with Lucius, even to let him come near her. It seemed a sacrilege, a sign of disrespect to her parents to take pleasure from Lucius' embrace. It would be months before she realized that she acted out of guilt and used continence as her punishment for surviving when they had not.

The night Lucius had come home to find that Mariaerh had moved her bed into Nimmuo's room, he had bolted from the house in a rage. He walked the streets, seething with anger and frustration, his mind wallowing in self-pity until all he could think of was some way to retaliate for the humiliation he suffered. He entered the first brothel he found and threw a few coins at the owner. The keeper snatched them up, seeing at once they were far more than the usual charge and offered Lucius the pick of his whores. Lucius did not care whose body he used. He grasped the nearest by the arm and pulled her toward a back room.

He was rough and brutal, his hands and mouth bruised the girl's tender flesh. He wanted to hurt and debase as he had been hurt and debased, and he punished the girl for the rejection he had received from Mariaerh. He finished with her quickly and flung her aside, feeling no relief from his pent-up frustrations or for his damaged self-respect. He yanked up his loin cloth, flung on his clothes and stormed out into the night. He found another tavern and drank himself to oblivion on cheap stale beer.

The next night Lucius did not even bother to go home, but went straight to the brothel. His rage had cooled to a calculating revenge and he took more care with his coins and studied the painted, scantily clad girls to make a selection. His eyes traveled over each of them, coldly judging as to which seemed the most desirable then came to rest on a face he knew. Lucius' expression did not betray his shock. He nodded his head curtly to indicate his choice then strode ahead of the girl to the back room.

Lucius stepped aside for the girl to enter then jerked the curtain closed and spun her around to face him.

"You are Celicia's friend, Judith! What in the name of the Almighty One are you doing in this place?" he demanded.

Judith wrenched her shoulders free from Lucius' grasp and tossed her head. "What are you doing in this place?" she asked defiantly. "I thought all you Nazarenes were above the sins of ordinary men!"

Lucius ignored her retort. "Does your father know you are here?"

Judith laughed. "Of course! Don't all whores get their fathers' permission before embarking on this trade?" Then, bitterly, "Don't be a fool! I've left my father's house."

A vision of Mary of John flashed through Lucius' mind. He gripped Judith's arm. "Then you are going back!" he ordered, and started to drag her toward the door.

Judith jerked her arm free and leaped back, confronting Lucius like a trapped animal with her teeth bared and her fingers curled into talons.

"Stay away!" she hissed. "I am never going back!"

Lucius forgot his own problems and his reasons for coming here in the first place. He regarded Judith weakly, bewildered and confused. "But Judith, you can't stay here. You aren't like those others out there. You commit a grave sin."

Judith's face purpled. "Sin!" she screeched. "Who speaks to me of sin!"

Lucius stiffened. "You are a woman. Your needs and . . . well . . . compulsions are not those of a man. God condemns the harlot!"

"Don't mouth pious words to me about God!" Judith spat. "Where was your God when you lured Celicia into your infamous sect, and where was my father's God when he set his self-righteous dogs upon my friend? What God? There is no God!"

Lucius was aghast. Never had he heard a Jew speak such blasphemy. The girl had to be hysterical, mad. He tried to calm her. "Judith. You don't believe what you are saying. You are distraught, overwrought by what happened to Celicia. God did not order that Celicia suffer as she did. He gave man free will, and by doing so cannot interfere, even when man chooses to use it for evil. Surely God knew man would abuse His gift and so provided for man's victims. Be assured that Celicia is in bliss, in heaven."

Judith began to cry. She clenched her fists and cried, "Heaven! I don't believe in heaven, only in hell and hell is here. I intend to reap whatever pleasures I can find in it." She collapsed in a heap on the dingy mat, weeping wildly and pounding her fists into the limp pillow.

Lucius went to her. His heart was wrung with pity. He awkwardly stroked her back as he tried to think of something to ease her distress, then gathered her into his arms to comfort her.

Judith did not resist. She wound her arms around

Lucius' neck and clung to him, sobbing. Lucius crooned to her, brushing her brow with his lips and smoothing her hair until Judith turned her face to his and met his willing mouth.

Their mutual need for comfort and understanding flamed into passion. They came together urgently, desperately, as if the physical act of love-making would erase all the weeks of pain and despair. When their passion was spent, they slept entwined in one another's arms, sated, content, their hunger for the warmth and companionship of another human being for the moment appeased.

When the night sky began to leaden with the coming of dawn, Lucius crept from the bed. He left some extra coins to satisfy the keeper for occupying one of his girls for the entire night, then stepped into the street and drew a long breath, more at peace within himself than he had been for weeks.

Each night Lucius returned to the brothel. He gave to Judith all the love and tenderness and comfort he had longed to give to Mariaerh. He poured out his heart to Judith, cleansing his soul of all the doubts and fears and bitter sense of loss he had felt since Stephen's death. Judith satisfied his need for someone to nurture and care for and counsel. She restored his self-esteem by obedient compliance to all his desires, and by expressing her gratitude in both word and deed. They healed one another.

## My Home in Jerusalem

*Am I wrong about Saul? Were the thoughts of my mind on the eve of Bethany's destruction, born of my own desire? Even as I write, Saul and his followers travel the road to Damascus to continue his vengeance against The Way. There was not time to warn them. We learned only today of his infamous plot.*

We were told that a man from Damascus complained to Caiaphas that the Brothers who fled to his city to escape Saul's persecution preach the Good News in the synagogue there and many of the citizens have come to believe. This man and others who are leaders in the synagogue have tried to dissuade the Brothers from speaking but, of course, to no avail. When Saul heard this, he went to Caiaphas and asked him for letters to the Synagogue in Damascus which would empower him to arrest and bring to Jerusalem anyone he might find living according to the new Way. Caiaphas honored Saul's request and even reenforced his band with recruits from the Temple police. Saul was well on his way before we heard of it, too late to send a warning. We wait in dread for news.

The return of our leaders is a welcome relief. Our despair is eased and our grief assuaged by the return of The Twelve. Their success in spreading the Good News uplifts us. They tell wonderful tales of miraculous escapes from the snares of Belial which restore our faith that recent events have caused to flag. We have also received word that Jonas, Susane, Ulai and Pathos reached Antioch in safety. Thaddeus and Jude ben Joseph received them with joy and they now labor together as servants in the Lord.

Philoas was successful in obtaining Pontius Pilate's recall. Pilate sailed from Rome as soon as The Great Sea was navigable, but we wonder if the temporary procurator will prove any better. Vitellius has sent a man called Marcellus to assume the post until a permanent procurator is appointed. No one in Judea knows this man and the city speculates over what his rule will bring.

We, too, are anxious over this appointment. While Pilate was certainly no friend of The Way, his wife was, and Cornelius, by virtue of his position, had more than a little influence over Pilate's policy regarding the Jews. Pilate, at least, was a known enemy. His reactions to The Way could be somewhat accurately charted by his attitudes in the past, but not so with Marcellus. We fear we shall learn soon enough. When Saul unleashes his vengeance against the Brothers in Damascus, Marcellus' response will indicate how the wind blows.

We await word from Damascus like condemned men awaiting the axe to fall. We curtail our activities. We avoid any publicity. We meet in secret and pretend we do not know one another when we meet in the streets. We greet one another with the innocent "peace be with you" and again draw the sign of the fish in the dust. I remember the days when I walked the streets of Laodicea as a free man. I feared nothing and no one. I spoke as I wished, journeyed to any city or land which captured my fancy without restraint. Will I ever know that freedom again?

\* \* \* \* \*

## Jerusalem

Saul's vigilantes have returned to the city without him! Is he dead? Did the Brothers rise up and slay him? Did he simply stay in Damascus after accomplishing his mission to gloat over his deed and receive praise from the authorities?

Rumors run rampant. We hear he is ill, is injured, turned coward, though the last we dismiss, knowing better. We hear nothing of substance.

\* \* \* \* \*

## Jerusalem

News at last from Damascus! Brothers from that city attended the Feast of Passover and tell a wondrous tale!

As Saul was approaching Damascus, a light from the sky suddenly flashed about him. He fell to the ground and at the same time heard a voice saying, "Saul, Saul, why do you persecute me?" "Who are you, sir?" he asked. The voice answered, "I am Jeshua, the one you are persecuting. Get up and go into the city, where you will be told what to do."

The men who were traveling with him stood there speechless. They had heard the voice but could see no one. Saul got up from the ground unable to see, even though his eyes were open. They had to take him by the hand and lead him into Damascus. For three days he continued blind, during which time he neither ate nor drank.

There is a disciple in Damascus named Ananias to whom the Lord appeared in a vision. "Ananias!" he said. "Here I am, Lord," came the answer. The Lord said to him, "Go at once to Straight

Street, and at the house of Judas ask for a certain Saul of Tarsus. He is there praying."

But Ananias protested. "Lord, I have heard from many sources about this man and all the harm he has done to your holy people in Jerusalem. He is here now with authorization from the chief priests to arrest any who invoke your *name*."

The Lord said to him, "You must go! This man is the instrument I have chosen to bring my *name* to the Gentiles, and their kings and to the people of Israel."

Ananias obeyed the Lord, and went to Saul and baptized him whereby Saul's sight was restored and his strength returned.

The Gentiles! Can it be that I was right, after all? Saul is my cousin. Can it be that the Almighty joined our souls by ties of blood so that one day we would join forces and together bring His word to the world?

The Elders do not share my excitement.

Vitellius also attended the Feast of Passover. The Jews turned out in a tumultuous welcome, hoping to win the Syrian proconsul's favor and promote Marcellus' good will. Vitellius was flattered by the magnificent display and rewarded the city by releasing her inhabitants from all taxes upon fruits that were bought and sold.

Vitellius deprived Caiaphas of the High Priesthood, and The Way, for a moment, rejoiced. Then we learned that he installed Caiaphas' brother-in-law, Jonathan, in his stead. Jonathan is a bumbling fool, a puppet in the hands of his father, Annas. He is clearly terrified of Caiaphas and will do whatever he says. We can see that only the name of the High Priest has changed and that the reins of power remain the same.

Vitellius also restored custody of the High Priest's garments to the Jews, an act so unexpected by the delighted priests that they refrained from voicing their objections to Jonathan, fearing that if they did so the president might change his mind and once again keep the garments under lock and key in the fortress, Antonia. Knowing the Roman mind, I believe it was a deliberate and clever move on Vitellius' part.

We had thought Saul's persecution would discourage believers but, happily, it is not so. The Elect who fled told the Good News to all their rescuers and many came to Jerusalem to attend the feast and hear more about the new way. They furtively seek us out, whisper to us the names and descriptions of our people to whom they gave aid. We meet with them in secret to avoid arousing suspicion.

For the most part, these inquirers are Aramaic-speaking Jews from Galilee, people whose blood has been mixed with Greeks for generations. They have ever felt despised and scorned by pure-blooded Hebrews. They are Jews but not Jews, Greeks but not Greeks, misfits in a society where the distinction between race and creed is clearly drawn. They are poor and uneducated. They have been told that without perfect adherence to every nuance contained in the Law, they are doomed forever. The daily struggle to stave off starvation drains their energies and gives them no opportunity to study and practice the Law. They live in despair, for themselves and their chidren and their children's children, for there is no escape from the iron-clad jaws of poverty.

They hear Jeshua's words like men dying of thirst who are suddenly come to a clear, running stream. "Blest are you poor; the reign of God is yours. It is not what goes into a man's mouth that makes him impure, it is what comes out of his mouth. This is my commandment; Love one another as I have loved you."

Love, patience, gentleness, kindly concern toward one another, these things they have always done, for one another is all they possess. They weep to hear that the Almighty One knows them and loves them, that He sent His son among them, clothed in flesh as themselves, poor and homeless, born in a cave, One who suffered and died like an ordinary man, but rose again and lived, a sign that all the faithful will live.

I watch their faces when I tell them the Good News. They are humbled and awed, awash in gratitude to a living, loving God who calls them, no matter that they are ignorant and tattered and wracked by disease. Jeshua speaks to their souls. "Come to me, all you who are weary and find life burdensome, and I will refresh you. Take my yoke upon your shoulders and learn from me, for I am gentle and humble of heart. Your souls will find rest, for my yoke is easy and my burden light." I watch the transformation of defeat to hope, despair to joy, and I, too, am humbled and awed.

Many stayed in Jerusalem, quietly melting into obscurity in Jerusalem's large population. They share with us the *Agape*, have joined home altars and circles of prayer, adding their voices to our own in our supplication, "Lord, Come!"

\*      \*      \*      \*      \*

# Chapter 19

Spring burst full bloom across the land. The earth blushed beneath the eye of the approaching sun and wrapped herself in a mantle of green, bedecked with the jewel-like lilies of the field to hide her winter nakedness. The air was balmy and filled with perfume. Lambs cavorted across the hills. Calves bawled and bucked their mothers' udders while new-born foals made valiant attempts to test their spindly legs. The ancient trees on the Mount of Olives spread forth their silvery leaves to provide a hiding place for the birds of the air to raise their nestlings in safety.

Jerusalem throbbed with life. The narrow, winding streets were nearly impassable, clogged with merchant trains bringing spices and perfumes and bangles of gold from the lands lying far to the east. Temporary corrals ringed the outer walls of the city and, when the breeze was right, the stench of dung and fodder and rank animal heat caused stomachs to heave and refined ladies covered their noses with perfume-soaked cloths and kept to the Upper City.

Fine yellow dust formed a haze above the city and filtered the rays of the bright, springtime sun until Jerusalem from afar seemed a glowing, golden globe. Inside the city the dust was an irritating, noxious enemy. It seeped through cloaks and skirts and veils causing eyes to tear and noses to sneeze and skin to burn and itch with its golden film. It dusted the honey cakes and dark, round loaves, and sifted into glasses of stale warm beer until nothing was eaten or drunk without the ever-present taste of grit.

The nettlesome dust was joined by the rank stench of garlic and onion and burning oil and stale wine and beer, of roasting meats and putrid fish and aromatic cakes and breads until man and beast were driven to a point of near madness.

The noise in the city was deafening. Merchants hawked their wares, the cords in their necks distended as they screamed to be heard over braying asses and barking dogs and camels that hacked and spat and lunged to bite. Entertainers ranged through the streets, jugglers, dancers, flutists, drummers, their colorful garb an abuse to the eye as they added their rhythmical beat to the cacophany booming around them.

The stench and the noise and the crush of bodies chafed against nerves and sapped a man's patience. Screaming arguments and vulgar street brawls were so commonplace that no one stopped to take note, let alone try to part the combatants.

Despite all the vexation and discomfort and sheer frustration, the city pulsed with an air of excitement. Everywhere the eye looked there were wonders to behold, wonders to send a man's fancy to dream of faraway places and exotic delights, and pleasures undreamed of before. And always the promise of riches and fame and power to be had if one used his courage and cunning.

The Way enjoyed peace. The Temple authorities were too occupied with the season of feasts and the political upheaval around them to pay any mind to the dispersed Nazarenes. Jonathan's inept rule had the Temple affairs in chaos. Old alliances fell apart, new ones emerged. Jonathan's weak attempts to wield authority caused heated arguments to break out, and the Sanhedrin became a battleground of debate.

The coming of more clement weather accelerated Herod's war with Aretes and brought the tax collectors out in force to check crops and cattle and market booths to be sure Rome got her due. The Temple authorities were inundated with complaints against Herod's coercions, graft, corruption and exorbitant taxes paid under duress, but with the political climate in a state of transition there was little they dared to do but fend them off with weak excuses and placate them the best they could.

The threat of further persecution from Saul seemed unlikely, at least for a time. The last word received from Damascus had Saul languishing in the house of Judas, still stunned by his vision and quaking in fear of the memory of his sudden blindness. It seemed he had entered that long, dark night of the soul that every intelligent, thinking man knows when suddenly confronted by truth. Old beliefs and preconceptions have to be discarded, old prejudices shed, and attitudes formed from childhood purged in the fire of faith. Yet the heart, mind, and soul of man cannot be left empty. New ideas have to be formed, new attitudes cultivated and brought to fruition, and new beliefs embraced to replace the old.

It was a terrifying experience. Friends and family once held so dear now turned their faces against such a man. He found himself reviled, condemned and cast out from his known society. He was beset by doubt, consumed by fear. Was it Satan's voice he heard, or that small, still Voice of the Father calling His child?

The Twelve and Elders in The Way knew full well the struggle Saul was going through, *if* it were not a sham, a cunning ploy of Belial to throw the Saints off guard. Each of them had known that long, dark night when fear and doubt and lack of courage waged war within their souls, but Saul was a formidable enemy and few were prepared to accept his change of heart. They followed James ben Joseph's advice. "Wait and see. Be wary and on guard. The fruit of his works will prove his sincerity."

Lucius remembered his thoughts about Saul on the night before the holocaust, and while others had grave misgivings on the outcome of Saul's spiritual struggle, Lucius felt like dancing through the streets, so convinced was he that Jeshua's call would be heard. He began to speak in Saul's favor, to expound upon Saul's virtues and talents, and describe a future for The Way with Saul as a friend and leader.

The Elect looked at Lucius with a wary eye. They shuddered in revulsion at the mere mention of Saul's name, and began to murmur among themselves over why Lucius would come to the murderer's defense. Only Peter and Barnabas heard what Lucius had to say with an open mind, and even they had reservations.

Lucius' expectation for Saul's conversion made his spirit soar. He felt buoyant, full of energy, and suffused with a zest for life. He threw himself into his work. He found homes for the new initiates, organized classes of instruction, even taught a class himself. He met with the Elders and basked in their high regard for his suggestions and opinions, and reveled in the knowledge that at last he was known as one of the leaders in The Way. The only cloud on his horizon was his separation from Mariaerh.

Lucius seldom went home to the house that he once felt held such promise, only once or twice a week and then merely for appearance' sake. The atmosphere between Mariaerh and him was strained to the point of being unbearable. They were polite, did not quarrel or fling accusing, sarcastic remarks at one another, but there was no topic on which they could safely converse.

Lucius' thoughts concentrated on his mission to the Gentiles. All his duties in The Way were carried out in the attitude of preparing himself for his ultimate work. He burned to discuss his plans and dreams with Nimmuo and Mariaerh, but all his plans included Saul, and the slightest allusion to Saul caused Mariaerh to pale and flee to her room and Nimmuo to fly into a rage.

Subsequently all conversation between them was stilted, constrained. They spoke on the weather, of whom they had seen or encountered that day. They exchanged bits of gossip about love matches and pregnancies, or related a comical phrase spoken by a precocious child. Mariaerh was again teaching a class of youngsters and Lucius patiently listened as she recounted her charges' accomplishments, but he found the antics of babes to be boring and could not disguise his disinterest. He tried to pretend an interest, and at times was effusive with praise for the work Mariaerh was doing, but his words rang false even to his own ears and more often than not he simply lapsed into silence and let the women chatter together.

Mariaerh never asked where Lucius spent his nights, a fact that Lucius found to be both a relief and a bone of contention. He recoiled at the thought of being confronted by his wife with his adultery, and yet it galled him that Mariaerh seemed not to care where he was or what he did. He fluctuated between guilt and rebellion, one moment resolving to give up his liaison with Judith and the next determined to do as he pleased.

Mariaerh guessed that Lucius had found another to share his bed. She did not know who or where, nor did she want to know. She also was suffused with guilt, knowing that if she would satisfy Lucius' needs he would not be forced to commit such a sin. She took his fault upon her own shoulders, condemning herself for his actions and praying night and day for the strength to beg his forgiveness and submit to his passion as any good wife would do. Her prayers seemed to go unheard. She could not. She felt herself separated from God, that her sin created a gulf between them and a dearth in her spiritual life. She was miserable, especially when jealousy coupled with guilt manifested as anger and self-pity.

At those times she blamed Lucius entirely for the situation. She railed at him in her thoughts, condemned him for his insensitivity toward her grief and need for privacy. She would brood over all the slights and thoughtlessness she had suffered at Lucius' hands. She remembered Celicia and all the other women whose names were linked with Lucius, and most of all she remembered Lucius' rejection of her and thought he would no doubt be unfaithful whether she submitted to him or not. She hated him then, and added that sin to all the others of which she felt herself accused.

There was no one to whom Mariaerh could unburden herself. She longed for her mother, fantasizing how she would lay her head in Marh's ample lap and pour out her heart to her sympathetic ear, disregarding the fact that if Marh were alive she could never speak to her of such intimate subjects. Marh would have been shocked, would have chastised her daughter severely and sent her home to obey her husband and perform every aspect of wifely duty. Mariaerh's idealized vision of her mother staunchly taking her side only increased the depth of her grief and widened the gulf between her and Lucius.

John Mark was the only person Mariaerh could even begin to confide in, but as he was male, there were definite limits as to how much she could tell him. She could pour out her grief and guilt over her parents and even her longing to have a child. She could faintly allude to the fact that not all was as it should be between Lucius and herself, but never could she say how repulsive she found Lucius' intimate contact.

Mariaerh put up a brave front in public. She convinced herself that no one in The Way knew of the estrangement between her and Lucius. She smiled at the proper times, pretended an interest in others' affairs, and spoke affectionately of Lucius as if all were well. It was a terrible strain for her to keep up such a sham and added to her already overblown sense of guilt. Dishonesty was also a sin, she believed.

The only time Mariaerh could relax and forget all her problems was when she was with the children. The children cared nothing for her sins or that she had failed as a wife. They only required her care and love, both of which Mariaerh had in ample supply. Yet the children revived her longing for a child of her own, and she lapsed into her old daydream of Lucius gazing adoringly at his wife and son.

Sometimes her need for a child was so great that she would resolve to swallow her pride, another of her sins, ask Lucius' forgiveness and return to his bed. At those times she would take special care about her appearance, letting her hair flow over her shoulders as Lucius liked, pinching her cheeks to bring some color to her pallid complexion. She would plan every word she would say to him, placing all the fault upon herself. By the time Lucius came home, she would be nearly ill with anxiety, trembling with fear of rejection, and weak with the strain of overcoming her acute embarrassment about any intimate conversation.

Each time she failed. Lucius would enter the house and greet her with a slight nod and a cool "Peace be with you," never noticing how she looked or recognizing by her pleading eyes or appeasing manner that she had something to say. He directed his conversation to Nimmuo and avoided any contact with his wife. Mariaerh's courage would wither at being ignored and she would feign a headache or weariness and retire to her bed where she would muffle her sobs in the pillow. Lucius usually left the house as soon as propriety would allow, never guessing that a chance for reconciliation had been lost.

*     *     *     *     *

James ben Zebedee and Nathaniel returned from Persia with wondrous tales of the Magi who through mystical means of the mind and spirit foresaw their arrival and met them on bended knee in reverence for the Word they brought. Those men of great wisdom were revered by the people of that enchanted land. Their tales of a babe born in a cave in Judea had long captivated the people's imagination and they flocked to James and Nathaniel to hear of Jeshua's words and deeds. Only urgent conditions at home in Jerusalem could have recalled James and Nathaniel from that land, and Nathaniel especially could hardly wait to go back.

With all of The Twelve in Jerusalem, the reorganization of The Way was consolidated and once more functioned as it had done before Saul's massacre. Saul's persecution had taught them a valuable lesson about security, and they exercised far more caution than they had before. The home altars became their principal places for worship. Small gatherings in private homes were far less likely to cause rumor and arouse suspicion than speaking openly in the synagogues or in the Temple courts. They kept to the practice of using their secret password and sign of the fish, and the Temple authorities had no clue that the Nazarenes were again a force with which to contend.

As the number of initiates grew, it became necessary to appoint new deacons to oversee the distribution of goods to replace those who were slain or were forced to flee. Lucius was sure that this time he would be named among them, but again he was overlooked.

Saul's obvious omission to include Lucius in his persecution led some of the Elect to question Lucius' loyalty to The Way. All the old objections to his elevation to leadership were again brought to mind—his reluctance to claim Mariaerh as his wife, his involvements with the Greek-speaking girls in the Synagogue of the Freedmen. Once more he was the subject of gossip. Some wondered to what extent Lucius' actions had influenced the drastic revenge taken against The Way. Others even went so far as to infer that his kinship to Saul had been the impetus for Saul's persecution, implying that Saul's hatred of The Way lay in his belief that its teachings had corrupted the faith of his cousin. When Lucius began to speak in Saul's favor and declare his belief in Saul's vision on the road to Damascus, there were many who were convinced that Lucius was not to be trusted. The final incrimination came when word leaked out that Lucius was involved in an illicit relationship with Celicia's Greek-speaking friend Judith. The Elect were convinced they were right and petitioned The Twelve to exclude him.

The decision came as a blow to Lucius. He could not understand why he was excluded, but pride prevented him from asking for an explanation. He decided again that it must be his Roman blood. He sulked for days, wounded to the heart that all of his work had gone unrewarded. When told that a man named Nicolas had been chosen to take Stephen's place as the keeper of the treasury for The Way, he seethed with the injustice.

Nicolas was of Greek parentage through his father. He was very rich and held in great esteem among society. One time he had approached Jeshua and asked the Master what he must do to gain eternal life. When Jeshua had told him to go and sell all his goods and give the money to the poor, Nicolas had sadly turned away, for he could not give up his possessions. Now he had returned, repentant and poor, and The Twelve had raised him to a high position. Lucius thought wryly to himself that Greek blood was obviously acceptable, but Roman blood was not. He withdrew into himself and found his only solace in a bottle of wine and Judith's willing embrace.

Philip went back to Samaria and with Luke's help, many Samaritans were baptized in Jeshua's *name*. For eight hundred years the Samaritans had been considered an outcast people by the Jews. They were the descendants of people from Babylonia, Cuthah, Avva, and other lands who were brought to Samaria after the Assyrians deported the Jews. They accepted the Law of Moses and believed in the God of the Jews, but staunchly refused to acknowledge the Jerusalem Temple as the true abode of God, or to bow to Temple authority. A feud had existed between Jews and Samaritans for generations, often erupting into violence. Border raids and skirmishes were commonplace and a man crossed from one land into the other at his own peril.

It was remarkable for the Samaritans to profess their faith in Jeshua, himself a Jew, and the Saints could not help but speculate what it could mean. Would The Way prove to be the common ground on which the Jew and Samaritan could meet in peace? The prospect was awe-inspiring. Peter and John went to Samaria and laid their hands upon the new believers and watched in amazement as the Holy Spirit became manifest in that hostile land by the speaking in tongues, prophecy, and the many other gifts bestowed by the Spirit.

News about Saul in Damascus was also heartening. Saul submitted his will to the Lord's and left Damascus without carrying out his intent to rid the city of the Greek-speaking Nazarenes. His followers and the Temple police had returned to Jerusalem disgruntled and furious at being betrayed by their leader. They accused him of cowardice, believed his blindness was only a result of one of his fits, a fit brought on by fear. They did not believe that Saul had seen a vision, and the light they all had witnessed they explained away as only an aberration of the sun's rays glinting off the desert sands. Their idol had disgraced himself, and they cursed him for his weakness and themselves for being duped. The sight of their once admired and exalted leader trudging alone and unarmed toward the desert like a common hermit, filled them with disgust, and they returned to Jerusalem, condemning him as a traitor. The Saints rejoiced. Surely the Holy Spirit protected them once more. The Way grew in peace.

Lucius did not rejoice. Saul's totally unexpected departure threw him into a fit of depression. He had been so sure that Saul's mission to the Gentiles corresponded to his own. He had even convinced himself that his rejection as a deacon was the direct interference of the Holy Spirit to free him for his ultimate work. Now all seemed lost. No one knew where Saul was or what he was doing, and certainly he could never return to Jerusalem as long as the Temple authorities considered him a traitor.

Lucius wrestled with doubt. He questioned the validity of his vision in Caesarea and wondered if his interpretation of its meaning had not been at fault. He even questioned his decision to come to Jerusalem in the first place, and the wisdom of joining The Way. What purpose had it been? The work he performed could be done by any number of men. His wife could not bear his touch and had thus far proved to be barren. The Elders suspected his Roman blood and did not trust him to manage the communal treasury, even though his qualifications were every bit as notable as those of the wealthy Nicolas, with the added advantage of six years spent in The Way.

Was it all a mistake? Did the Holy One punish him for neglecting his sons and for bringing grief to his parents in their advancing years? How easy life had been in Laodicea. He reread the latest letters received from Philippi and Merceden, of Lucia's ever-growing brood, of bountiful crops and flocks and warm sun and clean air and the continual irritations encountered with a house full of servants, and of course their repetitive plea that he and Nimmuo return to their father's house. The letters filled him with yearning for the simplicity and security he had known as a lad, and Jerusalem began to seem like a suffocating prison from which there was no escape.

The full blast of summer's heat descended upon the city, shimmering in waves from the glaring white limestone. The noise in the city was deafening, the choking yellow dust unbearable. Lucius longed even more for the crystalline air of Laodicea, for the soaring green hills that soothed the eye, and the cooling breeze that flowed through the valley. He hated Jerusalem. He hated the stench, the filth, the despairing, ever-present poor, the prejudices, the quarrels, the constant tensions and fears and juggling for power and prestige. It all unnerved him. He chafed with impatience with everything and everyone around him. Nothing pleased him. Nothing satisfied him. When the leaders decided that The Way was no longer under threat of persecution and they could safely resume their missions in the field, Lucius assumed he would be given a choice assignment and eagerly waited to hear where he would be sent.

Thaddeus and Jude arrived from Antioch with a list of the refugees now living there. Under Cornelius' protection they were trying to organize a community of Saints and Peter was sent to oversee their attempt. James ben Zebedee left for Spain to bring the Good News to the Jewish colonies settled there at the time of the exile. Thomas went back to Idumea, while Thaddeus, Andrew, and Nathaniel joined Philip and John in Samaria. The others went to the coast and to Galilee, full of enthusiasm for promoting the work of the Lord. They took their wives and families with them and each leave-taking was like bidding farewell to a holiday caravan off to vacation away from the city heat. Lucius was left behind.

By fall Lucius thought he could stand it no longer. Life was passing him by. He was thirty-seven years old and had accomplished nothing of value. The routine tasks he performed in The Way bored and stifled him.

His marriage was a failure. His infatuation with Judith had turned to disgust. She had nothing to offer but her body. Her conversation was vacuous, concerned only with lurid gossip or her own beauty or new forms of stimulation. She had no sympathy for Lucius' problems and his fits of despair, but would cut his lamentations short and draw him down onto the bed as if reveling in fleshly passion would solve everything.

Lucius went to the brothel less and less frequently. He found an accommodating inn in the Upper City that at least made an attempt at cleanliness, and found more comfort in a bottle of wine than he found in Judith's suffocating flesh. The wine dulled his despair and made him forget his loneliness, at least for the night, but night is followed by day and the days became intolerable. His old restlessness took root and grew until he was on the verge of bolting for freedom. Then Cornelius came to the city and Lucius' springtime sense of impending change was confirmed.

Tiberius had ordered Vitellius to give aid to Herod in his war with Aretas. His vast army prepared to march through Judea, but the principal men of the Jews forestalled him and pleaded with him not to bring the standards and ensigns that bore images into their land. Vitellius heard their plea and sent his army along the coast, while he and Herod came to Jerusalem to offer sacrifice on the Feast of Atonement.

Lucius was among the throngs who lined the streets to catch a glimpse of the Syrian proconsul and the Tetrarch of Galilee. It was an impressive sight. Trumpet players and drummers heralded their coming and led the procession into the city. Clear, piercing notes rent the air, deafening drumrolls reverberated from the cobbled streets and sent tremors through the spectators' feet. Herod and Vitellius were resplendent in richly ornate, royal robes of purple and gold and indigo blue, bedecked with silver chains and studded with jewels that flashed so brilliantly in the noon-day sun that the onlookers squinted their eyes and could hardly bear to look upon them. They rode noble steeds that pranced and danced in a sideways trot with their heads flung high and their nostrils flared as though disdaining the cheering crowds.

The royal guard was as wonderfully mounted, for the equestrian corps was inordinately proud of their regiment, and trained and cosseted their steeds with more attention than they gave to their children. Their precision in dress and armor was fabulous to behold. Red tunics blazed beneath fringed, leather vests, iron-soled sandals that laced to just below the knee, and dazzling golden helmets that caught the sun and tossed it back to the spectators' eyes. They held their shining spears aloft at an exact height and angle, and every knee was bent to the same degree. Their mounts put each foot down with the roll of a drum, as if all were one creature instead of many.

Cornelius rode at the head of his troops directly behind Herod and Vitellius. Only the insignia on his helmet and spear distinguished his dress from his men. He rode with dignity, his eyes straight ahead. Lucius knew those eyes missed nothing but were ever alert for the smallest sign of unrest, or the merest hint that an assassin lurked in the throngs.

The procession entered the courtyard of the Fortress Antonia with a clatter of hooves and a massive fanfare of trumpets and drums, then the great gates clanged shut behind them.

Lucius had taken particular care with his dress on this occasion for he wanted to see Cornelius and knew that his chances for admission into the Fortress were greatly enhanced if he appeared as a nobleman and not a poor Jew. He had rummaged through his belongings until he found his old pale blue tunic and the deeper blue mantle, and was pleased to discover they still fit after so many years. He had his hair and beard trimmed, and after scrutinizing himself in the barber's mirror, his spirits had soared for the first time in months. Lucius of Cyrene, son of Philippi, nobleman now of Laodicea, stared back at him from the burnished brass and Lucius welcomed him with an over-flowing heart.

When the gates closed behind the procession, Lucius turned against the crowd and made his way to a smaller gate where he would petition an audience with Cornelius. He had no trouble getting through the throng, for the people stepped aside and made way as it was obvious by his dress that he was a man of wealth and prestige. The guard at the smaller gate snapped to attention when Lucius approached. Lucius returned his salute off-handedly and said in an imperious tone, "Lucius of Cyrene, formerly of Laodicea and now of this city, to see the centurion Cornelius!"

Another guard was summoned and led Lucius to Cornelius' suite where yet another announced him, and Cornelius himself opened the door and greeted him expansively with a kiss on both cheeks.

"Lucius! Old Friend! Come in, come in. You anticipated my desire for your company!" He turned to a man servant. "Wine, refreshment! The dust of the road clogs my throat!"

He led Lucius to an inner chamber opulently appointed in tapestries, thick carpets and lush, soft divans. They ate and drank then settled back into talk of family, the latest controversies animating the senate, and all that had transpired since last they had met. Cornelius brought him up to date on his attempts to organize The Way in Antioch.

"There is much opposition from the Jewish leadership. They try to bar our Brothers from speaking in the synagogues and ridicule us in the streets. Some of them have even gone so far as to complain to me, not knowing of course that I too am one of the Christians."

Lucius' eyebrows raised. "Christians?"

"A title given us by the Greeks and understood by the Jews to differentiate us from themselves."

Lucius smiled. "Christos" transformed into Greek the well-known Hebrew word for the long-awaited "Anointed One," the Messiah. The word "Christian" meant a follower of, or believer in, Jeshua as *the* "Christos." An appropriate title, Lucius mused. He rolled the word about his tongue, tasting its very rightness. "I should not take offense at being known as a Christian," he laughed.

Cornelius leaned back on the divan and regarded

Lucius in silence for a long moment, then sat up and leaned forward, resting his elbows on his knees. He spoke with intensity, his lined face serious and his voice urgent.

"I intend to build a synagogue of our own when I return from this abominable war of Herod's, a place where we Christians can gather to worship in peace without harassment from unbelievers. I want it to be a synagogue free from prejudice of race, where Romans, Greeks, and Jews can come together in the *name* of the Christ."

Lucius' eyes widened. "Greeks and Romans? What will our leaders say to that?"

"Peter is now in Antioch. His heart knows I am right, but he falters when remembering the debate aroused over my baptism."

Lucius got up and strode across the room. "No one knows better than I how Roman blood generates distrust among the Jews," he said bitterly. "I am forever held under suspicion, always remembered for my father's blood and never for my mother's. Sometimes I despair that I will ever enjoy the full confidence of The Twelve."

Cornelius poured more wine and held a goblet out to Lucius. "Come to Antioch."

Lucius stared at Cornelius, ignoring the proffered drink. A hundred images flashed through his mind until it churned with excitement. Cornelius saw the interest his proposal provoked and pressed his point.

"We need a man of your knowledge, your experience, even," he laughed, "of your Roman blood. Why, your very being is symbolic of what I would like to do, joining Gentile and Jew in a common faith in the Christ. Think about it. Speak with your wife and let me know your decision before I leave Jerusalem."

Lucius' hand trembled as he reached for the goblet and quaffed down the wine. He flung the emptied goblet across the room and crushed Cornelius in a mighty embrace. "No need for thought!" he cried. "I will, and at once!" Then soberly and with his voice choked with emotion, "You have saved my sanity, friend. I shall never be able to repay you."

"Ah! Enough!" Cornelius said gruffly, "We are Brothers in Christ. What we do for one another we do for Him. Go then, and soon. Jonas and Susane will welcome you. Need you blessings from the Elders to go?"

Lucius shook his head sadly. "I doubt they care, they surely will not miss me." Then defiantly, "It matters not. I go!"

Lucius took leave of Cornelius and hurried toward his house, his thoughts flying before him. His heart sang with thanksgiving and gave wings to his feet. He flung open his door and strode into the house, his face flushed with excitement, startling Nimmuo and Mariaerh.

"We go to Antioch!" he cried. "Begin to pack what we need for the journey, for we leave as soon as we can make ready!"

The women stared in astonishment. Mariaerh was stunned and she winced as if struck a blow. Nimmuo gasped and clasped her hands.

"Antioch! Antioch of Syria? That great city? Lucius! Do not tease! Are you serious?"

Lucius grinned and swung her off her feet. "I do not joke. Cornelius is here and asked me to come to Antioch. He plans to build a synagogue just for The Way and I will be the overseer. Think of it! A synagogue of our own!"

Mariaerh stepped forward timidly. Her face was pale and she trembled with agitation. She gathered her courage and asked in a quavering voice, "Isn't this Cornelius a Roman centurion? By what authority does he select leaders in our faith?"

Lucius shot her a withering glance and answered coldly, "By his own authority, given him by the Holy Spirit as the first of the Gentiles baptized in the *name* of our Lord Jeshua."

Mariaerh plunged on. "Have you spoken with James ben Joseph or any other of our Elders of this plan? Do they give their consent?"

Lucius' countenance darkened. "I am not a slave. I have no need for their consent. I do what pleases myself and the Holy Spirit who guides me."

Fear, despair, and loathing to leave her native land threatened to overwhelm Mariaerh. She made a desperate last attempt to salvage the remnants of her known world. "But what of our work here?" she cried. "What of your classes and the children under my care? What of our home?"

"This house is hardly a home any longer," Lucius said harshly. "As for my class, anyone can take my place, and the same holds true for you. There will be no more discussion on this matter. Prepare to leave in a matter of days." He turned to Nimmuo. "There is much to attend to. Do what you can and I'll return as soon as possible." Without a further look at Mariaerh, he swung on his heel and left the house, leaving Nimmuo to cope with Mariaerh's tears and comfort her the best she could.

\* \* \* \* \*

Vitellius deposed Jonathan and installed his brother Theophilus in his place. Theophilus showed little of the weakness and ineptitude his brother had displayed. He did not fear Caiaphas, in fact looked upon his brother-in-law with faintly veiled contempt. He was a favorite son of old Annas and while he revered his father's wise advice, he did not fear to go against it. The Jews were content with Vitellius' choice and looked forward to some semblance of peace in the Sanhedrin.

Under Cornelius' urging, Vitellius instructed his new High Priest to release the Nazarenes arrested by Saul. Few had survived the dank, fetid, nether regions that contained the Temple dungeons, but those who did were embraced by The Way in gladsome celebration. They were taken to the homes of the Saints where they were tenderly nursed back to health, but none could overcome their fear of Jerusalem, and left that city as soon as they were well enough to travel.

On the fourth day of his stay in Jerusalem, Vitellius received letters informing him of the death of Tiberius. He called the city together and every inhabitant was obliged to take an oath of fidelity to Caligula, the new Emperor of Rome. The city was agog with the news. Rumor and speculation ran rampant. Business leaders met to discuss what effect a new administration would have upon commerce. Temple leaders anguished over Caligula's possible attitudes toward the Jews. The poor simply hoped he would let them live and not raise their taxes.

Vitellius recalled his army and turned them back to winter in Antioch as he had no instructions from Caligula to engage Aretas in war. Herod gnashed his teeth and tore at his robes, but there was nothing he could do.

Lucius received a message from Cornelius. "Come to the Fortress at dawn and make your journey under my protection." Lucius crumpled the parchment in his fist and pounded a table with joy. He was ready! There was nothing to detain him. He informed Mariaerh and Nimmuo of Cornelius' note then left to spend a last night with Judith.

Mariaerh spent the night staring into the dark. Her entire world had been destroyed. She was orphaned, and soon to be bereft of friend or even acquaintance, cast adrift in an alien, Gentile world with only a cold, uncaring husband to be her guide. She was numb with fear, rigid with terror at the prospect of traveling in the company of a Roman contingent. She prayed to the Lord to stop her heart and unite her with her mother, but at dawn she was still alive.

Nimmuo also lay staring into the dark, but her thoughts were not those of Mariaerh. She was filled with excitement and could barely wait for morning to come. A new life! A new place and new people, and the wonder and challenge of bringing new souls to faith! And Antioch! That famed city of riches and culture and cosmopolitan delight. Oh, how good was the Lord to lay this banquet before them!

Lucius slept the deep, profound sleep of a man untroubled by cares, his appetites sated by food and love. He had intended to tell Judith that she would see him no more, but her delight in his presence had been so endearing, he was reluctant to shatter her happy mood. He said nothing, but had been even more tender and lavish with his caresses than usual. He thought he might leave her a note, or if she chanced to awaken before he left, to tell her then. Better then than to endure a nightlong session of pleading and tears.

Lucius awoke hours before the first pale lavender ribbons of light began to streak across the sky. His arm ached and tingled. He pulled it from under Judith's sleeping form, careful not to awaken her. She lay on her side with her back curled against him, and Lucius eased himself away and got up. He paused for a moment to study Judith's naked, sleeping body, thinking it was the last image he would have of her. Her dark brown hair fanned out across her fleshy shoulders and tumbled down her back, limp and dull and in need of washing. Her buttocks were wide, round mounds, her thighs thick and sturdy. One arm pressed against her abundant breasts, pushing them up to an even more voluptuousness. Her face was pale in sleep, her lips slightly parted.

A sudden shudder of repulsion passed through Lucius. When first he had begun to share Judith's bed, he had found that abundant, yielding flesh to be a delight. She assuaged his loneliness, eased his need, and consented to erotic delights that he had learned long ago which were unacceptable to Mariaerh. But now he was sated with sex and he found Judith's excesses distasteful.

He thought of Mariaerh, how opposite she was to Judith. Mariaerh's cool, slim body contained not an ounce of extra flesh. Her narrow shoulders tapered to a tiny waist he could span with his hands, then fanned to finely molded hips and long, tapering limbs, while her small, soft breasts just filled his cupped hands. Where Judith pounced upon him with squeals of delight and threatened to smother him in her voluptuous body, Mariaerh trembled and approached him shyly, yielding to him in submission and modesty.

The memory of Mariaerh warmed his loins and he spun away from the sight of Judith and pulled on his clothes. He glanced around the dingy room to be sure there was nothing there that belonged to him and grimaced with disgust. The bedlinens were filthy, gray with grime, tattered and thin with age. The room stank of sex and sweat and stale beer and spoiled food. He himself smelled no better.

Lucius wondered how he had ever allowed himself to frequent such a place and to find pleasure in anyone as ignorant and coarse as Judith. He shrugged his shoulders and thought there was little to be gained in castigating himself for deeds done. Today was a new start, a new life. He would make amends to Mariaerh and become a model husband. What more could she ask than to be the wife of the overseer of the synagogue? He would make her the happiest of women, and she would regret that she had ever rejected him from her bed. He quietly left the tavern and stepped out into the silent street. He took a deep breath of the pre-dawn air and felt happy and free. He forgot to leave a note.

# PART II
# ANTIOCH

# Chapter 20

Mariaerh clung to her reins. Each plodding step her horse took sent a stab of pain shooting through her back. Her arms ached. Her legs were numb. Her blood-shot eyes burned from days of the sun glinting off the sea. Her throat was raw and her mouth filled with grit. She longed for a bath. She was covered with dust raised by the long line of mounted troops, and she stank of horse and her own salty sweat.

The last seven miles inland from the port of Seleucia had seemed to take forever, and she thought they would never reach Antioch. She squinted her eyes and tried to judge the time by the position of the sun. It hung low in the sky, and she prayed they would reach Antioch before night fell.

She could not bear one more night on the road. She had hardly dared to close her eyes throughout the journey lest one of those godless barbarians who rode behind her should invade her tent and do as he pleased. They were shameless! They had not even bothered to try to conceal their lust, and had brazenly stared at Nimmuo and her, then laughed and made ribald jokes at Lucius' expense. Romans! She knew in her heart that if Lucius had tried to stop one from molesting her, he would have been killed without a thought.

Nimmuo was riding at Mariaerh's side and Lucius was just ahead of them, riding abreast of Cornelius. He twisted in his saddle and pointed ahead. They saw a ribbon of flashing blue that had to be the wide Orontes.

Nimmuo said excitedly to Mariaerh, "We're almost there! Antioch is just across the river."

265

Mariaerh could only nod. She certainly did not share Nimmuo's enthusiasm at reaching their destination. Antioch was a pagan city full of danger and corruption. As Lucius' wife she had no choice but to follow where he decided to go, but that did not mean she had to be happy about it. Despite all of Nimmuo's assurances that they would be among friends, Mariaerh had dreaded every mile that had brought them closer to Antioch. The Hellenists who had fled Jerusalem were really Lucius' friends, not hers. Once they became aware of the alienation between Lucius and her, they would naturally sympathize with him and she would be no more than a tolerated outsider, the brunt of their gossip, the object of their curiosity.

As they neared the river, Mariaerh's miserable musings were interrupted by a low, rumbling roar that grew louder and louder as they approached the city. The sound was ominous. Mariaerh wondered what it could be until Cornelius called back, "Antioch celebrates the election of Caligula!" Mariaerh's heart quickened, and she felt a quiver of fear at the prospect of pagan celebrations.

They thundered across the great bridge that spanned the Orontes and were met by tumultuous cheers from the citizenry who lined the streets. Mariaerh clung even tighter to her reins, terrified that her horse would rear and bolt, but the disciplined beast merely raised her head and changed her gait to a high-stepping prance as if she knew she performed for an audience.

The city was a madhouse! Mariaerh gasped and paled with shock. People with their faces painted like grotesque, heathenish masks and dressed in outlandish, bizarre costumes danced in the streets. Sword-swallowers, fire-eaters, exotic dancing girls who wore little or nothing and made Mariaerh blush to the roots of her hair; jugglers, acrobats, clowns, mimes, fools, all whirled in a blur before her eyes. She stared in horror when she saw a parade of naked slaves being led to the circus where they would fight to the death to the glee of the crowd, then covered her mouth to smother a cry of dismay as they passed an auction block lined with nubile boys and girls being sold amidst maniacal bidding. Drunkenness was rampant. Men and women staggered and reeled and screamed with raucous laughter, while every tavern door was crowded with eager patrons scrambling to get in. Twenty-three years of savage rule under Tiberius had at last come to an end, and his subjects exulted in joyous acclaim.

Caligula was the darling of the people. His father, Germanicas, had been adored by the masses, and his untimely death, rumored to be by Tiberius' hand, had caused riots in the streets. Deprived of their hero, they sought solace in his son and had lavished upon Caligula all the love and devotion they had felt for his father. Now at age twenty-five, Caligula would rule as his father should have done before him, and the people looked for a benevolent, prosperous rule, a golden age not seen since the early days of Augustus.

They entered the courtyard of the fortress to a bacchanalian scene of unrestrained debauchery. Legionnaires swarmed in drunken disarray, waving wine flasks over their heads and toasting Caligula with shouts of "Hail, Caesar!" They stumbled and reeled and fell sprawled on the ground as their comrades cheered and applauded. Scantily clad females encouraged them, teasing and tempting the soldiery to take liberties that would never be permitted on an ordinary day. Naked bodies writhed in orgasmic ecstasy. Squealing girls half-heartedly fled their pursuers then laughed uproariously when caught and carried away.

Mariaerh covered her ears and closed her eyes against the sight of such evil. Nimmuo edged her horse nearer to Lucius, fascinated, yet repulsed and frightened by the blatant excesses. Even Cornelius was embarrassed and turned the troops over to another in disgust and hurried Lucius and the girls away from the orgy. He guided them through a maze of deserted back streets in the direction they had come until the ear-rending roar faded to a distant, muffled hum.

The sun was gone. Only a splash of purple and mauve remained in the darkening sky. Mariaerh swayed in the saddle, too numb to think and too tired to feel the pain in her back. Just when she thought she could not possibly endure any more, Cornelius drew in his reins and bellowed Jonas' name.

Narrow, one-storied limestone houses butted up against one another with their doorways leading directly onto the street. One door opened a crack and then was flung wide as an astonished Jonas bolted into the street to greet them. He fairly danced from one to another, crying, "Lucius! Nimmuo! Mariaerh! You, here? I can't believe my eyes!"

Lucius was already on the ground and the men embraced and pounded one another on the back. Nimmuo slid down from her saddle and flung herself into his arms as Susane came out of the house and the embraces and exclamations began all over again.

They seemed like actors in a play to Mariaerh, or else like a dream. She was not even aware that Jonas was lifting her down from the horse until she cried out in pain and felt her feet on solid ground.

Jonas laughed and swept her into his arms like a giant bear. "Poor child! It's torture to ride when not accustomed to it. You'll be all right as soon as your muscles have time to heal. Come in! Come in! Cornelius?"

Cornelius shook his head. "I must get back. I'll see you as soon as I can. My wife, Ex-elor, will expect you, Lucius. Bring Nimmuo and Mariaerh with you. I'll send a slave to show you the way in a few days."

Jonas ushered them into the house and Mariaerh limped along behind. She was trembling and weak, and could not bring her mind to focus. The others' excited voices buzzed around her head until she could hardly keep from covering her ears and screaming at them to be quiet. Susane flew to the task of preparing a meal, while Nimmuo set out dishes, and Lucius and Jonas did their best to out-talk one another. Mariaerh dutifully tried to help, but the very thought of food made her stomach roil. When a bowl slipped from her shaking hands and shattered on the floor, her tenuously held self-control snapped and she wept with uncontrollable abandon.

Nimmuo and Susane rushed to consoler her. Jonas fussed over her, taking her pulse and laying his hand on her brow in search of a fever, while Lucius watched in bewilderment. Susane led her to a mat and urged her to lie down. Mariaerh collapsed in a heap and in minutes was fast asleep. While the others talked far into the night, Mariaerh was sunk in oblivion, free from fear for the first time since leaving Jerusalem.

The rising sun spilled through a window and teased Lucius awake. He was up in a trice, loath to waste a minute of his first day in Antioch. The others still slept and he picked his way around them and went outside.

The day was glorious. The sky was the same depth of blue as the sky over Laodicea, and not a cloud was in sight. The air was clean and cool and smelled of trees and grass and over-ripe fruit. From the back of the house Lucius could see the wide Orontes through a stand of trees that grew between the row of houses and the riverbank. It was as blue as the sky, and flashed beneath the morning sun like a field of diamonds. Lucius raised his face to the sun and flung his arms aloft, letting the gentle breeze wash away the night's sleep and cleanse his body as if bathed in a tranquil stream. He wiggled his toes, reveling in the crisp, dewy grass beneath his bare feet, and the squalor and dust and stench of Jerusalem seemed like a nightmare forgotten. He found the water jars beside the door and washed his hands and intoned his morning prayers with the fervor of heartfelt thanks.

Jonas stumbled from the doorway, groggy and bleary-eyed from lack of sleep. Lucius waited until he had washed his hands and said his prayers, then slapped him across the back and cried, "Peace be with you, friend, and good morning!"

Jonas flinched and groaned. "May the Almighty One preserve me from high spirits at dawn."

Lucius chortled. "Are the women awake? My stomach demands food!" He shouted toward the house, "Nimmuo! Mariaerh! There are hungry men here!"

Jonas cringed. "Quiet, man! Do you want to awaken the dead?"

"Why not?" Lucius laughed. "This is a day to be alive! Look at that river! Smell that sea air! It is only you who refuse to come awake. How many glasses of wine did we drink?"

"Too many, as my head reminds me," Jonas groaned.

The women joined them at the water jars, then returned to the house and set out melons, figs, and flat barley cakes to break their fast. The night's sleep had restored Mariaerh. Her body was sore and stiff, but the prospect of a day free from the company of Roman soldiers made all her aches and pains seem inconsequential. She felt lighthearted for the first time since Lucius had announced his intention to come to Antioch. She watched him devour his food and could not help but be infected by his good humor and enthusiasm. He chafed with impatience to see his old friends, and as soon as their hunger had dulled, all but Susane hurried away to find them and to explore the city they now would call home.

The Jewish section of Antioch was large and not unlike Jerusalem, although better planned with the streets running in an orderly plot rather than the helter-skelter manner they did in Jerusalem. After weeks of seeing no one but Romans, it was a balm to Mariaerh's soul to see long-bearded rabbis with their phylacteries strapped to their brows, and carpenters hurrying to their shops sporting a curl of wood shaving over their ears. She was surrounded by Jews. It looked Jewish and smelled Jewish, and the demons of fear that had so plagued Mariaerh slowly vanished.

The Saints were scattered throughout the entire section and there simply was not time to see them all in one day. Those whom they did see reacted as Jonas and Susane had, with astonishment and joy and enthusiastic welcome. It was dusk by the time they turned back to the house, but Jonas insisted that they make one last stop along the way to see Pathos and Ulai. When they pushed open the gate to Ulai's walled courtyard, they stopped in their tracks and stared open-mouthed in surprise, for it was as if they were suddenly transported back to Martha's garden in Bethany.

The news of Lucius' arrival had spread by word of
mouth as though on the wings of an eagle. The
courtyard was awash in torchlight. Tables arranged in
a U shape were laden with delicacies that filled the air
with tantalizing aromas. A throng of smiling faces
stood before them as every Christian in Antioch had
gathered to share the *Agape* and welcome Lucius and
the girls to their community.

They stood rooted, speechless with surprise. Jonas'
face displayed a smug, self-satisfied grin while Susane
laughed with delight at the success of her planning. The
Saints surged forward. After a crush of embraces and
joyous greetings and many tears shed, Ulai demanded
they eat and led Lucius to the head table to preside over
the bread and wine.

The Saints scrambled for their places, and the garden
became hushed. Every face was upturned and glowed
with happy expectation for Lucius to begin. He stood
before them, but his heart was so full he could not speak.
His gaze traveled down the row of tables, alighting a
moment on each beloved face until his eyes swam with
tears and he could no longer see. So many faces he had
never thought to see again, but others he had loved were
lost, and the pain of their absence was so acute he could
almost see their ghostly faces intermingled among the
living.

The Saints understood, and their own eyes blurred.
They poured out their love and sympathy toward
Lucius, an emotional tide of such intensity that he was
nearly overcome. His hands trembled, his entire body
began to shake. He felt weak, faint, and thought his
knees would buckle. He struggled for breath. The world
seemed to spin around him and he was drawn into a
vortex of no time, no space, as his mind and spirit
stretched and expanded until he became one with all.

Mariaerh was seated at Lucius' side and she
somehow was not drawn into the trance-like state the
others shared. She watched, awed, reminded of those
times when Jeshua's presence was so evident in
Zebedee's house. A full moon sailed overhead. Not a
sound could be heard. Even the air held its breath lest it

disturb that holy moment when God communed with man. An aura of peace settled over them. Their rhythm of breath became one, their hearts beat in unison.

Mariaerh waited a few long moments, absorbing the peace, then touched Lucius' gently on his arm. Her touch brought him back to conscious awareness. He groped for her hand, then squeezed it and smiled down at her. An audible intake of breath issued from the Saints and time and space in the ordinary world resumed.

Lucius reached for the cup. His hands were now steady and sure. He raised the cup aloft and turned his face toward heaven. His voice was deep and vibrant and rang with conviction. The blessing resounded with power and might, and the Saints ate and drank without a shadow of doubt that they shared the body and blood of their Lord.

It was a night to remember, a night of sorrow and joy, of laughter and tears, and of grief and thanksgiving. Their hymns echoed in the air long after the last note was sung, as if caught and repeated by angels until they reached the ears of God.

The roll of the known dead was called, and prayers said for their souls, and each name was like a stab to the heart. Helene, Sylvesta, Celia, all asleep in the Lord, while others like Carvett, Sachet, Salome were lost, whether dead or alive, no one knew. Lucius was bowed by sorrow. He could almost hear the haunting notes vibrating from the harp under Sylvesta's and Celia's accomplished fingers. He could see Salome blushing under his praise for her beautiful lace, and Carvett's hands flying over a plastered wall, creating a scene of peace and beauty. Nimmuo brushed away bitter, angry tears when told how Helene died of cold and exposure because of the lack of food and healing assistance, and Mariaerh sat stoically dry-eyed when the toll taken in Bethany was read.

But not all were lost. Josida, Cerecea, Jacobean, Phoebe, Agnosta, and blessedly, Jeseuha and her babes had all made it safely to Antioch, and their reunion with Lucius and the girls was a moment of unforgettable joy. Even Philas was said to be safe, living quietly a few miles beyond Antioch as a tiller of the soil, his condemnation of The Way mellowed to an attitude of fatalistic acceptance.

It was nearly the midnight hour before they could bring themselves to part. After many prolonged and tearful farewells and promises to meet again, Lucius, the girls, Susane and Jonas followed the hushed, moonlit streets back to Jonas' house. They were bone weary, drained and emotionally spent, yet Lucius' mind spun with exhilaration. He wanted to talk, to spill out all his plans that tumbled about in his mind. The only response he could elicit from his weary companions were polite grunts and yawns they did not even try to hide. Lucius laughed at them and tried to raise them to his own state of euphoria.

"Why are you so tired? This is a great day! Have you no sense of adventure?"

"Day!" Jonas growled. "It is now the middle of the night and if you are not quiet, you will arouse a guard and your first adventure will be in the city jail!"

They faced an awkward moment when once in the house Susane showed Lucius and Mariaerh to a curtained alcove she had prepared for them to share. Susane had no way of knowing of the estrangement between them, and had gone to a great deal of trouble to rearrange her tiny house to provide them with a modicum of privacy. She stood by the curtain, smiling happily and waited for Lucius' and Mariaerh's expected delighted response. Lucius looked embarrassed. Mariaerh was dismayed. She closed her eyes for a moment and sighed. There was nothing to do except pretend that all was as Susane expected. She accepted the candle Susane held out to her and thanked her for her efforts, then held the curtain aside and motioned for Lucius to go before her. She let the curtain drop, and without looking at Lucius, extinguished the flame with her fingers. She removed her outer garments in the dark, then lay down on the mat without speaking a word.

Lucius hurriedly undressed and lay beside her, both

on their backs with their bodies touching since the narrow mat offered no room to lie apart. Neither slept. The tension between them grew unbearable, and their flesh seemed to burn where it touched.

Finally Lucius could stand it no more and turned on his side to face Mariaerh. "This is intolerable, Mariaerh," he whispered. "We start a new life in a new city, and soon in a new home. Can't we start anew with each other? Let us put the past behind us and live as God meant for man and wife to live."

Mariaerh did not move or speak. Lucius tentatively laid his hand on her shoulder, and when she did not pull away, began to caress her arm, then slid his hand across her waist and gently drew her nearer. Mariaerh did not resist, and Lucius grew bolder. He kissed her, gentle, fleeting kisses on her cheeks and eyelids and throat, and then full and lingeringly on her mouth. Only when his hand began to tenderly knead her breast did Mariaerh show any response, and then a mere intake of breath and a sudden stiffening of her body was all.

Lucius' passion became all-consuming. His caresses grew urgent. His body demanded immediate release and he pressed upon her, his senses drowning in the pleasure of Mariaerh's body. He took her quickly, his own impelling need mindless of any passion he may have aroused in Mariaerh, conscious only of the fire mounting within his loins and the waves of sensation produced by his body's thrusts.

When his passion was spent, he lifted his body away and lay on his back. He groped for Mariaerh's hand and said, "You are a wonderful wife, Mariaerh. No man can be more blessed than I." Then he was asleep.

Mariaerh lay a long time staring into the dark. She felt bemused, strangely peaceful. She knew the breach between them was once again healed, but the method of healing was an enigma to her. She was grateful, and offered a silent prayer of thanks to the Lord, adding a plea that this time it would last, but she thought she would never understand how one passionate embrace could instantly heal months of bitterness and acrimony. Did a man's love for his wife depend solely upon his access to her body? Was it only the strong drive of his flesh that compelled a man to marry?

Mariaerh thought of all the loving couples she knew. She remembered how she had envied Sylvia's obvious love for Jeseuha. Was that love because Jeseuha never turned away from the act of lovemaking? Surely two babes in three years testified that she did not. Mariaerh slid her free hand across her belly and wondered if her own child had been conceived, and prayed that it was so.

Lucius still clung to her other hand and she listened to his steady, rhythmical breathing and felt a surge of affection and pity for him. During the months of their estrangement she had missed his companionship, his support and approval and his tender assurances of his affection for her, and she was glad those lonely days were over. It was selfish of her to have put her own need to be alone in her grief before Lucius' need for her body. She had failed in her duty as a wife and had driven him out of her bed to the arms of another. To give him a child would make up for that failure and would also insure his love for her and her standing in The Way.

Mariaerh's eyes drooped sleepily. A little smile played at her mouth. Susane's unwitting mistake was actually a blessing in disguise. She slid her hand out of Lucius' and rolled to her side and vowed never to deny Lucius her body again. Her movement disturbed Lucius and he too turned to his side and flung one arm across her shoulders. She stiffened for a moment, wondering if he would awaken, then snuggled back against him, molding her body to his and fell asleep in the warmth of his arms.

# Chapter 21

The following days Lucius spent assessing the circumstances of his flock in Antioch. He listened attentively to each tale of woe and was appalled by what he learned.

When the Saints had fled Jerusalem and Saul's persecution, they had hoped to find in Antioch a safe haven. Antioch was the capital of Syria and the third largest city in all the Empire. Syria's proconsul, Vitellius, was well known for his sympathy toward Jews as long as they obeyed the laws and proved their loyalty to Caesar, and the city's large Jewish colony enjoyed nearly equal political and economic privileges with Gentile citizens.

The Saints arrived in Antioch with their meager funds spent. They knew no one in the city, were homeless, sick and exhausted. Many of them had been in shock, traumatized by terror and distraught with grief. It was traditional among Jewish people to extend aid and succor to the needy, and the Saints sought charity from the local synagogue, never anticipating that reports of Saul's persecution might reach Antioch before them. When the synagogue leaders learned that the refugees were a heretical sect and that Saul had acted with Caiaphas' blessing, they ordered their people to have nothing to do with the newcomers. The High Priest was not to be defied. Synagogue leaders also feared that any connection with the outcast sect might upset the tenuous goodwill extended by Vitellius. They turned the Saints away, refused to assist or employ them, and hoped to discourage them from settling in their city.

Cornelius had literally saved their lives. He found temporary shelter for them, fed and clothed them at his own expense until he found work for them among his friends. He used his influence to procure housing for them, but the houses were scattered throughout the Jewish section and whenever they ventured into the streets they were either avoided as if they were unclean or were met with jeers and taunts until they hesitated to go beyond their own doors.

The sense of community that was so vital to the life of The Way was nonexistent in Antioch. They seldom saw one another, even to celebrate the *Agape* or to meet for prayer groups and classes of instruction lest their hostile neighbors rise up against them as Saul had done. Each family had tried to establish a home altar and to celebrate the *Agape* alone, but the people were like sheep without a shepherd.

Lucius knew that without the continuous support and reinforcement of daily contact with others of like mind, the Saints' faith would become eroded and The Way would slowly disintegrate. The import of the revelation given to him in Caesarea that had led him to Mount Carmel had never seemed more clear. He drew upon his study of the Essene Code for Urban Communities and outlined a plan for establishing a camp removed from the Jewish section where the Saints could live and worship without fear. Cornelius applauded the plan and bought a plot of wooded land that lay to the south of the city wall between the Orontes and the main thoroughfare. He gave it to the Saints and, within days, the undergrowth was cleared and a city of tents sprang up beneath the sheltering trees.

Not since the days of rebuilding the City of Salt had the Elect been so united in spirit and ideal. The wide Orontes provided a plentitude of fresh fish and its banks furnished clay for pottery and bricks. A communal garden was planted. Numerous fig, hazelnut and olive trees grew among the towering oaks and pines, and they were pruned, pampered and made productive again. A few sheep were purchased for their meat and wool and some goats for milk and cheese. Lucius was elected overseer and every coin earned found its way to a strongbox kept in his tent for the common use of all.

Lucius knew his people well and drew upon their individual skills in organizing the camp. Pathos and Ulai were given charge of collecting and distributing the communal goods. Jonas and Susane set up an infirmary and Cerecea oversaw the communal dining hall. The Essene Rule stated that every child should receive at least ten years of instruction before becoming eligible for full status in the Congregation of God, and Lucius assigned Mariaerh to establish a school as she had done in Bethany. The Essenes also believed that the first tender years of a child's existence laid the foundation for one's entire life. To assure that every newly-arrived soul would be afforded the gentle guidance and loving atmosphere that was most conducive for spiritual growth, he appointed Jacobean and Jeseuha to the task of teaching young mothers the proper care and rearing of their babes.

The refugees spoke many different dialects. Intent on bringing Gentiles into the fold, he took advantage of Nimmuo's gift for languages and put her in charge of organizing adult classes devoted to the disciplines and tenets of The Way. He selected Josida as record-keeper, to document births and deaths, record initiate converts and carefully preserve accounts of visions, revelations, speaking in unknown tongues and other gifts of the Spirit manifested by the Saints.

Lucius plotted his little city after the orderliness and symmetry of Laodicia, with straight streets and equal-sized building sites instead of the jumble that distinguished Jerusalem. He had not forgotten Cornelius' dream of a synagogue which would admit non-Hebrews. In his plan, the synagogue received the most prominent place in the center of the camp, flanked on either side by the communal storehouse and dining hall. The infirmary and his own home would stand behind it, since the overseer's house would serve both as headquarters for the camp and as his private lodging.

# Discover the wealth of information in the Edgar Cayce readings

- **Dreams**
- **Soul Mates**
- **Karma**
- **Earth Changes**
- **Universal Laws**
- **Meditation**
- **Holistic Health**
- **ESP**
- **Astrology**
- **Atlantis**
- **Psychic Development**
- **Numerology**
- **Pyramids**
- **Death and Dying**
- **Auto-Suggestion**
- **Reincarnation**
- **Akashic Records**
- **Planetary Sojourns**
- **Mysticism**
- **Spiritual Healing**
- **And other topics**

## Membership Benefits You Receive Each Month

**EDGAR CAYCE FOUNDATION and**
**A.R.E. LIBRARY/VISITORS CENTER**
Virginia Beach, Va.
*OVER 50 YEARS OF SERVICE*

The entire public complex he set in the midst of flowing lawns and formally planted gardens which were intersected by yellow brick walks, graced at intervals by benches where the Saints could quietly study or pray or meet with friends.

Every man, woman and child took part in building the camp. Construction of permanent structures was immediately begun, and the mild coastal climate enabled them to build throughout the winter. Lucius' house was the first to be raised, then the infirmary, communal storehouse and dining hall and, one by one, the tents were replaced by durable homes.

The synagogue was left to the last. The very suggestion to build a synagogue that would admit Gentiles would have met with harsh opposition in Judea, but the Greek-speaking Saints in Antioch did not share their Judean brothers' intolerance for Greeks and Romans. They felt indebted to Cornelius, and rejoiced at discovering a way to prove their love and appreciation for him. With Cornelius providing the necessary funds, they built of limestone and granite instead of the yellow clay bricks that were used for the other buildings, and the synagogue soared two-stories high with a deep, columned, roofed porch surrounding three sides. It faced the rising sun which was traditional among the Essenes. Cornelius' dream had become a reality, and the synagogue came to be the heart and soul of the Congregation of God.

It took nearly two years to complete building the camp, and Lucius savored every day. He was up each morning before dawn, supervising construction, ordering materials and commissioning work that could not be done by the Saints. He often did not return home until late at night and then only to pore over his accounts and plans until sleep overtook him and he stumbled to his bed at the back of the house.

As overseer, every dispute and problem was laid at Lucius' door. Every question regarding The Way and Jeshua's teaching was brought to him to resolve, and only appeal to the Elders in Jerusalem or to one of the visiting Twelve would overrule his decision. He was priest, teacher, mentor and the leader of The Way. The Antiocheans considered Peter as their *Episcopos,* their Bishop, but in his absence, Lucius ruled.

There were no signs of a child for Mariaerh that first month in Antioch or any month thereafter. She secretly grieved over each onset of her menses but, after a day or two, swallowed her disappointment and told herself that, surely, next month God would bestow His blessing.

Once Mariaerh moved into her own house in the camp, she was surprised to find herself relatively happy. She felt safe in the camp. The horror she had experienced on first entering Antioch had faded over time, although she was still reluctant to venture far beyond the camp's boundaries. Her home was comfortable and furnished the way she wished, not as in Jerusalem where she had felt like a guest in Lucius' house.

She was no longer lonely, even though Lucius was seldom at home. She knew his absences were due to his work and that he was not in some brothel or tavern, for she had kept her vow to never again deny him her body, and he had no cause to stray from her bed.

She had no close friend, other than Nimmuo, but as the overseer's wife, she shared the honor and deference paid to Lucius by The Way, and her fear of being an outcast among Lucius' Greek-speaking friends had proven to be unfounded. Her reputation as one of the Holy Women was well known by the Antioch Saints, and they sought her counsel, deferred to her opinions and considered it an honor to have their child in her class.

The youngsters in her school made the lack of her own child more bearable. They shared their parents' deep distress caused by Saul's persecution, and nothing gave her more satisfaction than to see them shed their fears and bloom whole and trusting beneath her tender ministrations. She collected them each day from the dining hall after the morning meal and returned them in the evening for the *Agape.* They filled her days and consumed her thoughts and left little time to dwell upon her own disappointments.

Nimmuo shared their house and was a true sister to Mariaerh. She knew everything that took place in the camp and took great pleasure in relating all the latest tattle to Mariaerh. Her chatter banished the silence that would have driven Mariaerh to distraction with Lucius so often away, and her popularity drew the young people to congregate at the house. If Lucius came home out of sorts from a difficult day, Nimmuo could always be relied upon to restore his good humor. She continued to serve as a buffer between their disagreements, even when quarrels became more frequent once the camp was established.

At least once every week Lucius left the work at camp to others while he, Nimmuo and other chosen teachers went into the city to preach the Gospel to Cornelius' family and friends. Mariaerh refused to go with them. She had never forgotten her first introduction to Antioch and meant never to expose her eyes to such sinfulness again. Nor could she bring herself to enter a Gentile home, much less eat with them, for she might unknowingly eat meat that had been sacrificed to false gods! To Lucius' argument that Cornelius and his friends were Christians, not pagans, she retorted that she detested the word *Christian!* They were The Way, The Elect, not some word coined by pagan mouths. She was adamant, even when Lucius stormed and ordered her to go, shouting that as the overseer's wife she was obligated to support his position. Lucius finally admitted defeat and left her behind, but it became such a source of contention between them that the subject was totally avoided in their house.

Lucius found an eager audience among the Gentiles. The camp emerging outside their city walls had not only aroused their curiosity but it was also common knowledge that Cornelius championed the strange sect's cause and they vied for invitations to discover what it was that caught his attention. Each time Lucius preached, new faces came to listen, some out of simple curiosity, some only to ingratiate themselves and gain Cornelius' favor, but many left enrapt and awed by what they heard.

The mood throughout the Empire had been buoyantly optimistic since Caligula had risen as emperor, and the idea of a community dedicated to the spirit of brotherly love and service was in keeping with their expectations of Caligula's reign. They were weary of tyranny and oppression and fear, and the words of the Prince of Peace were comforting and full of hope. When rumor reached Antioch that Caligula believed himself to be a god, some of the more avid even wondered if Jeshua had come again in the guise of their beloved emperor!

The Good News spread from the wealthy, ruling class of Cornelius' friends to their slaves and servants and then to their families and friends. When the synagogue was finished and they learned that they would be welcomed, they flocked to the sanctuary to hear the Gospel and some settled permanently in the camp. Josida was kept busy adding names to her roster of initiates, and each week more shelves and bins in the storehouse were filled and Lucius' strongbox grew heavier.

Mariaerh's attitude toward the Gentiles was shared by Jewish leaders in Antioch. The burgeoning camp was an ever increasing irritant. It galled them that Jews turned blasphemers and heretics should thrive in such obvious prosperity. Their friendship with Gentiles was held abominable. Why, they even ate with them, worked side by side with them, visited their homes and invited them into theirs! To carry on business and trade with pagans was one thing, but to live among them as brothers was an outrage. They warned their people to stay clear of the camp and not to become tainted by the heresy of the sect.

When the Jewish leaders learned that Gentiles were admitted as full participants in the heretics' synagogue, they raised a general outcry. They complained to Vitellius who did not take kindly to their charge since he himself was a Gentile, and while he had no wish to partake of their synagogue worship, it angered him to know that these august men could not, would not, admit him. He chastised them soundly and warned them against causing any kind of disturbance, which enraged them all the more. The Gentile merchants added their voice of displeasure to that of Vitellius, and the Jews realized that their Gentile neighbors' goodwill for continued commerce was contingent upon their attitude toward the Christians. A prolonged, if uneasy, peace prevailed.

While Mariaerh refused to go into the city or to enter or eat in a Gentile's house there, she did accept them once they professed their faith in The Way and came to live in the camp. A number of their children attended her school and, to Mariaerh, a child was a child whether Jew or Gentile. She loved them equally. Her attitude pleased Lucius and the tension between them eased for a time until a young Roman began paying court to Nimmuo.

His name was Belden. He had been sent to Antioch by Rome to study the customs, traditions and religious beliefs of all the various races and creeds in that amalgam of a city, and then to advise those in authority on how best to rule. He questioned Cornelius on the sect of Christians and became intrigued by Cornelius' enthusiasm and devotion to the new superstition. He accepted Cornelius' offer to investigate the Christians for himself, but it was the overseer's beautiful sister who inspired Belden's devotion.

The first time he accompanied Cornelius to the camp, Nimmuo found herself blushing beneath Belden's admiring gaze. He was as tall as Lucius with raven ringlets that were clipped close to his head in the fashion of his countrymen. He was clean shaven, with a strong, square chin and a slow, teasing smile that seemed always to play at his mouth. His eyes were black, sometimes brooding when deep in thought, but sparkled with good humor whenever he caught Nimmuo's eye. Of all the young men who had sought her attention, Belden was the first one to stir her heart and she allowed him to become a regular visitor to Lucius' house.

Mariaerh voiced strong reservations about the deepening relationship between Nimmuo and Belden.

Not only was he a Roman, but he openly professed to a lack of any religious beliefs. "I put my faith in justice and law, not in gods," he would laugh whenever she spoke to him of The Way. She was appalled by his cheerful admission to atheism, and questioned the wisdom of encouraging him to come into the camp.

Lucius liked him. Belden reminded him of Philippi and he enjoyed their lively debates on the subject of religion. Once Lucius quoted Joshua, the son of Nun, "Others may do as they please, but as for me and my house, we will serve the Lord," and Belden had shouted gleefully, "Aha! My sentiments exactly! Let every man do and believe as he pleases!"

"Do those sentiments include women?" Nimmuo had asked.

Belden had sobered. He realized that Nimmuo's acceptance of him relied upon his answer. He thought long and carefully, then answered "Yes" with absolute conviction.

Mariaerh knew then that nothing she could say would sway Nimmuo from her chosen course, so she held her tongue and prayed Nimmuo would come to recognize her folly, but her prayers came to naught. With Lucius' blessing, Nimmuo accepted Belden's proposal and they sailed for Laodicea to gain Philippi's consent, leaving her and Lucius alone in the house, separated by an abyss of silence.

After Nimmuo was gone, Lucius and Mariaerh struggled to make conversation, but other than the news of the day, they had nothing in common. Lucius' interest lay in the growth of the camp, the progress of the Gentile initiates and his administrative duties. Mariaerh's focus was on the personalities about her, their changing relationships, their spiritual growth and, of course, her school. Lucius saw The Way in its totality, while Mariaerh saw the individual. They found little ground for agreement and, more often than not, their attempts to talk turned into a quarrel. They came to avoid any controversial subject until their only real contact was their nightly expression of love, and that too dwindled when they entered into the most serious quarrel of all.

The question of whether or not Gentile believers should undergo circumcision arose in the camp. Lucius said no. Mariaerh said yes. Peter's vision on Simon's roof in Joppa had not convinced her that the Lord meant all Gentiles to be shown The Way, and even if it did, she did not believe that it meant they were exempt from bearing the Sign of the Covenant. She accused Lucius of being lax in this regard and felt he should rule that Gentile initiates undergo the rite before being admitted into the Congregation of God. Lucius would not.

There were others in the camp who shared Mariaerh's views, who were willing to allow Gentiles to enter the synagogue but insisted they be circumcised before becoming full members in The Way. They added their voices to Mariaerh's and the dispute grew until the camp was split in two, half agreeing with Lucius and half with Mariaerh. The controversy raged until the first of the Gentile initiates reached that level of knowledge and spiritual growth when gifts of the Spirit began to manifest and the uncircumcised spoke and interpreted unknown tongues, prophesied and healed.

The Saints were amazed. If God made no distinction between those circumcised and those not, how could man do otherwise? For the Christians in Antioch, the matter was settled and a tenuous truce settled in Lucius' house.

Word began to spread among the Jews in Antioch of the remarkable events taking place in the camp. Some of the more venturesome visited the camp to satisfy their curiosity and were amazed by what they saw. Most of the curious believed the phenomena to be the work of sorcerers or magicians, but a few wondered and came back to learn more.

It was not long before Jonas' skill as a physician became recognized and he was often called upon to minister to the sick among the Jews. At first he was only called in desperation when no other physician was available, but such were his successes that soon he became the first choice for many. Those Jews who braved the camp to summon him told their friends of the welcome they received and gave expansive accounts of the kindness and concern they encountered. The Christians gained a reputation for charity toward all, and widows, orphans and the elderly who had nowhere else to go began to seek refuge in the camp.

Mariaerh worked hard to bring those Jews to The Way. She organized welcoming groups, made certain they were taught by Hebrews and eased their fears about living among Gentiles. She considered it a personal triumph over Lucius when Josida's records began to show Jewish initiates as well as Gentile.

Luke came to Antioch, bringing a collection of Jeshua's teachings, purported to be His very own words, compiled by their leader, Judith. It proved to be a boon in preaching the Gospel's good tidings. Until then, Lucius had relied upon his personal knowledge of Jeshua and upon his memory and notes of what he had been told. Often the initiates posed questions that Lucius and the other teachers could not answer, or their answers would differ according to memory or interpretation. At last they had a common source that permitted a uniform presentation of the teachings.

Luke's presence in the house eased the tension between Mariaerh and Lucius, despite the fact that he agreed with Lucius on most issues. He satisfied Mariaerh's hunger for news from Jerusalem and regaled her with tales of marriages and births and the events taking place in the lives of her friends.

All the Disciples were in Judea except James ben Zebedee who remained in Spain. James ben Joseph was living in Lucius' old house in Jerusalem. Philoas had been appointed to a high government position in Rome and Ruth was expecting their first child. Caligula had upheld Philoas' report on Pontius Pilate and that old enemy was permanently banished. The new procurator, Capito, was more sympathetic to the Jews and the church hoped to be free from persecution under his rule.

Other events which had taken place in Rome increased their hope for a more peaceful existence. The Tetrarch Herod Philip had died and Caligula had given his territory over to Herod Agrippa, the grandson of the Herod called "Great." When Herod Antipas sailed to Rome to protest, for he wanted Philip's tetrarchy added to his own, he found himself banished to Lyons for his effort and Agrippa was given not only Philip's territory, but also Perea and Galilee.

Mariaerh listened avidly to every word Luke spoke about Jerusalem, but when he began to tell of Saul, she paled and grimaced in hatred and had to steel herself against leaving the room.

Saul had returned from Arabia. His vision on the road to Damascus had left a lasting impression upon him and he was totally convinced that Jeshua was the Son of God. He had gone back to Damascus where he began preaching Jeshua's *name* in the synagogues, but Jewish authorities were outraged and considered him a traitor. They became so incensed that they sought to kill him, and only quick action on the part of The Way kept them from carrying out their threat. The Saints hustled Saul out of Damascus in the dead of night by lowering him over the city wall in a basket. He then fled to Jerusalem where he was no more welcomed than he had been in Damascus. He boldly proclaimed the Good News, and his former friends became dangerous foes.

The Elect did not trust him. Barnabas pleaded his case, and even though Saul spent two weeks conferring with Peter and James, the brother of the Lord, convincing them of his sincerity, the rest were not persuaded. When Saul dared to preach Jeshua's *name* in the Synagogue of the Freedmen, the Hellenists rose up in arms. Again The Way came to his rescue. They secreted him off to Caesarea and from there shipped him home to Tarsus.

When the Saints who had suffered from Saul's tyranny heard Luke's tale, they thought Saul's near escapes were just retribution. It served him right to fear for his life and to be forced to flee into exile. The image of the arrogant Saul ignominiously lowered in a basket sent them into gales of laughter, and for once they applauded the actions of the tradition-bound Jews. Mariaerh wished the Saints had left him to his fate, but

Lucius sensed Providence at work in the tale. He still believed that one day he and Saul would somehow work together in bringing the Gospel to the Gentile world. Tarsus was not far away, and he wondered how Jeshua would lead him to Antioch.

Lucius heard nothing more about Saul for months, even though visits by messengers were increasingly frequent. Wherever the seeds of faith were planted throughout the Empire the harvest of souls grew greater with each passing year, and each year more messengers were added to the network that traveled from land to land. These emissaries were men and women who had either been slaves themselves or were children of slaves and had been freed by Rome, or were Jews who, like Saul, had been granted citizenship in the Empire, thus were free to move about without interference from authority. Many were teachers, people who had completed several years of instruction in the tenets of The Way, and they not only carried letters from The Twelve and Elders, but were themselves qualified to settle questions of doctrine.

Judith's document was circulated among all the communities of believers and was a wonderful aid in insuring the uniformity of the Gospel. Without it, Jeshua's teaching could easily have been distorted or reshaped depending upon local beliefs and customs, and vestiges of false doctrine could become incorporated with the Gospel, leading to a confusion in Christian faith. Copies of the document were provided for all The Twelve and other teachers, and one copy stored for safety in the great library in Alexandria in case the others were lost in the great upheavals soon expected to herald Jeshua's return.

While the teaching was uniform, The Way in Antioch was unique among other communities of believers. No other group lived in an isolated camp or admitted Gentiles. And, with Vitellius' sanction and Cornelius' friendship, they enjoyed far less overt expression of scorn and harassment from non-believing Gentiles or Jews. Even those believers who did not live in the camp could establish home altars and prayer circles and classes of instruction in their homes without fear of jeers from censurious neighbors.

Under the influence of Gentile members, the *Agape* in Antioch became a joyous celebration which Mariaerh deplored, complaining that it had become more a Greek, bibulous dinner gathering than a meal in remembrance of the Lord. She was also shocked by the openly amorous displays she encountered among the young Gentile members whose behavior was often imitated by the Hebrew youth. She urged Lucius to exert his authority to bring discipline and sober decorum to the camp, but Lucius could not see that any great wrong was being done. They were, after all, Greeks and Romans with a zest for the pleasures of life, and not pious Judeans like Mariaerh. What harm did they do if they drank a bit too much wine at the *Agape,* or added some innocent entertainments to enjoy after the meal? What did it matter if the young people fell to temptation and found joy in one another's arms? He had been young once himself and his own passion had certainly not deterred his zeal for the Lord. The matter became one more issue for contention between Lucius and Mariaerh.

Lucius passed the fortieth year of his birth in Antioch. On that day he strolled through the camp and felt like one of the patriarchs of old. Children stopped their play and gathered about his knees, clamoring for his attention as he had seen little ones do with Jeshua. The women smiled and greeted him shyly and the men approached him with respect. They were his people, his tribe of Christians brought forth from a pagan wilderness, just as it was his camp, built under his instruction as Moses had built the tabernacle. He should be the happiest, most satisfied of all men, yet he sighed and knew he was not.

Nimmuo and Belden had wed in Laodicea and remained there until Belden was assigned to Jerusalem. They visited Antioch on their way to Judea, and Nimmuo's news of his family had filled Lucius with longing.

Philippi and Merceden were aging. Lucia's family

was nearly grown and many of her eleven children Lucius had never seen. And his own sons! Pebilus was a grown man and Thaddeus would soon reach the age of manhood. Belden said they were "true sons of Rome," adept at games and excellent horsemen. Vesta had seen to it that both boys received the finest education she could provide and her parentage and position gave them access to every advantage. Nimmuo said that Pebilus had shown an interest in The Way, but Vesta had discouraged his involvement. As for Vesta, she had never married, but, Lucius thought wryly, she no doubt did not lack male companionship. He told himself that he did not care whether she married or not, but in truth he was rather pleased. Obviously she had not found his match!

Nimmuo and Belden's short visit had awakened in Lucius a long dormant yearning for his family. The prime of his manhood had been spent in service to the Lord and, while he would have it no other way, it had cost him the life of a family man. He was forty years of age and his sons were strangers and would never be of comfort in his old age. Mariaerh continued to prove barren, a fact which had never caused him concern, but seeing the love and devotion that existed between Nimmuo and Belden made Lucius long for a woman who would show him a similar love and passion. Mariaerh was a good wife, tending to his needs in every way and certainly a perfect overseer's wife, but he wanted more from a woman. His loins remembered the passionate embraces of his youth and his heart the quickening when encountering the loved one's face. He also yearned to see Merceden and Philippi again, and feared they might die before he went home again.

With the camp running smoothly, Lucius' thoughts turned more and more to the void in his personal life. He was sometimes tempted to tell all and go home to Laodicea, but the prospect of shocked friends, their censure and the loss of his prestige and position deterred him. He would not acknowledge such self-serving motives, so he convinced himself that it was compassion for Mariaerh and devotion and commitment to The Way that kept him in Antioch.

Next year, he thought, next year I shall go home to see my sons when the faithful no longer need my guiding hand. But next year came and went, and then another, and then Barnabas came to Antioch and events took place that banished all thought of leaving from his mind.

Barnabas had been sent to investigate The Way in Antioch after the Elders in Jerusalem learned they were admitting Gentiles. He and Marcia and their children arrived in Antioch unannounced and were astounded by what they found. Barnabas sent a glowing report to Jerusalem, filled with examples of gifts of the Spirit being shown by the Gentiles, proof that the Lord called the Gentile as well as the Jew.

Barnabas stayed in Antioch and took over many of the demands the Saints made upon Lucius which gave him even more time to preach to non-believers. He spent a part of each day in the marketplace, preaching Jeshua's *name* to whomever would listen. He avoided the Jews who were still resistant to the Good News, and concentrated upon the Gentiles.

The Gentiles were an eager audience to Jeshua's message. Freedmen, citizens and slaves alike were desperate for something to believe in. The golden age they expected under Caligula's reign had failed to materialize and, in fact, they were worse off now than they had ever been in memory.

Caligula had come to be regarded as a madman. Within a year of his reign he had exhausted the treasury. He had come to believe that he was a god, and that belief led him to excesses never before seen in the Empire. He imposed exorbitant taxes on everything conceivable. He installed a brothel in the royal palace where even the senators' wives were forced into prostitution and, of course, Caligula took his share of the income.

The Emperor indulged in the most bizarre activities. He dressed as a woman, performed the most depraved sexual acts and forced others to do likewise. He married his own sister and slept with no end of others. He buggered men and young boys and boasted of regular intercourse with goddesses. As a god, he held human life in the lowest esteem, and the merest displeasure meant somebody's head would roll. He searched for the most brutal new methods of torture and butchery, and was fascinated by poisons that killed with the utmost agony.

The entire Empire was gripped with fear. Caligula was insane and no one dared to oppose him. The dream of the people for a just and benevolent rule turned to ashes, and across the Empire they turned to the Prince of Peace for surcease from their woes. The Christian following flourished. Their activities became better organized and more widely known. They came to be called the *church*—and adaptation of a Greek word which meant "a gathering of people"—and The Twelve were called *Apostles,* also a Greek term which recognized them as worthy persons setting forth to spread the Word.

In Jersualem, the growing recognition and acceptance of the church once again brought attention from Temple authorities. James ben Zebedee returned from Spain and his success with the exiled Jews spurred The Twelve and other teachers to redouble their efforts in Palestine. As they were seldom in the city, and the absence of daily leadership was beginning to weaken The Way, James and John ben Zebedee suggested that James ben Joseph be named leader of the expanding church. Who better to guide The Way than the Lord's own brother? James was revered by all Jews for his piety in fulfilling observances of the Mosaic Law, and his appointment seemed an astute political move to placate the suspicions of the Temple authorities. But the increasing popularity of the church had too far alarmed the Jewish leaders to be appeased by a change in leadership.

Outlandish tales of miracles and divine revelations were filtering in to the priesthood. One of the Nazarenes named Philip was said to have converted the treasury keeper of Ethiopia and then disappeared before the astonished man's eyes. Stories of instanteous healings, of demons cast out, of men and women caught up in ecstasy and speaking in strange tongues were bandied about the Temple courts. Not only the poor but, expanding numbers of wealthy, influential men in the Sanhedrin were proclaiming their faith in the Nazarene.

The Temple authorities felt compelled to take action. They complained to Agrippa, accusing the Nazarenes of promoting heresy and sedition among the people, but a crisis arose that made the activities of an outcast sect the least of Agrippa's worries and changed forever the Antioch church.

\* \* \* \* \*

## Encamped in Antioch

Desolation and weariness of spirit have stayed my hand from keeping an account of the last months' events. My people have scattered and I grieve as would the shepherd who, when upon rising, finds his sheep decimated by wolves during the night.

How did it happen? So quickly! To chronicle the events in their proper order may bring understanding to my troubled mind.

A tumult arose between the Greeks and Jews in Alexandria of Egypt. The Greeks there accused the Jews of debasing Caligula's divinity by refusing to swear by his name and to erect altars and temples in his honor. They sent ambassadors to Rome to present their case before Caligula, and the Emperor was so incensed that he retaliated against all Jews. He commanded every Jew in the Empire to bow down and worship his image, and ordered that his statue be erected in the Temple in Jerusalem.

The fool! He should have known that Jews would never allow the abode of God to be so defiled!

Men of reason did their best to dissuade him. The Tetrarch, Agrippa, was in Rome and tried to forestall the calamity. Vitellius, ever our friend, begged Caligula to rescind the edict, warning of civil war and riots and bloodshed in the streets, but his plea fell upon deaf ears for Caligula's insanity is beyond all reason! He recalled Vitellius, stripped him of his honors and sent the Commander, Petronius, to rule over Syria.

Cornelius warned us that Petronius is no friend of Jews and, remembering the torment they suffered in Jerusalem, our Hebrew Christians fled before the sword of destruction could fall upon their necks. Only Gentile believers remained in the camp.

Oh, my people, my people! The hardships they have known. They fled as the holy family had fled into Egypt, in small groups of families and friends to avoid arousing suspicion, braving searing heat and raging mountain storms, hunger and thirst and torturous terrain and the threat of robbers and bandits to be met along the way. But they were not alone. The Holy Spirit went with them. None were lost and we have received word that they have reached safety in Laodicea, but how many times must my people flee?

Our Brothers and Sisters had barely quit the region when Petronius swept into Antioch with a fanfare of pomp and ostentatious show. His personal guard and their mounts were decked out in full regalia, led by standard bearers and a small bugle corps who announced his arrival with long echoing blasts on their polished, brass trumpets. Only a token number of citizens lined the streets to hail his coming, mostly men of the ruling class who seek his future favors or rabble who look for excitement. The rest of Antioch stayed indoors, peering through windows and half-opened doors and, as I, were filled with a sense of impending doom. The whole city seemed to hold its breath in fearful anticipation, for no one knows Petronius' mind.

Petronius understands nothing of Jews. He thought it would take only a few days for him to cow them into submission and then he could march for Judea and install Caesar's image in the Temple. Folly! He mistook their adaptability to foreign rule for timidity, believing that a show of force would easily subdue them and a few hours in the torturer's hands would quickly persuade them.

He learned he was wrong! The Hebrews are men of honor and courage and my heart swells with pride for my mother's race. Every Jew in Antioch refused to bow to Caligula's image and no amount of persuasion or threat could sway them. When Caesar's edict was publicly read from the porch of the synagogue, the readers were met with shouts of "Hear, O Israel! The Lord, thy God, is One!" although the leaders died with that cry on their lips.

Petronius was enraged. His troops marched upon the Jewish quarter and death and destruction ruled the day. The synagogue was defiled and burned, shops torn down, their homes looted and vandalized. The Chosen of God were shackled in chains and led away to slavery. Blood ran in the streets and Vitellius' prophecy came true.

Cornelius tried to stop the destruction. He refused to carry out Petronius' order, but Petronius then led the troops himself and the mayhem was savage and brutal. It lasted for weeks and, when it was over, the Jewish quarter lay razed to the ground and the population indiscriminately killed. We Christians were able to save many by secreting them out of the city by night and hiding them in our homes by day, but the Jews' pocket of safety in a pagan world is destroyed.

Mariaerh and I, Barnabas and Marcia with their children took refuge in the city among friends. Our Roman citizenship protects us and Petronius has no interest in God-fearers, only Jews whom he identifies by race, not creed. When the carnage was over and Petronius had marched for Jerusalem, we went back to the camp and found that except for the synagogue, it was nearly intact. The Jews from the city turned to us for help and we turned away no one. Some think that God turned Caligula's heart against them as punishment for scorning The Way, and have come to believe.

The Antioch Jews were not alone in resisting. Pride in my mother's race compels me freely to record the events which occurred in Judea following our own time of travail.

No rain had fallen on Judea for nearly a year and the land lay parched and fallow. The rebellion in Antioch delayed Petronius' march on Jerusalem and he wintered the legions in Ptolemais which bought time for the Judeans to rally. Tens of thousands converged on Ptolemais to implore Petronius to change his mind. He could not ignore them, or force them to leave without risking another massacre. If the bloody affair in Antioch had taught him anything, it was that Jews would die for their Law and their God. He rode to Tiberius to confer with the Jewish leadership and discover if all of Palestine was poised to rebel, and was met with another multitude of Jews as determined as those he had left in Ptolemais.

For forty days, Herod's palace grounds in Tiberius were ringed with Jews lying prone on the ground with their necks outstretched, demonstrating their willingness to die before seeing their Temple defiled. Agrippa's brother, young Aristobulus, pleaded with Petronius to withdraw to Antioch, arguing that while those thousands of men lay prone in the courtyard, the land lay untilled, the flocks and cattle went unattended and the orchards and vineyards were left unpruned. Taxes would go unpaid. Famine and starvation would be rampant. The entire region would succumb to guerrilla warfare, prey to bandits and robbers. A total collapse of law and order would surely ensue.

Petronius, at last, realized that Aristobulus was right. To risk a war by forcing obedience to Caligula's edict, merely to satisfy the Emperor's mad ego, would prove too costly to his men and to the Empire. The rainless winter would wreak enough havoc with Palestine's economy, and Caligula's extravagance demanded every coin they could raise. After weeks of anguished deliberation, Petronius gave in to the Jews.

I must record that remarkable event.

As it had been for months, there was not a cloud in the sky on that day in Tiberius. Petronius had dressed in his full ceremonial uniform and addressed the Jews himself. He delivered a stirring, magnanimous oration which the Jews cheered and applauded as they praised Petronius' name. Petronius grandly accepted their acclamation. Then, just as he turned to leave them, the clear, blue sky seemed suddenly to be rent in two and a blessed, healing rain replenished the earth.

Petronius was awed. He thought the rain to be an omen, a sign of approval from the God of the Jews. He went back to his rooms and wrote to Caligula, knowing he no doubt signed his own death warrant. It would have been so had not Agrippa in the meantime persuaded Caligula to rescind his edict.

Agrippa's cunning is also worth noting. He had known Caligula since childhood, and was fully aware of the Emperor's enormous self-worship and his weakness for flattery. Agrippa prepared the most lavish, expansive dinner that Rome had ever seen in Caligula's honor, and the Emperor was so impressed by his display of love and devotion that he offered Agrippa whatever gift or favor he would name.

Agrippa wisely, at first, refused anything. He cleverly turned down Caligula's proffered riches and power, knowing Caesar would not allow someone to outdo him in generosity. When Caligula insisted and pressed Agrippa to name his gift, Agrippa asked no more than for Caesar to prove to the world the divinity of his nature by showing divine mercy to the stiff-necked Jews.

Caligula could not refuse. He wrote to Petronius and instructed him to leave the statue in the Temple if he already had it installed, but if not, to disregard the edict. Later, when he received Petronius' letter refusing to carry out his first command, Caligula was enraged and wrote again, demanding that Petronius take his own life for disobedience.

The God of the Jews rewarded Petronius for his mercy toward His people. Before that fateful last letter arrived, Petronius learned that Caligula was dead.

Those of us who remain in Antioch are safe for the time, but Jonas, Pathos and all our principal men are gone. Barnabas and I cannot lead our people alone. I told Barnabas of my conviction that one day Saul and I would work together in bringing the Word of the Lord to the Gentiles and Barnabas has sailed for Tarsus. The ways of the Lord are indeed inscrutable.

\*     \*     \*     \*     \*

# Chapter 22

Mariaerh hurried along the hard-packed street with her shoulders hunched, her head down and her eyes lowered. She had come from a house on the outskirts of the camp where she had counseled the parents of a child in her class and the hour was late. Visitors had arrived that morning from Jerusalem and Lucius expected her to be with him when he welcomed them at the *Agape*. She knew he would be disturbed by her tardiness but it could not be helped. The well-being of her little ones was more important than whether or not the overseer's wife was on time to greet dignitaries from Jerusalem

She was angry that the interview and others like it had become necessary. Ever since Petronius had wreaked havoc with the Jews, the children of The Way had been withdrawn and fearful. They saw the damage done to the synagogue and heard the talk of beatings and burnings and children orphaned or sold into slavery and were terrified of separation from their mothers. When left in her care, they clung to her skirts and cried whenever she left the room. They had nightmares and did not eat, and shrank at the sight of a stranger.

Mariaerh advised parents to exercise care over their speech when their children were present, to pay extra attention to them, fondle them often and constantly reassure them until their sense of security was restored. She felt partly to blame for their apprehension, for she too was afraid, and no matter how cheerful and reassuring she tried to be, she knew they sensed her fear.

The pogrom against the Jews had revived the memories of Saul's persecution that Mariaerh had struggled so hard to subdue, and Saul's arrival in Antioch had made these memories all the more vivid. She had begged Lucius not to send for him, wept and shouted and cursed the day that Saul was born, but all to no avail. When Barnabas had returned from Tarsus with Saul, Mariaerh had refused him entry to her house, threatening that if he took one step over her sill she would flee Antioch and Lucius forever.

Lucius could not understand her unreasonable fear of Saul. He had acceded to her demand that Saul never be brought to the house, but thought that once she saw him as a friend of The Way, her hatred and terror would disappear. It had not. If anything, her hatred had deepened. Fortunately, Saul had taken up his trade as tentmaker in a cleared-away part of the Jewish section and did not live in the camp, but nevertheless it was impossible to avoid him completely. She knew he would be at the *Agape,* but so would the entire camp and she could easily avoid any contact with him.

Mariaerh crossed the wide lawns in front of the synagogue and took the back path around it that led to her own house. She was still looking downward, lost in her thoughts, and did not see a man emerge from the porch and turn down the street toward her. Her feet automatically turned to cut across the grass and she ran into him when she veered across his path. She was knocked off balance and he caught her arm to keep her from falling, mumbling, "Sorry, lady," then hurried on his way.

Mariaerh steadied herself, then looked up to apologize for not paying heed, and gasped. It was Saul! She rubbed the arm that seemed to burn from his touch and stared at his retreating back, recoiling from the sight of his misshapen form and ungainly gait. She panicked, fearing he would turn back and see her stare. She fled down the walk to the safety of her own house, wrenched open the door and slammed it closed behind her.

She leaned against the door, ashen and trembling.

Marcia and Barnabas had shared the house since their arrival in Antioch and she heard Marcia call from Nimmuo's old room, "Is that you, Mariaerh? We were about to leave without you," but her throat had closed and she could not answer.

When Mariaerh did not answer her call, Marcia came into the room and, seeing Mariaerh's distress, exclaimed, "What's the matter, Mariaerh? Are you all right?"

Mariaerh's heart was pounding and she could barely breathe. She struggled for calm until she could finally croak, "Saul!"

Marcia was obviously relieved. She went to Mariaerh and put her arms around her, laughing, "Is that all! Mariaerh, you simply must get over this inordinate fear of Saul. He's not a monster. He won't harm you."

Rage restored Mariaerh's voice. "He did my mother!" she shot back.

"That was long ago. Saul has changed. Our people love him. Look at all the good he's done."

"He hates me!" Mariaerh cried. "He refuses to speak to me and avoids me whenever possible. He won't even look my way and some day he'll find a way to destroy me!"

"That's not true, Mariaerh. If Saul avoids you and is hesitant to meet your eye, it is out of guilt. He's said himself that he will never forgive himself for what he did in Jerusalem. He admits his guilt at every turn and it's his attempt to atone for his actions that makes him so zealous for The Way."

Marcia's children had come into the room and Mariaerh was forced to swallow her spiteful retort so as not to upset them. She disengaged herself from Marcia's embrace and said with feigned cheerfulness, "No matter. We must hurry. I've already made us late." She forced a smile and playfully ushered the children out of the house, trying to act as normally as possible until they entered the dining hall and she left them all with Barnabas.

Visitors from Jerusalem were always an occasion for celebration and the dining hall was packed. Still shaking, Mariaerh made her way through the crowd in search of Lucius and saw him seated, next to Saul, at the foremost table where he would bless the bread and wine. She knew a place was reserved for her at his other side but, when she saw Saul, she took a seat at the far end of the hall. The encounter with Saul had totally unnerved her. To see him across a crowded room or surrounded by admiring followers was one thing, but to meet him alone in the street and to bear his touch was quite another. Nor could she ever bring herself to sit at the same table with him. Lucius would be furious, but better to face his displeasure than to be in such close proximity to Saul.

The hall grew quiet. Mariaerh ventured a glance toward the speakers' table and saw Lucius was standing and ready to begin. She bowed her head and tried to concentrate on the prayers over the bread and wine, but her mind kept darting back to Saul.

Barnabas and Lucius thought Saul's presence was a gift straight from heaven. He preached, he healed, he drove out demons. He preached Christ's *name* with the same fire and passion that once he had debated Stephen and his energy was unflagging. His own illness and disability he ignored, although everyone said he suffered greatly. He was fearless and gave no thought to his own safety, inspiring others to his degree of valor. She listened as Saul prayed in his passionate, resonant voice and thought Marcia was right. The people loved him, and like it or not, Saul was here to stay.

The evening seemed interminable to Mariaerh. Voices and faces swirled about her head in a jumble of sound and form and her mind even wandered from the long orations given by the visitors. All she remembered later was that one called Agabus prophesied that the recent drought in Judea was only a measure of what was to come, and that The Way voted to set aside a part of their income to aid the Jerusalem church during the famine that was to come.

When Saul stood to preach, Mariaerh would have left the hall if the thought of Lucius' anger had not deterred her. She suffered through Saul's bombast on forgoing all pleasures for the sake of Christ and, just when she thought she could bear no more, she heard someone next to her mutter, "Ugly little fanatic! He can find no pleasures for himself and is jealous of others who can."

Mariaerh almost laughed aloud. She bit her lip and waited until her glee subsided, then chanced a sidelong glance to discover who would dare to say such a thing. She was shocked when she saw it was Cornelius' daughter, Celicene.

Celicene saw Mariaerh's shock and an impish grin spread across her face as she boldly met Mariaerh's amazed stare with a conspiratorial wink.

Without thinking, Mariaerh automatically returned the wink, then was aghast at her own temerity.

Celicene's face reddened with suppressed laughter and Mariaerh had to clamp her teeth together to keep from laughing herself. She did not trust herself to look Celicene's way again and, as soon as the final prayers were said, rose to leave before Lucius came looking for her. But Celicene detained her and offered a half-hearted apology.

"I'm sorry you overheard my remark about your friend, lady, but the sentiment was honest."

"He's not my friend!" Mariaerh snapped. Then, remembering her position, said in a more conciliatory tone, "It's quite all right. Saul does tend to be overly zealous at times, though I agree with him to a point. We must exert moderation in all things."

"Moderation I agree, but Saul teaches abstinence! That's not what I understood from Peter. He taught that the actions of the body were not so important as long as the motives and thought were in accord with your Christ. This Saul seems to think that everything enjoyable is sinful."

Mariaerh smiled. "The truth no doubt lies somewhere between, Celicene. My advice is to search your own heart and conscience, to pray diligently and let the Lord be your guide."

Celicene frowned. "I do not mean to offend, lady, but I find it difficult to pray to a criminal condemned and crucified. You say He died and rose again. I say impossible."

"Try, even though you do not believe. He will reveal Himself to you in some way, you can be sure."

"Perhaps," Celicene answered, doubtfully. "I see my mother and sister. Will you join us for refreshments?"

Mariaerh hesitated. She had forgotten Saul for the moment and was intrigued that Cornelius' daughter should express disbelief in Jeshua. She considered the invitation but then saw Lucius making his way toward her with a glowering face.

"No, thank you. I am very weary and planned for an early night. Another time, please."

Celicene shrugged and Mariaerh slipped out of the door before Lucius could reach her. She walked the short distance home alone and went straight to her bed. When Lucius came in a few hours later, she feigned sleep to avert the inevitable quarrel.

Mariaerh arose before dawn and left the house. Lucius would not find that unusual for she seldom saw him in the mornings of late. He enjoyed the gaiety that followed the *Agape,* and his overindulgence in wine and the late hour kept him to his bed until the sun had fully risen. Mariaerh did not mind. She took advantage of having the predawn hour to herself and each morning it had become her habit to walk to the river for a time of quiet reflection. The constancy of the river's flow and the surety that the sun arose, even though it might be hidden by overcast skies, reminded her that no matter how disrupted and uncertain her own life might be, God was the same, yesterday, today and every day. She was soothed by the thought and better prepared to meet the trials of each day.

On that morning she was more troubled than usual. She had not slept well. Lucius' body lying next to her had seemed to radiate his anger and disgust, and she had not dared to move lest he guess she was awake and draw her into an ugly confrontation.

Experience had taught her that it was useless to quarrel with Lucius. He stubbornly clung to his own position on any issue, even when she thought he must know he was wrong. The only time he gave way to her

judgment was when Barnabas or Cornelius or some
other Elder agreed with her. Sometimes she wondered if
it were not simply her gender that forced him always to
take the opposite view, for he was a proud man, too
proud to admit that a mere woman might know better
than he.

Mariaerh sighed. She found her usual place on a
grassy knoll and sat down with her back propped
against a tree. The cool, predawn air felt clean and fresh
against her face, and the rhythmic slap of the current
against the bank lulled her into a sense of peace.

The loneliness Mariaerh had known while Lucius
was in Caesarea had descended again full force since
Petronius' rampage. Her closest friends had been
among those who fled to Laodicea and with Nimmuo in
Jerusalem and mostly Gentiles in the camp, Marcia
was the only one Mariaerh could truly call a friend.

She would never understand the God-fearers, their
improper behavior, their lack of morality and sobriety.
Nor did they understand her. She believed that they
thought of her as overly pious, a burden for Lucius to
bear, that the men pitied him for his humorless,
unsympathetic wife and that the women secretly
scorned her barrenness. They treated her respectfully to
her face, but she thought that once her back was turned,
their whispers burned her ears. And Lucius did nothing
to change their opinion.

The chasm between her and Lucius seemed to grow a
bit with each passing day, and even the marriage act
was performed perfunctorily, without endearments or
confessions of love. When Lucius rolled to his side and
immediately fell asleep, Mariaerh was left with a sense
of emptiness, an awareness of loss, though she did not
know what it was for which she so yearned.

Saul's coming to Antioch had been the final proof of
Lucius' disregard. If he had any affection for her at all,
he would have understood her objection, not invited
him, and, if he had hinted at coming uninvited,
dissuaded him.

The memory of her encounter with Saul made her
shiver. What if such should occur again? If only she had

someone to talk to about Saul. Not Marcia, as she had learned. She, as everyone else, seemed to have forgotten the past and thought that now he could do no wrong. No one seemed to be able to see through his bombast and self-aggrandizement, or to share her avid dislike of Saul.

Mariaerh's eyes flew open. No one, she thought, except Celicene? She chuckled as she remembered Celicene's audacity. "Ugly little fanatic," she had called him. She was right about that, Mariaerh thought, ruefully. She closed her eyes again and tried to recall all she knew of Celicene.

Petronius had released Cornelius from house arrest upon his return to Antioch. His experiences in Judea forced him to admit that Cornelius had been right in defending the Jews, and since the new Emperor Claudius had deemed Agrippa an intimate friend since childhood, the temper of Rome was much more sympathetic toward the Jews. Nevertheless, Petronius could not forget the centurion's opposition to his methods, and Cornelius' influence in Antioch was vastly diminished. Petronius appointed a general called Shugard over Cornelius, and Shugard disapproved of Cornelius' involvement with The Way. He ridiculed the "tribe of Christians" and made no secret of the fact that he thought the building of a synagogue to be folly in the least, if not a near act of treason. It was no longer prudent for the Christians to visit Cornelius at his official residence, so he and his family instead came to the camp.

Celicene had become a familiar face in the camp. With Cornelius out of favor, her usual friends quietly shunned her and she was lonely. Her younger sister Leoda was an aide to Mariaerh at the center, and Celicene often came with her, more out of boredom than a desire to serve The Way.

Mariaerh had no objection. Celicene was good with the children. She was lively and gay and the children adored her. Mariaerh liked her, but she would never have entertained the idea of cultivating a friendship with her. Celicene was Gentile and even though she was

Cornelius' daughter, she made no secret of her skepticism regarding The Way. An intimate friendship between the overseer's wife and a disbeliever was out of the question. Mariaerh could just hear the talk that would cause, and Lucius would never condone it.

The sun, hot and bright upon Mariaerh's closed lids, told her that the children would soon be coming for class. She stood and stretched and gazed for a moment across the Orontes, then returned to the house to prepare for school.

The camp in Antioch had became a model for other camps which the Essenes foresaw would appear in the coming era of chaos. Monks from the City of Salt and Mount Carmel came to study its communal appeal and strength as did Elders and leaders from all the surrounding churches that were rising up. With Saul in the camp, many visited under the pretext of learning their secret when in fact they came to see how one who nearly destroyed The Way could have undergone such a change of heart. The story of Saul's conversion was recounted over and over again, each time leaving the listeners in awe over the power of the Lord.

Mariaerh was not awed. She thought Saul only told and retold his story to gain fame for himself, as though he were the only one sought out by the Lord. When visitors tried to discuss the matter with her, she found it intolerable and changed the subject or made excuses to leave the room. When Peter made a surprise visit to Antioch and Saul's popularity waned in the shining light of his presence, no one could have been more pleased than Mariaerh.

The mysterious ways of the Lord were never more evident than in His choosing Peter and Saul to lead His church. Two men of more opposite temperaments seemed never to have lived, yet share a common goal. Peter was the shepherd of his flock, compassionate and understanding of human frailties, strong and ironwilled in matters of doctrine, yet willing to bend to human need. He was modest to the point of self-effacement, yet ministered to the rich and prestigious with the same ease and confidence as he did to the poor. He was beloved by the people, but embarrassed by their adoration. When the Gentile believers showed signs of becoming overzealous in their high esteem for him, Peter would remind them that he was naught but a fisherman, and would order a boat be brought so that he might take them all fishing.

Saul on the other hand was fearless to the point of being reckless. His manner was haughty and authoritative and he brooked no compromise to the impossibly high standards he set for himself, while clearly expecting the same from others. He was highly educated and spoke with a sophistication that appealed to the thinking man, but his lofty rhetoric was sometimes lost on the more simple folk. When attempting to inspire by his own example, he often seemed boastful, too full of pride in his own accomplishments, yet all that he said was true.

Where Saul chastised, Peter forgave. Where Saul directed and ordered, Peter quietly led. While Saul held himself rigidly in check and guarded against all urges of his flesh, Peter enjoyed his body. He ate and drank with gusto. He spoke longingly of his years spent on the Sea of Galilee with the wind in his face and the sun on his back and the joy of pitting his strength against the unpredictable sea.

Saul saw himself as a soldier of Christ, bedecked in the armor of virtue, while Peter was the shepherd of a wayward flock, gentle, protective, guarding his lambs against the invasion of evil. Saul would compromise to no one, where Peter tried to be all things to all men.

Peter made no distinction between Gentile and Jew. He preached to both, he ate with both, but when some Judeans were sent to Antioch by James, the brother of the Lord, Peter refrained from dining at Gentile tables, lest he scandalize the pious men. His tact and sensitivity were lost upon Saul. Saul considered Peter's action to be hypocritical and felt no compunction in publicly berating an Apostle. Those who favored Peter were shocked by Saul's lack of respect, while those who felt closer to Saul argued that he was right. The camp was soon subtly divided between the two charismatic champions.

Lucius did not notice the division making its way insidiously through his church. As a favorite and protégé of Peter, and a kinsman of Saul, Lucius was revered by both sides of the issue. He basked in the reflected glory of both, and preened himself over the fact that he was the intimate and confidant of two such highly esteemed men. When Cornelius tried to warn him that trouble was brewing, Lucius brushed it away as nonsense.

"It's only natural that some should love Peter the more and others love Saul. When Peter returns to Jerusalem for the Feast of Passover, the whole matter will be forgotten."

Peter had brought his wife Cleo, his daughter Junie, and Andrew's son Ardoen and his wife Paula with him to Antioch. They were all staying at Lucius' house, and while there was barely room to walk, Mariaerh enjoyed them all immensely. They were a happy family, who teased one another outrageously, and the house was filled with laughter. It was impossible for her and Lucius to argue or to be at odds in such a carefree atmosphere. Their good humor was infectious. Mariaerh found Lucius teasing her as he used to do with Nimmuo, and she was happier than she had been in months.

Peter's easy way with Gentiles was thought-provoking and Mariaerh began to wonder if she had not been too severe in her judgments. When she saw how he could completely ignore whispered censure and did as he pleased despite disapproval from some who thought he should behave with more dignity, she began to wonder why she should not make friends with Celicene. Peter seemed perfectly confident in following his own heart and conscience, why could she not do so as well? If Peter's wife could act on her own without permission or approval from Peter, why could she not do the same? If Lucius did not like it, he would just have to find a way to accept it in his own mind, and if he became too angry, Mariaerh could always cite Peter as an example.

She began to seek Celicene out, to smile and offer a

pleasantry when they met, and to occasionally ask her opinion. To Mariaerh's delight, Celicene readily responded, although was as cautious as she.

At first they circumvented issues over which one thought the other might take offense, and were careful to avoid revealing their innermost feelings. But as time passed, trust in one another grew, and through tentative remarks dropped here and there to test the other's reaction, they discovered they had much in common.

Both were lonely. Both felt as if they were outsiders, tolerated only for their family ties. Both deplored the superior attitude of many men over women, and believed that women should be held equal and shown the same degree of respect as men. When Saul one night preached that women should hold their tongues and not participate in any meetings, but should rather ask questions of their husbands later in the privacy of their own homes, both Mariaerh and Celicene had publicly declared his teaching to be in error.

Mariaerh had cited the work of the Holy Women, intimate friends and family members of Jeshua himself, and never had He admonished the women to silence.

"I remember an evening in Bethany when Martha told us how she had complained to the Lord over Mary's preference in sitting at Jeshua's feet and asking questions instead of helping Martha to prepare the meal. Jeshua had answered her complaint by saying, 'Mary has chosen the better portion and she shall not be deprived of it.' "

As one of the Holy Women herself, Mariaerh carried more influence over the Antioch church than she had realized. The Saints sided with Mariaerh and women continued to participate actively in all areas of the church.

Saul accepted his defeat gracefully, although he never gave up his position on this and many other issues over which he and Mariaerh disagreed, and while Celicene applauded Mariaerh's courage in debating "the old bachelor," Mariaerh nursed her fear that Saul was only biding his time, and one day he would have his revenge.

Celicene increased her activities in Mariaerh's school. She watched Mariaerh's gentle guidance of the little ones and thought of her own childhood and the outbursts of her many nurses and tutors whenever her lively behavior had jangled their nerves. Where her own outrageous questions had been met with shocked chastisement, Mariaerh took such curiosity as a matter of course and answered the children with quiet honesty. She began to question Mariaerh herself, with growing confidence that Mariaerh would not belittle her or think her honest confusions to be a deliberate show of disrespect.

The developing friendship between Mariaerh and Celicene did cause talk, as Mariaerh had anticipated, and Lucius did disapprove, until Peter took him aside and reminded him of the many times when he, Lucius, had befriended a non-believer, only to turn him into a believer. Lucius had nothing to say to Peter's logic and grudgingly yielded, but he complained of Celicene's boldness and ready tongue, and believed she provoked rebellion within his wife.

By the time Peter returned to Jerusalem for the Feast of Passover, Celicene was a full believer in The Way and Mariaerh had the friend she so longed to find. Unfortunately, it was not to last, for even at that moment, the forces of darkness made ready to strike again.

# Chapter 23

Stuttering, some said half-witted, Claudius succeeded Caligula to Caesar's throne. Agrippa befriended the poor, bemused man and helped to reconcile the senate to his rule. Claudius rewarded Agrippa by bestowing upon him all the former kingdoms of his grandfather, Herod the Great.

Judea rejoiced when Agrippa became king. Nearly forty years beneath the thumb of a Roman procurator had come to an end and at last the land of their fathers was ruled by a king of their own people.

Agrippa was of the legitimate line of Hasmoneans through his grandmother, Mariamne, and that alone insured his popularity with the people but, at first, he further endeared himself by a public display of piety and devotion to God. He daily offered the proper sacrifices and performed all the duties prescribed by Law. He retrieved the priestly garments from the Fortress Antonia, and Rome would no longer depose or appoint the Jewish High Priest.

Daily life under Agrippa's rule was so much better than under Roman domination that the people thought it, by comparison, heaven on earth. Just prior to Agrippa's reign, the completion of the Temple had eliminated work for thousands of men and Jerusalem had become a city of abject poverty. Agrippa responded effectively by initiating many public building programs, the greatest of which was to expand and rebuild the city's walls. He released home owners from the crushing land taxes that slashed any profit to the bone, and his friendship with Rome was a boon to trade and commerce.

Agrippa knew that the tenure of his reign depended upon the peace and prosperity of his kingdom. If the Jews became disgruntled and complained to Rome, the kingdom he had obtained could just as quickly be taken away. He strove to please his subjects by acceding to their most outrageous demands, but once the economy was on solid footing and his popularity assured, Agrippa found the precise and specific Laws of Moses overly restrictive and intolerable. He began to spend long periods of time away from the city where he could indulge his passions and appetites removed from the watchful, censorious eyes of the Jews.

As his grandfather before him, Agrippa had a penchant for building. The majority of Jews would never tolerate the invasion of pagan games and plays into the City of God so it was the surrounding Greek and Roman cities that received the fruits of Agrippa's passion. He had a particular affection for Berytus in Syria and bestowed upon its citizens a theatre, an amphitheatre, baths and porticoes, then lavishly provided magnificent shows and entertainments.

The Jews were not happy that the funds which flowed from Palestine into the king's treasury should be spent in foreign cities to further pagan debaucheries. They were more incensed when Agrippa took up residence in Antipas' palace in Tiberius and rumors of unholy revelries began to filter into Jerusalem. When Claudius learned that Agrippa was rebuilding the wall that encompassed the city, he ordered Agrippa to stop, fearing such fortifications could be used against Rome. Agrippa obeyed, no matter the outcry from the thousands who were again without work, and the Jews viewed his action as proof that he cared more for Rome's disposition than for that of his own people. Agrippa's popularity was on the wane and the Nazarenes would be used to regain it.

Years had passed since Caiaphas had been stripped of the High Priesthood. He was old and sick, and only his bitter hatred for the Nazarenes, whom he blamed for his fall from power, kept him alive. When the Apostles named James ben Joseph as head of the Jerusalem church, Caiaphas had flown into such a rage that his family feared he would suffer a stroke.

Caiaphas hated James. James' striking likeness to Jeshua was a constant reminder of the Nazarene Caiaphas had allowed to die, and the nagging doubt that He might just possibly have been the true Messiah, drove Caiaphas to the brink of madness.

As a Sadducee, Caiaphas did not believe in the continuity of life but, as each year drew him closer to death, he began to fear that he might be wrong. To spend eternity in the flames of Gehenna because of the role he played in the Nazarene's death terrified him. He became obsessed with proving that Jeshua was a fraud and that he had been right in disposing of Him, for only then could he die in peace. Caiaphas believed that the extinction of Jeshua's followers would be that proof and that he had followed God's will in handing over the Nazarene. As long as the Nazarenes flourished and grew, it seemed that God was on their side, but if they were destroyed, it would show that God found the sect an abomination.

As the Jews became more and more disillusioned by Agrippa's actions and neglect, Caiaphas saw his chance. He began a campaign of slander against the Nazarenes. A hint dropped here and there of pagan rites and atrocities, a whispered tale of sexual perversions, an expression of concern over the Nazarenes consorting with Gentiles—Did they plot the overthrow of the King?—and soon the calumny spread from the tables of the rich by their servants through the lower classes until The Way became suspect throughout the city. The authorities became alarmed. Then, when the normally heavy winter rains refused to fall and only an occasional shower settled the dust on the thirsting land, the common people sought the cause for God's displeasure and many looked only as far the infamous Nazarenes.

The approach of Passover brought thousands of pilgrims into the city and old Caiaphas seized the opportunity to bring his carefully laid plot to fruition.

He waited until Agrippa and his retinue were installed in the Hasmonean Palace then sent agitators to the outer Temple courts to jeer and harass the preaching Nazarenes. He counted on the highly-charged, emotional atmosphere of Passover week to aid his lackeys in stirring the Jews to passion, and he was right.

Day after day the agitators heaped abuse and ridicule upon the followers of The Way. They accused them of blasphemy, of consorting with Belial, and declared Jeshua a criminal accursed by God. The people chose sides, those who shouted that the Nazarenes be barred from speaking and those who cried for their right to be heard. Finally Caiaphas' hoped-for riot occurred and all went according to his plan.

The High Priest sent to Agrippa for troops to quell the riot. Agrippa's guard marched into the melee with clubs raised and swords drawn and, before the hour was out, the courts ran red with blood and the severed head of James ben Zebedee stared in mute testimony to the cruelty of man toward man.

Josie, the handmaid to the Mother of the Lord, died when her skull was crushed by the blow of a club. Sopha, the Baptiser's ancient nurse, was trampled to death by the crowd. Thaddeus, son of the Other Mary's old age, died broken and bloody in his mother's arms. Justin, the beloved of Judith, the beloved of all the Saints, lay sprawled with his Roman blood pouring out on the Temple floor to mingle with that of his beloved Jews. Zebedee's heart refused to suffer more grief and he joined his loved ones in the sleep of death.

The Saints reeled with grief and despair. Why had God not warned them?

The Temple authorities lauded the King for his quick action in quelling the riot. Agrippa had received little approval from his subjects' leading men of late, and when he saw how pleased they were, he quickly acquiesced to Caiaphas' suggestion that he arrest the leader of the troublemakers and run his subordinates out of the city. To rid the city of a despised, heretical sect seemed little price to pay to insure the continued support of the ruling priests.

Caiaphas knew better than to name James ben Joseph as the leader of the Nazarenes, for James' popularity among the people would cause a general outcry of dissent, so he named the rough-cut Galilean, Simon ben John, instead. Peter was arrested and thrown into jail and the other Apostles given twenty-four hours to clear Jerusalem of their stench.

The dead were buried by sunset. There was no time to grieve, no time for friends and families to join together in prayer and mutual comfort. The principal leaders of the church gathered at Marcus' house and labored throughout the night and into the next day preparing for the Apostles' departure.

The women packed leather pouches of food to sustain them for part of their journey. Money and extra clothing were drawn from the storeroom beneath the house. False identities were created in case they were stopped and questioned by frontier guards and lists of trusted Brothers who would help them along the way were memorized by each fleeing Apostle.

Judith worked with James ben Joseph and the Apostles in plotting their itinerary and in reorganizing the network of messengers to insure that a continuous communication flowed between The Twelve and the church. Her unwavering faith and acceptance of God's will inspired and gave strength to them all. She subjugated her own grief, burying it beneath her brusque, authoritative command, and only her haunted, pain-ridden eyes betrayed the depth of her sorrow. When someone ventured to remark upon the extent of her courage, Judith answered, caustically, " 'Let the dead bury the dead,' the living must live for the living."

Nimmuo helped with the preparations and watched Judith with a lump in her throat and an ache in her heart. She felt empathy to Judith. Wed to a Roman herself, she could well imagine what Judith must feel. She identified Justin with Belden, and if Belden confessed his faith in The Way out of his love for her and then was slain because of it, Nimmuo thought she would be wracked with guilt, no matter how irrational it might be. She felt an inner compulsion to share her understanding with Judith, but the frantic confusion of those few hours gave her no opportunity.

When the last Apostle and his family had been kissed and blessed and sent on their way, and the remaining Saints gathered in Marcus' upper room to pray for Peter's deliverance, Nimmuo still did not seek out Judith. She needed to see Belden, to hear his voice and to sleep in the circle of his comforting arms and pretend for a time that nothing would ever part them. John Mark took her home, hurrying through the dark, deserted streets, hearing nothing but far away night sounds, lonely sounds, sorrowful sounds, the sigh of an ancient city bereft of the best of her men.

Nimmuo returned to Marcus' house at dawn and, after a quiet exchange with Peter's wife, went, at last, in search of Judith. She found her alone in a room at the back of the house, staring out of a window. Nimmuo hesitated a moment, wondering if she should intrude upon Judith's thoughts, but the memory of Belden's arms and the knowledge that Judith would never know that pleasure and comfort again, impelled her to follow her intuition. She quietly entered the room and gently laid her hand upon Judith's arm.

Judith turned her face to Nimmuo and Nimmuo's eyes welled. Judith's face was ashen, haggard. Black circles ringed her eyes that normally were as blue as the sea, but now were as pale as ice. Her mouth was pinched and her shoulders sagged. She shook her head sadly and turned back to the window.

Nimmuo let her hand slide down Judith's arm until she found her hand and squeezed it, saying nothing, just pouring out all of her love to the beloved teacher of them all. After a few moments, she said, quietly, "These last hours I've wondered if it's wise to love a Roman and teach him to love The Way. If Belden should sometime meet Justin's fate because of me, I think I'd not be able to bear it."

Judith did not move. Nimmuo sighed. "Then I thought, would it be better for him to die an old man in his bed and never have known the Lord?"

She made a gesture of helplessness. "How is a woman to know? Belden has a mind of his own, as you of all people know all Romans do. I might plant the seed of faith in his mind, but it would be his soul responding to Jeshua's call, not to my wifely nagging."

Judith frowned at Nimmuo, but a bit of color shone in her eyes. "So, a mere snip of a girl hands out bits of wisdom to me, eh?" she said irritably. She turned back to the window and her tone turned wistful and heavy with sorrow. "My son Phinehas was in the Temple. He blames me. He's gone, and vows never to return or to see me again."

Nimmuo could feel her temper rise. How dare any pass judgment on Judith! "It seems to me as if your son should grow out of his childishness before he dies of old age!" she retorted. "Both your sons seem ever to look for somewhere else to lay their faults than upon their own shoulders where they belong!"

Judith's eyes widened. Nimmuo swallowed. She shrank a bit, wondering if perhaps she had gone too far, but then her sense of injustice overcame her timidity, and she plunged on.

"Really, Judith! Your sons are grown men. You yourself teach that man's will can overcome any obstacle. So what if you made mistakes in raising them? As grown men they should be able to understand why and come to terms with it. Each soul shapes its own destiny. To blame others is only to avoid meeting ourselves."

Judith snorted. "So the student is sent to lecture the teacher!" she said testily, but her eyes danced and her voice contained a hint of humor. She studied Nimmuo, her brow knit, her eyes probing. "You have fire as well as wisdom, then. Your Belden must lead an interesting life."

Nimmuo grinned. "I hear few complaints."

Judith actually laughed. "I would guess not!" Her eyes became wet, and Nimmuo watched, fascinated, as they became an ever deepening blue. "You've eased an old woman's burden," she said gently. "Come. The others pray in the upper room. Let's see what we can do for Peter."

Peter's trial was delayed until after the Feast, and for the next few days the gathered Saints held a continuous vigil of prayer. Hour upon hour they sat in a state of deep meditation, their silence broken only when one was moved to pray aloud. When one grew weary and needed a rest another would quietly take his place and the circle was never broken.

Another night had fallen. Nimmuo had been sitting for hours. An ache between her shoulder blades was becoming unbearable and her hand held by John Mark was numb and drenched with sweat. Her body rebelled, and she could no longer still her thoughts to hear the Lord. Her mind wandered, going back over the week's events.

The whole thing seemed like a nightmare relived. The riot, the funerals, the grief and despair, it was Saul's persecution all over again. This time Nimmuo had felt nothing but a sense of inevitable resignation instead of the anger and hatred she had felt then. She was coming to believe that to follow The Way sometimes meant to follow Jeshua all of the way, even to violent death. That night at Zebedee's when the martyred Saints had been laid to rest, Salome had told how she had once asked Jeshua if her sons could have the places of honor at His right and left hands.

"Can you drink of the cup I am to drink of?" Jeshua had asked. Well, James had gotten his wish, and the content of that cup was bitter indeed. How many more would be required to drink?

Nimmuo's eyes traveled around the circle. Martha of Nicodemus held tightly to her other hand, her daughter Rebecca next to her with her head resting sleepily on Silas' shoulder.

A love match blooming there, Nimmuo thought. Silas had made his home with Nicodemus since Saul's persecution, and the lonely, orphaned boy had sought solace in Martha's toddler. Rebecca adored him, and now at thirteen, her childish adoration was growing into a woman's love. Nimmuo felt a pang of loneliness for her own small daughters who were safely at home with Belden.

The riot had horrified Belden. "What if you had been there!" he cried. "You could have been killed!" When Nimmuo had simply shrugged her shoulders, he had been aghast. "Would you give up your life for this Jeshua?" he asked in amazement. "Would you give up yours for Rome, or would you betray her to save yourself?" Nimmuo had replied.

Poor Belden. He had looked so defeated, so helpless. He feared her coming to Marcus', but he did not forbid her. He never interfered in her activities in The Way, even though he did not believe himself.

A warmth spread through Nimmuo. Who could compare to Belden? Justin could. What if that had been Belden lying in his own blood on the floor of the court? She could not have borne it! Well, on second thought, she probably could. What choice would she have? After all of these years in The Way, she had come to know that one could bear whatever is set before one. They had all surely had enough practice, she thought ruefully.

She shook her head, scattering such thoughts before they could make her throat ache and her eyes burn. Her gaze passed over the others in the circle: Nicodemus, Marcus, Josie, Mary, Cleo, Junie, John Louie, Ardoen and Clement.

Poor child! Clement was frightened to death. James ben Joseph had sent his little son to Marcus' to insure his safety. No one knew if Agrippa's men would invade James' house and carry James off to jail also, and it would be a terrible thing for a child to witness. He was pale and drawn and struggled to keep awake, but would not lie down to sleep. Nimmuo wondered if perhaps it might be worse for him to be separated from his family and not know what was happening.

Judith began to intone a hymn, and Nimmuo marveled. Her firm, vibrant voice was more that of a girl of twenty than a seventy-year-old woman who had just lost her husband of nearly fifty years. She listened to the hymn Judith chose and a lump grew in her throat, for it was a cry from a weary, grief-stricken heart.

"Lo, I am stricken dumb. What can I say against this? I have spoken but according to my knowledge and only with such sense of right as a creature of clay may possess. But how can I speak except Thou open my mouth, and how understand, if Thou give me not insight; or how content, save Thou open my heart; or how walk straight save Thou guide my feet? How can my foot stand, how can I be strong in power, how can I endure save by Thy grace?"

What would it take to shake Judith's faith? Nimmuo's head was bowed and she smiled into her lap. If she had ventured that question to Judith herself, she could just hear that wonderful, joyous, infectious laugh, and would be treated to marvelous tales of when Judith was wracked by doubt.

Someone tapped Nimmuo's shoulder and she raised her head and met Belden's anxious eyes. She relinquished her place to Rhoda's husband and followed Belden downstairs where he drew her to a corner and pulled her into his arms.

Their embrace was passionate and desperate with fear. Nimmuo melted against his familiar, hard body, reveling in his strength and the knowledge of his love. She was overcome with emotion and could not trust herself to speak. She clung to him, wishing he would never let go, then suddenly remembered her daughters and pushed herself loose from his arms.

"Why are you here? Are the girls all right?"

Belden cupped her face with his hands. "They are fine. Do not worry," he soothed. "I had to see you. Are you all right?"

Nimmuo nodded, relieved. "Of course. I'm so glad you are here."

Belden drew her to a low bench and kissed her again. "I miss you. The girls miss you."

"What did you tell them?"

"The truth, though I don't know how much they understood. I was going to make up some story, but one day they will hear the truth and wonder why I lied."

Nimmuo grimaced. "I now understand why Mariaerh was always so angry when children were subjected to fear."

Belden changed the subject to take Nimmuo's mind off the girls. "I've spoken to a few people about Peter, but without a military force in Jerusalem, there is little the Roman authorities can do. They have to tread softly where Agrippa is concerned. He is a friend of Claudius, and no one knows how far the breach in their friendship goes over Agrippa rebuilding the wall. Our officials are in a tenuous position since Judea became a kingdom. They really don't know where they stand or what powers they have."

Nimmuo gripped his hand. "Thank you for trying. How can I ever tell you how much I appreciate your understanding?"

Belden grinned. "I could think of a way."

Nimmuo laughed. "We'll discuss it when I return home."

Belden held her tightly, then whispered. "I must get back to the girls. I don't want one of them to awaken and call for me and find me not there."

Nimmuo reluctantly let him go. They lingered at the door, loath to part, but after a final embrace, Belden's sturdy back disappeared in the darkness.

Nimmuo had something to eat and rested a bit before going back upstairs where she relieved Josie. The night wore on. The silence lay thick about them until a knock at the door downstairs startled them all wide awake.

They held their breath. Footsteps came running up the stairs and Rhoda burst into the room.

"It's Peter! I recognize his voice!"

"It can't be!" Marcus gasped.

Again the knock, louder and urgent.

"It must be his angel," Junie cried.

They raced for the stairs, hearts pounding. They huddled in the entry hall and stared at the door until Nicodemus stepped forward and cautiously pulled it open.

It was Peter! And not his angel. Nicodemus pulled him inside to astonished cries of disbelief.

Marcus hushed them and herded them back up the stairs.

"I can't stay. I must leave Jerusalem tonight," Peter said.

"How did you escape?" John Louie asked.

Peter grinned. "As I escaped once before. The Lord sent an angel who freed me from my chains and led me out of the jail. Report this to James and the Brothers. I must go. The sun will soon be up and I must be out of the city by then."

Cleo began to hurriedly gather her things together, but Peter stopped her. "You can't go this time," he said gently. "Agrippa will search for me high and low, for the High Priest will be furious and blame Agrippa for the incompetence of his guards. I'll be safer alone."

Cleo drew in her breath to protest, but saw Peter's expression and did not argue.

"Take me," said John Mark. "Two pairs of ears and eyes are better than one."

Peter hesitated. He searched John Mark's youthful eager face and looked at Cleo whose eyes pleaded with him to consent. With a quick jerk of his head, he said curtly, "Come!"

Rhoda was waiting at the door with a leather pouch filled with bread and cheese. Josie clasped John Mark to her breast, weeping, then released him to Rhoda and Mary and then to Marcus, while Peter's family exchanged their prayerful farewells.

The lamps were extinguished. Nicodemus opened the door and listened for any sound of movement, then they slipped out into the night and the door closed on their backs.

Agrippa made an extensive search for Peter. The hapless guards were executed, but the feast day arrived and the grandeur of Passover drove the incident from everyone's mind. The Apostles were gone. James ben Joseph ruled over Jeshua's flock and the forces of darkness were given their due and their day.

# Chapter 24

## The Inn in Seleucia

I am weary. My hand trembles and my eyes blur as it is past the midnight hour and I have known no sleep since before the dawn. The drought in Judea has reached disastrous proportions. Relief and aid has been sent from all over the world, but it cannot begin to feed thousands of starving Jews. Saul, Barnabas and I sail to deliver the relief fund we have accumulated since Agabus prophesied the drought. It will sustain James and the Saints in Jerusalem until God finds it fit to again bestow the blessing of rain on this evil world.

I set this account down tonight, for only God knows when or if I write again.

The camp is flooded with refugees. Agrippa's persecution of The Way in Jerusalem gave unwritten license for others throughout Judea and Galilee to follow suit. The impudent rabble jeered and mocked them in the streets. Tax collectors boldly demanded of them double what was due and pocketed the excess for themselves, knowing they had no recourse for complaint. They were overcharged for purchases, underpaid for their goods. Greedy landlords happily raised their rents while money-lenders raised their interest then confiscated their properties when they could not pay. Employers cut their wages. Innkeepers refused to serve them. Their shops and booths were boycotted and they had no market for their wares. They were denied the right to speak in the synagogues and their sacrifices were refused as unclean. Our Brothers and Sisters in Jerusalem could only meet under the cover of night and acknowledged their friendship with "Peace be with you" and used again the secret sign of the fish.

They were not without friends. The poor remembered the healings received and the aid and succor given in times of distress, and many priests, Pharisees, even scribes, recalled the stir in their hearts when they heard the words of our Lord and were moved to sympathy for the plight of His followers. A loaf was brought in the dark of night. An interest-free loan offered with no questions asked. A barn to hide in, an ass to ride upon, sometimes a blessing given and a prayer said were all they could give, but given it was.

Christians fled Judea, to Damascus, Caesarea and here to Antioch. John Louie came to us, bitter and distraught, driven from his home in Capernaum because his uncle, Simon ben John, our Peter, is a fugitive from the law. Andrew's children, Dora, Ardoen and Ardoen's wife, Paula, came with John Louie. Silas led the Other Mary and Timothy here, away from the scene of their grief, but there are tens upon tens that I never knew.

I was amazed, as I interviewed them and recorded their histories, at the number who had as children been blessed by the Master. I have heard tale after tale of the touch of His hands, of His gentle voice, His love-filled eyes, described in a manner which made me know these accounts have been told and retold again and again. I was also amazed that a childhood encounter could so change their lives, for they have never forgotten, will never forget and are compelled to share the experience. When they found they could no longer tell their tale without risk of ridicule and censure, they quitted their villages and homes and friends to seek out new, willing ears, ears that would know, would understand that the hand of God had touched men.

Does Pebilus remember? Does he feel the humbling, profound sense of gratitude that these young people feel? Does his flesh still tingle from the Master's touch and his soul still vibrate from hearing His voice? Ah, that I could know, but I digress from my history.

Claudius replaced Petronius with Marcus. It was Marcus who informed the Emperor that Agrippa rebuilt the wall and insinuated—calumny that it was—of its possible use against Rome. Marcus despises Jews. He imagines that rebellion lies hidden in every Jewish heart and thinks it an ever-constant threat to peace within the Empire. He hoped to suppress that threat by planting the seeds of distrust against Jews in Claudius' mind, whereby he and others of like mind could keep the Jews in their place without fear of repercussions from Rome. Marcus' attitude filtered down through the ranks until even servants and menial laborers emulated their masters' behavior and speech. Now the lot of Jews, whether Christian or not, is no better in Antioch than in Judea.

Marcus encouraged tax assessors to inflate our worth. Farm produce is either over- or under-estimated according to whether the land is owned by a Jew or rented from a friend of Marcus. If owned, more bushels for each parcel of land are calculated or a few extra sheep added to the count of the flock so a greater amount of tax can be wrenched from the hapless farmer. If rented, they rate the harvest below what it actually is and recommend to the landowner that he hire a better manager. If we protest, we find ourselves in court, pleading our case before a judge who is urged and sometimes bribed to find in favor of the defendant. There are yet a few just men who remember Rome's heroic days when law and order and justice for all were revered but, for the most part, they give way to fear and pressure exerted by Marcus or to the lure of financial gain and the approval of their friends.

Cornelius covertly works to sway lawyers and judges and other civil authorities to render fair treatment. He stays within the law and does not overstep his authority, but his subtle interference has not gone unnoticed and has earned him the ever-increasing displeasure of his superiors. Marcus has now been recalled and we do not, as yet, know if the new proconsul will be any more kindly disposed toward Cornelius.

Agrippa died suddenly in Caesarea. Claudius deemed the king's son too young to assume his father's throne and a procurator again reigns over Judea. Legionnaires again patrol the streets of Jerusalem and the authority to inflict the death penalty is back in Roman hands. Claudius gave King Agrippa's brother, Herod of Chalcis, control of the Temple. Herod appointed Joseph ben Camus to the High Priesthood and, since Caiaphas is dead and Joseph has no familial connection with that old enemy's house, it was safe for Peter and John Mark to return home. Claudius recalled Marcus out of respect to Agrippa's memory.

Cornelius does not know the new proconsul, Longinus, so we

cannot guess what his attitude toward us will be. Longinus has yet to arrive in the city and these weeks of transition are a welcomed respite from oppression. I hope to return from Jerusalem before his new policies are put into action.

Dawn awaits upon the horizon. My body cries out for rest and my eyes are blinded by sleep, but my mind churns with thought and my heart is full. Nimmuo walks in Jerusalem and, though she is unaware of my coming, I anticipate seeing her beloved face.

May the Almighty One watch over and protect my flock in my absence.

\* \* \* \* \*

Lucius, Saul and Barnabas debarked at Ptolemais and followed the route through Galilee and down the Jordan to Jerusalem.

Lucius was shocked by nature's mutilation of the land and the ravages drought could have on a people. The famed vineyards of Galilee had shriveled and died. The lush green fields had turned to a powdery dust that was scooped up by the parched desert winds and hurled across the countryside to settle in drifts like snow in the mountains. Pasture lands lay curled and crisp beneath inches of dust and were strewn with the putrefying carcasses of their once proud, fat sheep and cattle. The ancient olive trees thrust their roots deep into the earth in search of water, but the fruit they produced was wizened and useless.

The air was an impenetrable haze, as smoke, that burned eyes and throats and stung raw any exposed flesh. Every step sent eddies of silt up legs and under clothes to itch and irritate, and women wept in despair and flung their brooms away.

The wind never let up, whipping across the land day and night, its endless roar and scorching heat crazed both man and beast. No fires could be lit outside. Beleaguered women were forced to cook in the sweltering confines of the house, for the merest spark would soon grow into a raging fire. Despair and hopelessness were as thick as the dust in the air.

Wells had run dry. Creek beds were cracked into geometrical shapes as hard and gray as sun-bleached bones. The Sea of Galilee had recoiled from its banks and lolled beneath a cover of stagnant, green slime. Her fish suffocated from the lack of aerating rain, and fishermen died of hunger. The river Jordan was shrunk to a narrow, sluggish stream that pushed its way through the ooze and mire that stretched yards away from its banks. Drinking water was sold at exorbitant prices, wine and beer so dear that only the rich could slake their thirst with the cooling fruit of the vine.

Hunger and disease stalked the land. Epidemics followed. The roadways were choked with thousands of homeless, starving peasants who roamed the countryside scavenging for any edible root or shoot, begging for scraps, stripping the trees of their leaves for food. Crime increased on a massive scale as men turned to thievery to feed their families, or committed any violent act in a mindless attempt to avenge themselves against the tyranny caused by nature.

Peasants fled to the cities. A tide of human misery poured through Jerusalem's gates, but their hopes for food and shelter were quickly dashed. The heat and disease were worse in the city than in the country. Old people and children died without a struggle for life. The streets were clogged, made impassable by squatters who lolled in quiet desperation and silently begged with their eyes.

Vileness and squalor, despair and defeat. Lucius recoiled from the wretchedness and fought an overwhelming urge to flee with his hands over his ears to stop the low, never-ending drone of suffering, with his eyes squeezed shut against the obscenity of filth and starvation, and with his breath held against the overpowering stench of decay.

When they reached Jerusalem, Lucius was crushed to learn that Nimmuo and Belden had sailed for Laodicea only a week before his arrival and the repressed yearning in his heart for his family and city burst asunder. After days of looking upon naught but destruction, his eyes ached for the green expanse of his childhood valley, for the sparkling freshets cascading from the ring of hills; for white, puffy clouds skimming across an azure sky, chased by breezes as cool as the marble on his mother's atrium floor.

In Jerusalem, Lucius felt suffocated, caged, imprisoned in a desolate, burning hell that if he did not flee at once, he would not escape. The sky over the city was white hot, the wind like a blast from the ironsmith's forge. When he dreamed one night that Jerusalem burned and he was caught in the conflagration, he recognized it as a dream he had known before, and was desperate to flee the city. He turned the relief monies over to the presbyters and urged Barnabas and Saul to leave at once for home.

Barnabas invited John Mark to come with them. He eagerly agreed and they boarded ship at Caesarea and sailed for Seleucia. Lucius stood on the deck and watched the coast of Judea recede. A weight lay upon his chest as if a great stone pressed against his lungs. Jerusalem was finished. In some secret recess of his mind, he knew that he witnessed the beginning of the end, that the present suffering was only a taste of what was to come. He mourned Jerusalem. He grieved for her past glory, her rich history, for the saints and devils she had spawned and the wonders and depravity that had occurred within her walls.

Jeshua's words when he too mourned Jerusalem sounded over and over in his ears. "O Jerusalem, Jerusalem! How often have I wanted to gather your children together as a mother bird collects her young under her wings."

The Master knew. He had wept then as Lucius wept now. The disease and corruption and death and decay of the city only matched the plight of its people. Who would save them? Who would feed the children of God the bread of eternal life? Would they eat when offered?

Lucius' thoughts were continually interrupted by John Mark who fairly danced from one end of the deck to the other as he excitedly pointed out one view after another for Lucius to see. It was his first sailing and his exuberance made even dour Saul smile, but he made

Lucius feel old which depressed him even more. He watched him and wondered where his own youth had gone, when he had lost his own optimism, his joy of discovery, his delight in simple pleasures.

Lucius turned his gaze back to the sea, entranced by the wake left by the great ship. He had seen too much. He had looked behind smiling friendly faces and found hatred and bigotry and self-serving motives festering in the souls of men. He had left the wide, tree-lined avenues of his youth for twisted dark alleys and found evil and filth and depravity. The world was a garbage pit of wickedness. Was it beyond saving? If so, why should he care? And yet he did care, so much that it broke his heart.

Lucius' mood lasted throughout the journey and did not lift when they reached the camp and Mariaerh gasped and cried out in sheer joy when John Mark leaped across her doorsill and swung her off her feet and danced her around the room. When he put her down, she rushed to fix him a meal, then sat across the table from him and bombarded him with questions, starved for every tidbit of news from home. She feasted her eyes upon him as if she could never drink her fill.

Lucius ate in silence and watched Mariaerh. Years of unhappiness had fallen from her face. She was animated, glowing, her voice light and excited. Her hands fluttered as she spoke and her body leaned toward John Mark in eager anticipation of his every word. It was as if she were sixteen again, the lively girl he had only seen when in Martha's class.

Lucius' appetite fled and he wanted to weep. He pushed his bowl aside, made an excuse and went to his study in back of the house. The table that served as his desk was piled high with lists and reports and messages that had accumulated during his absence, but he ignored them. He straddled the cushionless, three-legged stool and sat at the table, his heart laden with regret and his thoughts a march of sins of omission.

How had he failed to evoke the happiness and spontaneity that he had just witnessed in Mariaerh? How beautiful she had looked, how alive and alluring!

Why had he never been able to love her as she should have been loved? He did love her, as a father for a daughter or a teacher for a favored student, but it was a joyless love without the heat of burning passion or the depth and need and longing that moved a man to the roots of his soul.

Lucius buried his head in his hands and shook his head sadly. He had been right in the beginning. He was too old for Mariaerh. She should have wed someone who saw the world fresh and new, not like himself whose sight had already been blurred with disillusionment, his heart already burdened with the cares of the world. He had spent his youth and deprived Mariaerh of hers. He had put his work first and foremost and ignored the happiness of his wife.

The heavy, stagnant smell of the river and the sounds of early evening drifted through the opened window upon a soft, unhurried breeze. The light of the day had faded and the room was shadowed and filled with ghosts. Merceden and Philippi, young and vital as his mind's eye last saw them. Nimmuo, carefree and happy, the apple of Philippi's eye and the beloved torment of his own youth. Lucia, heavy with child, dreamy-eyed with love for her young, plodding Jesua.

His own city, picturesque, sunwashed, nestled contentedly on the valley floor, her pulsating movement of life hidden from his view by a canopy of jewel-like rooftops. And Vesta, golden, lighthearted Vesta, with Pebilus snuggled happily at her breast.

Lucius Ceptulus of Cyrene put his head in his hands and wept.

\* \* \* \* \*

Longinus turned out to be as hard-hearted toward Jews as Marcus had been. He was enraged that a Roman centurion should encourage Greeks and Romans to worship the Jews' God, and peremptorily sent Cornelius packing to Rome. He enforced the restrictions and proscriptions against Jews, and included the tribe of Christians in the edicts.

It was a difficult time. Ignorance, bigotry, lust for

power and self-exaltation pressed close from every side, and the Saints drew together to resist the frightening tide of hate. They turned inward and relied upon the Holy Spirit for guidance in every matter. They heeded Saul's advice to avoid unbelievers, to accept their lot when need be, and to settle disputes among themselves. They wanted for nothing, for their practice of sharing all things in common insured that no one went hungry or cold. Freed from the daily concerns of the world, they turned their hearts and minds to things of the spirit, to consolidating and solidifying the tenets and practices of faith they had learned.

John Mark played a major role in bringing the Saints to a fullness of faith. He told endearing tales of Jeshua's love and humor as seen through the eyes of a growing boy, and his homely anecdotes gave flesh and life to the teachings they had embraced. John Mark's love for Jeshua was unencumbered by ritual and dogma and pious subservience. His love was childlike, joyful, totally free from fear and self-recrimination. He preached Christ's *name* with laughter and easy, affectionate irreverence, delighting his audience and drawing them into his own intimate, personal fellowship with the Lord. They wept when told how Jeshua wept, sighed in sympathy when Jeshua became bowed and weary with cares. They clenched their teeth and grimaced as they shared the Master's frustration and dismay, and nodded in understanding when His temper flared. They cheered and applauded when Jeshua laughed and joked, even on the way to the cross.

The profound deepening of love for Jeshua broke down all the barriers created by fear and opened the door to the Lord. His spirit poured down upon them, coursed through their souls and temples of flesh until they were made anew. For a time, a sense of peace and quiet joy settled over the camp, an island of calm in the midst of a turbulent sea.

The Essenes taught that two spirits resided in man, the spirit of truth and the spirit of perversity, and even those who practiced righteousness were liable to the sway of error. The carnal man resists the advance of the spiritual man and clings to its old, familiar ways out of fear of extinction, refusing to believe that only in its death is true freedom found.

The Saints were not immune to this process. Like the Master, they were in the world, even though they were not of it, and the temptations and pull of the world were as strong these days as in the days of Adam. Old habits of attitude and thought were not easily set aside, and as time passed, the camp came to know its own measure of internal discord.

The manifestation of spiritual gifts became a yardstick for holiness. If one did not speak in tongues, he was considered unworthy before the Lord, and was looked at askance and thought to have sin on his soul. They began to grade the Lord's gifts. The gift of prophecy was more important than the gift of teaching, healing more important than prophecy, and they used the gifts to jockey for positions of prestige.

By placing so much emphasis on the outward display of spiritual growth, they fell into the same old trap that Satan had laid for those among the Pharisees who were given to follow the letter not the spirit of the Law. Good works were performed to gain a reputation of charity. Long faces and pious postures replaced initial smiles of joy. They made public display of spiritual disciplines, boasted of callouses on their knees and weight loss from days of fasting. Such contests for recognition bred envy, and envy bred hatred, and that in its turn bred decay of the spirit.

John Mark ignored all such nonsense. He trod the earth with joy and full confidence in the Lord. He embraced the world with all its pleasures, and indulged his appetites so long as they never distressed another. He exemplified the whole man, a balance of flesh and spirit, but the Saints, caught up as they were in a wave of self-righteousness, failed to recognize him as such, and he became their target for gossip.

John Mark was exceedingly popular with the young girls in the camp. His happy-go-lucky personality and cherubic good looks, coupled with his familial ties to the Master, made him the most eligible bachelor ever to appear in the camp, and the girls vied for his attention. He was flattered by their adoration, and happily succumbed to their generous offers of favors. His many liaisons became a scandal among the pious Christians, but he turned aside their barbed criticism with laughter, quoting the Master, "The Son of Man came eating and drinking, and you say, 'This one is a glutton and a drunkard, a lover of tax collectors and those outside the law!' Yet time will prove where wisdom lies."

The Saints complained to their leaders. Barnabas pleaded with John Mark to set a better example. Lucius remembered his own passionate youth and chose to turn a blind eye. Saul was furious and preached lengthy sermons on the virtue of chastity, but John Mark blithely continued to lavish his affections upon one and all. When Lucius emerged from his meditation during a prayer service with instructions from the Lord to send Saul and Barnabas on an evangelizing journey, Barnabas seized upon the chance to resolve the problem. He suggested that John Mark go with them as their recorder and secretary, and although Saul complained and grumbled, Lucius agreed. After a preparation period of prayer and fasting, Lucius laid hands upon them and sent them on their way.

Internal difficulties within the camp were only minimized by external harassment. With Cornelius recalled to Rome, the centurion who replaced him thought that Longinus' restrictions did not go far enough to dissuade Greeks and Romans from becoming enchanted with the Christian sect. He gained Longinus' permission to dismantle the camp, to disperse the Gentiles throughout the city where the lack of close proximity would discourage their active participation in the church. The Gentiles were evicted, and nearby Jews forced to occupy their homes. The Hebrew Christians were scattered throughout the Jewish section where they bore the brunt of the Jews' anger for bringing the wrath of Rome upon them. The centurion ordered the synagogue opened to all Jews, not just to Christians, and deterred any Gentile from entering. The communal storehouse was plundered.

Every wall painted with murals depicting the life of the Master was whitewashed. Any private school "teaching an aberrant philosophy" was ruled illegal, and all books and scrolls and teaching aids were burned.

Lucius' Roman citizenship prevented his home from being confiscated, but as the overseer, he was subjected to a maddening subtle harassment. He was under constant surveillance, brought before the centurion for "questioning" over and over again at any time of day or night. He was ordered to stop spreading his "subversive views," and anyone he visited became suspect and faced the same grueling interrogation.

Mariaerh was paralyzed with fear. Everywhere she went she was followed by a legionnaire, stopped and questioned as to where she was going and why. The house was watched day and night and she kept the curtains drawn and the door locked, a prisoner in her own house.

It was a long and bitter winter. The Saints found themselves in dire straits as employers found excuses to dismiss them, and buyers shied away from purchasing their wares. They shared what they had with one another, but even meeting put them at risk. Lucius used the privilege of his citizenship to plead for the rights of his people, but loopholes in every law he cited were found, and every petition denied. There was nothing he could do. His presence in Antioch put every friend in danger, and he knew that for the good of all he must leave. He asked for an audience with Longinus and gained his permission to meet with the church one last time, and to allow any who wished to go with him.

They met in the vacant dining hall that only a few short months before had rung with joyful hymns and vibrant, confident prayers as the faithful joined hearts and minds in the harvest feast of the Lord. Now it rang with silence. The walls were bare, the tables gone, an empty expanse of broken dreams. The Elect stood before Lucius in quiet grief, their faces downcast with eyes staring at the floor, unable to meet one another's gaze or to view the evidence of their undoing.

Lucius' throat constricted. He tore his eyes from the sea of bowed, defeated heads and let his gaze travel across the barren walls. When he could trust himself to speak, he spoke quietly, with gentle, loving assurance.

"The church is not a building. The church is in the hearts and minds of all the faithful throughout the world. Our enemies may raze our buildings, burn our scrolls, and rob us of all our worldly goods, but never can they destroy the *church*. The Kingdom of God is within. Our bodies of flesh are His temple, and just as the Temple in Jerusalem has been leveled then raised again, so the People of God.

"His Light is in the world. You are the Lightbearers. Hold that lamp high. It matters not if the Light shines from the highest mountain or in the poorest hovel. It matters not if many Lights shine together and light up an entire nation, or if one tiny flame glows in the darkest cave, it matters only that the Light shine forth in the darkness.

"We are uprooted, scattered and transplanted in hostile soil, but our Light is not extinquished. Grow where you are planted. Bloom, even though your roots touch rock and stone, and remember, He is with you always.

" 'If I go up to the heavens, you are there, if I sink to the nether world, you are present there. If I take the wings of the dawn, if I settle at the farthest limits of the sea, even there your hand shall guide me, and your right hand hold me fast.' "

Every face was now upturned. Lucius watched defeat and despair turn to resolve. Slumped shoulders straightened, dulled, vacant eyes became light. His own voice gathered strength and sounded a note of hope.

"I must leave you. My work among you is finished, and I go to my own city to further the work of the Lord. You will never be far from my heart, and your faces shall ever be held in my memory." He raised his hands over them, " 'The Lord bless you and keep you! The Lord let His face shine upon you, and be gracious to you! The Lord look upon you kindly and give you peace!' "

Most of the Hebrews, particularly those who had

recently fled Agrippa's persecution elected to go with Lucius. The Gentiles voted to stay in Antioch, to preserve their church as best they could, for Antioch was their home, the place of their birth, and they loved it as Lucius loved Laodicea.

They left in early spring as soon as the road was passable. The church treasury was gone and there was no money for passage aboard ship, so the Saints went overland, slogging through mud and braving the last of winter's mountain storms, a band of pilgrims who like the One they followed had nowhere to lay their heads. They watched the walls of Antioch grow small and fade from sight with heavy hearts, but not so Lucius. Lucius of Cyrene was going home at last.

# PART III
# LAODICEA

# Chapter 25

Lucius could see Philippi through the tall, double, wrought iron gate that shielded the estate from the street. He was sitting on the wide portico that stretched the breadth of the house where, as Merceden later said, he had held vigil for two days awaiting his son's arrival. Lucius' heart lurched. His shaking hands fumbled with the latch until he drew it toward him with a harsh rasp of metal scraping metal. Philippi came to his feet. His body bent forward. He peered down the long, brick-paved walk, his ears straining and, as Lucius could guess, holding his breath in anticipation.

Lucius swung the gate open. Philippi took a tentative step forward then, as Lucius came through, hurried down the portico steps, stumbling in his haste with his arms already outstretched. Lucius hesitated, watching, heart pounding, then ran.

They met in fierce embrace, with the force of their coming together knocking them off balance. They clasped, held, overwhelmed with emotion, without words, only a low groaning that rumbled from Philippi's throat that after a moment Lucius understood as "my son, my son." They parted and gazed into one another's face, then Philippi grasped Lucius' head and kissed both his cheeks, then full upon his mouth.

From over Philippi's shoulder, Lucius saw Merceden waiting on the portico. Her hands twisted a bit of linen, her body swayed slightly as if ruffled by the afternoon breeze. Lucius disengaged himself from Philippi and walked slowly toward his mother, feasting his eyes, his whole body taut and charged with anticipation. He paused at the bottom step to the portico. Merceden's mouth worked. Her hands increased the speed of their twisting. Tears streamed unchecked down her face.

Lucius' vision blurred. He groped for the railing and pulled himself up the steps, his legs suddenly as tentative as a new-born calf. He took the piece of twisted linen from Merceden's hands and wiped her face, gently, carefully, as if she were a little child, then drew her head to his shoulder, swaying with her, holding her, gingerly, tenderly, fearful of bruising her with his strength. Her scent played tricks on his mind. He was three, held in his mother's arms with his fingers entwined in her heavy, luxurious hair, her full, soft breast a pillow beneath his bony chest, her arms safe and comforting, and her scent his alone. He groaned and closed his eyes, wanting to cherish the memory forever, until he heard movement about them and reluctantly let her go.

Lucia was there, weeping, and Jesua, smiling, embarrassed, wondering what to do with his hands so he awkwardly patted Lucia's shoulder. Nimmuo, biting her lower lip, clutching Belden's hand with one of her own and pressing a tiny girl's head to her thigh with the other.

Children, a whole school of them, the largest a boy of near manhood who for a fleeting moment Lucius mistook for his dead brother, Antonius. One after another he embraced them. The children were shy, blushing, ducking their heads when he teased, standing on one foot and then another, anxious to be off and away from the adults' overwhelming emotion.

Philippi's voice boomed. "See here! Mother! See who I found!"

Mariaerh was crushed under Philippi's massive arm. She was dwarfed by her towering father-in-law, pale and trembling with anxiety. Merceden's face dissolved into sympathy. She rushed forward and rescued Mariaerh from Philippi's grasp.

"Dear child!" she cried. "How lovely you are, and how weary you must be. Come in where it's cool."

She ushered them all into the shaded atrium, cool as

she had promised, with fruits and nuts and salted olives waiting in great heaps, and servants scurrying about pouring cider and wine and sweetened lemon juice into tall frosty glasses. The younger children vied for the glasses, gulped hurriedly and stole handfuls of treats then fled away to play, relieved to be excused from the onerous duty of greeting relatives from afar. The older ones stayed, curious. They sipped their drinks slowly and stared at the uncle they had never seen, and listened to their elders' talk with genuine interest.

They reclined at the long table. The couches were faded, worn, in some places nearly threadbare, but the same as Lucius remembered. The atrium rang with the babble of voices. Philippi told of their excitement when a messenger brought Lucius' letter saying he was at last coming home. Lucius was urged to recount their journey, and Lucia was full of her children's accomplishments. Jesua was giving an account of past harvests, of yields and weather conditions and fluctuating market prices. Lucius pretended an interest, nodding politely and making appropriate remarks, but his mind was not on farming. He was watching Lucia's oldest son, Antonius, across and farther down the table from him.

Antonius was a handsome lad, tall, broad shouldered and thick necked, like Philippi. He reclined with a cat-like grace, relaxed, comfortable, yet muscles tensed to spring in a moment. His hair was black and curled in tight ringlets. His skin swarthy, tanned bronze by the sun. He was just a bit younger than Pebilus, and Lucius wondered if the boys looked anything alike.

Antonius felt Lucius' eyes upon him and lifted his head. Lucius smiled. "You are well-named, Antonius. For a moment on the portico I thought you were my brother."

Antonius returned the smile, open and confident, with not the slightest embarrassment. "Thank you, Uncle. I've heard that sentiment often. I hope you will tell me more of the one for whom I am called."

Lucius nodded, pleased, liking the lad. Antonius turned his attention back to the conversation, but

Lucius could not dismiss Pebilus from his mind. Pebilus was twenty-one years of age now, and attended the great university in Alexandria. Hopefully he was home for the summer. What was he like? Lucius wondered. What had Vesta told him of his father? How would he receive him, with joy? With polite reserve? With hatred?

Mariaerh's soft, faltering voice broke into his reverie, answering some question Nimmuo had put to her regarding her school. Lucius' head began to ache. How was he going to tell Mariaerh that he had a son? Two sons! He had nearly forgotten Thaddeus. How old was he, sixteen? Lucius glanced at Lucia's son, Ceptulus, the child she carried on their journey to Jerusalem. The boys were near of an age. Did they know one another? The thought frightened Lucius. Suppose Ceptulus inadvertently mentioned his cousin before he had a chance to explain to Mariaerh?

"Lucius." Merceden's voice jerked him back to attention. "I've prepared your old rooms for you and Mariaerh to occupy."

Mariaerh was standing, Nimmuo at her side. Apparently they were leaving the atrium and going to his old apartment, no doubt so Mariaerh could rest.

Lucius scrambled to his feet, feeling a flush of guilt. He had hardly spoken to his wife since they arrived. He hurried to Mariaerh and put his hand possessively on her arm to atone for his neglect.

"That's fine, Mother. Thank you." Then to Mariaerh, "Rest well, my dear. I'll be in later. I want to talk to my father for a time."

The family dispersed. Merceden to the kitchens, Lucia to check on her brood, Jesua to tend his beloved fields for it was planting time, and the older children seemed simply to have melted away. Belden took his leave and went down to the city, and Philippi and Lucius were left alone.

Philippi led the way to the garden. They settled on cushioned settees and regarded each other, absorbing the changes sixteen years had brought.

Philippi's hair was iron gray, not so thick, but still tightly curled. He was thinner, the heavy muscles gone, but not gone to fat. His stride was less long, and his back not quite as straight, but for a man nearing seventy, he was yet a fine specimen. Lucius felt the rush of pride and affection he had always felt when he studied his father.

Philippi was taking his own measurements and did not like what he saw. Lucius' face was lined, care-worn. His eyes held a perpetual sadness, like a man who has never recovered from a mortal grief. His hair was beginning to show a few strands of gray, more in his beard that needed the attention of a good barber. His clothes were poor, almost shabby, but the thing that disturbed Philippi most was a sense of despair, futility, aimlessness, that emanated from his son.

He addressed Lucius gently, as he did when Lucius was just a boy and cried over some childish hurt or disappointment. "You are not happy."

Lucius twirled a wine goblet between his palms and smiled crookedly. "Is any man?"

"Every man has his measure of happiness, some more, some less. If not happiness, contentment at least."

Lucius sighed. "Not all men are as blessed as you, Father."

"True. The gods have seen fit to be good to me, else to ignore me." He gave a short laugh. "But seemingly less fortunate men than I find their own happiness. What causes one man happiness does not necessarily do the same for another."

Lucius did not answer, just studied the wine whirling in the glass.

"I sense more than the lack of happiness. Is there a definite cause for unhappiness? Is it Mariaerh?"

Lucius shrugged his shoulders.

"Have you lost confidence in this Nazarene you put such store by?"

Lucius' head jerked up and for the first time Philippi saw fire in his eyes. "No!" His answer was emphatic and Philippi believed him.

Lucius set the goblet down, stood up and paced the lawn in front of Philippi. "I don't know, Father," he said irritably. "Everything just seems so futile. I teach loving kindness and service to one another but it's like trying to empty the sea with that goblet!"

Philippi laughed. "You try to change the world in a day. Did not your God take six days to make it? And do not your scriptures say a day is as a thousand years to your God? You are a greater man than the Olympians, greater even than your own God if you think you can do in one short lifetime what it took Him six thousand years to accomplish."

Lucius grinned. "You know our scriptures well for a pagan."

Philippi snorted. "Remember, I have lived with a pious Jewess for nearly fifty years. What of this camp in Antioch that Nimmuo raves on and on about? She tells me that you have a whole village of people converted to your way of thought. I'd think that would dispel any sense of futility."

"Gone. Longinus disapproved and scattered my people all over the city. He pressured me into leaving by punishing anyone I contacted. A few came here to Laodicea with me."

"I see. And those left behind, have they discarded your teaching? Do they no longer believe in this Christ?"

"No!" Lucius exclaimed. "If anything, their faith is stronger than ever."

"Then what's the problem?" Philippi demanded. "Every man chooses his own standard to live by. He doesn't need a whole community of like-thinkers to be his neighbors. The test of a man is to live as he believes when surrounded by those who oppose him. To do less is weak, cowardly. I'd say you've accomplished your objectives, if I understand them correctly, which are to bring men to believe in and follow this one you call the Christ. Do you expect the whole world to suddenly believe as you do, just because you say so? If so, you are no better than any other who tries to force his own ways upon others. You set before you an impossible task and you should know you will fail. You are too intelligent for this nonsense. What else troubles you?"

Lucius sat down again and resumed twirling the goblet. He could feel Philippi's eyes boring into him and knew there was no way he could avoid telling him the truth. He kept his head bowed over the wine, and said, softly, "Have you seen Vesta's sons of late?"

"Ah!" Philippi breathed. "*Vesta's* sons! Yes, as a matter of fact, I saw them only a few days ago and told them you were coming."

Lucius' head flew up. "You told them? What did they say? How did they react?"

"Of course I told them! What do you think? They were interested, but not particularly eager. Why should they be? They don't know you. You have no part in their lives."

Lucius groaned. Philippi frowned. "Is that it? Guilt over your sons? So, it is done! Circumstances lead us to do many things we regret. The thing is to know it and do something about it. You cannot change the past, you can only refrain from making the same mistake in the present and future. To wallow in guilt and self-pity is useless. Nothing destroys a man faster than guilt."

Lucius did not respond. Philippi sensed he was not convinced and groped for another way to present his case. He pitied Lucius. He wanted to ease his burden, but felt inadequate to the task until he remembered some of Nimmuo's incessant babbling about the Nazarene.

"Your sister tells me that this man you believe to be the Son of your God allowed Himself to be crucified in order to atone for the sins of man. Do you believe this also? If so, then the One you follow has already atoned for your sin, and all you can do is to go on from today. Would you in your arrogance attempt to redo what He has already done for you? I'd say forget it, and refrain from giving the man cause to hang there again!"

Lucius looked at Philippi with amusement. "You preach my faith better than I, Father. Has Nimmuo converted you from your pagan gods?"

"Never!" Philippi snorted.

They sat in easy silence for a time. Lucius was deep in thought, but no longer seemed so dejected and filled with gloom. His mood was lighter, although still troubled. He finally spoke. "There is more. Mariaerh does not know of the existence of my sons."

Philippi drew a long breath. "Ah, so Nimmuo has said. I thought you would have told her by now. She seems to be a reasonable girl; after all, this liaison with Vesta occurred long before your marriage."

"You don't know Mariaerh. Multiply Mother's piety and strict morality a hundredfold."

Philippi winced. "That bad! Well, you have your hands full, I can see. A veritable storm brewing, without a doubt, but it will blow over. Be as gentle and contrite as possible. Play on her sympathies. Women can never resist forgiving a repentant man."

Lucius was not so sure if this held true for Mariaerh, and if the truth were known, he cared little. He was concerned over his sons' reaction and acceptance of him. He wanted to be a father to them, to have them love and respect him as he loved and respected his father. How to win them over was his first concern, then Philippi voiced his second.

"How do you feel about Vesta?"

Lucius' loins warmed. His face colored and he was grateful for his beard that hid the flush from his father's eye. "I, I haven't given Vesta any thought," he stammered. "I would guess she'll be difficult about my seeing the boys just to spite me, to have her revenge, but it won't last."

"She's very beautiful," Philippi warned.

"No doubt," Lucius said wryly.

"And strong willed."

"She hasn't changed, then."

"I'd take care and not give Mariaerh new cause for distress or yourself new reason for regret."

Nimmuo left Mariaerh in Lucius' former apartment under the care of a servant girl, who much to Mariaerh's chagrin offered to help her undress. Mariaerh had never disrobed in the sight of anyone in all of her life, let alone a total stranger, and she shrank away from the girl in horror.

"No!" she cried, then embarrassed, stammered, "I

prefer to see to my own needs. Thank you. You may go."

The girl gave Mariaerh a look of disdain, clearly disapproving of her peasant dress. She nodded in sham subservience and left the room.

Mariaerh gazed around the room in wonder. The sleeping room was mammoth, larger than her entire half of the house in Antioch. A huge, canopied bed commanded the room, draped in shimmering silks of cool, pastel colors, high off from the floor, and fashioned of ornately carved lemonwood. Plush chaises and deeply cushioned chairs were scattered about in casual but orderly arrangement, while chests, a fine writing table, nooks for scrolls, and curio cabinets filled with shells and colored stones and other objects that spoke of a young boy's interests were conveniently placed along the walls. Two sides of the room were windowed from ceiling to floor, giving a panoramic view of Laodicea's hills.

Mariaerh crept through the room on tiptoe, scarcely daring to breathe in such luxury. She pushed open a louvered door and gasped when she saw the bath. It too was huge. Gleaming mosaic tiles covered the floor and walls. Steps led down to a marble tub that was recessed into the floor. Gold plated faucets and copper pipes, one leading up beyond the ceiling tile and one to a copper reservoir with a brazier beneath to heat the water. A latrine was hidden behind a screen. A barber's chair, a massage table, weights and pulleys for exercising. Mariaerh did not even know what to make of the strange fixtures.

She saw another door and pushed it open a crack and peered into the dressing room. Row after row of rich tunics, blouses, togas, robes and cloaks, long and short, could they all belong to Lucius? Surely the whole family must store their clothing here!

A movement caught her eye and she cried out, startled, until she saw that she faced a mirrored wall and the movement she saw was her own. She stole inside, fascinated, and took a critical look at her own appearance.

The face that stared back at her seemed ten years

older than it should have been. Her face was pale, pinched, stern and forbidding. Tiny lines etched her eyes and mouth, and her lips thin and drawn and severe, humorless, as though they had never learned to smile. Her hair was pulled back so severely that it drew her eyes into an Oriental slant. She was thin, shapeless. Her neck, what showed above her high, tightly laced bodice, was scrawny, like a chicken, she thought with disgust. Her hair was without luster, her eyes dull. Why, I am old and ugly, she thought with dismay. No wonder Lucius cannot love me, who could?

She swung her back to the offensive image and fled through the bath to the sleeping room. She sank to the bed, shaking, but its softness surprised her and she leaped up again before it swallowed her whole. She chose a safe-looking chaise and lay back. How had she come to look so bitter? She began to weep. Lovely, Merceden had called her. She had lied! Mariaerh burned with shame and rolled to her side and drew her knees up. She was an embarrassment to Lucius' family! Not only was she unpresentable, she had no child! Lucia had eleven children, Nimmuo, three, but Philippi's son presented him with a barren wife!

She gazed upon the exquisite room in near panic. How could she ever live here? Why had Lucius never told her that he was as rich as a king? She sobbed aloud, flooded by despair. She wept until she slept from exhaustion.

An hour later, Nimmuo found her still asleep. She gently shook her awake to give her time to prepare for the evening meal, and as soon as Mariaerh opened her eyes and saw Nimmuo, the flood of tears began again.

Nimmuo was alarmed. She tried to soothe Mariaerh and kept prodding her to tell the cause of her distress until finally the whole sorry tale came spilling from Mariaerh's mouth.

Nimmuo could not help but laugh. She threw her arms around Mariaerh and cried, "Is that all! You are so tired you are not thinking straight. You've just spent weeks on the road under the most dreadful conditions. Do you think we expected a ravishing beauty to emerge from that? I know you, Mariaerh, remember? You certainly are neither old nor ugly. Come with me!"

Nimmuo pulled Mariaerh into the bath and overrode her blushing protests. She drew the bath, adding oils and scents from an array of exquisite bottles. She washed Mariaerh's hair, rinsing it with lemon juice to restore its sheen. When finished, she conceded to Mariaerh's painful modesty and turned her back until Mariaerh was wrapped in the embrace of a lavish robe. She handed her a vial of rose-scented oil, demanding, "Rub this into your skin, all over, for it is dry and chapped from the wind and sun, then put this on." She handed her a colorful, woolen robe that was many sizes too large. "I'll be back in a moment."

Mariaerh dutifully obeyed. Nimmuo returned with a servant who dressed Mariaerh's hair, brushing it to a high sheen until it flowed in deep waves down her back, then using a curling iron, made long, tight curls that she brought to the crown of her head and caught with an emerald velvet ribbon, letting the strands and the curls tumble to Mariaerh's shoulders. She left Mariaerh's high brow clear and smooth to accentuate her large, doe-like eyes, but allowed gentle waves to wing back over her ears, softening the sharp planes of Mariaerh's face.

A seamstress appeared with an altered dress of Nimmuo's, pale green as seafoam, cut of floating, gossamer layers of silk, and festooned with lace the same emerald hue as the ribbon. Matching satin slippers completed the ensemble, and when Nimmuo led a reluctant Mariaerh back to confront the mirror, she at first gasped, then blushed with pleasure at her own transformation.

Nimmuo observed her critically, then went back to the bath and returned with a small, alabaster jar. She dipped into the jar with one finger and began to apply dabs of red ointment to Mariaerh's pale cheeks.

"Nimmuo! I can't wear paint!" Mariaerh wailed.

"Pooh!" Nimmuo scoffed. "A little help to nature never hurt. Who ever saw a pale, peaked baby? We're born with rosy cheeks! Weariness and distress make us pale, and God does not intend us to be either!"

Mariaerh could not argue with that point, even though she knew it was ridiculous. She laughed. "Nimmuo! Such nonsense!"

Nimmuo grinned and continued her ministrations. "See! When you smile you are beautiful. Look," she cried, pointing at the mirror. "Now tell me you are old and ugly!"

Mariaerh looked and blushed crimson, but her eyes shone and her shoulders straightened. She lifted her chin and twirled around like a young girl. "No, I am not," and her voice carried conviction.

Mariaerh's appearance at the dinner table caused a furor. She could hardly bring herself to look at Lucius, and when she did, she saw the same astonished approval she had seen on his face the day of Naomi's wedding. Philippi paid her grand court. Jesua blushed, and Belden bowed over her hand and called her "My Lady." Lucia and Merceden exclaimed and marveled and the younger children crowded around their beautiful, new-found aunt.

Lucius watched her throughout the meal with a sinking heart. How much easier to tell stern, petulant Mariaerh of his sons, than this smiling, beautiful young woman. His passion stirred, and he squirmed nervously on the couch. His food was tasteless. He drank more wine than he should have and avoided meeting Philippi's eyes. By the end of the meal he was nearly drunk, and his desire for Mariaerh had become a burning flame. He pleaded weariness from the long day, and led Mariaerh back to their apartment.

He made love to her in the great, billowing, cloud-soft bed. Mariaerh, still euphoric over the effusive praise of Lucius' family, responded more warmly than ever before, and Lucius' intention to tell her of his sons fled on the tide of passion. He would wait until tomorrow when his head was clear and his tongue less influenced by wine. He rolled to his side and dreamed of making love to an ardent Mariaerh who eerily turned into a laughing, sardonic Vesta.

He did not tell her in the morning. He arose before sun-up and left her sleeping, nearly buried in the deep, feather-filled mattress. He went into the city as soon as the sun arose and wandered through the marketplace and clean, swept streets, reacquainting himself with his childhood home. He found Jehul's shop and shared a welcoming glass of ale with him and Rhea, then visited other Saints who now lived in Laodicea. Through all the reunions with old friends, Jonas and Susane, Pathos and Ulai, his mind wrestled with Vesta, his sons, and Mariaerh. When the sun had completed its journey across the sky, he climbed the wide staircase with slow, dragging steps. He came to the landing which, if he turned right, would lead him to Vesta's villa, but shook his head and continued his upward climb. He would not see his sons until he confronted Mariaerh.

The evening meal was torturous. Mariaerh was as lovely as the night before. She was animated and talkative, asked pointed questions of Merceden about running a Roman house, and sparred delightfully with Philippi's wit. Lucius inwardly groaned and regretted ever having returned to Laodicea. Had he been mad? Why had he not considered the consequences more carefully! If only he had been truthful with his wife from the beginning! He was on the verge of deciding to leave, to go to Jerusalem or Caesarea to aid in the churches there, when Antonius and Ceptulus engaged him in conversation about Judea.

The boys were eager for knowledge about the land of their ancestors. As Lucius described the land and its people and expanded upon his experiences there, their eyes glowed with admiration, and their remarks hinted at near hero-worship for their adventuresome uncle. Lucius basked in their adoration and imagined it was Pebilus and Thaddeus who regarded him with such high esteem, and his resolve of a moment ago to leave Laodicea evaporated. He would stay! He would cultivate his sons' love and respect and Mariaerh would just have to accept it!

When they retired to their rooms, Lucius waited while Mariaerh modestly disappeared into the bath to change into her nightdress. When she returned, wearing a soft, flowing gown that revealed the slim lines of her body, and her hair falling free in shining waves to her waist, Lucius wavered. His body remembered her warm response the night before, and his eyes darkened with desire. Mariaerh blushed and quickly slipped into bed and drew the coverlet up to her chin.

Her action irritated Lucius. Damn her prudishness, he thought. He dragged all the other occurrences of his wife's childish retreats behind her overly-exaggerated modesty to his mind, all the times she had stopped his hands and mouth from finding full pleasure in her body, all the times she had withheld her body to punish him for some slight. He prodded his irritation to bloom into anger, and used the anger as courage to say what he had to say.

He stood over her with his hands clasped behind his back. His voice was business-like, formal. "There is a matter that demands discussion between us. I would appreciate your attention for a moment."

Mariaerh, happily remembering Lucius' passion of the night before did not notice the coldness in his eyes or the stern tone of his voice. She smiled shyly, expecting a compliment, or a remark on her popularity with his family.

Lucius ignored her smile. "Many years ago, before I came to Judea, I had a casual liaison with a local woman of Greek ancestry. The union resulted in the birth of two children, sons, my sons. One is a young man of twenty-one years, the other sixteen. I have never seen the younger, though of course I knew the first-born. I had thought never to come back to Laodicea, that Jeshua's return would be more immediate and I would never see Laodicea again, thus I saw no reason to cause you distress by this revelation. But since the Master seems to delay, and circumstances have brought me once again to my own city, I deem it my moral duty to cultivate the friendship of my sons. I expect you to understand my obligation and to accept and support my responsibilities as you have so ably done in the past."

The smile on Mariaerh's face remained frozen. Her head spun with Lucius' spate of words and would not absorb their import. She could feel her body shrinking, shriveling into one tiny particle hidden beneath the sheets. One word kept repeating in her mind.

"Sons?" she whispered.

Suddenly she sat bolt upright, her face twisted, ugly with rage. "You have sons by a Greek woman and give me none?" she shouted.

Lucius' head snapped back as if she had slapped him. He was offended by her unreasonable fury. "You cannot fault me for your barrenness. My sons are proof that the failing does not lie with me."

Mariaerh would have been less wounded if he had flogged her back into bloody ribbons. She whimpered and drew her knees up as though to fend off another attack.

Guilt forced Lucius to defend himself with cruelty. "Your behavior is unbecoming in a woman of your age and station. I must say I expected a more mature response from my own wife."

Mariaerh stared at him, hating him, then a new thought formed in her mind. "Does your family know of your sons? Nimmuo?" She could tell by his face that they did. "How long has Nimmuo known?"

"What difference does that make?" Lucius said irritably.

"How long!" Mariaerh demanded.

"She's always known, of course. How could she not!"

Mariaerh closed her eyes and wished she would die. Nimmuo's betrayal was worse than Lucius'. All the rage seeped away and she felt numbed.

"Go away," she mumbled.

Lucius tried to retain his anger, but it too evaporated, and his conscience began to be heard. "Mariaerh," he began lamely, but she did not allow him to finish.

She opened her eyes and looked directly at him, her voice wooden. "Get out of my room. Go to your Greek or any other whore you fancy at the moment, but get out of this room and leave me alone."

Lucius retreated, backing toward the door where he paused as if to say something further, then sighed, left the room, closing the door quietly behind him.

Mariaerh watched the door close without moving. She looked at the luxury and affluence around her and felt as though she were in an alien world. What was she doing here? What made her think that she could belong in such a setting, belong to such people? She was betrayed, humiliated, made a fool of!

She flung back the coverlet and marched into the dressing room and rummaged about until she found the worn bundle of her own clothes. She searched through it, pitching unwanted garments wherever they happened to land until she found her old, high-necked, coarse sleeping gown. She yanked Nimmuo's altered bit of froth over her head and donned the old one. Then she found a brush and furiously pulled her hair back into a severe bun.

She returned to the sleeping room, but grimaced in distaste at the inviting bed. She pulled the thick cushions off from a chaise and lay down on its hard surface. She would sleep here tonight, but tomorrow she would find Jonas and Susane and ask for refuge in their house. Most of all, she would not cry!

But she did cry. Great wracking sobs that tore her throat raw. Scalding hot tears of shame and remorse and betrayal and despair. She wept until she made herself ill and was forced to flee to the latrine where she retched. Her head throbbed without mercy. Her eyes burned and her mouth was swollen. She was weak and trembling and groped her way back to the bed chamber. She stumbled onto the chaise, and fell into a deep, death-like sleep.

After a few hours she awoke. It was still dark. A full moon shone through the tall windows, and the sky was ablaze with stars. She got up and opened the window, letting the soft breeze cool her burning face. She was stiff and sore from lying on the bare chaise and she replaced the cushion, took a pillow from the bed to support her back and lay down again, watching the beauty of the changing night sky.

She was calm now, drained of all the emotions that had raged through her heart. She could think clearly, and did, her mind flying from one solution to another until when the stars began to fade against the leaden sky, her decision was made. She drew her own bath, bathing carefully, adding oils and salts as Nimmuo had done for her. She dressed her own hair, drawing it up into a soft chignon, leaving it loose and waved over her ears. She donned one of Nimmuo's dresses, a simple, lemony yellow that set off her olive skin.

The sun came up. Mariaerh scrutinized herself in the mirror. She looked like a serene young matron, assured of her place, except perhaps, a little pale. She retrieved the paint-pot, added a little color to her cheeks, then a bit of kohl to her eyelids, more out of defiance than anything else. Satisfied, she went back to the bedchamber, replaced the pillow and threw back the coverlets and disturbed the sheets so the servants would not guess that no one had slept there. Then she went down to her morning meal.

Lucius had hardly slept at all. He had found a guest chamber where he spent the night but the ugly scene with Mariaerh haunted him and made sleep impossible. The water pitchers were empty since no one supposedly occupied the room, and he did not dare to disturb Mariaerh, so he was forced to resort to the kitchens to wash his face.

The servants stared. Lucius mumbled something about rising early for a walk, then cursed the servants' penchant for gossip under his breath. He needed fresh clothes, but those could only be had by going back to his own apartments and he would be damned if he would return until Mariaerh had left them, if she did! It would be more like her to stay in there and sulk for days, an embarrassment to the whole family!

His stomach rumbled. He went to the small eating porch where the family helped themselves to an informal, morning meal, prepared to use the excuse of an early morning walk to explain his disheveled appearance. He stopped short, amazed as he saw Mariaerh. He stared and was about to flee when Merceden's voice stopped him.

"Lucius! Heavens, Son! You look terrible! Did you sleep in your clothes?" she cried.

Mariaerh turned slowly and looked serenely into
Lucius' eyes, waiting like the others for his explanation.

Lucius was furious. He said, without taking his eyes
from Mariaerh. "Of course not. I arose early and went
out for a walk. I simply put on the attire I discarded the
night before."

Mariaerh smiled sweetly. "Lucius is always
considerate. He didn't want to disturb me by stumbling
about in the bathing room. He is disoriented in the early
hours and quite clumsy. His noisy maneuvers
invariably awaken me."

Merceden laughed. Lucius glowered. His appetite was
gone and he took only a few pieces of fruit on his plate.
Mariaerh brought her meal and sat next to him, and he
saw that her appetite seemed unaffected. When no one
was paying any attention to them, Mariaerh said in a
quiet tone so none could hear, "For the sake of your
family's harmony, you may share the apartment with
me and we will continue as we always have. Do as you
will with your sons, but never bring them within my
sight. As for the woman, do as you like, but if I ever hear
of your alliance, I shall leave you, no matter the
scandal."

Lucius' heart sank. This was a new Mariaerh and he
was more than a little frightened. He could read nothing
in her face, and her voice was reasonable, but there was
something about the way she chose her words and held
herself in control that made him believe that he had
pushed her too far. He flushed and stammered,
"Mariaerh, give me a chance to explain more fully. Last
night we were both angry, not . . ."

"We will never speak of this again," Mariaerh
interrupted. "Nor do I wish to hear of it!" she hissed,
then pushed her uneaten meal aside and left the porch.

Lucius sighed. He would leave her alone for a day or
so, let her come to her senses, then when she was in a
more conciliatory mood, he would make her
understand. He pushed his own plate away and went to
his rooms for clean clothes. Today he would see his
sons.

Mariaerh did not go back to the apartment. She went

to find Nimmuo, knowing how she hated to rise early, guessed she would still be abed. She knocked on Nimmuo's door, then went in without waiting for Nimmuo's answer, knowing Belden was already up and gone.

As she guessed, Nimmuo was still in bed and turned sleepily and opened her eyes when Mariaerh came in.

"Good morning," she yawned. "What are you doing here so early?"

"I came to talk to you," Mariaerh said coolly. She stood at the foot of Nimmuo's bed, clasping the brass rung until her knuckles were white. "Lucius told me last night that he has two sons. I loved you as if you were my own sister. I trusted you, and confided in you, but you betrayed me. You aided Lucius in this monstrous hoax and I can never forgive you. I shall treat you in a civil manner, but I shall never consider you as a friend again."

She spun on her heel, then as a parting shot, spat scornfully, "You and your brother! Your faith in The Way is sheer hypocrisy!"

"Mariaerh!" Nimmuo wailed, but too late, for the door slammed on Mariaerh's back.

# Chapter 26

Lucius paced the marble floor of Vesta's atrium. His neck and shoulders were taut with tension and his palms were damp. He had been waiting for Vesta for some minutes and his nervousness grew with each passing moment.

How like her to keep him waiting, he thought irritably. Only one of her many ploys that put a man at a disadvantage. He dipped his hand into the bubbling fountain then wished he had not for there was nothing to wipe it on except his tunic and Vesta's critical eye would be sure to take note of the stain. He shook his hand furiously, hoping it would dry before she appeared.

A servant brought a tray of figs and grapes surrounding a silver carafe and, Lucius noticed, a lone goblet. For a moment he panicked. Did she not intend to receive him?—then cursed beneath his breath and realized it was one more trick calculated to increase his agitation. The servant bowed and backed away without a word.

Lucius ate a few grapes, splashed some wine into the goblet and drank as if he were dying of thirst, but in reality hoped the wine would calm his nerves. The wine was good, very good, of a wonderful vintage, and he poured another portion and sipped slowly, savoring its delicate taste and aroma. Only the best for Vesta, he thought ruefully.

He heard her voice and quickly set the goblet aside.

She was giving an order to her servants, her voice gay and breezy as though she had not a care in the world. Lucius' stomach tightened and his mouth went dry. He licked his lips and straightened his shoulders as Vesta floated into the atrium. He sucked in his breath and almost groaned aloud.

She was beautiful! She carried herself as regally as ever, more so. She wore her frothy gown like another skin, and the golden mass of curls piled high on her head was as brilliant as the sun. A ruby pendant flashed, drawing his eye to her long, ivory throat then downward to her lush, blue-veined breasts that were barely covered by the shimmering silk. Her eyes were awash with amusement, and her voice merry.

"Lucius! How delightful to see you after so many years!"

She kissed the air alongside his cheeks. Lucius winced at her reference to his long absence. Her scent stirred memories of heated passion, and her breasts, fleetingly brushing his chest made the palms of his hands run wet. He wiped them on the sides of his tunic, forgetting about stains, and took the hands she held out to him. They were soft beyond measure, long and narrow, fine bones he could easily crush, yet her grasp was firm and with surprising strength.

Lucius' voice was husky. "You are more beautiful than even I remember, Vesta. The years have served you well."

"Why, thank you, Lucius. I'm surprised you remember at all!"

"Stop it, Vesta. Your barbed remarks are not necessary."

"Oh, dear, must I be subjected to a Jewish sulk in the first moments of your arrival? I'd hoped you'd outgrown such nonsense." She drew a finger lightly across his brow, fully aware of the effect her touch had upon him. "You scowl like a petulant boy, Lucius, though I will admit it is one of your more endearing traits," she said softly.

Lucius' brow burned from her touch. His face reddened, then suddenly he threw his head back and laughed delightedly. "You have not changed at all, Vesta. You are still maddening. You still have the capacity to anger me beyond words!" He drew her into his arms and hugged her fiercely. "There is not another like you in all the world."

Vesta laughed with him and returned his embrace, then leaned back in his arms and regarded him wickedly, "Not even your wife?" she teased.

Lucius laughed again. "No. She is as ponderous and humorless as I, I'm afraid."

"A good match then."

"Hmm. In some areas, yes."

"And in what areas is she not?" Vesta asked coyly.

Lucius refused her sly invitation to discuss the sexual aspect of his marriage. "Never mind about Mariaerh." He frowned. "It was wrong of you not to tell me you were carrying my child."

"Was it!" Vesta said icily. "Would you have forgone your trip to Jerusalem, or returned in time for his birth?"

Lucius floundered. "You don't understand, Vesta. You don't know what drew me, or what held me in Judea."

"Your betrothed, I assume," Vesta said bitterly.

"No!" Lucius rubbed his hand across his eyes and groped for some way to explain. "I never gave Mariaerh a thought. I was shocked when suddenly confronted with a girl I never knew, whom my mother had arranged for me to marry years before."

"And yet you married her."

"Not willingly!"

"Lucius," Vesta chided, "this is Vesta to whom you speak. You know better than to try to deceive me. I know you are never forced to act against your will."

"It's very complicated. Of course I decided to marry Mariaerh, but the reasons for that decision are complex and many."

Vesta stretched out on a chaise and regarded Lucius through thick, curled lashes. "I would be most interested to hear them."

Desire stirred beneath Lucius' tunic. Vesta's skirt

was split nearly to her thigh, and one, long, slim leg was totally exposed. The gossamer silk fell away from one breast and he could see just a hint of the dark aureole that circled her nipple. His voice thickened. He turned his back to regain his composure.

"I don't know if I can make you understand. It's Jeshua, the Nazarene. When I reached Judea, I learned that He was dead, crucified, yet His followers, Mariaerh included, had seen Him alive again. He arose to heaven, and promised to return. I could not leave! I had to be there when He came! As for Mariaerh, not to marry her would have been tantamount to divorce, cruel, and would have caused no end of a scandal. If I stayed, I had no choice but to accept her, and I could not leave."

Lucius turned to Vesta. His voice was pleading, his eyes haunted by remembered emotions. "I cannot describe the hold Jeshua has upon me. I love Him, Vesta, more than Mariaerh, more than my family, my sons, more than my very life!"

Vesta frowned. She was not unmoved by Lucius' impassioned cry, but neither could she let him off so easily. "And did your master return?" she asked, knowing he had not.

"No," Lucius said miserably. Then eagerly, "But there is a reason, a purpose, and I am part of that purpose. I must fulfill the destiny the Master has laid before me."

Vesta sighed. She swung her long legs from the chaise and sat up. She admired Lucius' dedication to a cause, no matter if she found that cause to be folly. His stubborn insistence to hold to his own beliefs was one of his attractions. If he had been easy prey to her beauty and wiles, she would have dismissed him from her mind long ago. His will was as strong as her own, the only man she had ever known whom she could not completely control. She could make him squirm, which she did with delight, but she could never bend his will to her own.

She studied him with respect and admiring appraisal. He was handsome in his maturity. The boyishness was gone and he seemed a man of substance, world-worn, tempered by suffering, a man who had known loneliness and grief and confusion and doubt, yet did not succumb. The sprinkling of gray in his hair and beard lent dignity to his appearance. His body was lean and hard. His legs and arms muscular, not gone to flab like many men his age who lived out their lives in luxury.

She shivered, remembering those arms and legs, taut and trembling around her body. She raised her head and met his eyes. They were naked, begging for understanding. Her heart softened. Her sympathy went out to him. He was still vulnerable, still, in many ways the innocent. She relented her brittle, accusing stance and said softly, "Perhaps I can understand, somewhat. Pebilus has never forgotten his meeting with your Nazarene, though he was so young it amazes me how he remembers so clearly. He speaks of it often still, and always with awe and wonder. If this Jeshua could make such an indelible impression upon a child, then perhaps I can guess at the hold he has over you."

Lucius' vision blurred. "He does remember, then," he breathed. "Has he sought out anyone here in Laodicea who could tell him more of Jeshua?"

Vesta frowned. "I've discouraged such action. His father's obsession with this charismatic figure is enough. I do not want my son involved."

"Where is Pebilus?" Lucius asked, then added, "And Thaddeus?"

"Out. Either at the gymnasium or the riding academy, or possibly both. I'd rather you didn't see them until I talk with them about your return."

"They know I am here, or at least that I was coming. Philippi told them."

"I know. So they told me, but I wanted to see you first, to discover your intentions. What do you intend to do, Lucius? Are you here for a short time and then off again on your adventures? I would be very displeased if an affection for you arose in my sons and then you desert them again—the gods only know for how many years. That can be a shattering experience."

"Was it shattering for you?" Lucius asked, softly.

Vesta laughed. "I was not lonely for long. Do I look as though I have pined away for you?"

Lucius' loins warmed again. He returned to her first question to distract his thoughts from the disturbing train they were taking. "I am home to stay. There are many believers in Laodicea. I intend to organize the church here as I did in Antioch. I would like my sons to join me."

"I do not approve of religious fanaticism, Lucius. My sons," she stressed *my,* "are Greek and have been raised as Greeks. I do not want them changed into pious, overbearing Jews."

"They are Jewish and Roman as well! You cannot deny them their choice of heritage."

Vesta was angry. "Why not! You denied them that choice for sixteen years!"

Lucius winced. "I cannot argue that with you, but that is past. This is today."

"You shrug off your responsibilities so easily, Lucius. I wish I had your lack of conscience."

"My conscience is more disturbed than you may think. I not only deprived myself of the company of my sons, but also bore the burden of excruciating guilt. The past sixteen years have been quite painful for me."

"Yet you did nothing about it. Your argument is weak."

"I could *do* nothing about it." Lucius rubbed his hand over his face. He looked weary, beaten. Vesta again felt a stab of pity for him. "Please. Let us not quarrel," Lucius pleaded. "I cannot best you in a battle of words. When may I see the boys? This evening?"

"Better tomorrow. I'll speak with them tonight. Call in the afternoon, about this same time, and I'll try to see that they are here to receive you."

Lucius left the villa and walked slowly along the horizontal, terraced path, deep in thought, trying to sort out the myriad emotions evoked by his meeting with Vesta. Sorrow over years lost, regret over the anguish he caused to Mariaerh, excitement over the propsect of meeting his sons, and fear that they might reject him. But he was most disturbed by the impact Vesta had made on his senses.

It seemed as if he had never been away. Her beauty inflamed his passion. Her gaiety delighted him, her caustic tongue was as much a challenge as it had ever been. The smoldering sensuality that lurked just beneath her cool, Grecian exterior was evident in her eyes, exposed in the fluid movements of her body, and betrayed its existence in the timbre of her voice. Even now, just thinking about her made his genitals flare. His heart pounded and beads of perspiration blossomed on his brow.

He must resist his body's demands. A renewed love affair with Vesta would be disastrous to his already tenuous marriage. His prestige in the church would be destroyed, and the love and respect he had earned from the Saints would change to disgust. Adultery was a serious sin! It had not seemed so when he had frequented the brothels of Jerusalem, or even when he had indulged himself with a prolonged liaison with the slut Judith. Why would lying with Vesta be any different?

He knew the answer without having to think. It was because his heart was involved. The others had meant nothing, bodies coming together in mutual need and pleasure, but Vesta he loved, and it was that love which would destroy Mariaerh.

He reached the landing where the stairs led upward to Philippi's estate. Philippi was returning from the city and Lucius waited to walk the rest of the way with him.

Philippi wiped his face. "Not yet summer and already hot. We need rain." He glanced back along the path that led to the villa. "You've seen Vesta?"

Lucius nodded. "I'll see the boys tomorrow."

"You've told Mariaerh?"

"Yes. She's . . ." he hesitated. "My having sons has made her feel her barrenness more keenly. She has always longed for a child."

Philippi's eyes clouded. "I had not thought of that. Be especially kind to her, Lucius. Make her feel that she is of great value to you in other areas. We have the finest medical academy in all the world here. Perhaps the highly trained physicians could discover the cause of her barrenness. Suggest to her that she allow herself to be examined. It may give her hope and ease her sorrow."

Lucius nodded, but thought that even if Mariaerh would consent to an examination, which he doubted her extreme modesty would permit, she could hardly conceive when she refused to allow him to touch her. It was worth a try, though, and might be the means to melt the wall of icy silence she had erected between them.

Lucius had no chance to broach the subject to Mariaerh that night. When they retired to their rooms, she stated imperiously, "I wish to see Jonas and Susane tomorrow."

Lucius nodded. "I'll take you in the morning."

"No. I am occupied in the morning hours. I wish to go in mid-afternoon."

Lucius' heart fell. "I'm sorry, Mariaerh. I have an appointment in the afternoon."

"I'm sure you can change it if you wish."

"I can't," Lucius said miserably. "Let me take you earlier in the day."

"No. That's impossible. I see no reason why you cannot let me accompany you to the city. Surely a few extra moments won't matter."

Lucius stammered. "I'm not going into the city."

Mariaerh regarded him coldly. "Where are you going, then?"

Lucius sucked in his breath. "I meet my sons tomorrow."

"I see." Mariaerh climbed into bed and clung to the edge as far away from Lucius as she could get and turned her back to him.

Lucius propped himself on one elbow. He reached for her shoulder but decided it was wiser not to touch her. "Please try to understand. They are my sons! Have you no sympathy as to how I feel?"

"Having no child of my own, how could I?" Mariaerh shot back.

Lucius sighed and tried again. "I want them to come

to know you, Mariaerh. You gave so much to Barnabas' children, they learned so much from you. I want my sons to have that opportunity. I want them to know of Jeshua, to follow The Way. There is no one better suited to instruct them and to serve as an example of the Lord's teaching than you."

Mariaerh was quiet, almost seduced by Lucius' complimentary plea. Her silence encouraged him to continue.

"Pebilus, the oldest, was blessed by the Master as a child, like the others we met in Antioch. Vesta tells me that he has never forgotten."

If Mariaerh had been close to relenting, the mention of his Greek woman's name quickly changed her mind. "*Vesta* tells you!" she said acidly. "Then let *Vesta* teach your sons!"

Lucius gave up. "Very well. I shall take you to Susane's and return for you before the evening meal."

"Never mind. I shall find my own way," Mariaerh said, stubbornly.

Lucius sighed and no longer argued. "Do as you wish," he said crossly, then turned his back as she had done.

They avoided one another in the morning, both hurt and angry and disagreeable from a restless night. Lucius watched how Nimmuo struggled to make friendly overtures to Mariaerh, and ground his teeth at Mariaerh's open rebuffs. Lucia was nervous and spoke too loudly with a false ring of cheer, while Philippi and Merceden chattered nonstop in a clumsy attempt to disguise the undercurrents of dissension and anger that tore at the family unity.

Lucius escaped the intolerable tension and went to the city where he wandered aimlessly until noon. He went back to the house and insisted upon taking Mariaerh to Susane's, and since no one else knew where Susane lived, Mariaerh relented. He accompanied her to Susane's door, and left without either one of them making reference to his destination.

There was no cooling his heels in the atrium this time. His sons were waiting, as eager as he for their meeting.

Lucius was flooded with pride when he saw them and had to grasp the back of a chaise to steady himself against the tide of emotion that swept over him.

His eyes flew to Pebilus. He was tall and slim like his mother, taller than Lucius. His hair was light brown, gently waved, but close to his head in the Greek style, and his face was clean shaven. His eyes were blue, clear and candid. His jaw firm, and his mouth full and turned up in a smile. In three fluid strides he was in front of Lucius and kissed his cheeks.

"Welcome, Father."

Lucius' knees nearly buckled. Father! His eyes blurred. His impulse was to crush Pebilus in his arms but he feared an over-display of emotion would embarrass the lad. He did not know how to respond, and his voice stuck in his throat.

Pebilus sensed the force of Lucius' emotion and stood back, smiling, and motioned to Thaddeus to approach.

"This is Thaddeus, Father. He's a nuisance at times and quite uncontrollable, but likeable."

Lucius noted how Pebilus' eyes darkened with affection and heard the same sentiment in his voice. He turned his eyes to Thaddeus and saw that he neither blushed nor ducked his head, but grinned and accepted his brother's teasing in the light for which it was intended. Lucius cleared his throat and started to speak, but his eyes widened and he caught his breath as he realized he saw a miror-image of himself at Thaddeus' age. The identical build, the same black ringlets and dark skin, the same shape of head and face, and even Lucius' thickly-lashed black eyes.

He was speechless. Both boys began to laugh. Thaddeus stepped forward and embraced Lucius. "Mother said you would faint when you saw me. She said she gave you no clue as to how I looked."

Pebilus broke in, "You see, Father, whenever I wanted to remember what you looked like, I only had to look at Thad to refresh my memory."

Lucius was overcome. He let the tears flow freely down his cheeks and gathered both his sons into his arms. He still had not spoken, and was too full to try.

Vesta's entrance gave him time to get his emotions under control and find his voice.

"What a touching familial scene!" Vesta cried gaily. "A pity there is not an artist here to capture it on canvass."

The boys laughed. Lucius released them and flushed, embarrassed by his blatant display of emotion, but his sons were not at all embarrassed.

"I surprised him just as you said, Mother. He was stunned when he saw me," Thaddeus laughed.

Vesta smiled and joined them. "So, I have all my men together at last. Tell me, Lucius. Do you approve my sons?"

"*Our* sons!" Lucius corrected. "More than approve! They are wonderful! My eyes cannot get enough of them. Pebilus! You are a grown man! Whenever I've thought of you over the years, which was daily, I saw you as yet a boy, no higher than this," he measured with his hand, "and with golden curls falling into your eyes." He turned to Thaddeus. "And you!" He rumpled Thaddeus' hair playfully. "Since I had no memory of you, I assumed you looked like your brother."

He looked past the boys at Vesta who watched them fondly. His voice softened, trembled at bit. "You've done exceedingly well, Vesta. Better perhaps than if I had been here to interfere with your methods. I am grateful, eternally so. No man had finer sons."

Their eyes locked in a long moment of shared memories. The boys lowered their gaze. Lucius went to her and took her in his arms and kissed her lovingly, without passion, a kiss tender and cherishing.

Vesta broke the embrace gently. "I'll leave you alone to get acquainted."

Lucius turned back to the boys. "Tell me about yourselves. What do you do? What do you enjoy? What interests you? I have sixteen years to catch up on."

It was an exhilarating, memorable afternoon. Lucius was loath to have it end and found his sons' plea for him to stay almost impossible to refuse.

"Nothing would please me more, but I promised Mar—" he stopped. No mention of his wife had been made throughout the afternoon. He did not even know if they knew he was wed. He was flustered, then relieved when Pebilus forced the subject to open discussion.

"Mariaerh? Your wife?"

Lucius was not sure what to say. It was an unusual situation to face one's sons with the fact of a wife who was not their mother.

"We know about Mariaerh. Does she know of us?" Thaddeus asked.

"Yes."

"What does she think of us?" Thaddeus pressed on.

Lucius hesitated. He studied Thaddeus' eager young face and then Pebilus, also waiting for his answer, although more soberly, knowing his father's response would have serious implications for their relationship. Lucius wondered how truthful he should be, then sensed that Vesta, being Vesta, would never be less than frank and he dared to be no other way. He chose his words carefully.

"I made the terrible mistake of not telling Mariaerh about you until recently. She was hurt and angry. She felt, and rightly so, that I somehow betrayed her by my silence. She has been unable to have a child, and to learn that I have children is a terrible blow. She is a fine woman, and one day will forgive me and want to know you, but," he made a gesture of futility.

Pebilus laid his hand on Lucius' shoulder. "We understand, Father. Perhaps she will feel differently when she meet us."

The thought of their meeting at this juncture horrified Lucius. "I think it wise to wait a time. Let her pain heal."

Both boys nodded in agreement, much to Lucius' relief, but then Pebilus asked, with a hint of accusation in his tone, "Why didn't you tell her, Father? Would she have refused to marry you? Did you love her that much?"

Lucius turned away from them. How could he tell them the truth when he hardly knew the truth himself? How could he admit to motives less than honorable when the high esteem of his sons meant more to him than anything in the world? A bit of his conversation with Vesta the day before came sharply into his mind. "I love Him, Vesta, more than Mariaerh, more than my family, my sons, more than my very life." He turned back to his sons. His voice was steady and his eyes were clear and untroubled.

"A young man once approached the Master, seeking to become His disciple, but asked to be allowed to bury his father first. The Lord said to him, 'Let the dead bury the dead. Come, follow me.' Another time Jeshua was preaching in a house and when told that His mother and sister and brothers were asking to see Him, said, 'Who is my mother? Who are my brothers? Whoever does the will of my heavenly Father is brother and sister and mother to me.'

"The love of our Master—Christ—takes precedence over all earthly loves. He promised to return again, and I burned to see His coming. I thought, wrongly, that it would be impossible for me to marry Mariaerh if she knew, and impossible for me to become a part of The Way unless I married her."

He took a deep breath and plunged on. "I was weak and selfish. I feared censure by the very group I so desperately wished to join, and my fear drove me to commit a drastic error. I paid for that sin by cutting myself off from my sons for sixteen years, and I pay for it now by witnessing the pain I cause to Mariaerh. I was right to stay. I was right to follow the course my life has taken. But I was wrong to deceive another."

Pebilus and Thaddeus were silent. Thaddeus' face reflected his bewilderment, his lack of understanding much of what Lucius had said, but Pebilus knew. His scalp tingled. He felt again the Master's hands upon his head in blessing, and understood the power that held his father captive. He went to Lucius and wordlessly embraced him, and sixteen years of yearning was suddenly washed away.

Lucius took his leave and went to collect Mariaerh. They walked home in silence. She asked nothing about his meeting with the boys, and he volunteered no information. The ghostly presence of Lucius' sons created a chasm that neither believed would ever be bridged.

# Chapter 27

## Return to Laodicea

My cup runneth over! I rejoice to be in my own city, to bask in the sights and sounds of my youth and to dwell with my family and friends I have known from childhood. To see and know my sons! But to write of them here would digress from my history.

My scattered flock is back within reach of my staff. My eyes caressed their beloved faces as I raised the cup and broke the loaf before them, and could not drink their fill. I am a Job, once writhing in agony over the loss of all I possess, only to have it restored twofold. Thanksgiving to the One who bestows such blessing upon me.

We organize again, though not as in Antioch. We shall build no isolated, exclusive camp to provoke the suspicions and envy of non-believers. We will mingle with our neighbors and live among them, as any new citizen would do. We will not preach Christ in the synagogues and public places that risks the ire of our brother Jews, or overtly and publicly try to sway Gentiles to our faith. We will live by our faith and impress non-believers only by charity and good deeds. Those whom God calls will recognize that we are Christians by our love and come freely, stirred by the Truth which reigns in their hearts.

I know my city well. Its people, for the most part, are of ordinary means, comfortable and content, happy to live where fear and want and risk of robbery and murder are nearly unheard of. Work is plentiful and employers are encouraged to pay a fair wage. A beggar in the streets is rare and slavery is kept to a minimum. A few in the wealthy class own slaves, brought with them when they first came to the city, but the practice is not encouraged and there is no auction block to outrage Mariaerh's sensibilities. We shall be left in peace, for there are none with rebellion in their hearts to lead them to find a scapegoat for their discontent.

The city lies on the main trade route between east and west and its citizens are accustomed to seeing strange peoples and beasts and exotic goods. The economy relies upon the constant traffic of foreign merchants and they cannot afford the luxuries of intolerance, bigotry and suspicion. People from every land and race and creed live intermingled in harmony and peace, and Laodiceans are not shocked by unfamiliar beliefs. Jehul reports only an isolated case where The Way was jeered for their belief in the risen Christ.

Rome considers Laodicea a backwater, a small, unimportant city that holds no promise for the politically ambitious. Government officials who are assigned here are men who look for a life of ease and go out of their way to see that no dissension or complaint blemishes their record and causes their recall. They look for ways to keep the citizens happy. Minor infractions of the law are overlooked, but serious crimes, though few, are given harsh and swift determination which pleases the citizens for it insures their safety. Taxes are kept to a minimum and their assessments and collections are fair. Civil suits are judged upon merit and not influenced by race or creed.

I am convinced that The Way can prosper and flourish here as in no other city if only we take a moderate stance, obey the laws and participate in local customs. My people agree. Those who are natives to this city have always lived so, and the others have had their fill of persecution and scorn. They gladly embrace a proposal that promises freedom from fear and peace. My life has come full circle. I am eager to begin.

\*　　\*　　\*　　\*　　\*

The sun set early behind the towering hills that ringed Laodicea but reflected its light from the high, puffy clouds and favored the city with long, shadowed evenings that had always been Lucius' favorite time of the day.

The bustle of business transactions came to a halt when the sun went down, and the marketplace was transformed into a season-long carnival. Tents and portable booths appeared in the streets as if by magic, filled with nuts and sweets and every good thing to eat and drink, and some overflowed with household goods and clothes crafted by the local women. Games and races were held on the riverbank. Jugglers and acrobats and dancers performed their arts. Musicians wandered through the crowds, and games of chance and skill drew anyone with a spare coin to try and win a prize. Actors staged dramas and comedies on folding platforms. Challenged by an audience of myriad tongues, they showed consummate skill in telling their tales without the use of words.

Mariaerh disapproved of such frivolity. After being persuaded to go one time, she staunchly refused to go again, and Lucius was for once happy that she carried her piety to such lengths. Without Mariaerh, he was free to meet his sons, and each evening they strolled the carnival grounds together where they pitted their luck against games of chance, indulged in the sweets and exotic foods from faraway lands, and joined the onlookers around the performing artists. Antonius and Ceptulus often joined them, and Lucius delighted in cheering them on when the four young men entered the games on the riverbank. Sometimes he joined them, feigning an exaggerated, embarrassed outrage when trounced by young men less than half his age.

Lucius had never known a happier time. Sometimes they would loll on a grassy knoll and just talk, coming to know one another by sharing thoughts and feelings and personal experiences. All four boys displayed an intense curiosity about Lucius' life in The Way, and the discussions invariably turned to the teachings of Jeshua.

Lucius avoided any encounter with Vesta. He was shaken by the attraction she still held for him, and did not trust himself to exercise prudence and self-control as long as Mariaerh held herself at a distance. He would meet the boys at the landing, and leave them there upon their return, but memories of Vesta's body continued to haunt him day and night.

Mariaerh guessed that Lucius spent each evening
with his sons, and tortured herself over the possibility
that Vesta was with them. She had hoped by refusing to
attend the fair that Lucius would feel obligated to stay
at home with her, if not out of consideration for her
objections, then at least from his sense of propriety.
When her ploy did not work and in fact Lucius seemed
relieved that she refused to go, Mariaerh suffered untold
anguish, but stubborn pride refused to allow her to
change her mind. She retired to her rooms as soon as the
evening meal was ended where she often wept in
frustration and despair, then feigned sleep when Lucius
returned.

She was miserable and lonely. She had never
forgiven Nimmuo, and Nimmuo no longer tried to
placate her anger. She avoided any intimacy with
Lucia, for Lucia's preoccupation with her youngsters
only served to remind Mariaerh of her own barrenness.
She could not complain to Merceden about her own son,
and was too ashamed to discuss her infertility.

There was no one to whom Mariaerh felt she could
turn for understanding and comfort. She had met
Lucius' suggestion that she consult with a physician
over the cause of her barrenness with such bitter acidity
that it was now impossible to relent her stance enough
to even confide in Jonas or Susane. She was isolated
from all friendships and human compassion by an
impenetrable wall of silence and withdrawal, the
products of her own creation.

Mariaerh's loneliness eased when the Saints began
organizing the church. Lucius grasped the opportunity
to breach the wall that loomed between them by seeking
her opinion and drawing her into conversation regarding The Way. He asked her to locate a suitable site for a
storehouse and meeting hall, then publicly credited her
with making a wise choice. He urged her to once again
begin a school, stressing in glowing terms his high
regard for her former success, and little by little the icy
silence between them thawed but any intimate,
personal topic was strictly avoided.

They did not always agree. Mariaerh expressed her

concern that Lucius was possibly sacrificing strict adherence to the tenets of The Way for the promise of an easier life and wondered if even a casual participation in local events and customs might not lead to moral laxity among the young. When Lucius seemed determined to set a more subtle, lenient tone for the church, she held her tongue rather than quarrel, but decided that she, for one, would set an example of righteousness.

Mariaerh began her school for the youngest children and helped the Other Mary begin one for the older, teenage youngsters, which earned them the good opinion of the Laodiceans. As the seat of the famed medical school with its lesser schools in philosophy, history, mathmatics and astronomy, intellectuals and scholars came to the city from all over the world and they held education in high regard. Where citizens in larger cities stressed financial gain, social position, and athletic and military prowess, Laodiceans admired learning and wisdom, thus nodded approvingly when the new sect of Christians held classes in their homes.

The God of the Jews was no stranger to Laodiceans. As every other city, Laodicea contained many God-fearers, men and women who listened from the synagogue porch. When these people heard that the Christians worshipped the God of the Jews and did not require painful circumcision as a condition for admission to the faith, many were intrigued and approached the leaders expressing a wish to learn more. New teachers were added, and the number of initiates steadily increased without overt, public evangelizing. It was true that the vast majority were Gentiles, but even an occasional Jew whose heart longed for the promised Messiah, came to believe that the Nazarene was indeed the Christ.

The long, twilight evenings were ideal for holding prayer meetings, for study, for the practice of spiritual disciplines, and of course, for sharing the *Agape*. Freedom from stress and fear of persecution made way for long hours of contemplation and solitary meditation, and the seed of profound spirituality sown in Antioch found fertile soil in which to grow.

As the spiritual disciplines were practiced and perfected, the gifts of the Spirit seemed to bloom uncontained. Healers, prophets, teachers and preachers became numerous and well-known. Even non-believers came to have their ailments cured or to learn what their futures held, and anyone in need soon discovered that a Christian would never turn a deaf ear. The Christians became honored for their gifts, respected for their wisdom, and admired for the love and charity they showed to all.

It was an idyllic summer. Lucius' initial anxiety over the Saints' reaction to his sons proved to be largely unfounded. The older Judeans who had known about Pebilus from the beginning had never been certain if Mariaerh knew or not, and the affair had been forgotten for years until Lucius announced his intent to return to Laodicea. Upon their arrival, they had been shocked to learn that Lucius had not one son, but two, but when they saw how the always cool and formally polite relationship between Lucius and Mariaerh remained unchanged, their whispered speculations subsided and they accepted the situation for what they thought it was, a mistake made long ago and best forgiven and forgotten. A few, such as Ulai, deplored Lucius' former behavior, but even Ulai held her tongue, believing, as the majority in the church, that all sins committed before confessing Christ had died on the cross with Jeshua.

Mariaerh never acknowledged the boys' existence, and the Saints took her lead and never mentioned them in her presence. They sympathized with her barrenness, and understood the pain she must feel to know that Lucius had sons and she had none. No one knew that she burned with jealousy, or that she was consumed by fear that Lucius might turn to Vesta again, for she confided in no one. The church admired her ability to forgive and forget and, out of kindness and affection for her, the matter was overlooked.

Lucius was overjoyed when Pebilus and Thaddeus expressed a desire to take part in his activities. He arranged for them to attend the class taught by the Other Mary, and introduced them to Susane who put them to work in the communal storehouse. He took great pains to assure that the boys and Mariaerh never accidentally met and, with no new incidents to fuel the fires of gossip, the boys were absorbed into the church with little or no comment.

As the sons of the overseer, the boys were at first given deferential treatment by many in the church, but it was not long before they were accepted and liked for their own merit. Pebilus was a serious-minded young man who showed an astonishing understanding for the tenets of The Way. The Other Mary was surprised and pleased when Pebilus told her that he had searched out and studied the prophecies and records of Jeshua's life that the Essenes had filed in the great library in Alexandria, but when he also told her how he had been blessed as a child by the Master, she understood the source of his interest. No one who had felt the Master's touch could resist the pull of the Lord.

The Other Mary quickly realized that Pebilus' knowledge and innate understanding of the Master and His teaching were far in advance of the introductory classes she taught. She recommended that he join an adult group that studied the more mystical and esoteric interpretations of the Gospel where his grasp of the spiritual meanings and his ease in learning the disciplines of deep meditation and other phenomena of the spirit were soon the talk of the church.

Mariaerh could not help but overhear bits of such talk, and despite her resolve to never have anything whatsoever to do with Lucius' bastard sons, she was curious. As Pebilus' reputation grew, she sometimes found herself wishing that she could somehow relent her stand. The boys were a constant source of tension between herself and Lucius, and now that they were active in the church, it was increasingly difficult to enter into any discussion and not make mention of their names. Their formal exchanges were becoming increasingly stilted, until silence threatened to close in upon them once more.

Mariaerh dreaded lapsing into that strained, hostile silence again. She was in no way prepared to openly forgive Lucius, but she unconsciously watched for some opportunity where they could speak of his sons without fear of open warfare. When the opportunity did present itself, Mariaerh's pride and pain of rejection almost let it go by.

Thaddeus became the Other Mary's favorite. He reminded her of the son she had lost, for not only did he bear the same name, but was close in age, and displayed a similar brashness and boyish exhuberance. He made friends with ease. His quick wit reflected Vesta's wry sense of humor, and his timely quips during class not only relieved the tension and reverence the students felt due to the topic they studied, but often shed light on a particularly difficult utterance of the Lord. His compositions showed a real gift for writing. He could record an event in the life of the Master in an interesting and humorous style that inspired his reader to learn more. The Other Mary encouraged his gift, and suggested he write stories about Jeshua's life that small children could easily understand. She was delighted with the results, and without thinking, took them to Mariaerh to be read to her tots.

Mariaerh gasped and recoiled from the scrolls the Other Mary so enthusiastically thrust upon her when she heard the name of their author. It was the first time anyone had spoken to her of Lucius' sons, and she was shocked by the Other Mary's bluntness. She saw and heard the Other Mary through a haze of bewilderment and pain that quickly turned to resentment and anger. The Other Mary was acting as if she expected her to share her excitement, to react with the same enthusiasm, and Mariaerh was hurt beyond measure. She clenched her teeth upon the scathing retorts that flew to her mind, and accepted the scrolls with a mere nod of her head and a half-hearted promise to read them.

The Other Mary left and Mariaerh closed and barred the schoolroom door behind her, then flung the scrolls onto a table. She was incredulous and shaking. Hot, angry tears blurred her eyes and she was awash in self-pity. Was there no one who considered her feelings? She could not believe that even the Other Mary would take Lucius' side. His sons were causing favorable comment from everyone in the church, and while he could bask in fatherly pride, she could only drink the bitter dregs of her childlessness.

Mariaerh sank onto a chair and lowered her head to her arms on the table. She sobbed aloud. It was not fair! The Saints seemed to find it more laudable to have children out of wedlock than not to have them at all. Why was she being so punished? What sin had she committed that could be worse than Lucius' sins of adultery and deceit? To be denied a babe to fill her empty arms was surely punishment enough, was she also expected to quietly accept everyone's indifference to her plight? She moaned in despair. She hugged her stomach and rocked her body and wept until the font of her tears ran dry and she was trembling with exhaustion.

She heard the faint sounds of merriment outside in the street as the booths and tents were being raised for the nightly fair. She slowly raised her head and pressed her fingers against her aching eyes. The sun was gone. She knew she would be late for the *Agape* if she did not leave soon, but she could not face another evening of forced sociability. Her prayers of late had been nothing but mouthed repetitions anyway. No wonder the Lord ignored her pleas.

She pushed herself up from the chair. She bathed her face and felt somewhat revived. She had to go home. She could not stay here all night, and there was nowhere else to go where she would not be expected to offer an explanation. She unbarred the door and paused to glance around the room, for even in her numbed state of mind, her mother's training would not allow her to leave it untidy. Her eye fell upon the discarded scrolls and she sighed in resignation. She went back and retrieved them and took them home to read as she had promised the Other Mary.

Lucius, as usual, did not come home. Mariaerh

ordered a tray brought to her room, and after a bath and a light meal, she settled on a chaise before the tall windows to read.

Halfway through the first scroll, she became so caught up in the stories that she forgot, or at least no longer cared, who the author was. They were good, very good! Her little ones would love them! They were filled with tales of Jeshua's own childhood, of His friends and pets, and His schooldays on Mount Carmel. There were also accounts of His love for children when He had grown and become a man, accounts that deeply moved Mariaerh and somehow brought healing to her own troubled heart.

She laid the last scroll aside, her mind a sea of confusion over Thaddeus. What sort of boy, and only sixteen, could convey the Master's love in such a simple and yet profoundly moving manner? Who taught him such things? Surely not his Greek mother! And the other, Pebilus. Some went so far as to call him *holy*. How could a bastard child born out of carnal lust be *holy?*

The teachings of the Essenes tumbled through her mind. There are no accidents. Each soul is born with a purpose, and the conditions for its entry into the earth are prearranged to further that purpose. There was no denying that Lucius' sons were touched by the Holy Spirit, but why did they carry the blood of a Greek and not her own? What plan was unfolding and, as Lucius' wife, what role was she to play?

She thought of Judith whose single-minded devotion to Jeshua had forced her to shunt her own sons aside. Mariaerh had often thought that she could never have done so. Was this why she was childless? Was she to somehow help shape Lucius' sons to assume a place in the church, and would her preoccupation and devotion to her own children have deterred that purpose? And what of all the little ones she had taught and molded and planted within them the seeds of faith for all these many years? Would she have invested the vast amount of her time and energy and emotions if she had a houseful of children at home? Lucia's entire world revolved around her brood of eleven, and Mariaerh knew in her heart she would have been the same way.

Mariaerh quivered with a tremor of excitement. Perhaps she was not being punished! Perhaps her childlessness was a sacrifice she had willingly made, that when this time came her heart and mind would be free to promote her purpose. Denying Lucius' sons and nursing her wounded pride, anger and bitter resentment, and grieving because Lucius did not love her, had brought her nothing but misery. Was it because she was thwarting her life's purpose? Her mind wove a fantasy of the joy and contentment she could feel as she and Lucius worked side by side in guiding the spiritual growth of his sons. She must find some way to let him know that she accepted his sons, and forgave him his past indiscretion. A scroll rolled from the chaise to the floor and Mariaerh bent to pick it up. She held it in her hand and smiled, and knew she had found the way.

Lucius and the boys had shared the *Agape* that evening at Jehul's house, and after a leisurely stroll through the fair, had said goodnight at the landing. As always, their parting left Lucius regretful and depressed, for his heart went home with his sons, and only the empty husk of himself trudged wearily up the remaining stairs to his father's house and his cold, unforgiving wife.

Mariaerh was waiting for him. Lucius looked surprised to see her still up and hesitated as if to speak, but changed his mind and went into the bath. Mariaerh thought he looked unduly weary. Sadness clouded his eyes, and an aura of remorse and dejection overshadowed him. She was stung with a pang of pity for him, and for the first time considered the possibility that he might be as miserable as she. She waited until he finished his preparations to retire, and when he came back to the sleeping room, she handed him the scrolls and said quietly, "I'd like you to read these. The Other Mary brought them to me today for she thought I should read them to my children. They are written by your son Thaddeus."

Lucius was startled. He paused a moment, waiting for

the scathing remark he was sure Mariaerh had prepared for him, but when she remained silent and he could see no sign of angry resentment in her expression, he cautiously took the scrolls from her hand and drew a chair close to the lamp. He fumbled nervously with a scroll. He scanned it quickly, then another, seeing that they were harmless stories of Jeshua's childhood. He was puzzled, wondering what Mariaerh had found objectionable.

"Read them carefully, Lucius," Mariaerh urged. "I want to know your opinion."

Lucius sighed, resigned, and did as she bid, and was soon absorbed in the tales, sometimes smiling, sometimes shaking his head in amusement. They were wonderfully written. He could hear Thaddeus' voice as he read, and see his eyes shine with that particular light that seemed always to appear when they spoke of the Master. He finished the last and laid it aside. Mariaerh had not spoken all the time he read, but had carefully watched his reactions. Lucius was at a loss. He made a helpless gesture with his hands and said, "Mariaerh, I don't know what it is you want me to say."

"I would like your opinion."

Lucius blew out his breath and strode across the room, then came back. He feared to start a quarrel if he praised Thaddeus' work too highly, and knew Mariaerh would know he was lying if he made light of it. He tried to find an acceptable, middle ground.

"They are fine tales. The boy shows a bent for writing," he said lamely.

"Is that all?"

Lucius rubbed his hand across his eyes. "Mariaerh, please!" he groaned. "It is very late and I do not want to quarrel with you. God knows I've had enough of quarreling and anger between us. Why do you give me these? What do you want me to say or do?"

Mariaerh's throat thickened. She too was sick of quarrels and anger and hostile silence. She swallowed and chose her words carefully, deliberately calling Lucius' son by his name instead of her usual, acid "your son."

"I thought Thaddeus' stories were extraordinary. I found it hard to believe that a boy of his age could express himself so movingly. He brings Jeshua alive in such a way that my children can easily come to know Him, and each one subtly teaches a spiritual truth. I was so moved, and thought that you, as Thaddeus' father, would especially enjoy them. You should be very proud of him."

Lucius was astounded. He did not know what to say. Wild hope leapt in his heart that maybe Mariaerh would at last relent. If only she would! If only she would return to be his wife in every sense, perhaps he would no longer find his thoughts filled with Vesta. He looked at Mariaerh with eyes so filled with gratitude that she looked away in embarrassment. His voice cracked when he spoke, so thick with emotion that he had to exert himself to speak above a whisper.

"I am proud of him. He's a fine, sensitive, affectionate lad. I'm not surprised that he writes so well, for he writes as he speaks."

Mariaerh asked, "How has he learned so much about Jeshua in such a short time? He has only been in the Other Mary's class for a matter of weeks."

Lucius was surprised that she knew that, and wondered how much more she knew. "I'm sure Pebilus has told him many things about Jeshua, and the boys are close friends with Antonius and Ceptulus. Pebilus read our records in the Alexandria library and no doubt he discussed what he found with Thaddeus."

Mariaerh's eyes widened. "Why would Pebilus do that?" she asked.

"He was blessed by the Master. Remember the young people in Antioch, how they still could feel His touch? Pebilus never forgot either."

Mariaerh remembered. She had been so angry when Lucius first told her that he had taken Pebilus to see Jeshua that it had not registered. A blessing by the Lord Himself explained Pebilus' easy advance in matters of the spirit. How mysterious are the ways of the Lord, she thought.

She was suddenly very tired. It was extremely late

and she felt strangely at peace for the first time in weeks. She knew she would sleep without the disturbing dreams that had plagued her lately, and her body ached for the bed. She held her hand around the flame and blew out the lamp.

"Come to bed, Lucius. Morning will come too soon as it is. We can speak of this at another time."

Mariaerh was immediately asleep, but Lucius lay awake, too bewildered to sleep. He wondered about Mariaerh's sudden change in attitude and what it would mean for the future. He even dared to hope that one day his wife and his sons might be friends.

Mariaerh stirred and rolled over, and one hand fell upon Lucius' chest. He covered it with his own, and then he too slept.

# Chapter 28

Autumn appeared at the mountaintops and crept insidiously into the valley to warn the sons of man that the gods of the north were awakening and would soon be on the march. The motionless hills of summer began to quiver in anticipation. Winter wheat was sowed. Hordes of reapers devoured the golden waves of summer grain, followed by colorful gleaners who vied with the birds of the air for the bounty left behind. Big-wheeled, ox-drawn carts jounced over the rocky paths, creaking and complaining beneath their burden of barley and rye. Millstones screeched and groaned when separating the seed from the chafe.

The marketplace became chaotic. Camel trains and strings of asses jostled for a place in line, their masters cursing in a cacophony of foreign tongues and whistling their whips through the air to urge the beasts on before a chance early snow made their mountainous route impassable. Fierce, stern-faced nomadic tribes, their women hidden behind heavy black veils, invaded the city to trade their strong, foul-smelling cheese and woven goods for vital supplies before fleeing to winter camps.

The city-dwellers too heard the warning of autumn. Roofs were rethatched or broken tiles repaired, stone walls were rechinked and shutters made tight against winter's wind. Servants and housewives rushed to stock winter larders. Woolen blankets and cloaks were mended and hung out to air. Mattresses and pillows were filled with fresh, warm down or straw, and thick reed mats were woven to keep the cold stone floors from penetrating tender feet.

The days grew short. The twilight hours steadily decreased, and the carnival dwindled in size until one night it simply was no more.

Like all Laodicea, the church also made ready for the changing season, and the frantic pace left little time or energy for intimacy between Lucius and Mariaerh. They seldom saw one another during the day, each absorbed in their own field of endeavor, and by night they were both too exhausted to risk the added strain of quarrel by entering into a discussion of a personal nature, so the subject of Thaddeus and Pebilus was shelved for the time.

Peter added to their already, overburdened schedule by making a sudden, unexpected visit to Laodicea. He was on his way to Rome where Ruth, Philoas, and Cornelius had made great strides in convincing both Jews and Greeks that the Messiah had come and soon would come again. The worldly, openminded Jews of Rome were far more willing to accept the concept of God Incarnate than their rigidly pious Judean brothers, and to preach Christ's *name* in their synagogues did not cause the outcry that it did in Jerusalem. Legionnaires returning from Judea over the years had told wondrous tales of the gentle Nazarene, and their friends and families were eager to hear more. Many had been baptized in Jeshua's *name,* and now awaited Peter to impose hands upon them and baptize them in the Holy Spirit.

Peter's visit threw the church into a frenzy of excitement. The new members hung back in timid silence, awed by the presence of one of the Master's chosen, while those from Judea and Antioch rudely pushed each other aside as they pressed to come near and let everyone know that Peter was considered a personal friend, then flushed and preened with pride if he called them by name. As overseer, Lucius was always at Peter's side, smugly imperious with his exalted position, while Mariaerh looked on with disgust. The Saints clamored for private interviews, argued over whose guest he would be, and his public addresses were crowded to an overflow capacity. Lucius was hard-pressed to see that no one was slighted and that no accusations of favoritism could later be charged.

As Lucius' wife, Mariaerh was compelled to oversee the festivities. She had to make certain that each *Agape* Peter attended contained all of his favorite foods, and that singers and musicians were present wherever he appeared. The storehouse was raided for embroidered linens, thin, hand-blown glassware, and fine, translucent plates and bowls that were free of cracks and chips. She commandeered artists to beautify each home he would visit, and borrowed suitable benches and tables when the homeowner had none.

Mariaerh begrudged each task she performed. She was embarrassed by such ostentation. She knew Peter better than any, and knew that the rugged fisherman of Galilee would have been far more content with nothing but the barest necessities, but Lucius and the Elders insisted that only the best be provided for an Apostle of the Lord. She did as they wished, but was resentful, and thought it all nonsense and hypocritical, a case of self-aggrandizement on the part of the church. As she watched the Saints compete for recognition and to be accorded a place of prestige, she was often reminded of Jeshua's parable of the guest who took the least place, and was then raised by his host to the seat of honor. She was dismayed that His message of simplicity and humbleness seemed to have fallen upon deaf ears. As the hectic days wore on, Mariaerh found it almost impossible to continue the pose of a loving, dutiful wife. Fortunately, the threat of winter cut Peter's visit short, and Mariaerh heaved a sigh of relief when he left for Ephesus where he would sail to Rome.

Throughout Peter's visit, Mariaerh had watched for a glimpse of Lucius' sons, thinking that he would surely present them to Peter, but if he did, it must have been in private, for she saw no one who answered their description, although she easily could have missed them in the abounding confusion. She fantasized chance meetings with Thaddeus and Pebilus, accidental encounters in which she comported herself with dignified magnanimity and Lucius was humbled in pentitent gratitude. When her chance encounter did finally occur, it was not at all as she had imagined.

It was a fine autumn day. The hills were ablaze in red and gold, and the crisp, fallen leaves formed a coppery carpet that rustled beneath Mariaerh's feet. It was warm. The shawl she had tugged tightly around her shoulders that morning now hung over her arm, a useless burden in the afternoon sun. The sky was cloudless, deep blue, the sun benign, a globe of light and mellow warmth, and the air smelled faintly of dust and burning leaves.

Mariaerh meandered through the streets. Her class was dismissed for the day and she carried a bundle of shirts she had hemmed to deliver to the communal storehouse. She had taken a circuitous route to savor the gift of a last summer day, and her thoughts floated as lazily as the falling leaves. She hoped Susane was still at the storehouse, then they could walk together to the street of the weavers to share the *Agape* with Jehul and Rhea. She wondered where Lucius was and if he would be at Jehul's. She hoped so. With Peter gone and things returned to normal, maybe they could resume repairing their faltering marriage.

She wished their marriage were like that of Jonas and Susane. They too were childless, and yet seemed content, their love for one another and their shared devotion to The Way enough to bring them joy. If only she and Lucius had a similar well of love to plumb, perhaps she would not feel the burning need for a child. Mariaerh shook her head. No, she would still want a babe of her own, even if Lucius loved her wholeheartedly.

Mariaerh's musings were disrupted by a sudden spate of shouts and laughter. A group of youngsters spilled pell-mell from a doorway up ahead, and she realized with a start that she had wandered onto the Other Mary's street and it was her class of teenagers that noisily rejoiced at being freed for the afternoon.

Mariaerh gasped. Her pulse raced and she clutched at

the bundle of shirts in her arms as Thaddeus' name flashed into her mind. She was seized by panic. Her eyes cast about, seeking a place to hide, and she almost fled back down the street, but months of suppressed curiosity kept her rooted. She slipped behind a tree, wanting to see but not to be seen. She peered around the gnarled trunk, watching, wondering which one could be Thaddeus, and if she would recognize him if even she saw him. Her ears strained to hear lest someone should call him by name. She stared, searching every male face for some vestige of Lucius' features, when a deep voice behind her startled her so she jumped and cried out aloud.

"He comes now. The dark-haired one at the door in the purple tunic."

Mariaerh spun to the voice. A young man stood behind her, tall, slim, light-haired. His blue eyes shone with amusement, yet were filled with sympathetic understanding.

Mariaerh's heart plummeted. Her face flushed crimson. "Wha-what?" she stammered.

"My brother, Thaddeus, there, coming toward us."

Mariaerh wished the earth would open up and swallow her whole. She was physically ill with shame. She started to push by Pebilus, to pretend she did not know him or understand his meaning, but he stepped in her path and blocked her way.

"Please, Lady. Do not leave yet. Thad and I have wanted to meet you. We've seen you often." Pebilus laughed gently, also a little embarrassed. "You see, we've secretly sought you out and watched for you too."

Somehow his confession eased Mariaerh's acute embarrassment. She looked into his face. He was smiling and his eyes sparkled, inviting her friendship. She relaxed a bit, but still clung to her bundle as if it were some sort of shield.

"I didn't realize where I was. I truly did not come here deliberately," she explained lamely. Her hot face flushed even deeper. "I'm horribly embarrassed. You must think me ridiculous, hiding behind a tree, but I was so shocked to see where my wanderings had brought me, and hid impulsively before Thad, your brother, chanced to see me."

Pebilus laughed, a fine, open, joyous laugh without a trace of mockery. "I think Thad and I would have perished if the tables were turned and you had caught us. Please don't be embarrassed. Let me call Thad."

Mariaerh was torn. She wanted to stay, to satisfy her curiosity over Lucius' sons, and yet to do so was to capitulate to Lucius' deceit and betrayal. She hesitated, chewing her bottom lip, trying to decide what to do. Pebilus said nothing more, letting the decision be hers alone and the thought crossed her mind that Lucius would never have done so. He would have taken immediate command of the situation and called out to Thaddeus without even consulting her. She was grateful to Pebilus for putting her wishes before his own. She raised her eyes to his face and saw the eager, hope in his eyes and could not refuse him. She swallowed her pride and nodded her head.

Pebilus smiled and touched her hand briefly, a simple gesture of gratitude that conveyed the thought that he understood her dilemma. He stepped around Mariaerh and used his body to shield her from the other students' notice and called out to Thaddeus. Mariaerh was again touched by his sensitivity. If the other youngsters saw her with Pebilus and Thaddeus, the talk would rage through the church like a grass fire.

Thaddeus answered Pebilus' call and bounded up to them. He opened his mouth to speak to Pebilus, but when he saw Mariaerh, his eyes widened and his face exploded in happy surprise.

"Mariaerh!" he gasped, then at once looked chagrined and embarrassed by his rude familiarity. "I mean, I'm sorry, Lady, I," he stammered.

Mariaerh did not notice. She was staring, speechless with amazement at how much the boy looked like Lucius. Some students were coming toward them and Pebilus deftly maneuvered Mariaerh to the other side of the tree. After they had passed, Pebilus explained to Thaddeus.

"The Lady Mariaerh was passing by while I was

waiting for you and I found courage to speak to her. She kindly consented to wait and meet you also."

Mariaerh shot him a look of pure gratitude for not exposing her silly spying from behind the tree.

Thaddeus groaned. "Father will have a fit." He turned to Mariaerh. "He ordered us not to distress you by ever coming near where you were."

Mariaerh suppressed a laugh. A fit, she thought. Well, she knew well enough what he meant by that. She had a sudden urge to defend the boys against their father, and said consolingly, "Never mind. It's my fault. I was taking these shirts to the storehouse and took a long route to enjoy the fall day. I didn't take note of the time, or pay attention to where I was. I'll explain to your father. I'm sure he won't be angry with you."

Mariaerh was surprised at how easily she had said *your father*. The Saints were right. The boys were charming. She suddenly felt buoyant, adventuresome. She looked from one eager young face to the other and felt totally at ease, even, she thought with a sense of shock, motherly!

They all stood in silence, grinning inanely at one another as if they were conspirators who had just perpetrated a harmless hoax. Mariaerh began to giggle like a schoolgirl. Months of crushing tension caused by her dread of meeting the boys dissolved away and she felt free and light as if a great burden had been lifted from her back.

"What suffering and anguish we cause ourselves by giving way to our fears," she said wonderingly.

Pebilus nodded gravely. "We feared you would hate us and reject us in anger."

"And we felt guilty," Thaddeus added, "because father . . ." he blushed and looked down, not knowing how to express in words their illegitimacy.

Mariaerh understood what he was trying to say and felt sorry for him. She shifted her bundle to one arm and laid her hand on Thaddeus' arm. "I don't hate you and am not angry. Any anger I felt was with Lucius, not you. And you must never feel guilty. None of this is of your doing. 'The sins of the fathers are visited upon their children.' This does not mean that God punishes the child for the wrongs of the parents, but that the poor innocents always suffer the results of their elders' misdeeds."

The relief on Thaddeus' face was heart-rending. Mariaerh silently chastised herself and Lucius for causing the boys to know such confusion.

Pebilus reached for the bundle in Mariaerh's arms. "Let me carry that for you, Lady," he said gently. "May Thad and I walk part way to the storehouse with you?"

Mariaerh surrendered the bundle and flexed her arms that had stiffened from its weight. "Yes, please do, I'd be happy for your company."

The sun was perched at the crest of the hills and threatened at any moment to tumble down the far side and plunge the valley into darkness. Mariaerh and the boys hurried toward the storehouse, Mariaerh between them, swinging her head back and forth to answer Thaddeus' exuberant chatter, then Pebilus' grave pronouncements. She was happier than she had been in months. She felt bold and strong and full of courage. When the boys slowed their pace not far from the storehouse and Pebilus offered to return her bundle and leave her before they were seen, she suddenly no longer cared how much gossip she caused. She shook her head and refused the bundle. She looked from one to the other and a mute understanding of her intent passed between them. They grinned at one another in conspiracy and affection, and marched boldly together into the storehouse.

Susane had already gone. The boys waited while Mariaerh delivered the shirts, enjoying the whispers and stares they provoked. Mariaerh ignored the shocked surprise and the stammered answers to her statements, and behaved as though not a thing were amiss. When she finished her business, she led the boys outside and politely invited them to accompany her to Jehul's house but was relieved when Pebilus declined.

"I think we caused enough uproar for one day," he said amicably.

"No need to give Father an attack of his heart,"

Thaddeus teased.

Mariaerh agreed. She was still amazed by the turn the day had taken, and even more amazed by her audacity in bringing the boys to the storehouse, but she lacked the courage to suddenly face Lucius with his sons at her side.

"May we see you again, Lady?" Pebilus asked.

"Whenever you wish. You are always welcome, both of you. And please, call me Mariaerh."

She bid the boys a good evening and parted with "Peace be with you" that came from the depths of her heart.

Lucius was not at Jehul's. The beauty and perfection of the fine autumn day had enticed him to abandon his duties and lured him away to the hills. He followed the rocky, winding field paths to a place high above the city which he had frequented as a boy, and sat with his back to a tree, filling his eyes with the panorama of the blazing hills and the picturesque city below.

It was peaceful and quiet. Only an occasional bleat of a sheep or the deep, cajoling voice of a shepherd drifted by on a breeze to momentarily shatter the silence. Squirrels scampered nearby, gathering nuts to store for the winter, and at first had chastised him soundly for daring to enter their private domain, but when they saw he was harmless, they quietly resumed their task and ignored him as part of the landscape. Bees droned, sucking the dregs of nectar from summer's last blooms, lulling him nearly to sleep with the monotony of their song. Spider webs rode the gentle air waves, and delicate air-borne seeds floated by. Lucius faced the sun, his eyes closed, watching the ever-changing shapes made by the light filtering through his lids and let his thoughts roam free.

He was weary, his nerves on edge. The last hectic weeks had drained his energy and left his emotions frayed and raw. He was lonely. An empty, yearning, void yawned wide within his breast, despite his many friends and the companionship of his sons. He needed, wanted, longed, yet knew not for what. He sighed and wished, but did not know for what he wished. He felt melancholic, sad, and tried to shake it off by taking pleasure from the scene around him, but its beauty only increased his sense of dissatisfaction.

The sun was hot. Lucius removed his shirt and the warmth caressed his skin like the sensual, tantalizing hands of a woman. Lucius' loins warmed, and his thoughts turned to Vesta.

He had brought her here once, long years ago, and they had made love on this very spot. How young they had been, and free and innocent, their passion as natural and wild as the primordial hills that had watched them. Lucius groaned in pain at the vision that memory provoked, and tried to cast Vesta out of his mind by thinking of Mariaerh.

At least they were now friends if not lovers, but, Lucius sighed, they had never been truly lovers. He wondered why not? Why did one woman sate his desire and another leave him partially empty? Mariaerh was like winter, coldly intellectual, a background of unobtrusive white that did not distract, did not demand, a sound, hard footing on which to accomplish his work. Vesta, on the other hand, was summer's heat, luring his thoughts from purpose, burning his body, sapping his strength, a shifting sand that tossed his emotions from ecstasy to despair and promised never-ending days of warmth and pleasure.

Lucius' eyes flew open. He was bathed in sweat. His heart pounded and his manhood was hard and erect. He wiped his face with the shirt and jerked it on, angry, disgusted, rebellious, sick of self-sacrifice, tired of loneliness, stretched to the limits of his endurance in denying the natural function of a man. He would go to Mariaerh, settle this estrangement between them once and for all and demand his rights as her husband.

He hurried down the rocky path, mindless of the sharp outcroppings that cut through the soles of his sandals, chasing the lengthening shadows that raced before him across the valley. He entered the city, breathless and sweating, threading his way through the crowded market that was busily closing up shop for the day. He glanced toward the street of the weavers, but decided not to attend the *Agape* at Jehul's, his determination to confront his wife would not be put off.

The sun plunged behind the hills, taking its warmth with it and Lucius shivered with a sudden chill. Halfway up the terraced stairway it occurred to him that Mariaerh would not yet be home. He slowed his pace, disappointed, wondering if she were at Jehul's and regretting that he had not gone there. His determination evaporated. He plodded up the stairs to the landing and sank down upon the stone bench.

The shadows deepened. The evening star winked solely in the sky, as cold and lonely as himself. He was overwhelmed with longing. The emptiness in his heart stretched and widened, threatening to encompass his entire being and suck him into the vortex of swirling, black void.

Lucius covered his face with his hands and moaned, his head swinging back and forth as if detached from his body. He sat thus until the cold, damp night air prodded his body to move. He struggled to his feet, weary to the marrow of his bones, old, defeated, devoid of love and companionship. He looked toward his father's house and found no surcease for his misery there, then his feet turned with a mind of their own and carried him off toward Vesta.

No words passed between them at Vesta's door. The naked need in Lucius' face said all, and Vesta came into his arms, and the void was held at bay. He found life in her body, life that restored and renewed, that healed and soothed and solaced and filled him with ecstasy and joy. He plunged deeper and deeper, drawing her strength and her love into himself with every desperate thrust until his emtpy heart was full and his soul at peace at last.

He left her reluctantly, wanting to stay, knowing he could not, grateful that she did not urge him. He let himself out, leaving her smiling and languid upon her bed. His feet floated home. His stomach rumbled with hunger. He stopped at the kitchens and tore at a loaf of bread, wolfing it down with gusto, laughing aloud at his ravenous hunger.

He let himself quietly into his bedchamber, then stopped short. Mariaerh was awake, obviously waiting. A candle burned on a table by the bed. She was sitting up, smiling, her eyes aglow, her hair tumbling in dark waves over her shoulders. The sleeping-gown she wore, surely one of Nimmuo's, was cut low, sheer, exposing the soft mound of her breasts.

Lucius sucked in his breath and began to tremble. Mariaerh held out her hand, a gesture for him to draw near. Her voice was low, inviting, forgiving, and thick with promise.

"I met your sons today, Lucius. They are wonderful young men, and we are friends. Indeed, I felt almost like their mother."

# Chapter 29

It was cold. Lucius shivered and drew his woolen mantle close and scanned the sky. The air was damp and smelled of snow. The sky was milky white and low, obscuring the gently rounded hills in an eerie mist. The sun shone weakly, a glowing orb diffused by haze that shed no warmth. A sudden gust of wind tugged ineffectually at Lucius' mantle then sobbed and slunk away as though ashamed of its lack of strength.

Lucius stamped his feet and wished he were still in Vesta's warm bed. He winced as the wave of guilt that always assailed him when he left the villa slammed into his chest, guilt that over the weeks had eased, yet still left him shaken and filled with remorse. He shook his head, remembering the Master's words to Peter when he slept in Gethsemene, "The spirit is willing, but the flesh is weak." So true, he thought, with a sigh of helplessness.

He started down the staircase, wishing he could simply take the horizontal path to Philippi's house, but he could not afford the risk of being seen by one of the family as he came from Vesta's villa. He thought it little enough penance to be obliged to go all the way down to the city then cross through the streets and come back up Philippi's stairway. Some day he knew he would be called to account for the full extent of his subterfuge, "as you sow, so shall you reap," either in this life or in the next. Lucius shivered again and fervently hoped it would be in the next. Adultery was a serious sin, more condemned by the Jews than by the Gentiles in the church, but nevertheless he could imagine the furor it would cause if his infidelity became known. Merceden would be livid, and Mariaerh?

Lucius groaned and huddled deeper into his cloak. He had to stop seeing Vesta before Mariaerh found out, but even as he thought it, he knew he would not. He was powerless against Vesta's charms. He was addicted to her as some men were addicted to wine, and once he had tasted the pleasure of her body again, his passion for her was insatiable and he returned to her bed as often as he could slip away.

He hurried through the streets, anxious to be home, hungry as always after Vesta's embrace. Twice he was stopped by friends in the church and was forced to tarry and exchange a few words, and each time his guilt had flared anew as he saw in their eyes and heard in their voices, their unexpressed admiration that their over-seer was out and about tending his flock on such an intemperate day. He wondered what they would think if they knew that his loins still throbbed from Vesta's touch and his skin smelled of her scent? Romans or Greeks would probably wink an eye and feel envy, but Jews and Christians?

He let himself into Philippi's garden, then into the house where he surrendered his cloak to a man-servant and hurried into the low-ceilinged, south-facing room where the family convened in the winter. He paused at the entrance. Braziers burned brightly, filling the room with light and warmth. Mariaerh was surrounded by a circle of Lucia's youngsters, reading to them from one of Thaddeus' scrolls. Philippi and Jesua pored over their accounts. Nimmuo and Lucia giggled like girls as Merceden feigned shocked disapproval while Julia modeled the latest fashion in hair arrangement. It was an idyllic family scene, one that Lucius had yearned to see during the long years of his absence, but now he cringed, knowing how tenuous their contentment was in view of his affair with Vesta. He took a deep breath and strode into the room, smiling broadly and rubbing his hands together.

"It's freezing out there!" he exclaimed with more bravado than he felt. "I'm also starving. Is there anything to eat?"

The family paused in their various involvements to bid him welcome. Mariaerh quickly laid the scroll aside and approached him, her face wreathed in smiles and her eyes aglow with happiness. She raised her face for a kiss, which Lucius dutifully planted upon her cheek, then blushed. Mariaerh filled him a glass of warmed wine and spread a layer of honey on a plate of fresh barley cakes. He accepted them with murmured thanks, swallowing his irritation at her reddened cheeks.

"Have you had a busy day?" Mariaerh asked.

Lucius nodded. He avoided looking at her, ridiculously afraid that she would somehow be able to see the image of Vesta still mirrored in his eyes. He ate hungrily, and looked around the room.

"Where are the boys?"

"Somewhere in the house with Ceptulus and Antonius. In the game room, I would guess."

Mariaerh had steadfastly ignored any gossip or speculations in regard to her friendship with Pebilus and Thaddeus. She had offered no explanations, allowed no discussions concerning her reversed stance, but she left no doubt in anyone's mind that the issue was closed, that the past was not only forgiven, but forgotten. She had set an example for the entire church, and even Merceden had felt she could do no less and the boys had become regular visitors to Philippi's house. Lucius was overjoyed that his sons had at last become an active part of the family, but Mariaerh's largess needled him, for she destroyed his only plausible excuse for continuing his liaison with Vesta.

Servants were setting the table for the evening meal. Belden returned from the city, and the boys were called from their games. Remote from them all, his duplicity and guilty secret alienating him from the ones he loved, Lucius watched the mass confusion of Philippi's large household preparing to dine with the observant eye of a stranger. Pebilus approached him, and Lucius' heart sank as he asked in his grave, serious manner,

"Will you bless the bread and wine for us, Father?"

Lucius nodded as his guilt made inroads on his

network of nerves, but he could see no way to refuse.

He went to the head of the table and lowered his eyes to the ruby-red wine and the dark, round loaf that awaited his blessing. He closed his eyes and groaned. His mind went back to a time at Martha's house when he had vowed never to approach this holy meal with sin on his soul, but he had no choice. "You shall not commit adultery." Was it adultery when his heart and mind were in accord with his body?

Lucius sighed and placed his dilemma at the feet of his Lord. Forgive me if I sin. Have pity upon me, in my confusion. His prayer was silent and was wrung from the depths of his soul, but he felt no peace that told him that Jeshua had heard and had answered.

He raised his eyes and sought out each anticipating face. Merceden, flushed with brows knit in concern, wondering if this new rite she allowed beneath her roof were not blasphemous. Philippi, unbelieving, but patient, willing to indulge his children in their new fancy. Lucia, Jesua, and all their offspring, Nimmuo clutching at Belden's hand as she cast a warning eye upon her squirming little daughters. His sons, Thaddeus smiling, eyes aglow, Pebilus, grave, still, waiting for the mystery that changed the bread and wine to the body and blood of his remembered Lord.

Mariaerh. Lucius tore his eyes away from her as he was suddenly choked with resentment. It was because of Mariaerh that the *Agape* was held in his home and he was forced into this corner, compelled to compound his sins by presiding when his heart and mind were in turmoil. He was aghast that such thoughts should emerge at this time. He banished them and made himself look at Mariaerh with tenderness and compassion, and his hands began to tremble.

Mariaerh's face was suffused with love, a love so powerful that it poured forth from her as an invisible energy that rocked him on his feet with its strength. He recoiled against it, ashamed to be the recipient of such adoration when his heart was filled with deceit and hypocrisy. He mentally deflected it to the goblet and loaf and began to intone the prayers.

Mariaerh watched him. The force of her emotions was like warm, liquid bliss that coursed through every cell in her body then rushed from a never-ending font to envelop the entire world. Her heart was bursting with gratitude. The Lord had answered her every prayer and His presence overshadowed her like a warm, protective cloak. She felt approved, loved, and blessed.

She had never known a closer walk with the Master, not even when she stood beside him in the flesh and knew the force of his love from his own living eyes. She felt she had been tested, and had emerged victorious. She had overcome pride and self-pity, banished resentment and hurt and the urge for revenge by sowing forgiveness and understanding and acceptance in their stead, and the harvest she reaped was abundant beyond her wildest imaginings.

As Lucius raised the loaf aloft, she watched with a heart overflowing with tenderness. The change in Lucius could only have occurred through the direct intervention of the Lord, and tears of humble gratitude blurred her sight. She took the loaf from his hand and pulled a small piece away and put it in her mouth, moved to her roots by the knowledge that she melded her soul to the Lord. She passed the loaf to Nimmuo and waited in silence until all had eaten their share, trying to still her mind and emotions, but Lucius' presence so near made her tingle with joy and her mind refused to empty.

How disappointed she had been when on that first night Lucius had not embraced her as she had hoped. She had struggled to keep from weeping in frustration and failure, but by morning she realized that she had expected too much too soon. Lucius also had his pride, and months of rejection could not hope to be healed in one night. It had not taken long. Mariaerh had persevered and after a few nights of subtle encouragement, Lucius had been convinced of her sincerity and had come to her willing arms.

Mariaerh felt her face warm and ducked her head. She blushed every time she thought of their lovemaking.

Lucius had become so solicitious of her wishes, and so sensitive to her needs. He only reached for her body once a week or less, and then no longer made embarrassing demands or behaved with unconcealed lust. He was gentle and modest. He averted his eyes while she donned her nightdress and pinched out the candle when she asked without argument. She thought the change in Lucius was no doubt, at least in part, due to his age. A man of mature years had more important things on his mind than the demands of his flesh, and it seemed reasonable to expect that his blood would be less hot than in his youth.

Lucius was blessing the wine and Mariaerh turned her mind away from thoughts of the flesh and tried to concentrate on the blood of the Lord. Her eyes met Pebilus' who reclined across the wide board from her on Lucius' other side, and she smiled at him and again felt a warm rush of love.

She loved Lucius' sons as if they were of her own flesh. She often pretended that she was their mother, a secret game that she played with herself, but it served the purpose of banishing her longing for a child of her own, and certainly caused no harm. The boys made it easy to do so. They treated her with such respect, almost reverence, as their father's wife, and displayed such affection and concern for her welfare that they made her feel as if she were their mother. They tactfully never mentioned their real mother, and of course Lucius did not, and Vesta had become in Mariaerh's mind, some shadowy, ghostly figure who had no real existence.

Thoughts of Vesta caused Mariaerh to bristle. Whatever reason their paths had intertwined was over, and never again would she intrude into Mariaerh's life.

The cup was passed. When everyone had taken the token sip and it was returned to Lucius, he chanted the final prayers and the *Agape* was ended. The servants were dismissed, and the family relaxed to enjoy the rest of the meal.

Throughout the blessing, Lucius had been acutely aware of Mariaerh's attention. It made him uneasy, and he found it difficult to concentrate on the solemnity of the rite. It irritated him, both because it distracted him from the holy office he performed, and because despite himself his body responded to her obvious love and the promise it implied.

He reclined on the couch and deliberately turned his back to Mariaerh and chatted with the boys in a lame attempt to keep from thinking about it, but his thoughts kept going back to Mariaerh.

Ever since Mariaerh had come to her senses and accepted the fact of his sons, she had changed, and Lucius was not at all sure he liked those changes. Her long, dark hair had taken on a sheen like satin, warm and alive and silky to his touch. Her appetite had returned. The sharp, angular planes of her body had disappeared, and now soft, tempting flesh filled out all of her hollows. Her breasts were full and womanly, her hips and arms round and pleasing. Her skin glowed and her eyes shone. His loins warmed and came alive every time he looked at her until he remembered how stiff and unresponsive that tempting body became whenever he tried to awaken her to the pleasures of love.

Her physical changes he applauded, but there were other, deeper changes that he did not like, even— although he hated to admit it—feared. She had become confident and self-assured. She walked with her head erect and her eyes wide and alert. There was a new spring to her step and her stride was longer and sure instead of the faltering, almost shuffling pace he was used to seeing. It had always irritated him that his wife walked with her head down and her eyes focused on the ground, picking her way with care as if she feared to fall or to step into something distasteful, and now her new, swinging, carefree gait perversely irritated him just as much.

Her whole attitude had changed. She no longer cowered beneath his instructive criticism, but faced him with candid explanations in her own defense. She still blushed far too often, but now laughed at her own reddened cheeks and could banter Philippi with ease. She went her own way, made her own decisions, and no longer deferred to his wishes as she should. Lucius felt slighted and somewhat diminished. He felt he had lost control, and he was at a loss as to how to handle this new Mariaerh.

Lucius did not like to think of himself as unable to govern any situation, and it rankled him even more when it was his own wife. He could not admit that he harbored such petty vanity within himself and sought other motives to justify his ire.

It really was Mariaerh's fault that he found himself in such an intolerable state. It was her rejection that forced him into Vesta's arms in the first place, and her damnable, pious, inhibited attitude toward sex that kept him there. Her cringing distaste for lovemaking reduced one of God's most precious gifts to nothing more than the rutting of animals. With Mariaerh there was no give and take of pleasure and joy, no blending of minds and spirits that soared as one on the wings of ecstasy. It was all one-sided. She reluctantly submitted while he perfunctorily did his duty. Lucius shuddered. He felt used, like a stallion at stud. No wonder his seed refused to take root!

Lucius turned his attention to a conversation taking place between Mariaerh and Thaddeus before his rising indignation got out of hand. Mariaerh met his gaze and smiled shyly. He recognized the smile as her awkward signal that his advances would be welcomed later. His stomach muscles tightened and the organ between his legs moved. He thought ruefully, in this case, it is the body that is willing and the spirit that is weak.

Philippi arose and announced it was time for bed and the family bid their goodnights. Lucius took Mariaerh's hand as they walked down the long, cold passageway to their own apartment. His heartbeat quickened and his manhood rose and he shook his head in wonder at the eagerness of a man for a maiden.

# Chapter 30

John Mark sprawled on a deep chaise in Lucius' rooms and gaped at the lush furnishings in awe.

"You're as rich as a king, Lucius! I take my hat off to you for giving up all of this and living in poverty all those years in Jerusalem."

Lucius was embarrassed. "It belongs to my father, not me. I live here only to please my mother. I'd be just as happy in a cottage in the city." He changed the subject. "Are you alone? Where are Barnabas and Saul?"

John Mark grimaced. "I left them. Saul is now called Paul. The Greeks he is so fond of would have it no other way and he seems to like it better."

"Why did you leave?"

John Mark squirmed. "Saul-Paul and I didn't see eye to eye on a number of things."

"Such as?"

John Mark slapped his knees and stood and began to pace the room. "His overbearing, self-righteous attitude got on my nerves. He thinks the vision he saw on the road to Damascus sets him above everyone else, as if he is some especially chosen apostle of the Lord."

"He could be right."

"Nonsense!" John Mark exploded. "Jeshua calls every man and woman to the priesthood of Israel."

"Doesn't Saul prove that by preaching to the Greeks?"

"I think he preaches to the Greeks because the Jews hate him. He won renown as a student of Gamaliel, and the Jews view him as a traitor to the faith of our fathers.

The Greeks are awed by his bombast and his ability to heal, and they treat him as one of their lesser gods."

"I think you misjudge Saul, or else there is more that you haven't yet told me."

John Mark ran his fingers through his blond, unruly curls. "He misinterprets Jeshua's words. He puts too much emphasis on behavior and appearance, and doesn't discover what lies in a person's heart and soul. Like some of the Pharisees, he makes rules and regulations, establishes standards and rituals to be observed until the essence of the Gospel is lost in the maze. All Jeshua asked was that we love one another and believe in Him."

"That's too simplistic, John Mark. There is more to being a Christian than just a public proclamation of faith! The Way is to be lived. We are to mold our life to Christ's as closely as possible."

"Even to the exclusion of women?" John Mark snorted. "Saul-Paul thinks so!"

It was Lucius' turn to squirm. He poured them each a glass of wine and wondered how to answer. He chose his words with care, unconsciously trying to absolve himself as well as defend Saul's position.

"Jeshua was unique. He knew his days on earth were numbered. He knew he must die on the cross as the supreme sacrifice that all men might live. For Jeshua to marry and bring souls into the earth would have been cruel, knowing he'd leave them orphaned in such a short while."

John Mark frowned. He knew Lucius to be a brilliant theologian. Now he too was being simplistic and John Mark wondered why. He shot Lucius a quizzical look, but Lucius rushed on before John Mark could form his question.

"Knowing you, my guess is that the females found you irresistible, and of course you could not disappoint them, and Saul would not allow it."

John Mark grinned. Lucius laughed: "So! I am right!"

John Mark fell back onto the chaise in a slouch. "Paul knows nothing about women. He views them as less than men. He exhorts them to obedience. He allows them no mind of their own. He'd separate them in the church as the Jews do in the synagogue, and chooses to ignore the fact that Jeshua recognized their true worth and saw them as more capable and faithful than many men."

"And you, of course, recognize their value also, and show your gratitude by lying with any who are willing."

John Mark flushed, angered. "That's not true! You make it sound like I indulge in Roman-style orgies! I simply do not see what is wrong when a man and woman come together in mutual pleasure. If a man has a wife, then he should remain loyal to his wife, as you do with Mariaerh, but if not, as I don't, then I think Paul should hold his judgment. My own conscience is my guide, not Paul!"

Lucius turned his back so John Mark would not see the guilt that he knew must be evident in his eyes. He did not know the answer for John Mark, and God knew he wrestled with the same thing long enough. He tried to side-step the main issue and bring the matter to a close.

"I have no directive for you, John Mark. I ask only that you be discreet and not cause a scandal while in Laodicea. We Christians are in good standing in this city, but the memories of persecution are ever in our minds. We live in peace and are free from scorn and ridicule. Please do nothing to bring censure upon us by non-believers."

John Mark laughed. "Done! I get along very well with non-believers. I even have changed a few into believers before I've been through."

Lucius shook his head and laughed, believing him entirely. John Mark could charm Belial if he set his mind to it.

Later that afternoon Lucius lay naked beside Vesta and described to her his conversation with John Mark. She smiled with a glint in her eye, and said wickedly, "This John Mark sounds fascinating, Lucius. You must introduce me to him soon."

"You? Never! John Mark holds far too much attraction among the young women now; think how he would be if he fell into your expert hands."

Vesta giggled and pulled at Lucius' hair, drawing his head down to her lush breasts. Lucius nuzzled them and ran his hand down her satiny skin, reaching for her silken mound of maidenhair, but his hand stayed at her belly. He was quite still. He held his breath and moved his hand slightly back and forth, feeling, but disbelieving the firm fullness where before had been a deep hollow.

Vesta did not move. Lucius' heart raced. He felt hot, then cold. He refused to entertain the thought in his mind. He tried to remember when Vesta had last bled and could not. He took his hand away and raised his head, his eyes alone asking the question that his tongue could not form.

Vesta smiled. "Do you mind? I considered an abortion, but really, I would like another child."

For the next few months, Lucius was unaware of the passing of time. He moved through a dense fog of terror and despair, his hands and mouth moving automatically, conditioned by years of performing the same tasks and speaking the same words in service to the church.

The Way commemorated Jeshua's resurrection in a day-long festival of prayer and thanksgiving. Thirty-two initiates were baptized by immersion in the icy river, a testament to the strides the church had made in only a year, but Lucius' thoughts were only on Vesta.

Lucius had considered every possible way to keep Mariaerh and the church from learning of Vesta's pregnancy. To his horror, his desperation had almost led him to press for abortion, but he had immediately recoiled, for to thwart the purpose of an entering soul by destroying its channel for expression was not to be considered. Whatever consequence he would face for his actions, he could never face the Lord with such a confession on his tongue.

His sons already knew. How could they not? They did not pass judgment, not a word of censure had left either boy's tongue, but an awkwardness existed between them, unspoken thoughts and unexpressed feelings that produced a tension that grieved him. He knew the boys were torn between their loyalty to himself and their mother and their affection for Mariaerh. He sensed that they found him lacking in courage and honesty by his failure to tell his wife, but they were young and inexperienced, and could not possibly know the disastrous results of such a disclosure.

Time was his enemy. Soon everyone would know and he had no answer to forestall the calamity. Why had he never considered the possibility that Vesta could conceive again!

He had to tell Mariaerh soon, or someone else would. Philippi moved in the same social circle as Vesta and it was surprising that he did not yet know. He would soon, and then so would Merceden, then Lucia and Nimmuo and the children and someone was certain to speak of it where Mariaerh would overhear.

Perhaps, by telling Mariaerh himself, he could make her understand. She had eventually accepted two sons, why not three? She would be angry, of course, and no doubt withdraw her companionship from him for a time, but if he handled it right, it might not be for too long.

What of the church? They would expel him as overseer, of that he was sure. Some of the more pious, as Ulai, would seek his expulsion from the Community of Saints, but they would most likely be overruled by the more liberal majority. He could bear the humiliation of losing his position as just punishment for his sins, but to lose the respect and good opinion of his flock was almost more than he could bear.

The opportunity for telling Mariaerh never seemed to arrive. Vesta's girth swelled until she could no longer hide it behind flowing gowns and, as Lucius guessed, Philippi was the first in the family to know.

"Are you mad?" Philippi stormed. "Did you never give thought to the consequences? You are nearing fifty years of age and still cannot control your lust! I do not understand you. Sleep with the woman, yes, if you must, but in the name of the gods, don't leave your seed! Plow the field if it gives you pleasure, but do not sow it unless you intend to reap the harvest!"

Lucius let Philippi rage without interrupting, offering no defense in his own behalf. His head was bowed and his hands dangled between his knees. Philippi paced and ranted until his anger lost its steam, then he sat on the bench beside Lucius and threw up his hands in defeat.

"I will know no peace from your mother until they lay me in my grave."

Lucius could not help but smile, despite his misery. He kept his head lowered and seemed so forlorn and beaten that Philippi was moved to pity. He patted Lucius awkwardly on the shoulder.

"Ah, well. What is done is done. Do not take it so to heart. Your mother will come around, no doubt. After some time," he added without conviction. "I assume Mariaerh does not know. What then? What do you plan to do? Will Vesta leave Laodicea to have the child?"

Lucius shook his head. "I don't know the answers to any of your questions, Father, except that Vesta will stay in Laodicea. The child is mine and I want it."

"Will you divorce Mariaerh?"

Lucius shrugged his shoulders. "I think for Mariaerh that divorce would be worse than my adultery."

"You could deny parentage. Vesta is not known as a vestal virgin."

Lucius shook his head again. "I would lose the last shred of respect my sons have for me. They would never forgive me for accusing their mother of playing the harlot."

Lucius rubbed his hands over his face and finally raised his head. "As you with mother, I will just have to weather the storm and wait until Mariaerh can once again find it in her heart to forgive me."

The next day Lucius faced a similar confrontation with Merceden which was more difficult than the one with Philippi. Men understood such things, whereas— women! Merceden wept and blamed herself for her failure to instill a better sense of righteousness in her son, which broke Lucius' heart. Lucia was furious and used little constraint in speaking her mind, but

Nimmuo's disillusionment was the hardest of all to bear.

"I stood by your side once, Lucius," she said quietly. "I kept your secret and defended you against gossip and it cost me Mariaerh's trust and friendship. I will not deceive her again. You will tell her tonight or I shall tell her myself, but whoever tells her, this time my support is with her."

Nimmuo left Lucius no choice. He waited until he and Mariaerh retired to their apartment for the night, and watched Mariaerh's face for a clue to her thoughts as he poured out his confession and declared his need and affection for her, and finally his vow to remain faithful evermore, and a cold knot of fear formed in his stomach. Mariaerh's expression did not change. She listened quietly, without comment. Only the pallor that drained her face of all color, and her eyes, dulling and darkening with pain, betrayed that she felt or thought anything at all. When Lucius had finished, she wordlessly left her bedchamber and did not return, while Lucius waited throughout the night, awash in despair and shame.

Mariaerh went to the same room that Lucius had found the night he told her of Pebilus and Thad. She closed the door quietly and leaned against it in the dark. She was numb and her mind a blank. She groped her way to the bed and sat down. She began to shake. Her throat ached and her eyes burned with unshed tears, but she refused to weep. She took a deep breath and tried to relax her body that ached and throbbed in every part, talking aloud to herself in a vain attempt to bring order to her thoughts.

"This should not be so shocking! You knew this! The clues were everywhere, but you refused to acknowledge them. The look in Pebilus' and Thaddeus' eyes whenever you mentioned their father, their pitying, protective, even guilty attitude of late. And Lucius! Why did you deceive yourself by believing his reduced interest in your body was out of consideration for your wishes? You would not admit to the possibility that he satisified his needs elsewhere. Day-dreamer! Fantasy-builder! Do you so much want his love that you are willing to pretend and fabricate where there is no substance?"

Mariaerh was filled with self-loathing. She cradled her head in her hands and rocked her body back and forth, refusing still to weep, wanting to laugh at her own self-delusion, but fearing to go mad if she did.

The door opened. Mariaerh raised her head and saw Nimmuo, carrying a lamp that lit her face and revealed her own sorrow and grief. Nimmuo raised the lamp and swept the room with its light until she saw Mariaerh hunched over on the bed. She set the lamp on a table and sat next to Mariaerh, taking her hand but could find no words to speak.

Mariaerh managed a tremulous smile. "Do not be distressed for me, Nimmuo. I'm not nearly as shocked and surprised as you might think. I've known for weeks that Pebilus and Thaddeus had something on their minds that they could not tell me, but I wouldn't let myself even form the thought of what I somehow knew it must be. Not that their mother was with child, *that* never occurred to me, but that Lucius was seeing her again. I also sensed lately that something was amiss here in the house. Too many sympathetic looks, and you all were suddenly far too polite and solicitous."

Mariaerh's face twisted and her eyes became so filled with pain that Nimmuo was forced to look away.

"It's the child!" she wailed. "Oh, Nimmuo, I want a baby so badly. I try to be so good, to do everything I think the Lord wants of me, and Lucius sins and he gets a child and I remain barren!"

Tears flooded Nimmuo's eyes and she flung her arms around Mariaerh, her heart wrung with pity by Mariaerh's poignant, yearning cry. They clung to one another, both weeping, until Mariaerh broke the embrace and angrily dashed her tears away.

Nimmuo sniffed and blew her nose. "What will you do?"

Marierh shook her head. "I don't know. I know what I *won't* do! I will not hide in my room, the poor, betrayed, embarrassed wife! I will not sever my friendship with Thaddeus and Pebilus and punish them for their father's behavior. I will not cringe from his family for fear they blame me for driving him into that harlot's arms, and," she gave Nimmuo a pointed look, "I will not blame others for my misery and add to it by depriving myself of my friends."

"Oh, Mariaerh!" Nimmuo wailed. "Don't chastise yourself for being angry with me. I always understood how you must have felt."

Mariaerh squeezed Nimmuo's hand. "I know that now. You were right not to betray Lucius, but I have learned a great deal in this past year and I don't intend to make the same mistakes again."

Her face turned defiant and her eyes blazed with anger. Her tone was deadly serious and totally determined. "Another thing I will not do is to continue to share Lucius' bed. I am also not going to be the one to leave the apartment. He can go to the trouble of moving his things and using a guest bath down the hall. You can tell him that for me, Nimmuo. I would myself, but I am too angry and would say more than I should. I will sleep here tonight, but tomorrow I want him out!"

"It will be a pleasure," Nimmuo said grimly. "Lucius is my brother and I love him, but this time he has gone too far."

Nimmuo looked at Mariaerh as though debating whether or not to speak, then asked, "Do you love him, Mariaerh?"

Mariaerh sighed. "I wish I could say 'no' for the sake of my pride, but yes, I do. I would not hurt so much if I did not. I would not be so jealous, so insecure, so fearful of displeasing him if I did not. How I wish that I did not!" she cried. "All that loving Lucius has ever brought me is pain and heartache and misery, and yet I love him!"

She stood and strode across the room, then came back to stand in front of Nimmuo. "You are so blessed with Belden. Never take for granted the blessing it is to be loved and wanted and needed by the one you love. It is too terrible when your love is not returned. I've tried to stop loving Lucius many times, but always I fail. Do not blame him over-much. I think you cannot force yourself to love someone any more than you can force yourself not to love someone. Lucius has tried to love me, I'm sure, but he cannot."

She released Nimmuo's hand and a shadow of infinite sadness passed over her face. "It seems my testing is not yet over."

"Testing?"

Mariaerh shook her head as if to clear it of some unwelcomed thought. "Never mind. Please speak to Lucius in the morning. And Nimmuo? Thank you for coming to me tonight."

Nimmuo embraced Mariaerh and bid her a tearful goodnight. After she was gone, Mariaerh turned down the coverlet and dropped to her knees. She said her nightly prayers as usual, adding an extra blessing for Nimmuo, and asked for courage and fortitude and patience of heart in facing the coming days. She crawled wearily beneath the coverlet, and surprisingly fell immediately to sleep.

Lucius could not believe that Mariaerh demanded that he leave the apartment. Anger, outrage, tears, then weeks of petulant, wounded silence he had expected, but not this! He strode down the hall, trying to dismiss the rising fear that this time Mariaerh would not be cajoled. Of course she would! Despite her many faults, Mariaerh had always been obedient and reasonable. Her past threat to leave him if ever he resumed his liaison with Vesta had only been anger speaking. Her devotion to duty and wifely responsibilities would never allow her to dissolve their marriage, and if that were not enough, her meekness and many fears would surely dissuade her from taking such a step.

He reached Mariaerh's door and knocked forcefully. He did not wait for her to answer, but strode inside and said in an annoyed and admonishing tone, "What nonsense is this, Mariaerh? My feelings for you have not changed. I have no wish to sleep apart from you."

Mariaerh looked at him in amazement. For all his wisdom and learning and love for the Lord, he had no understanding of what took place in a woman's heart. She answered him slowly, forming her words distinctly as she would to a child who had difficulty understanding.

"But I wish to sleep apart from you, Lucius. 'What God has joined together, let no man put asunder.' I cannot share you with another woman. It is not lawful that a man should keep two wives, and I cannot be a party to such behavior. You must decide between the mother of your child and me."

Mariaerh lowered her head and closed her eyes. She twisted her hands in agitation, struggling to bring herself to say what she had decided the Lord would want her to say. Her heart rebelled, but she raised her head and forced the words to form on her tongue.

"You should go to her now. She will need your support and companionship over the next few months until her child is brought forth."

Her eyes suddenly flashed with anger. "We will decide upon a course of action at that time, but for now, I will not and cannot share a room with you!"

Lucius' mind could not comprehend that Mariaerh was actually suggesting that he be with Vesta. He passed over her statement and retreated to her reference to the Law.

"I do not pretend to have two wives, but in any case, you forget that the patriarchs of old often had concubines and it was not considered a sin."

Mariaerh retorted with irony. "It didn't work too well, did it? Sarah banished Hagar and Ishmael to the desert, and Jacob's preference for the sons of his most loved incited the others to attempted murder."

Lucius clenched his teeth in frustration. He should have known better than to engage Mariaerh in a contest of scripture. His mind raced to find some way to regain the upper hand, and after a moment, said imperiously, "I fear you have not stopped to think about the consequences of your actions. What will the family think of such a move? And what of the church? Surely you know that it won't be long until everyone knows you have ejected me from our living quarters. Are you prepared to be the object of gossip?"

Lucius was dismayed as Mariaerh began to laugh with abandon. It struck her as enormously funny that Lucius should think that her prime concern was what others might think, when her heart was breaking because he could not love her and because she could not give him a child. She struggled to control a rising hilarity lest she become hysterical, and finally gasped, "Oh, Lucius! I do not care what your family or the church thinks or says. You obviously do not, so why should I?" She sobered, suddenly depressed by the futility of it all. "It's useless to continue this discussion. If you wish to remain in the apartment, you need only to say so and I will have my things brought here. I can understand your attachment to the rooms you have occupied since you were a boy."

"The apartment!" Lucius croaked. "Mariaerh! This is not a discussion about who will occupy the apartment! This is a discussion about whether or not we continue as man and wife! Do you think I care about the apartment? It is you whom I am concerned about!"

Mariaerh gave him a long, considering gaze then closed her eyes briefly and shook her head. "I'm sorry, Lucius," she said gently, "but I cannot believe you have any concern for me." Her eyes saddened, and her mouth trembled in an attempt to smile. "I would like to believe you. You don't know how much I would like to believe you, but I do not. I cannot share the bed of a man whom I believe feels no more than a casual friendship for me. By doing so I betray myself and all the ideals that I hold dear, and that I cannot and will no longer do."

Lucius' scalp prickled with fear and his mouth went dry. He took a step toward Mariaerh with his arms outstretched as if to take her in his arms, but Mariaerh sidestepped his proffered embrace. Her expression was hard, and her eyes warned him to keep his distance.

Lucius stopped his advance, shocked. They stared at one another, their eyes locked in a battle of wills. Lucius lowered his gaze first, defeated by his wife whom he felt he longer knew.

"I'll do as you wish," he said dully, "but if you change your mind . . ."

But Mariaerh shook her head and his half-spoken sentence hung awkwardly in the air. His shoulders sagged. He made a gesture of helplessness, then turned and left the room.

Mariaerh watched the door close behind him with a mixture of pity and sorrow, yet with a curious sense of relief, and surprisingly, felt no desire to weep.

# Chapter 31

Provincial, conservative Laodicea was rocked by scandal as the news of Vesta's latest romantic escapade raced from the mansions on the terraced hills through the marketplace in the heart of the city until even the lonely shepherd tending his flock in the high rocky pastures shook his head and grinned wickedly, wishing it had been he who warmed the notorious Greek woman's bed.

The entire city was agog. Vesta's relationship to the Caesars assured her the highest position in Laodicean society, and her friendship was courted by every class to insure that her reports to Rome were to the city's advantage. Her every move was noted and commented upon. She set the pace for fashion and new forms of entertainment, and an invitation to her home was a coveted prize. Her flagrant disregard for polite society's standards of propriety had ever provided the gossip-mongers with hours of happy prattle, and the impending birth of her third illegitimate child set tongues wagging at a furious pace.

Speculation over the child's sire ran wild. Everyone knew that the son of Philippi had fathered her sons, and his timely return to Laodicea put him in the forefront of Vesta's many suitors. Lucius' name became a byword in every household, and even the gamesters at the carnival took odds in his favor.

Philippi came to dread going to the baths or other public houses where men of his class gathered, for they baited him unmercifully with coarse, ribald jokes over his son's conquest of the colorful Greek. Merceden was in disgrace at the synagogue. Her Jewish friends snubbed her, while her Gentile acquaintances suddenly became frequent and uninvited visitors on the pretext of commiseration, but in truth to glean any further details they could carry back to their friends.

At first the church withheld judgment, unwilling to even entertain the thought that their overseer could be involved in so shoddy an affair, until one of Merceden's serving girls carried tales that could not be ignored.

The girl, Josephine, had been among the newly-baptized, and had endured considerable teasing from servants in neighboring estates over her devotion to the new superstition. When the scandal over Lucius and Vesta broke, the teasing turned vicious, and Josephine found herself the object of ridicule and scorn. She was cast off from her former friends, and blamed Lucius for her plight. She sought to make new friends within the church by drawing notice to herself and, at the same time, punish Lucius for the suffering he had caused. She whispered into any willing ear that the gossip about the overseer must be true, for what better reason could her sweet mistress have for ejecting the young master from her bed? The Saints added Josephine's conclusive bit of information to the mounting evidence against Lucius, and the church exploded in shocked dismay.

No outside persecution could ever have come so close to destroying the church as did the controversy over Lucius' infidelity. "A house divided cannot stand," and the church in Laodicea was divided into warring camps.

Some Gentile members, native Laodiceans who knew and admired Vesta, could not fault Lucius for desiring her over his pious, humorless wife, and thought he should divorce Mariaerh and marry Vesta, thus giving all three children the benefit of his name. Others wondered, why the fuss? It was natural for men to desire more than one woman. Many men supported a mistress, but that did not take anything away from his legal wife! Lucius should remain with Mariaerh, but no one should mind if he found a bit of pleasure beyond his gate.

The Jewish members cried, "You shall not commit adultery!" but even they were divided. Some, as Jonas and Susane, and Jehul and Rhea, cautioned, "Judge not, lest you be judged"; while another faction, led by Ulai, was outraged and demanded that Lucius be held to account for his actions. He was called to appear before the Elders where he admitted his guilt, but would offer no defense other than, "No one knows the way of a man with a maid," an ambiguous statement that did little to appease the wrath of Ulai and her friends.

Nimmuo was besieged by every group seeking her support for their point of view. She hotly defended all parties involved, refused to take sides, then wept angry, frustrated tears onto Belden's breast at night. Lucia retreated into bewilderment, and Jesua denounced both Lucius and the church.

Mariaerh watched the black, lowering clouds of scandal form over Laodicea with a sense of impending doom, and braced herself to once again face curious stares and whispers behind her back, but she was in no way prepared for the storm that broke loose. She was shocked by the intensity of the Saints' reaction. She gasped in stunned disbelief when she chanced to overhear a heated discussion in which Lucius was viciously maligned and Vesta scathingly condemned, shocked to her very core by the lack of charity shown by those who professed to follow The Way. She recoiled from being the object of pity, and could hardly keep a civil tongue when an overly solicitous friend clumsily offered her sympathy. She found those who burdened her with part of the blame easier to bear, for then at least she could vent her righteous anger. She wanted to flee to her rooms, to retreat into solitary hiding until the matter became resolved, but her firm belief in the Essene creed that nothing in life befalls man that he has not at some time brought upon himself, forced her to brave each day and carry out her usual duties as normally as possible. Her heart went out to Thaddeus and Pebilus who were as deeply affected as she, and she followed their example in exhibiting a public show of bravado.

As the Saints coalesced into bitter, arguing factions, Mariaerh began to fear for the unity of the church. She sought out Jonas, Pathos, the Other Mary, anyone whom she thought to be of influence and wisdom who could bring order out of the chaos, but they as everyone else, with the exception of John Mark, had formed their own opinions and would not give way to seeing another point of view. John Mark refused to take part in the fray at all. His own reputation with the opposite sex was causing him enough trouble and he was not about to champion Lucius' cause and bring more calumny down upon his own head.

John Mark was living with the Other Mary, and was in great demand as a speaker. His travels with Saul and Barnabas had been exciting and eventful, and the church clamored for every detail. The Hebrew members were thrilled to hear how Jews of Cyprus, Barnabas' former home, had welcomed them in their synagogues, and how many now believed in the Lord. The favorite tale of the Gentiles was the conversion of Sergius Paulus, the Roman proconsul at Paphos, and all the Saints gaped in wonder when John Mark told how Saul had blinded his court magician.

Barnabas and Saul were thought of as heroes, and John Mark's friendship with them served to elevate his already magnetic attraction. The unwed maids vied for his attention, and their jealous pursuits led to quarrels and back-biting until even their mothers were combating one another in the contest to find him a wife.

The church was falling into disrepute. The infighting among the Saints caused talk throughout the city. Lucius was an object of laughter and vulgar wit wherever he went, and Gentile mothers warned their daughters against John Mark's Jewish charms. The synagogue leaders grasped the opportunity to issue lengthy harangues over the immorality of the Christian sect, and warned their congregations to avoid all contact lest they be tainted by the sin and blasphemy that invaded their ranks. The Saints had been known for their love and charity toward all, but that reputation was now forgotten and *Christian* became synonymous with licentiousness and discord.

Mariaerh could not bear it. The church had been the focus of her life from her fourteenth year when she had seen the Master enter Jerusalem to the glad hosannas of thousands, and to see all the souls gained in Laodicea lose The Way because of her and Lucius, bowed her with grief. There was nowhere to turn, no one to bring the Saints to their senses, except perhaps, herself. She set aside her timidity and swallowed her pride and innate distaste for the merest hint of notoriety, and determined within herself to set the example for all the church to follow.

Mariaerh made it a point to be seen with Lucius, and addressed him with the same friendliness and wifely concern as she always had. She spoke kindly and lovingly of him on every occasion. She refused to countenance derogatory remarks about Vesta, and cut short every attempt to offer her sympathy. She created opportunities to speak on forgiveness, patience, and long-suffering, on the need and obligation for the Saints to strengthen and uplift one another in times of trial. She tried by the sheer force of the love and reverence the Saints held for her to hold the church together, and she might have succeeded if Saul had not come to Laodicea.

The peak of summer's heat was on the wane when Barnabas and Marcia brought an ailing Saul to the mountain air of Laodicea. John Mark had left them in Perga, a fever-infested town in the low-lying region of Pamphylia, and Saul's ever precarious health had fallen prey to the miasmic environment. When the first onslaught of fever and chills struck, Barnabas pleaded with Saul to quit the area for higher ground, but Saul refused. He had bitterly accused John Mark of abandoning their mission, and he would not follow suit just because of a fever! When attack followed attack, and it became obvious that Saul's life was in danger, he submitted to "God's will" and allowed Marcia and Barnabas to lead him to Laodicea. Barnabas brought him to Lucius, literally carrying Saul on his back when chills and weakness made it impossible for him to walk, and it was a thin, ravaged Saul who appeared in

Merceden's atrium.

Saul was enjoying a respite from fever the day they arrived, but even so, Merceden was aghast. She had always pitied Rachel's son. Even as a child his deformities and abrasive, superior attitude had made him the butt of ridicule and teasing from his schoolmates and cousins, and the middle-aged man before her seemed no less deserving of her pity.

Saul's eyes were sunken and burned brightly, as much from fever as with religious zeal. His bony skull was nearly void of hair except for a fringe of thinning gray. His beard was straggled and unkempt, his clothes ill-fitting, old and worn, no better than those of the rare beggar in Laodicea's streets.

Merceden sent a servant racing to the city to summon Lucius and Jonas, and another to fetch Philippi's tailor, but Saul insisted that he could not stay.

"We will find lodging in the city where I can ply my trade and work for my keep. I do not accept charity."

"Do not be foolish," Merceden chided. "A commendable virtue, I'm sure, but you are ill and will stay here until you are fully recovered."

A battle of wills ensued. They argued back and forth until Merceden simply ignored him and ordered a sumptuous meal to be prepared according to Law, and commanded a sputtering Saul to eat while she readied her finest guest room.

Barnabas and Marcia attacked the repast with gusto, but Saul grudgingly picked at the vast array of succulent dishes. As soon as he declared himself satisfied, Merceden unerringly propelled him to his room where the tailor waited with measuring tape in hand and a nubile servant girl stood beside a steaming bath, eager to assist the poor ailing guest in washing away his journey's dust.

Saul gaped wide-mouthed in shock. He looked about the lavishly furnished room and thundered, "The One I follow had nowhere to lay his head! I cannot . . ."

But Merceden interrupted. "Then he would be overjoyed to see you so well taken care of since he knew the hardship of being without shelter."

Lucius and Nimmuo had arrived and followed Philippi to Saul's room just in time to witness his horrified reaction to the prospect of being bathed by a girl. Lucius struggled to contain his mirth. Philippi grinned openly and Nimmuo fled down the hall to laugh uproariously without being heard.

The tailor began measuring Saul, wrinkling his nose in obvious distaste while Saul brushed his hands away and backed off, trying to avoid him, until he was trapped against a wall.

"I cannot wear finery when I preach to the poor," Saul cried desperately.

"Nonsense!" Merceden soothed. "Who listens to a beggar? I'm sure your Nazarene did not go about in filthy rags."

Saul opened and closed his mouth like a fish as Philippi added, "Perhaps if he had presented himself as a man of means and influence, the authorities would have thought twice and he would be walking the earth today."

Saul's eyes bulged. He shot Lucius an accusing, disbelieving look, then croaked, "You do not know why our Lord was lifted up? You do not understand the fulfillment of the scriptures?"

Philippi shrugged his shoulders. Merceden replied amicably, "This is a tolerant household, Saul. Philippi is a Roman and I a Jew. Our own beliefs are not affronted by our children's fascination with the Nazarene."

Saul stopped struggling against the hapless tailor and closed his eyes as a man reluctantly accepting defeat. When he opened them, he said quietly, "I accept your invitation to be a guest in your house. Clearly the Lord has guided me here."

Merceden glowed with the pleasure of her victory, and Philippi shook his head in amusement, gratified that he was not the only one who could not withstand his wife's indomitable will.

They left Saul to the chagrined ministrations of the fastidious tailor. Saul consented to a bath, but not before he ordered the serving girl from the room. When

Jonas arrived, he meekly submitted to an examination, and swallowed the prescribed potions without protesting. He even agreed to weeks of inactivity and rest, bewildering Jonas who knew Saul's stubbornness well, until Saul asked him to summon Nimmuo and Lucius, and Jonas discovered what motivated Saul's sudden change of heart.

The door had not closed behind Nimmuo and Lucius before Saul launched an angry tirade over their failure to bring Philippi and Merceden to faith in the Lord. He paced the floor, punctuating his words with exaggerated gestures, upbraiding them in no uncertain terms and citing his easy success with his own mother as the example they should have followed.

Nimmuo thought she would burst with forcibly contained rage. Lucius let him rant on until Saul boasted of his easy conquest of Rachel, then laughed, "Come Saul. I should think that your encounter just now with our mother would tell you that Merceden is not Rachel."

"I am now called 'Paul.' I have put on the 'New Man' and it is fitting that I should have a new name!" Saul reminded them imperiously. "And it matters not that Merceden is of a stronger mind than Rachel. They are both women, are they not? and Jews!"

Nimmuo snorted. "Your attempt at bringing the Word to Jews has not always been so successful, we've heard. And if my mother can be so easily swayed, why aren't you making tents instead of living here in luxury?"

"I would be! But it seems I must stay here and perform a task that you should have done."

Nimmuo was livid. Lucius threw her a warning glance that told her to hold her tongue, and she threw up her hands in disgust and stomped from the room. Jonas followed, amazed that one with Saul's mind and learning could be so blind to the sensitivity of others.

Lucius turned to Paul and said wearily, "Have you no tact, Saul? Pardon me, Paul? Do not speak so disparagingly of women when in their presence."

Paul's brows shot up and he looked genuinely

surprised. "I? How could I do so? There is no male or female in Christ. All are one!"

"Your tongue says so, but your tone and attitude belie your speech."

"Nonsense! You simply misunderstand me. Speaking of women, where is your wife?"

Lucius was taken off guard. "My wife?" he repeated dumbly.

"You are wed, are you not? Where is our devoted Sister in Christ?"

Lucius coughed. His mind flew to find a plausible answer, and he stammered, "She . . . Mariaerh is in her rooms. You'll no doubt see her at dinner with the family."

"Her rooms? You do not share a room?"

Lucius' heart sank. He did not want to be called to explain the complexities of the latest event in his tenuous marriage at this juncture, and wondered how by all that was holy he could ever explain it to Saul, but before he could speak, Saul rubbed his hands together in satisfaction and exclaimed, "Ah! I see! You have set aside fleshly passion! My heart rejoices that the carnal man in you has died to Christ and only the spiritual man lives on! A victory, indeed!"

Lucius gulped in amazement and sputtered as he started to refute Paul's bizarre assumption, but Paul's ungainly gait was already taking him through the door, and Lucius sank to a chaise, held his head in his hands and groaned.

Mariaerh did not join the family for dinner that evening or any other evening as long as Paul was in the house. Her hatred and fear of Paul had not diminished over the years, and she had fled to her rooms the moment she heard he had arrived. She was horrified to have him under the same roof, and no amount of argument from Merceden, Nimmuo, or Marcia could persuade her that Saul was not the arch-enemy she believed him to be. She fled to her class at the first streaks of dawn, then spent the remainder of the day in the storehouse or at the Other Mary's home where Barnabas and Marcia were living as well as John Mark.

She would not return to the house until the long twilight deepened into dusk and John Mark took her home.

If it had not been for John Mark, Mariaerh doubted if she could have gone home at all. He seemed to be the only one who understood about Saul. Since accompanying him on this missionary journey, Marcia championed Saul more now than she had in Antioch, and the Other Mary, out of the sheer goodness of her heart, thought the past should be forgotten. John Mark's own memory of Stephen's agony while Saul looked on in self-satisfaction was still vividly painful, and he realized that while his memory was based upon his own eye-witness, Mariaerh was forced to rely upon her imagination of the agony her family had suffered. He knew that fantasies of the mind were often far worse than reality, and he tried to ease Mariaerh's distress by banishing some of the phantoms her mind had created. He explained how in all probability Marh and Jochim had succumbed to smoke long before the flames had reached them, and that their deaths had no doubt been painlessly easy, a simple lapse into unconsciousness, then a joyful rise to the arms of the Lord. He told her again how Stephen's face had become suffused with ecstasy, and how he had cried out that he saw the heavens open and Jeshua standing at God's right hand. Surely death was but a moment of bliss.

Mariaerh looked forward to the nightly walks through the gathering dusk with John Mark. They spoke of many things, of problems within the church, of personality clashes and family disputes among the Saints, of matters of theology, and the different interpretations of Jeshua's words espoused by the various Apostles.

Age and years of marriage had eased Mariaerh's acute embarrassment over any subject that hinted at intimacy, and she was surprised to find herself confiding to John Mark her heartache and anger over Lucius' affair. For the first time in her life, she openly discussed her turbulent marriage, pouring out years of bitterness and hurt and disappointment into John Mark's sympathetic ears, until she felt purged and light-hearted, and at last at peace with herself. She came to think of John Mark as a brother, protective, understanding, unwavering in his support, even when he did not necessarily agree with her. She could say what she would to him without fear of losing his affection or regard, and she turned to him more and more for solace and counsel, never once thinking that their friendship might be misunderstood.

Mariaerh successfully avoided Paul, and he was too involved in his campaign for the salvation of Philippi and Merceden's souls to notice the absence of Lucius' wife. His illness confined him to the house, and since Jonas forbade visitors until he was fully recovered, there was no one to carry tales of the scandal that was rocking the church. Even Josephine held her tongue out of fear of Merceden's wrath, and Lucius gave thanks unto God for each day of reprieve from Paul's self-righteous fury.

Paul was an impressive addition to Philippi's household. His penetrating eyes and deep, resonant voice, and his absolute conviction of purpose commanded everyone's respect. Lucia's children took care to guard their behavior in his presence. The servants regarded him in awe and fled to anticipate his every wish. He fascinated Lucia. Jesua feared him and did not disclose his disenchantment with The Way. Belden admired his ability to overcome his physical defects and Philippi admired his keenness of mind. Although Lucius and Nimmuo did not always agree with Paul's understanding of the Word, they gave him his due for practicing what he preached and for his total devotion to Christ.

Paul preached Christ's *name* during every waking moment. He was a formidable orator, parrying every argument with conviction and finesse until even Philippi was forced to admit that there might be more to the risen Nazarene than he had formerly thought. Merceden was uneasy. "Son of God" sounded blasphemous to her pious, Jewish ears, but Paul's proof-texts from the scriptures could not be denied.

His fervor was contagious. When he led the family in

prayer and meditation, and Merceden and Philippi witnessed their own children speaking in tongues and prophesying, they could not deny that surely the Spirit of God was upon them. They began to believe, and by summer's end were baptized in the *name* of Christ Jeshua.

For the rest of the summer, Philippi's house was like an island of peace in the midst of a threatening world. Every word spoken and every thought formed centered upon the love of God. The world outside was forgotten, unimportant, unreal, their only reality the Kingdom within and Jeshua's speedy return. The specters of scandal and ruin were held at bay, but as Paul's health improved, and Vesta's confinement drew near, Lucius knew that those peace-filled days were numbered.

The days grew shorter. The surrounding hills exploded into a riot of color. Vesta grew cumbersome and anxious, and Paul declared he was well enough to carry on his work for the Lord. He summoned Barnabas and ordered him to find him a room in the city where he could work at his trade and spread the Good News. Lucius watched him prepare to leave and his heart sank and his soul shriveled with dread, for the storm that had hovered so low over his head was about to erupt in full fury.

# Chapter 32

Paul's move to the city caused such excitement that Vesta and Lucius were temporarily forgotten. Barnabas found him lodging at the river's edge where a cluster of small cottages housed the trade of tent-makers, and the Saints ignored the stench of drying skins and fetid litter of Laodicea's poorest section and flocked to hear the Word of God preached by His foremost disciple.

There was no middle ground of feeling where Paul was concerned. He was either hated, or loved to the point of adoration. He was either feared or revered, and his teaching repulsed as outrageous or embraced as inspired truth. He was either a saint or a devil, depending upon the individual view, and there were precious few who, as Lucius, could accept Paul for the man that he was, a man of zeal and dedication with a deep and abiding love for the Lord, yet with all the faults and weaknesses of other men.

The Gentile Christians rejoiced to have a pillar of Paul's stature and reputation visit their church, but their Jewish brothers and sisters, particularly those who had fled Judea, were wary. They stayed at the fringe of the crowds and searched Paul's words for signs of error. They disagreed with him often, and complained among themselves, but few found courage to openly debate him.

For all their suspicion and distrust of Paul, the Hebrews could not deny that the Spirit of God was upon him. He preached with forcefulness and conviction, drawing Christian and non-Christian alike to thrill to the wonder of his oratory. His gifts of healing, prophecy, and of speaking in tongues, awed and amazed his audience, and soon the entire city stirred with excitement.

The crowds grew larger with each passing day. The Jewish leaders became alarmed. They complained to the authorities, then warned their congregations that Paul was an agent of Satan, but still they came, and many went away healed and believing. The Romans watched with amusement. They thought of Paul as a talented magician, and as long as the crowds were orderly and no evidence of swindle was observed, they left him alone and cautioned the synagogue leaders to do likewise. Merchants passing through Laodicea carried tales of the wonderworker to other cities, and soon Laodicea thronged with pilgrims from neighboring towns who came to see for themselves. Laodicea's merchants and money changers rattled their coinbags with glee and added their voice to the police that Paul should go unmolested. Mariaerh avoided Paul at all costs, and John Mark too stayed away, knowing Paul would not hesitate to publicly upbraid him for abandoning him in Perga.

Paul quickly took stock of the spiritual state of the Laodicean church, and while he was generous in his praise for the work Lucius had accomplished in little more than a year, he found much that displeased him. Even though he saw himself as the reaper of Gentile souls, Paul was not happy to see Christian and Gentile living side by side, working together and sharing the mundane details of their lives. He feared that daily, casual contact with pagan thought and custom might influence the church and pollute the pure message and practice of The Way. He would not accept Lucius' explanation that tolerance bred peace, and friendly impartiality opened the door to seekers, but instead declared such attitudes a sign of weakness. He cited himself as one whose faith overcame all fear, and preached that the Saints should happily embrace any persecution in Christ's *name*.

Paul especially deplored what he saw as the lack of

vigilance over snares of the flesh. He frowned upon the flirtatious conduct he observed among the young, and disapproved of any public display of affection, even between man and wife. He chided Lucius for being too lenient with the Saints in that respect, and declared that the church needed a firmer hand, someone less prone to overlook their weaknesses, and who better qualified than himself?

Paul began to preach lengthy sermons on the temptations of the flesh. He demanded that all females dress modestly, cover their hair, and comport themselves with chaste humility. The men he admonished to exercise authority over their wives and daughters, and to set the example by being constantly on guard against any occasion of sin.

The young people resented Paul's interference in their social lives. The women felt he placed too heavy a burden of guilt upon them for the behavior of men, but Paul's more ardent admirers absorbed every word, and not only policed themselves, but also their friends and neighbors. The Judeans cautioned against the dangers of judging one another, and wondered if Paul were not more a hallow Pharisee than a Christian.

Lucius, Jonas, and Jehul warned Paul that he risked losing souls already gained by taking so rigid a stance, but Paul scoffed, "They are but children of Christ, and as children are subject to correction, even chastisement if need be!" and would not be deterred from attempting to bring the Saints to a more sober grounding in faith.

It was inevitable that in the growing atmosphere of watchfulness that someone should point a finger to the overseer's lack of virtue. Paul was stunned to learn that Lucius was the father of grown sons by a pagan Greek who at this moment carried his third child. He stormed into Lucius' office, demanding an explanation, and was in such a state of agitation that one of his fits assailed him and Lucius sent for Jonas.

Paul's seizures were of short duration, and by the time a servant returned with Jonas, Paul was lying quietly on a couch, pale and exhausted, but his body free from spasms. He brushed aside Jonas' attempt to examine him, growling impatiently, "Leave me be. I am all right. It is an old affliction that I know well, a cross to bear for the Lord."

Paul struggled to his feet, knocking away Jonas' hands as he tried to help him, and turned blazing, angry eyes toward Lucius.

"Tell me about this fall from Grace!"

Lucius winced at Paul's choice of words, and Jonas intervened, "Come, Paul! I think this is a private matter between Lucius and . . ."

"Private?" Paul cried. "He holds a sacred office and assumed the responsibilities that go with it. You were entrusted by the Lord to be a bearer of Light, to be His shepherd in His stead, and you allowed that Light to become extinguished!"

"That's not true!" Lucius shouted. "I lead this church well, as you yourself have said. My love for a woman in no way jeopardizes my love for Christ, if anything, it enhances it."

"You shall not commit adultery!" Paul cried exultantly.

"Who shall judge! You? What do you know of human love? Have you ever loved anyone? Has any woman offered you warmth and comfort and gentle respite from the cares of the world?"

The argument was getting out of hand. Paul's face was purple and he was shaking with indignation. Jonas feared another seizure and stepped in between them.

"Stop this! You are acting like children. Paul, I insist that you calm yourself before you are overcome again. And Lucius, leave it for now and resolve this debate at a later time when your emotions are under control."

Lucius flung himself from the room and fled to his favorite place in the hills. The autumn wind was chill, and Lucius turned his fevered face to allow its coolness to soothe him. He was trembling with anger. His fists were clenched and the cords in his neck were distended. He sucked in great gulps of the crisp mountain air in an effort to still his pounding heart and ease the tension across his shoulders.

Paul's accusations rang in his head. Was Paul right? Had he betrayed Jeshua? Did his love for a woman make him unfit to do the Lord's work? Had he really extinguished the Light of Christ within him?

Lucius moaned in despair. Gossip, scorn, and censure from his peers he could bear, but to have cast himself off from his Lord was insupportable. He tried to pray, but his mind could not find words to express the agony he felt. The tension and anger slowly drained away and he sank to the ground beneath a tree and great, rasping sobs tore at his throat.

The storm of weeping passed, and Lucius washed his face in a nearby stream. He drank deeply of the sparkling water, then returned to the tree and sat with his back against its trunk, spent and heartsick, but somewhat at peace.

The wind had abated. The receding sun cast long shadows across the autumn-browned hills. A few small clouds scudded across the sky as though in a rush to find shelter before the curtain of night rang down.

Lucius could pray now. He prayed from the depths of his soul, his heart reaching out to the words of the psalmist to form his plea.

"O God, you know my folly, and my faults are not hid from you. Let not those who wait for you be put to shame through me, O Lord God of Hosts. Let not those who seek you blush for me. Out of the depths I cry to you, O Lord; Lord hear my voice."

Lucius watched the sun disappear and the stars emerge from their hiding place. A sliver of moon shed its weak, cool light on the long, twilight hour. Lucius waited, waiting for that small, still voice that comes not from the wind, nor is found in the roar of thunder, but comes from the altar of God within. He was cold, but did not notice. He was hungry, but did not care. His mind cried out, "Tell me what I should do!" and he waited until at last Isaiah spoke in his heart.

"Though he was harshly treated, he submitted and opened not his mouth; like a lamb led to the slaughter or a sheep before the shearers, he was silent and opened not his mouth."

Lucius got to his feet and went home.

Jonas argued with Paul in Lucius' defense for more than an hour until he realized his effort was in vain. He left Paul, saw a few patients, then went home, overcome with gloom and foreboding. He gathered Susane to his breast, laid his cheek on the top of her head and said wearily, "There is trouble ahead. Pray that the church survives it."

Laodicea busily prepared for the long, isolating winter. The excitement over Paul abated as his presence among the Saints became accepted as commonplace, and the influx of pilgrims from neighboring towns dwindled to a meager few brave enough to risk being caught in a sudden early storm. Paul's harsh exhortations against all forms of intimacy were unsettling, and his popularity waned until Vesta gave birth to a baby girl and the smoldering embers of scandal were fanned into flames of war.

Lucius looked down at the tiny form of human flesh cradled in her mother's arms and wondered how such a small innocent thing could be the bone of contention for so many. What soul abode there? What lives had been lived to merit such an ominous beginning, and what purpose could be attained by entering into a hostile, unreceiving world?

Lucius tried to feel love for the child who was his daughter, but only pity came forth from his heart. He tried to feel joy and gratitude and tenderness toward Vesta, but his passion had drained as unmistakably as had the waters that gushed forth during birth. Lucius kissed Vesta's brow and cupped her cheek for a moment in his hand, and her eyes told him that she too knew their love had died. He turned away, empty and saddened, and went to find Mariaerh.

Mariaerh felt her heart crack like the ice in spring on the frozen river, as she heard Lucius say quietly, "A girl. Vesta calls her Susana." It felt as if a chunk of her heart broke off and scraped through her veins until raw, bleeding pain filled every cell of her body. She did not, could not speak, but only nodded dumbly while her eyes betrayed the depths of her heartbreak.

Lucius began to weep, and for a moment, Mariaerh's own pain was nearly forgotten. She made a hesitant move to console him, then stopped and turned, and left him alone.

Mariaerh did not weep until she saw John Mark and then her rain of tears was so violent that John Mark was frightened and wondered if he should send for Jonas.

"I want a little girl! I want a daughter!" Mariaerh sobbed. "Why does she have it all and I nothing? My arms ache for a babe. My breasts burn to suckle and my womb contracts with emptiness. I hurt, John Mark, I hurt! Oh God, my God! Why have You forsaken me!"

John Mark held her, rocked her, crooned soothingly into her ear, but Mariaerh could not be consoled until she was spent and weak with exhaustion. She lay against John Mark's breast, shuddering as the last dry sobs escaped from her throat. When she was still, he lifted her up and looked solemnly into her face.

"Dearest friend. Only you have the answers within. God does not forsake, not even His son who cried out the same from the cross. He passed through His trial and was given life, as will you, yea, all of us in His due time. In the fullness of days all will be revealed, even the cause of your barrenness, and on that day you will rejoice in His wisdom and mercy."

Mariaerh disengaged herself from John Mark's hold and sighed deeply. She forced a tremulous smile to her lips and said, "I know you are right. My mind says you are right, but my heart despairs and quakes with fear. Can I endure this testing? Will I be steadfast and faithful and recognize His work?"

"Yes! Nothing is given that we cannot bear. Everything you need to carry you through this time is within; you must only dig down and search for it."

John Mark smiled. "You have never failed yet, beloved girl. Backslide a little from time to time, as we all do, but always you are victorious. Each time of testing earns us new strengths until we reach that state where Jeshua promised there are no tears, no pain, no doubt or fear or broken hearts."

Mariaerh grimaced, then said wryly, "How long, O Lord, how long!"

John Mark laughed. He took Mariaerh home in the chill dusk and they shivered against the wind that heralded the coming of winter. Mariaerh raised her eyes to the cold stars and the icy sliver of moon, and said, "A harsh season is upon us. I feel this winter will be long and fraught with misery. Goodnight, John Mark, and thank you. You are a gift from God. Peace be with you."

Mariaerh's prophecy came true. An early blizzard raged in from over the northern hills, blanketing Laodicea in inches of snow, blocking the mountain passes and stranding a few lagging merchants in the city until spring. And it was only a taste of what was to come. It seemed as if the elements were as disturbed and volatile as the emotions in Laodicea. Freezing temperatures never abated to give the citizens a respite from frostbite and cold. Storm after storm assaulted the city until Laodicea was inundated with snow, and to leave one's home was a major undertaking.

The river froze hard. Holes had to be cut in the thick ice for water. Fuel supplies ran short. Sickness was rampant. Colds and raging fevers invaded every house and the elderly moaned in arthritic misery. Death from exposure and over-exertion became an everyday occurrence. Jonas, Lucius, Paul, anyone blessed with the gift of healing, slogged through the drifts from house to house bringing surcease from suffering and pain.

Paul declared that the wrath of God was upon them, and only by turning from their evil ways would the sun of His mercy shine again. His sermons became harangues, long diatribes against licentiousness and sexual indulgences, strident calls for the strictest of moral conduct. The desperate, winter-weary Saints took his warning to heart, and Lucius became the symbol of all that provoked God's displeasure.

Ulai and her friends called for Lucius' immediate dismissal. Jeseuha, Archar, Dorochen, and more, demanded that Lucius renounce Vesta and her child and publicly pledge his fidelity to Mariaerh. Others insisted that Lucius divorce Mariaerh and legitimize his offspring, while Jonas and Jehul and other more liberal souls insisted the church had no right to judge. Some abandoned The Way altogether.

Lucius bowed his head and accepted every angry accusation, every caustic, sneering remark, and every blatant gesture of disapproval and censure as only his due. He brushed aside any attempts by Jehul or Jonas to offer him support. He went to his office each day and buried himself in his work, the only panacea he found to relieve his guilt. He was sunk in depression, had never felt more alone and outcast in all of his life. He clung to his vision in Caesarea as his only hope that his service to the church had not come to an end. There were days when he even doubted his vision, days when he wondered if even the Lord had abandoned him in disgust, and those were the worst days of all. Then thick, black despair would descend upon him and suck the last vestiges of hope from his mind and his soul would cry out in anguish.

He was friendless. Shame isolated him from the company of his sons. Guilt over the suffering he caused to his family barred him from his father's house. He visited Vesta and tiny Susana out of duty alone, and could dredge up no love or joy, no matter how diligently he searched his heart.

He longed for Mariaerh. He hungered for the sound of her gentle voice, for her quiet ways, her wise counsel and her gift for seeing to the heart of a matter. He wanted to lay his weary head upon her breast, to feel her small, soft hand against his cheek, and hear her say he was forgiven, but guilt and shame and the deep conviction that he must bear his cross alone and without complaint prevented him from going to her and begging her pardon.

Mariaerh's heart ached for Lucius. She seldom saw him. He never came to the house, and to greet him in public seemed only to fan the flames of scandal and give ammunition for talk among the various groups. She avoided him for his sake, defended when she could, but her kindness was no antidote for Paul's increasingly righteous sermons.

By midwinter Paul began to preach against marriage. He declared that all leaders, teachers, and Elders in the church should remain chaste and unwed. He went so far as to declare that it was better for everyone to remain in the single state if possible, and that even those who were already wed should live as if they were not.

The Hebrews, to whom marriage and family were sacred, were outraged. The Gentiles, who from birth were taught to revere the body, were aghast, but Paul was persuasive, and the unnatural climate that raged over the city lent credence to his words. Marital arguments became alarmingly heated as one spouse agreed with Paul and the other did not. The joyful, loving marriage-bed became a battleground in many homes, while young lovers argued over whether to marry or not.

Mariaerh took Paul's unprecedented teaching as a direct assault against her barrenness. She burned with shame and kept to her rooms for days at a time unable to face what she felt was public reproach. She turned to John Mark more and more for support, and Belial chortled with glee and whispered upon the cold winter wind that another illicit affair was in the making.

The uncommonly harsh winter bred a disastrous spring. The friendly, life-giving river became a torrential foe, raging across the valley floor and taking with it anything within its reach. The shops of the tentmakers were wiped out. The house where Paul stayed trembled and collapsed and went swirling away to the sea. The city was flooded. Homes and places of business were knee deep in cold, muddy water, and the loss of life and possessions was horrendous.

The countryside fared no better. Every creekbed and normally beautiful freshet joined forces with the angry river, uprooting trees, washing away precious topsoil, tumbling boulders and rocks down the mountain as if the gods played a dangerous game of field-ball. Cattle and sheep were destroyed, and their bloated, spinning carcasses churned through the city, leaving a legacy of stench and disease. Torrential rains added to the carnage, and when it was finally over, a weary, heartsick and grieving city began to rebuild.

The stunned Laodiceans searched for a reason for such devastation. The pagans shook their heads in impotence and laid the cause to the caprice of the gods. The Jews saw the face of God turned against them, no doubt because they suckled the heretical Christians to their breast. The church recognized the first of the woes foretold by the Lord that would herald His promised return, but an increasing number of Saints began to pay closer heed to Paul, and wondered if he were not right after all, and the Lord was indeed purging the church of sin.

Accusations against Lucius grew bolder and stringent. The sight of Mariaerh and John Mark working side by side in clearing away the flood's ruin confirmed their suspicions that adultery again threatened the People of God. It was, after all, inevitable. What woman, accustomed to the pleasures of the marriage bed then estranged from her legal companion, would not succumb to temptation from a man, particularly a man of John Mark's reputation? Mariaerh was a young woman, and the overseer had passed his prime. Could one really fault her for paying Lucius in kind? And what of John Mark? A feather in his cap indeed to capture the affections of the overseer's wife.

When the mountain passes cleared and travel was possible again, tales of licentiousness and immorality flew to Perga, to Paphos, winging their way even to Antioch and Tarsus, anywhere the messengers of the church carried the astonishing news. Those communities also took sides and expressed differing views on what the teaching should be. Gossip, moral outrage, suspicious distrust, and self-righteous accusations threatened to destroy The Way as surely as the flood had destroyed Laodicea.

When Mariaerh heard the malicious tales being circulated about her and John Mark, she knew she

could no longer remain in Laodicea. Her old homesick-
ness returned. She longed again for those carefree days
when she was safe and secure in the love and respect of
the Holy Women. She wept for her mother, then
remembered the softness of Elizabeth's breast and her
gentle wisdom that had once given her strength. She
went to John Mark and asked him to take her home,
home to Judea, to Galilee, to Capernaum where she
would find Elizabeth and Mary, the Lord's mother.

John Mark agreed. He was fed up, disgusted. Paul he
believed to be soiling the Good News with his adamant
case for virginity. Barnabas he thought weak in not
standing up to Paul, and Lucius he deemed a fool for
choosing another over Mariaerh.

Mariaerh went to see Lucius and told him she was
going. He paled, and turned his head away, but did not
try to dissuade her. She said a tearful goodbye to
Merceden and Nimmuo, then she and John Mark
boarded ship at Ephesus and sailed into the sun for
Ptolemais.

# Chapter 33

Laodicea put forth a massive effort to clear the city of the flood's devastation, and by the time the first caravans arrived for the new trading season, no one could have guessed that only a short time before the city had been awash in mud and debris. The tentmakers optimistically rebuilt on their former site and became a symbol of courage and hope, and Laodicea set aside its grief for the dead and its anguish over lost possessions. Cold and misery were forgotten, and the hardy Laodiceans looked to the dawn of a new day.

Lucius made no move to organize a joyful celebration to commemorate Jeshua's resurrection as he had the year before. There were no new initiates awaiting baptism. The Christians had become a pariah in Laodicea, and no Jew or Gentile was anxious to be numbered among them. The Saints were at such odds with one another that to throw them together for a common cause was asking for trouble, and Lucius had seen enough trouble to last him a lifetime.

Lucius had no heart for celebrations in any case. Mariaerh's departure had left him with a depth of emptiness he had not thought possible, and he no longer cared about anything. He felt spiritually and emotionally dead, as if only his body continued to function, and many a time he wished that it too would cease its struggle. He was without hope or direction. His wife was gone and his sons despised him. His beloved church was disintegrating before his eyes and he was helpless to stop it. Vesta no longer loved him and his daughter could not move his heart. He was a failure, as a husband, a father, as a disciple of Christ. All told, he had failed as a man.

Lucius was not the only one affected by Mariaerh's flight. Merceden and Philippi were heartsick. Lucia and her brood were saddened and missed her greatly, and Jesua declared he was right in denouncing The Way. Nimmuo was furious, and placed most of the blame upon Paul, while Thaddeus and Pebilus saw Lucius as the culprit.

Mariaerh's departure sobered the church. Many privately cringed with shame at the role they had played in causing her such distress that she found it no longer possible to remain in their midst. Marcia and the Other Mary wept, and wondered if they should have spoken up and defended Lucius and Mariaerh before matters had gone so far. Even Barnabas, for all his admiration of Paul, wondered if this time his hero were not in error. Susane, Jeseuha, and Rhea felt nothing but disgust for all the gossip-mongers and wanted to wash their hands of them all. Everyone waited for Lucius to take some action to bring Mariaerh back, but Lucius remained impassive and seemed not to care.

Ulai and her friends thought Mariaerh's flight, and with John Mark, was proof that they were right about the relationship between the two, and said so at every opportunity, while Paul declared that both were souls lost and warned the Saints against the outcome of sin.

All the differences of opinion pooled into two schools of thought, those who believed Paul and Ulai were right and that definite rules for conduct should prevail in the church, and those who believed God alone should judge such matters. The two factions argued furiously, sometimes even coming to blows among the men. Families were divided, friendships dissolved, until Nimmuo and Merceden took separate steps to bring order out of chaos.

One bright morning Nimmuo was in the storehouse taking inventory of the shelves that the harsh winter had nearly laid bare. She worked alone, quietly intent upon her task, hardly aware of the two men who spoke in hushed tones on the other side of the shelves until she heard Paul's name spoken and her reed stopped in mid-air and she crept closer to hear. She recognized their voices, Elders, older men who had been married for many years to dutiful, loving wives, Hebrews to whom God and family were the supreme reason for being alive. Their complaint was the same she had heard before, Paul's radical call for chastity among church leaders.

All through the wretched winter Nimmuo had listened to many Saints express their disapproval of Paul's teaching, but always behind his back and never in open confrontation. She had watched the Elders docilely follow Paul's directives, unconvinced of their validity, but too timid to oppose his powerful tongue. She was sickened by their weakness, dismayed that they should have so little faith in their own conscience that they would choose error rather than risk reproof, and as she listened to the sorrow and despair and fear that betrayed the voices beyond the shelves, her sense of justice and fair play was outraged beyond endurance.

Nimmuo waited until the two went on their way then emerged from her seclusion behind the shelves and pitched the reed and tablet onto a table, trembling with angry indignation. Well, she did not fear Saul-Paul! If the Elders were so afraid of that bandy-legged fanatic that they could sit by while the church was destroyed, she was not! She had fought Saul before, and by the Almighty One she would fight him again, and again and again if need be!

She stormed from the storehouse, slamming the door behind her and marched to the river's edge and the tentmakers' quarters. As usual, a crowd of admirers encircled Paul. She pushed her way to the forefront, and the sight of their rapt, adoring faces served to strengthen her resolve and fired her anger to ever greater heights.

She reached Paul and waited impatiently until he had finished a long exhortation, her fists jammed into her sides at the waist and her foot tapping the ground. She wrinkled her nose against the acrid stench that pervaded the area, and thought, "a fitting place for

Saul. The air is as foul as he!"

Paul paused for breath, and Nimmuo seized her opportunity. She leaned forward and spoke through clenched teeth, her voice cold and hard.

"I'd have a word with you, Paul. Privately."

Paul looked up. A look of genuine surprise passed over his face as Nimmuo had never come to him before. He saw the anger in her face, and noted her tone of voice. He frowned.

"There is nothing you can say to me that cannot be said publicly," he said mildly.

"The wretch!" Nimmuo thought. "He thinks because I am female that I am too fearful to create a scene."

"Very well," Nimmuo said with relish. "It shall be as you say. You, Saul, teach in error. You boast of the vision you saw on the road to Damascus, and you in your pride think that one brief encounter with the Lord sets you above all others. Well, I say you are wrong! Your promotion of chastity, your down-grading of women, your absolute audacity in passing judgment upon others is in direct opposition to the life of our Lord. *Never* did He teach such ideas! *Never* did He relegate women to a lower position! Who were His most faithful supporters? Who raised the money for His ministry? Who followed Him to the Place of the Skull while the men hid in fear? Where was His first public wonder performed? At a wedding! Perhaps you do not know that He officiated at His own sister's marriage!

"You preach continence! What of the children Jeshua so loved? Your way would deny entry into the flesh for all waiting souls and deprive them of fulfilling their purpose!

"How dare you say that Mariaerh and John Mark are lost! How dare you pass judgment upon Lucius! Do you know his heart? Do you know all of his lives and the lives of all involved to even guess at the purpose for their coming together?"

Nimmuo was out of breath and shaking with anger. Paul had recoiled from the onslaught of her tongue, while the listening Saints drew together in stunned amazement.

Paul's eyes bulged. His face was white and his mouth worked at trying to form some defense. He was flustered with embarrassment. He never knew how to confront women except from a position of authority, and his furious, daring kinswoman completely undid him. He swallowed, stammered, then finally gathered himself together and said imperiously, "You forget your place, Nimmuo. You are given to hysteria."

"My place!" Nimmuo fairly screeched. "Just what is my 'place,' and who appoints it, you? And don't throw that old charge of female hysteria at me."

The Saints began to murmur among themselves and cast wary glances in Paul's direction. Paul could feel that their temperament, particularly that of the women, was leaning toward Nimmuo. He tried to regain his loss of credence. He drew himself up and glowered.

"I teach what I hold to be true. The Lord Jeshua would never condone lechery. He warned against the fires of hell and the loss of one's soul through sin."

"I do not argue that," Nimmuo countered, "but I argue who shall judge what is sin, what is lechery and what is human love. How do you know that you do not sin by your judgments, by your public condemnations that drive people from the community of Saints? I warn you, Saul! See to the purity of your own house before you deplore the state of another!"

Nimmuo's anger was spent. She turned to go, but Paul called out angrily, "I am no longer Saul! I am Paul!"

Nimmuo smiled. Her back was to Paul so he did not see, but the others did. She turned to face him, and said sweetly, "My father is a Roman. As the child of a Roman, I am well schooled in his tongue. One of the meanings for the name 'Paul' is, 'runt of the litter.' "

Then Nimmuo spun on her heel and walked away.

Within hours the entire church had heard about Nimmuo's row with Paul, and not only the church, but much of the city, since Paul's fellow tentmakers lost no time in spreading the choice bit of gossip. Philippi's business associates chortled with glee and wondered what his notorious children would do next. The fine ladies sipping wine in their mansions shook their heads in mock dismay and said they knew Merceden had always been far too lenient with her youngest child.

The Saints could hardly believe their ears. They were astounded that Nimmuo would speak so to a pillar of the church, and were just as amazed when the next day she went even further and took to task every Elder who in any way abetted the decay of The Way. It was unheard of for any young person, much less a female, to speak with authority to those more advanced in years, and her unprecedented act bewildered and confounded them.

The women applauded the stand Nimmuo took for equal status for females involved in the church, but feared the added responsibility it might evoke. The men were uneasy. They feared a loss of power over their wives and daughters, and worried lest they follow Nimmuo's lead. Most Saints agreed that Nimmuo had shown a gross lack of womanly constraint, but no one denied her courage, and after the shock of what she had done began to abate, her motives and message were thought-provoking. More than one began openly, if cautiously, to question Paul's teaching, and to take a more sympathetic view of the matter of Lucius, Vesta, and Mariaerh.

Paul's more ardent followers were aghast and called for a public rebuke of Nimmuo by the leaders, and Ulai was in the forefront of that movement. For all that Ulai despised Paul for his persecution of the Jerusalem church, she did share with him a common background of rigid, pharisaical thought. Adultery was a major sin; barrenness a punishment for sin. Fornication, desertion of husband and home, disrespect for one's elders, any aberration from prescribed rules of conduct must be dealt with at any cost lest the fabric of righteous living be abolished entirely. She made a convincing argument for Paul's defense, and the progress Nimmuo made to bring peace to the church might have proven futile if Merceden had not intervened.

Merceden invited Ulai to her home, and Ulai readily accepted, confident that a Jewish woman of Merceden's generation would be a staunch ally, and her confidence increased when Merceden greeted her warmly and led to her own small private sitting room that adjoined her bed-chamber. Ulai's eyes widened, and she could not help but nod in approval at the soft colors, and the rich but comfortable and serviceable furnishings that Merceden provided for her own private use. Her eyes absorbed the unaccustomed wealth.

Tall, slender vases of garden blooms chosen for their harmonious colors were artfully arranged and wafted their sweet scent throughout the room. An open cabinet for scrolls, a wonderfully carved, fragile desk, a tall unit that held precious objects, all caught Ulai's admiring eye. She noted Merceden's talent for needlework in the embroidered pillow tops, the thick, knitted foot-throws, and the gossamer doilies that adorned every table. She also noted with satisfaction, that despite the affluence, no human image blasphemed Merceden's quiet retreat.

Merceden urged Ulai to make herself comfortable, and waited as a young serving girl brought a tray of sweets and nutmeats, and a carafe of mild wine and placed it on a small table before them. The girl darted a curious glance in Ulai's direction, then blushed prettily when Merceden gave her a motherly pat on the arm. As soon as she was gone, Merceden poured Ulai a small glass of wine and said in a friendly, confidential tone, "I'm sure you know why I invited you to see me, Ulai, and I am grateful that you are here. As a mother, I am most concerned with what is taking place."

Ulai's defenses began to rise, a fact that did not escape Merceden's watchful eye.

Merceden sat back and smiled. "Believe me, I understand your anxiety over the current state of affairs, but I thought, as Sisters in Christ, we could reason together and come to a mutual agreement as to what should be done."

Ulai relaxed. Merceden continued and sighed sadly.

"My dear Ulai. You must guess how many anguished hours I have spent in communion with our Lord seeking a mother's direction over the waywardness of her children."

Ulai nodded, full of sympathy.

"Nimmuo has always been such a headstrong girl. From the time she was a child, her father encouraged her to speak her mind and to act upon her own convictions. I felt that Philippi gave her far too much freedom, but," Merceden sighed again, "I must admit that had he not been so indulgent, she would not have gone to Jerusalem for Pentecost so many long years ago, and none of us would be followers of Christ today."

Merceden smiled. "Our Lord does plant His seeds early, does He not?"

Then her face saddened again. "Lucius. You cannot know what my son has meant to me. Did you know that we had another son? Antonius was taken from us in his twenty-third year. So young! I thought my heart would break, and I clung ever closer to Lucius for my comfort."

Ulai dabbed at a tear, and Merceden frowned and her voice hardened. "I never approved of his dalliance with Vesta. I deplored his conduct, so much that I did not acknowledge Pebilus and Thaddeus until last year when Lucius returned from Judea.

"Oh, Ulai! All those years that Lucius and Nimmuo were so far away, laboring in the Lord's service! How lonely I was! How I longed to see all of my children's faces around my table again. I am an old woman, and my heart was torn by the thought that I might never see them again!"

Ulai sobbed audibly, and Merceden closed her eyes and rested her hand upon her heart as if the memories were simply too much to bear.

"I was so happy when they came home. I thanked the Almighty One over and over for returning to me what was lost. I embraced Pebilus and Thaddeus, and such joy they have brought to my old age. I know now that I was wrong to disavow them. Forgiveness is surely the way of the Lord!"

Merceden stood and gazed out of a window. "How sad that we do not learn from our past mistakes and must face the same conditions over and over until we finally get it right."

She returned to her seat. "When Lucius took up with Vesta again, I was heartsick, angry, furious, ready to disown him as my son! How could he do so? And this time he had a wife!"

Ulai nodded emphatically and started to speak her approval, but Merceden rushed on.

"Believe me, Ulai. I did not know what to do. I had nowhere to turn. Then God in His mercy sent Saul, Paul to our home. Oh blessed day!" Merceden exclaimed with hands clasped. "Paul brought Christ our Lord into our home. He taught us the meaning of 'Lift up thine eyes unto the hills whence shall come thy help.'

"Much have I received from my meditations, thoughts I would like to share with you as one more experienced and wiser than I who am new to The Way."

Ulai was flattered, and intrigued.

"First," Merceden continued. " 'If your brother does wrong, correct him; if he repents, forgive him. If he sins against you seven times a day, and seven times a day turns back to you saying, *I am sorry,* forgive him.' "

Ulai began to squirm and did not like the turn Merceden's discourse was taking.

"Again, 'If you want to avoid judgment, stop passing judgment.' Both obvious and self-explanatory. It is the third that I do not understand, a teaching of which I am not familiar. 'Nor do I condemn you. You may go, but from now on, avoid this sin.' "

Merceden looked steadily at Ulai and asked quietly, "Is this an utterance of our Lord? And if so, upon what occasion did He speak so, that I may better understand its meaning?"

Ulai had paled. She gazed at her hands folded in her lap for a long moment, then raised anguished eyes to Merceden's face.

"It was when Mary of Syrus, the adulteress, was brought to Him by the Pharisees," she murmured.

Merceden looked puzzled, then she allowed acknowledgment to dawn upon her face.

"Mary of Syrus, now Mary of John ben Zebedee. Of course! The Other Mary has told me of her. A Saint, blessed of the Lord!"

Merceden frowned as if deep in thought, then said thoughtfully, "She also told me how disturbed you were that one who had lived so debased a life should be totally forgiven and even become a favorite with Jeshua."

Merceden's voice was filled with pity. "How difficult a time that was for you." She patted Ulai's hand as she had done the serving girl. "If only we weak temples of flesh could have faith and confidence when all seems at odds around us. I can surely understand how at the time it seemed that the Lord made an error in judgment. But now! Mary of John is considered the holiest of women, surpassed only by the Lord's own Mother!"

Ulai's face was crimsom. Her heart sank and guilt was so strong she could almost taste it in her mouth. She could not look at Merceden. Her mind rebelled against the conviction of her spirit that again she had been proven wrong.

The room suddenly was suffocating to Ulai. The blooms' sweet scent redolent with violets nauseated her. She sprang to her feet and could hardly keep from bolting. She invented an excuse of a pressing appointment and begged her leave.

Merceden saw her to the door and kisssed both her cheeks. "Thank you, dear friend. My meditations revealed that you were the one to bring me comfort and enlightement. The Lord in His mercy never fails those who seek His way. Peace be with you, my dear."

Ulai fled down the terraced stairs as if a legion of demons snapped at her heels. She raced to her own house and shut herself up in her bed-chamber, shaking and distraught. She closed her eyes, but saw Jeshua's face, His eyes filled with pity and love, drawing from her very soul compassion and understanding. Ulai's eyes flew open, but still she saw that face, pleading, beckoning, just as she saw It once long before. Ulai covered her eyes with her hands and wept as though her heart would break.

Merceden watched Ulai's flight, then closed her eyes and clasped her hands in a pose of prayer. "It is up to you now, Lord," she whispered.

She turned back to the house and called for Lucius' man-servant. She ordered him to fetch a basket, then led him to Lucius' office in the storehouse.

A startled Lucius stared as Merceden marched through his door and ordered his servant to gather and pack his clothes.

"Mother! What are you doing? What is the meaning of this?"

Merceden pursed her lips. "You are coming home! I have had enough of this nonsense."

Lucius wilted. He shook his head. "I can't, Mother. I can't face Lucia and Antonius and Julia, or even Jesua. I can't face Mariaerh's empty rooms."

"I did not raise a coward. You might be many things, Lucius Ceptulus, but a coward you are not! I may be old, and you may be a middle-aged man, but you will obey me, and you *are* coming home!"

The embarrassed servant had finished packing. Merceden strode to the door and held it open. She nodded in Lucius' direction and commanded, "Now!"

Lucius was brought up short, then he began to laugh, the first time he had laughed in months. He laughed until tears rolled down his cheeks, then swept Merceden into his arms.

"You are incorrigible, Mother," he gasped. "How does Father manage you?"

Merceden snorted and said loftily, "I manage him!"

Lucius went home with his mother. Lucia welcomed him with happy tears, his numerous nieces and nephews clustered about him, and even Jesua shyly clasped his hand. He moved back to his old rooms, struck to the heart by their echoing silence, yet comforted by the few possessions Mariaerh had left behind, as if they mutely promised that some day she would return.

Merceden visited him late in the evening. She settled herself on a soft chaise and asked, "What are you going to do about the church?"

Lucius looked surprised, then cast his eyes downward and shook his head. "Nothing," he said sadly.

Then he told Merceden of the message he had received that day in the hills. "Though he was harshly treated, he submitted and opened not his mouth."

Merceden considered what he said for a moment, then said firmly. "Well and good for yourself. You deserve everything that has come your way, but I do not speak of you, but of the church. The sheep have scattered, some lost and may never be found. The shepherd remains silent and watches impassively as wolves devour his flock."

Lucius started. His eyes widened.

Merceden went on. "To remain silent and accepting when only you are maligned is commendable, but does one stand by and let friends drown? What did Jeshua do to the money-changers who polluted the Temple? What did He say to those Pharisees who preached one way and practiced another? Unless I am wrong, Our Lord did not always hold His tongue."

Lucius paced the floor and considered what Merceden said. When he stopped, he faced Merceden with determination set on his face.

"You are a wise woman, my Mother. Of course Jeshua was not always silent."

"You must speak to Paul," Merceden urged. "His teaching on marriage and chastity are not to be borne. The union between male and female in the flesh is a natural occurrence, created and sanctified by God, though as with every good gift, to be used wisely and soberly, and with responsibility toward the results of the union."

Lucius flushed, but did not defend himself against his mother's subtle chastisement. "I can handle Paul, but I'm not sure about Ulai and her supporters. I fear I have lost all credibility there."

"Do not worry about Ulai. She is a good woman. A bit rash in her judgments, perhaps, but once she gives sober consideration to a problem, she invariably sees the right path to follow. You are the overseer of this church. If you lead with confidence and authority, the others will follow, for the Spirit will bear witness to their spirits, that truth is being told."

Merceden stood to take her leave, but at the door, paused, and left Lucius with a final thought.

"I would ask Saul if his teachings were received from the Lord. I would wager not."

# Chapter 34

Capernaum was a small fishing village nestled at the foot of the Galilean hills on the northwest shore of the Galilee. The houses were small, either of rough dark stone or whitewashed mud bricks, and the streets narrow and twisting, a maze of blind alleys and dead ends where a stranger was easily lost.

The people were poor. The market stalls were few and ill-stocked. Tax collectors managed to ferret out any stray coin, and the people had little to spend on such luxuries as oil and flour. Fish was the main staple of their diet, and even this modest fare had often to be smuggled home in the fishermen's shirts without catching the managers' notice.

Fishing was Capernaum's main source of livelihood, and nearly every man was employed by rich owners who lived in Jerusalem and only occasionally visited the source of their wealth, preferring to hire a manager to make certain their laborers earned their day's pay and kept their boats and nets in good repair. John ben Zebedee was an exception. The large summer house he had built beyond the city and to the north had become his permanent residence, though he went to Jerusalem often on business matters, both for the church and to consult with his customers.

Mary, the Mother of the Lord, lived with him, as did his own mother Salome, Salome's sister Elois, Judith, and of course his wife Mary. Naomi lived within a few minutes' walking distance in the village with Elizabeth and Adahr, but it was John's house where the Holy Women met for daily study and prayer. Its comparative isolation, hidden from the sea by a grove of trees, and protected by the Galilean hills, created a quiet retreat conducive to spiritual endeavors and shielded them from idle talk and curious stares and possible censure from the synagogue leaders.

While most of Galilee was of Gentile blood or a mixture of Jew and Gentile, Capernaum's population was almost entirely Jewish. They were a devout, God-fearing people who strictly observed the Law and loyally supported the Temple. Many remembered the carpenter's son who had created such a stir. They remembered. His beautiful sister Ruth who scandalously married a Roman, and His brothers, Jude who still lived among them, and James, the holy Essene of Jerusalem who could pass as Jeshua's twin. And of course, gentle Mary, the ethereal, ageless woman who lived in quiet isolation on the shore of the sea. They respected the family, had witnessed too many miracles to discount the Power of God, but neither could the greater number declare that Jeshua ben Joseph was indeed the longed-for Messiah. They reserved judgment, waited, watched to see if He came again as His followers declared, and in the meantime, left His family and friends in peace.

Mariaerh loved Capernaum. It was so like her own childhood village of Ain Karim deep in the Judean hills, except that the Judeans were shepherds, not fishermen. She felt at home in Capernaum. She was more at ease among the poor than she was trying to live up to expectations of Philippi's daughter-in-law or the overseer's wife. In Capernaum she dressed simply, in shapeless, drab, home-woven wool, and no one could tell her from any other woman who came to the market for oil. She basked in anonymity, enjoyed haggling over the price of figs, and giggled like a girl in the jostle to claim the freshest fish.

John Mark had brought her to John ben Zebedee's then went on to Jerusalem, and the Holy Women had taken her in with no questions asked. They gave her a room to herself, and tactfully left her alone to work out whatever problem had brought her to them. They brought meals to her unasked. Sometimes they sat with her for an hour or so without speaking, but their love and concern were as tangible as the bits of embroidery they worked in their hands, and their presence a comfort.

Mariaerh came and went throughout the house and grounds as she wished. She wept without the need to explain why, but there were always welcoming arms and a sturdy shoulder to absorb her tears. She took long walks along the seaside, mostly alone, but occasionally Judith or Elizabeth, or even Adahr would walk quietly at her side. Mariaerh had the eerie sense that each time one of the Holy Women offered her silent comfort, a bit of her burden was lifted away as though each one now carried a share.

Within a week's time Mariaerh felt somewhat restored. The gentle, constant lap of waves against the shore soothed her troubled mind, and the steadfast outpouring of love from the Holy Women healed her spirit. In the hushed serenity of John's house she found herself again, not the wife of an overseer, not the teacher, not the struggling stepmother of grown sons, or the injured wife or the alleged adulteress who fell prey to John Mark's charms, but simply Mariaerh, a child of God. She was still confused, still grief-stricken and lonely, still feeling rejected and unjustly maligned, but the bright sun glinting from the blue Galilee promised hope and an eternal tomorrow.

Gradually Mariaerh began to reveal the events that occasioned her flight from Laodicea. The Holy Women listened without judging, offering sympathy and understanding when needed, but took no sides. Never did they declare that Mariaerh was justified in leaving, but never did they say she did wrong. Nor did they condemn or applaud Lucius, but shook their heads sadly and also shared in his pain. When she asked for specific advice, they answered in generalities, always urging her to search within, to set an ideal, a standard by which to live, and then to compare her actions to that ideal and assure they were in harmony.

Judith tramped through the sand on the shore of the

sea beside Mariaerh and spoke to her about discovering and holding to one's ideal. Judith had passed her seventieth year, and her once glorious golden tresses were now gray and haphazardly drawn to a coil at the nape of her neck. Her ample breasts still rode high and defied her shapeless dress to conceal them. Her face was lined, her eyes a bit duller since Justin's death, but her back was straight and her long legs strode quickly and surely.

Mariaerh was soon breathless in trying to keep up to Judith's pace. She is dauntless, she thought, and soon had to beg her to stop and rest for a bit.

Judith frowned at Mariaerh's plea and cast a critical eye over her body. "Youth these days have no stamina," she groused, but gave way to Mariaerh's request.

The hot sand felt good on the backs of Mariaerh's aching legs. She leaned back on her elbows and turned her face to the sun. She closed her eyes and sighed contentedly. "Please finish what you were saying."

Judith lowered herself to sit beside Mariaerh and brushed the sand from her hands. "Very well, but I think more clearly when on my feet.

"First, you must analyze yourself. What is your spiritual ideal? What is your concept of spiritual perfection, and what is its source, where does it come from? It is helpful to write it down, to give it names. Once that is clear in your mind, test that perfection against various experiences in your life and see if you have attempted, by your actions and response, to live up to that ideal. Let us say that Jeshua is the ideal. When you meet life experiences, then ask youself, 'What would the Master do? What would the Master say?'

"Then analyze and set into words your mental, intellectual ideal. This should include all manner of anxieties, sorrows and joys. Then test them, also, against your ideal. Your thoughts precede action and build your experiences in the physical world. If you dwell upon fear, telling yourself repeatedly that you are afraid of someone or something, when you meet that which you have dwelled upon, you will be terrified. If you constantly think about how miserable you are and dwell upon the cause for your misery, you will be miserable. You can make yourself just as happy or just as miserable as you like, depending upon where you allow your thoughts to take you."

Judith looked directly at Mariaerh and asked pointedly, "How miserable do you want to be?"

Mariaerh grimaced.

"Do you want to worry about everything that comes along? Do you enjoy contending everything with everyone else? Does it give you satisfaction to be jealous of every person you see or every woman who speaks to your husband? If so, you'll be in misery!"

Judith's words stung, and Mariaerh looked away in embarrassment, but Judith patted her hand and said cheerfully.

"Be joyous in the Lord! Love others as you would have them love you. Then as to how happy or miserable you desire to be you create in your own environ. The Lord will not withhold any good thing from those who love Him or love His coming."

Mariaerh mumbled: "I have no child."

"So? They are not always a blessing," Judith said grimly. "See first to your ideal. Search self and discover what you hold dear. Then examine why you so desperately want a child and see if it is in harmony with your ideal. You may discover that your motives for desiring a child are out of step with what you believe."

Mariaerh's eyes widened.

Judith stood. "Think on it. Put some effort forth and not in just feeling sorry for yourself."

Mariaerh watched Judith's long strides carry her quickly out of sight, then lay back on the sand with her hands behind her head. The sky was bottomless blue. The far hills were a dusky mist rising out of the sun-washed sea. Mariaerh closed her eyes and sighed. Judith did not sweeten the impact of her words with polite evasion. "How miserable do you want to be?" she had asked. I am miserable, Mariaerh thought, and I hate it. I shall try Judith's way.

Another time it was Elizabeth who presented Mariaerh with food for thought. Elizabeth was of the same years as Judith, though seemed older. She brought her needlework to Mariaerh's room and they sewed together in companionable silence until Elizabeth finally said, "For more than five decades I have observed the attraction of young lovers for one another and am ever amazed. The attraction they have for one another does not seem to depend upon whether or not their ideals are the same at the time of their meeting, but rather on what they have done in regard to their ideals during their associations with one another in other lifetimes."

She gave Mariaerh a side-long glance and her eyes twinkled. "Whether these have been for weal or woe does not prevent the attraction. Whether the attraction is to be for growth or the undoing in themselves depends upon what is the ideal of each."

Mariaerh thought with envy of Jonas and Susane. "It seems that few couples find the same purpose or hold to the same ideal," she said, sadly.

Elizabeth considered a moment then said, "You think of yourself and Lucius. Perhaps you are closer in thought than you know. Have you ever discussed it with him? Few couples seek to know how they can use their knowledge and understanding to the glory of the Father as shown by Jeshua. I think you and Lucius do this, but as individuals, not as two become one."

"What of Lucius and Vesta? If they are as one in purpose and ideal, then what of me?" Mariaerh cried.

Elizabeth shook her head. "This can only be answered from within by each. Physical intimacy should be the outcome, not the purpose, of a soul answering to a soul. If that intimacy is entered into only for the satisfaction of self, then it becomes vile in the experience of those who join in such relations.

"Have you not experienced, at odd moments, an awareness of a presence of power, a presence of beauty, patience or kindness? It is as the leaven, as Jeshua said. You will find peace, not as the world knows peace, but the peace that comes from the awareness of the presence and promises of Jeshua, that He has chosen you as a messenger, as a light, that you may give strength and blessing to others.

"Beware that you do not stumble or grow faint in well-doing. If you know that there is a mission, work diligently in spirit, mind and body and He, as His promise has been, will not leave you comfortless, but will come and abide with you."

Mariaerh wondered how she could ever live up to such saintly virtue, how anyone could, and yet she saw that she lived in a house where everyone did, and easily. Kindness, gentleness, patience; these women were such. Could she ever be?

Peace! How she longed for it! Peace of mind, peace of soul, peace from her body's ache for a child. But how to know peace with Lucius as a thorn in her heart! Perhaps Saul was right. Perhaps to be holy it was better to remain virgin. She broached the subject of chastity with Adahr who had never wed.

Adahr's stern face softened in reflection. "There are those for whom it is best that they keep a life of celibacy, owing to their circumstances and their activities, but it is more advisable that each individual fulfill the purpose for which it entered the earthly experience. All the desires of the body have their place. These are to be used, not abused. All things are holy unto the Lord, that He has given to man as appetites or physical desires, yet these are to be used to the glory of God and not in that direction of selfishness alone.

"There are many various phases in the development of the body, mentally and spiritually through celibacy, yet the lack of a companion sometimes brings a dissatisfied feeling in a portion of the body's reactions. This must be judged by one's self alone, as to what would be most advisable for the best development."

"Saul teaches continence for everyone," Mariaerh said bitterly, "particularly for those who lead the church."

Adahr frowned. "Well for Saul, well for me, but not for everyone. To strenuously combat the body's natural urges and appetites can sometimes prove to be too great a stumbling block. The expression of love, which is God, is sometimes necessary in a physical manner for the wholeness of the entity.

"It is true that there are problems related to children, related to family relationships, but these should not be a burden, rather opportunities for growth. Speak to Mary, the Lord's Mother, on this subject. There is no one who has combined family and devotion to the will of the Lord better than she."

Mary of John was unwell, and the Lord's Mother was her constant companion and nurse, leaving Mary's bedside only in the hour before dawn when she would walk on the shore of the sea in communion with the Lord. Mariaerh watched for her there, waiting until the sun exploded in brilliant hues over the deep, blue Galilee and Mary began to retrace her steps toward the house. She approached Mary shyly, awed as always by the presence of the most holy woman of all, but her shyness fled when Mary saw her drawing near, and smiled and held her arms out in anticipated embrace. Mariaerh's heart sang. She ran through the sliding sand straight into the safe warm haven of those waiting arms, and her full heart spilled over in salty tears.

Mary laughed softly, a sound like faraway music riding in on the waves of the sea. She raised Mariaerh's head from her breast and looked long and lovingly into her eyes.

Mariaerh's bones seemed to give way. Her heart nearly stopped and she sucked in her breath, for looking into those gray-blue eyes was seeing the eyes of the Lord. She felt an urge to fall to her knees and clasp Mary's ankles in homage, but instead cried, with her voice thick with love and tinged with wonder, "Oh, Mother Mary, I love you so! How I have missed you!"

"And I, you, my child. You left us as a mere bride, and now you return as a woman."

Mariaerh's face clouded with sorrow. "Not a woman, Mary. I have no child. God seems to have withheld from me the gift of womanhood."

Mary studied Mariaerh for a long moment, then said gently, "Perhaps. But for a purpose. Remember, always for a purpose, a lesson to be learned, an awareness to be gained."

Mariaerh flushed. "Someone once suggested that perhaps in another time I abandoned my child. Oh, Mary! I cannot think that I could do so!" Mary sighed. "There are those who must look for lack, for a debt to be paid, a punishment merited. It is not usually so. More often it is a sacrifice, a willingness of a soul to enter under conditions of hardship and sorrow to bring blessings to others."

A faraway look passed over Mary's face, as if remembering. She said musingly, "They forget to look to Jeshua. Was He hung up for lack, for payment upon debt? Did the Father mete out punishment to the Son?" She smiled and briefly touched Mariaerh's cheek. "He came and suffered willingly that all generations might see and know The Way.

"Once He was asked if a certain man was born blind because of his sin or that of his parents. Jeshua answered, 'Neither. It was to let God's works show forth in him.' "

Mariaerh pondered. "My barrenness could be such?"

"Only you can answer. Search within, honestly, diligently, no matter how painful. Be watchful for God's works showing forth in your life."

Mariaerh hesitated, wanting to ask Mary's advice on what to do about Lucius, but shame stayed her tongue. She could not bring herself to admit her failure to one who exemplified perfection in home and family. She asked instead about Mary of John.

Mary's face softened with quiet acceptance. "Her purpose in entering the flesh is ended. Her soul prepares to return to its true abode, which is with God."

Mariaerh's eyes blurred. "Does John know?"

"Yes. It is hard. His heart grieves but his soul rejoices at Mary's triumph. He loves her dearly and will miss her sorely, yet knows one day they will be reunited in the Lord."

Mary looked out over the sea, again seemingly remembering. "We grieve for ourselves. We fear the aloneness that lies ahead, and long for the day when we too can lay down our burdens and flee to the Lord." She smiled. "We must treasure our loved ones while they are with us, overlook their faults, and see only the divine within. Then when the time of separation is upon us, we will have no regrets and draw comfort in the promise of reunion."

Mariaerh did not detain Mary longer. She stayed by the sea and pondered the import of Mary's final words, wondering if she could overlook Lucius' faults. The sun was fully risen. Mariaerh gazed out over the Galilean hills that stretched as far as the eye could see. Lucius was so far away, yet he stood beneath the same warm sun. Did he think of her? Did he feel an emptiness, a sense of being incomplete? Was he lonely as she was lonely? A solitary tear crept down Mariaerh's cheek. She brushed it away and sat down on the sand to think.

By mid-summer, Mary of John's condition had not improved but neither had it worsened. Mariaerh took her turn each day to sit by her bedside, sometimes reading to her, praying with her, but most often sitting in silence. Mary seemed to draw strength from her presence and Mariaerh to draw comfort from Mary's serenity.

Mariaerh watched the process of dying with a sense of wonder, marveling at Mary's total lack of fear, and amazed when at times Mary's spirit seemed to be in another realm and only her body breathed on. At those times Mariaerh wondered where she went and what she saw, for Mary's countenance would become ethereal, glowing with some inner light, and her eyes, while blind to the room around her, would be filled with joy. Whom did she see? With whom was she so obviously in communication? The earthly realm shrank in size and importance as the reality of a greater, eternal world was etched into Mariaerh's mind.

The long, mellow, summer days seemed endless. Lucius, Vesta, Saul, the turmoil of Laodicea, seemed nothing more than a bad dream, over and best forgotten. The house in the grove by the sea became the entire world, a world of peace and love, a safe haven where cares and burdens could not reach, until John came home from Jerusalem and said that James was summoning all church leaders to the city for a council, and Mariaerh's heart leapt as she knew Lucius would be among them.

# Chapter 35

The gods seemed to have wearied of amusing themselves by exciting the elements of nature to torture man, and summer throughout the Empire was benevolent and calm. The sun shone brilliantly every day, while gentle, life-giving rains waited until the cool, quiet hours before dawn to fall lest they spoil the carnival or hinder the business day. Crops flourished. The famed black sheep grew sleek and fat, their wool, the best in the world at the worst of times, was thicker and softer and more shiny than ever from the abundance of tender green grass.

The ideal weather tempted an unprecedented number of merchants to try their luck in foreign markets. More inns and taverns were built. The vast array of exotic goods offered in the growing marketplace burgeoned as a plentitude of coins was available for exchange, and Laodicea's bankers and tradesmen congratulated one another in delight at their mutual good fortune.

The increased number of merchants carried tales of the Laodiceans' hospitality throughout the entire area, and visitors came from far and wide to participate in the games of chance and to test their athletic skills in the sporting contests held nightly on the river's bank. The carnival was a huge success, drawing actors and performers of every ilk to display their talents before an increasingly large audience, hopefully gaining the fame and financial sponsorship necessary to be invited to Rome.

Laodiceans of every class knew prosperity that summer, from prostitutes and the occasional beggar in the streets to the richest owner of a mansion on the terraced hills. A full belly, the clink of extra coins in a pocket that gave access to a few luxuries in life, combined with the balmy, benign weather, did wonders for the Laodiceans' dispositions. The passions of anger, hatred and fear that had held Laodicea in their grip for so long were dissipated. Smiles replaced scowls. Accusations and fault-finding gave way to cheerful greetings and enthusiastic exchanges over the fine weather of the day. The deprivations and sufferings and feuds of the past were forgotten as the friendly sun and starlit skies enticed Laodiceans to thoughts of love, and betrothals and weddings were celebrated weekly, uniting former warring families by a mutual concern for their young.

Lucius took advantage of nature's benign influence to reassert his leadership over the church. He heeded Merceden's advice and abandoned his guilty, penitent attitude and let it be known by manner and voice that despite his failure to live up to the Christian ideal, he was the overseer, the one whose judgments could only be overruled by appeal to the Elders in Jerusalem. He particularly reminded Paul of his authority, and demanded that he distinguish between which teachings came from the Lord, and which were his own conclusions.

He reinstated classes that had disbanded because of conflict, and insisted that each begin with group meditation to bring their hearts and minds into harmony. He instigated a weekly community *Agape,* held at the storehouse where every Christian was expected to attend and leave their differences beyond the door as they came together in the *name* of the Lord. He preached love, mercy, forgiveness, and stressed the Lord's admonition to feed the poor, heal the sick, visit the prisoners, and support the widows and orphans, inspiring the leaders and teachers to labor in a true spirit of service.

The conflict-weary Saints were relieved to have the reins of the church back in the overseer's hands. The Judeans had never quite lost their mistrust of Saul. The

Hellenists and Gentiles found Paul's directives harsh, difficult to integrate into their accustomed way of life, while Lucius, they thought, had a broader view, was more understanding, and took individual circumstances into account when making a ruling. Paul was still thought of as a pillar of the church and was greatly revered for his gifts, but the last word on any question was conceded to the overseer.

Lucius and Paul led the church in friendship. Ulai and Pathos had returned to the church in Antioch shortly after Ulai's meeting with Merceden, and when Pathos wrote that some men from Judea had come to Antioch insisting that only the circumcised be baptized, Lucius, Paul, and Barnabas joined forces against this stricture and wrote to James in Jerusalem asking that those men be recalled. Lucius was more convinced than ever that his vision for the future had been correct when he had first heard about Saul's conversion, for surely now they labored together to bring Christ's *name* to the Gentiles.

By mid-summer the church was again becoming a vital, living force in Laodicea, and was slowly regaining its lost reputation for brotherly love and charity toward all. Lucius knew that he should have been the happiest of men, but his victory was hollow without Mariaerh to share it with him.

Mariaerh was never far from Lucius' thoughts. Healing the emotional wounds of the church meant reconciling Gentile, Hellenist, and Hebrew minds, and while his Roman heritage made it easy for him to understand the Gentiles and Hellenists, the Hebrews left him at a loss. He realized now, too late, how often he had relied upon Mariaerh for understanding of her race, and hardly a day passed when he did not wish he could seek her advice.

The pressures of playing the peacemaker in his heterogeneous church were horrendous. He longed for Mariaerh's sure-footed common sense to calm the anger and frustration he felt, and castigated himself for ever considering that trait as exasperating and dull. In fact it seemed that everything that annoyed him about

Mariaerh now seemed to have been a hidden treasure. When he had regaled her with his grandiose plans and she had failed to respond with excitement, he now saw that instead of disinterest, she had been acting as a sounding-board so that he could hear the flaws for himself. When his anger and self-pity had met with naught but an unsympathetic shrug of her shoulders, she had only allowed him to vent his spleen to one who could be trusted not to whisper the content of his ire into enemy ears.

Such opposites in nature and temperament they were—not unlike Hellenists and Gentiles contending with the Jews—and yet one without the other was incomplete, and it took the talents and virtues of each to make a strong, cohesive whole.

Lucius began to study the Essene teaching on balance, how man and woman function at opposite ends of the pole, but by uniting and working together, they meet in the center to become the ideal. He and Mariaerh were a prime example of that theory. Where he was strong, Mariaerh was weak, and where he was weak, she strong. Mariaerh was timid and fearful, he adventuresome, and while he drew her out of herself and forced her to experience the world, her caution and reticence more than once deterred him from error. Her excessive piety offset his lack of self-control. He knew in his heart of hearts that if Mariaerh had been more tolerant of his taste for strong drink, he might have found himself in its clutches with his mind dulled and his body ravaged as so many others he saw, and his sexual appetite might easily have raged out of control, drowning him in the fleshpots of the world without the restraint of her cool reserve and thinly-veiled repugnance for the marriage bed.

He visited a class being held for the young who were entering marriage, and heard, "The passions of the flesh must not become the primary concern when choosing one's life-companion. Oneness of purpose, oneness of ideal, the complementary balance of weaknesses and strengths, these are those things that make for a successful sojourn in the earth."

It grieved him to think that he and Mariaerh had cast away such an opportunity. They had used their differences as stumbling-blocks when they should have been used as stepping-stones. Could he make Mariaerh understand this view? Could he make her understand that Vesta was only a symptom of the greater ill of thinking only of self?

Lucius seldom saw Vesta. His occasional visits to her villa were nothing more than duty calls, awkward moments that embarrassed them both and filled each with a sense of relief when over. All of Vesta's former passion was channeled into their child, and the price paid for his lust had killed all vestiges of Lucius' desire. They were friends, but not lovers. Their mutual love for their sons would be a life-long bond, but beyond that there was nothing.

Lucius regretted that he could feel nothing more than a passing interest in little Susane, but it was as if the months of scandal and ostracism and pain caused to others had excised any paternal feelings he might have had. He wished her happiness and health, but felt no desire to take part in her upbringing. He wanted only the church, and Mariaerh working quietly at his side, his companion and helpmeet who did not distract by igniting the fires of passion. He searched for some way to bring Mariaerh home, and found that way in James' summons to Jerusalem.

The end of the sailing season was near when Paul, Lucius, and Barnabus set sail for Ephesus. It was a rough crossing. Lucius' stomach rebelled most of the time and his legs were wobbly when at last they disembarked at Caesarea. They tarried a few days with Philip the Apostle, who now led that church, until John Mark came down from Mount Carmel and Pathos arrived from Antioch to join them.

John Mark and Lucius had not seen one another since John Mark and Mariaerh had left Laodicea together. It was an awkward meeting. The gossip and speculation over the relationship between the Lord's young cousin and the overseer's wife had ranged even to Caesarea, and both men hesitated, embarrassed, knowing that every eye watched for some sign that would either prove or disprove the rumors. When Lucius held out his arms and offered John Mark the kiss of peace, he could almost hear an audible sigh of relief come from the onlookers, and he hoped that his public display of affection for John Mark would lay that nonsense to rest once and for all.

Lucius kissed John Mark and said loudly enough for all to hear, "It is good to see you, old friend! How is Mariaerh? Have you seen her of late?"

John Mark shook his head. "Not for a matter of weeks, though when I left her at Capernaum she was well, but lonely."

John Mark frowned and said seriously, "I think she misses you sorely, Lucius."

Lucius lowered his head and said sadly, "No more than I her." He glanced at those who watched, and his brows raised, as if he were suddenly aware that they had an audience. He pretended embarrassment, and said with what he hoped was false heartiness, "We'll speak of it later. Tell me what you do at Mount Carmel."

"What you did once, I'm told. I'm studying the records kept by Judith on the life of our Lord, and am compiling an account to be used for instructing the Gentiles."

"Ah!" Lucius exclaimed. "Paul and I will be most interested to see what you have done. The Lord calls more and more Gentiles to faith, though if James and the Elders decide for circumcision, I fear we will lose many."

Paul snorted and limped off. He had not yet forgiven John Mark for leaving him at Perga, and his rebuff let it be known that he did not countenance a document written by one not constant in the Lord.

The trek to Jerusalem was rewarding. At Joppa and at every small village along the way, they were welcomed expansively by Brothers thrilled to be visited by pillars of the church, and who stared in unabashed curiosity at Paul, a former enemy turned champion of The Way. Lucius renewed his friendship with many that he and Peter had brought to Christ, and gave thanks unto God as he baptized their children and grandchildren.

Evidence of the great famine was everywhere. Dead trees marred the western slope of the Judean hills. Flocks were uncommonly small. They came across tiny abandoned villages, overgrown with weeds and crumbling from disuse. In every settlement the stark absence of the very old and of children newly born bore mute testimony to the disease and starvation and death that had occurred. It was a sad sight, a frightening reminder of the impotence of man when confronted by the forces of nature. The arduous climb over and around the desolate, forbidding, Judean hills increased their sense of isolation and death, and they gratefully descended into the Kidron Valley and approached the teeming melee of life in Jerusalem.

They entered Jerusalem through the Essene gate, the area where Lucius had spent so many years of his life, and he was surprised at how painful his memories were. He averted his eyes at the Synagogue of the Freedmen where the death-knell for Stephen had first been tolled. Veronica's house was gone. His own house, the one he had bought for Mariaerh, was barely recognizable. New additions jutted out at odd angles and a second story had been added to the roof. James still lived there, but it was also the headquarters for the Jerusalem church, and expansion had obviously been needed.

They went home with John Mark to Marcus' house. Old Cleopas was dead, as were Alphaeus and Mary Salome, and Joseph of Arimathea, so many original Saints now slept in the Lord. Josie and Marcus were old, Nicodemus seemed ancient. Lucius wondered how so many years had slipped by unnoticed. Silas had wed young Rebecca of Nicodemus and they now had a child of their own which made Lucius feel as old as Nicodemus looked. Rebecca's brothers were nearly grown men, and Clement ben James was almost sixteen. A whole new generation of Christians was approaching adulthood.

So many changes had taken place. John ben Zebedee had sold his father's home and lived exclusively in Capernaum. Bethany had been rebuilt, but was inhabited strictly by orthodox Jews and was no longer the refuge and haven for the followers of Jeshua.

Some things had not changed. The stench was as acrid and the dust as thick as ever. The famine had increased the number of beggars, prostitutes and thieves, and the congested streets were barely passable. Rome's continual rape of the country's resources left little for the city fathers to spend on repairs and new building, and Jerusalem looked shabby and old.

The political environment had only deteriorated. A self-proclaimed prophet had promised to part the waters of the Jordan as Moses had done the Red Sea. Hundreds of hopefuls had followed him to the river, only to be met by Fadus' troops. Many were slain, more taken prisoner, and the prophet had lost his head.

A riot had erupted in the Temple during Passover when a soldier had dropped his undercloth and desecrated the holy feast by exposing his private parts. The procurator, Cumanus, sent the legion to bring order, and thousands were crushed in the ensuing stampede.

Every incident served to widen the breach between Rome and the Jews. The country was a cauldron of unrest, a rumbling volcano, a festering boil making ready to burst. Lucius shivered with dread and again had the sinking feeling that he witnessed a land in the throes of death.

The council met for a number of weeks. All of the Apostles were there, Peter from Rome, Thomas and Thaddeus from Babylon, Andrew and Nathaniel from Persia, and the others from Galilee and Samaria. All Elders and presbyters who had a voice in decision-making took part. Luke, the Lord's brother Jude, Cephas and Naomi, Lia and others from the City of Salt, Brothers and Sisters from Mount Carmel, and of course, Judith. How could any deciding council sit without Judith! James presided over that diverse lot with a skill that evoked Lucius' admiration, and for the first time in his life, he had no higher ambition. Trying to steer the Laodicean church on a steady keel had been challenge enough, he had no wish to try the same with the entire church.

Mandatory circumcision was not the only issue to be decided upon. Dietary laws were debated vehemently. Standards for sexual behavior were argued for days, a topic that caused Lucius no little embarrassment. Uniform rituals for baptism, the laying on of hands, confirmation of the Holy Spirit, all the important signs for sanctity were hotly debated, finally agreed upon, and drawn up. New bishops, presbyters, and overseers were appointed. Lucius was nominated to the bishop's seat in Laodicea, and the old, worn question of his Roman blood nearly undid him until Peter and Paul and the Elders in the Caesarean church argued in his behalf and finally carried the day. Pathos won the same title for Antioch, and the two old friends celebrated their victory together.

Of all the issues, the most thought-provoking and emotionally satisfying was the congruence of under-standing received through reason with the revelation granted by the Holy Spirit. Not one discrepancy was found. The meaning of Jeshua's life, death, and resurrection was agreed upon by all, and the Saints rejoiced in their re-confirmed faith that the Holy Spirit led them.

The council ended with victory for all of Lucius' views. Gentiles would be embraced without undergoing circumcision. Only meat sacrificed to idols or from strangled animals must be avoided. The sexual standards were vague, broad. The faithful were admonished to abstain from "illicit sexual union," but what was "illicit" was not defined. Lucius saw nothing that would be objectionable to his racially mixed church.

The council adjourned in mid-winter. Most of the Apostles and Elders stayed on in Jerusalem until spring made it possible to return to their churches, but Lucius bid a final farewell to Jerusalem, hired a horse, and rode by himself to Capernaum.

# Chapter 36

Lucius left his hired horse at a livery in Capernaum and went down to the harbor. The wind was strong and blustering and raw. High seas pounded the fleet of boats tied securely to the moorings, making them buck and bob in a frenzied, pagan dance. Lucius watched them. Shivering with cold and hunched deeply into his winter cloak, he marveled at how Jeshua had once calmed those turbulent waters and walked upon the surface. No wonder Peter had lost his courage and nearly drowned until the Lord had come to his rescue. Lucius smiled to himself and shook his head, then sighed and wished the Lord would come to *his* rescue.

He was dawdling and knew it. Now that he was so near to Mariaerh his eagerness to see her had fled, taking his nerve with it. He was shaken by doubt. What if she rebuffed him? What if she hated him? Mariaerh was capable of hate as her attitude toward Saul attested, and he had given her enough cause to hate, God knew.

Lucius tried to recapture his confidence by remembering Judith's and John's encouragement. Judith had poked her bony finger into his chest and ordered, "Go to your wife!" Surely she would not have said so unless she were sure he would be received, and John Mark had assured him that Mariaerh would come back to him if she were convinced of his sincerity. But what if he could not convince her?

James taught that man was justified by his works, but would Mariaerh grant him the time to prove his affection and faithfulness by his works? The thought of seeing Mariaerh's eyes grow cold and turn away from him in rejection made his stomach knot.

What could he say to her? How should he approach her? Should he be contrite, penitent, pleading? Or should he be firm, exert his authority? Perhaps he should play the wounded husband, abandoned, mistreated by an unforgiving wife, relying upon Mariaerh's sense of guilt to bring her back.

Lucius spat in disgust and pitched a stone out to sea. Games! Deceit and subterfuge! To use such childish methods was to build the foundation for the rest of his life upon sand!

The sun hidden behind the lowering clouds was speeding toward the west, and the temperature was dropping. Lucius' ears tingled and his hands and feet were numb. If he stayed any longer he would turn into ice. He sighed resignedly and turned toward the house in the grove, dragging his feet and still mulling over and over in his mind what he would say to Mariaerh.

She was smiling! Lucius' heart pounded and saliva flooded his mouth. Stern Adahr had admitted him to the house and her frown and unwelcoming tone of voice had done little to bolster his confidence. The wait as she went for Mariaerh had been interminable, stretching his nerves to the breaking point, and he had sweat beneath his cloak despite his chill, but now Mariaerh's smile caused a surge of hope to rush through his veins.

She looked wonderful! The bony shoulders and sharp, harsh planes of her face had disappeared beneath soft, pleasing flesh, and the pinched, unhappy look she had worn in Laodicea was replaced by serene contentment. Her mouth was full and tempting, and her enormous dark eyes were peaceful, not haunted by pain and grief. Her hair was drawn back in its usual heavy coil at the nape of her neck, but softly, with gentle waves that covered her ears, and the strands of gray that had appeared since he had last seen her were becoming, giving a look of maturity to her child-like gamin's face.

Lucius wanted to say how lovely he thought her to be, but compliments for his wife had seldom left his tongue throughout the years, and contrarily refused to do so now. Instead he stammered an innocuous, "Peace be with you, Mariaerh. You are looking well."

Mariaerh had been taking his measure also. His hair was completely gray and his beard nearly so. Deep lines grooved his face, and he was thin and looked weary. But even so, Mariaerh thought he was still the handsomest man she had ever known.

When Adahr had come for her, Mariaerh's legs had felt infirm. How often she had pictured their meeting again in her mind! She had trembled, so happy that he had come at last. She had hurried to him, eagerly anticipating his first embrace, and the approval and admiration she saw in his eyes urged her to fly into his arms. But then he spoke, and his words were stiff and formal and his arms at his sides offered no invitation.

Mariaerh stopped, uncertain, embarrassed by her display of eagerness. She was sick with disappointment, then angry at herself that once again she had allowed her fantasies to raise false expectations.

Lucius was shivering, both from the cold and from nervousness. Mariaerh choked back her disappointment and mimicked his reserve.

"Peace be with you also, Lucius. Let me take your cloak. Come to the fire and warm yourself."

Lucius gave her the cloak and followed her to a glowing brazier where he held out his hands and let the blessed heat warm them. He remembered Peter doing the same when Jeshua was brought to trial and wondered if Mariaerh could forgive his betrayal as the Lord had forgiven Peter's. The possibility was heartening and loosened his tongue.

"Capernaum has been good for you. You are quite beautiful when you are happy."

His smile faded. "There have been few times while married to me that you have been beautiful," he added mournfully.

Mariaerh drew in her breath in exasperation. Again he used the ploy of self-blame as a bid for sympathy! She would not be taken in this time, nor absolve him by refuting his words. She did not answer him, but raised her eyes to his in an expression of candid agreement.

Lucius flushed. He lowered his gaze and concentrated on warming his hands, not knowing what next to say. An awkward silence ensued until Mariaerh said in a conversational tone, "I am surprised to see you. I had thought you had no doubt returned to Laodicea before the sea closed for the season. Will you stay in Judea until spring?"

An angry knot twitched in Lucius' cheek. Mariaerh's casual tone riled him. She spoke as if he were merely an acquaintance, not a husband whom she had not seen for months. She could have at least expressed some pleasure at seeing him again, and her assumption that he would return to Judea seemed to suggest he would not be welcome in Galilee. He answered her shortly, unable to hide his pique.

"No. I intend to stay in Capernaum. This separation is intolerable. I want to come to an understanding with you and reconcile our differences. If you do not want me to stay here, then I will stay with Naomi and Cephas."

Mariaerh's own anger rose. She did not mean to imply that he was not welcome. Why did he always read meanings into her words that were not there! She clenched her hands and made an extreme effort to keep an even tone and not provoke a quarrel in the first moments of their meeting.

"Our differences are many, Lucius," she said quietly. "It will take great effort on both our parts to come to agreement. It might be wise for you to stay with Cephas. When you and I are together for any length of time we invariably quarrel."

Their eyes locked in hostility across the brazier, each thinking the situation to be hopeless until Lucius diverted his eyes first and let his hands drop to his side. He could not let his mission fail so quickly, even though it galled him to concede to Mariaerh's stubbornness.

"You are right," he relented. "We are together less than an hour and already we quarrel."

He left the warmth of the brazier and began to pace. "Why do we quarrel so? Before I came here I thought I knew. I thought I had discovered the root of our mis-understanding. I thought I would come here and explain my insight and all would be well and you would come home and be my wife as before."

"It's not that simple, Lucius. I cannot be your wife 'as before.' There must be a new understanding to replace the old mis-understanding." She went to a divan and sat down. "Explain to me these 'insights'."

Lucius faltered, not knowing how to begin, then awkwardly tried to tell her of his studies on the Essene teaching of balance. His confidence grew as he spoke and he became carried away by his own rhetoric. Soon he was striding back and forth, gesturing widely, emphasizing important points by counting them off on his fingers.

Mariaerh contained her mirth as long as she could, then burst into laughter. Lucius broke off in mid-sentence and stared in amazement, wondering what she could possibly find so comical. Mariaerh put her hand over her mouth to stifle her glee and said contritely, "I'm sorry, Lucius, but you look like a grand orator holding forth in the library at Alexandria!" She sobered. "Sit down. I am your wife. You are not teaching a class. Can you imagine Jonas speaking so to Susane, or Philippi to Merceden? I am the one you should be most at ease with, yet I am the one you treat with the most formality. Why can't you be yourself with me? Why must you always use such an imperious, authoritative tone with me and treat me like a wayward student?"

Lucius did as she bid and sat beside her, shaking his head in bewilderment. "I don't know. But you are right, I do."

"You have two sets of behavior, one for me and another for your family and friends. I watch you with others and my heart swells with admiration and affection for the kindness and wisdom and under-standing you display, but when I need those same qualities from you, I receive only cold disapproval. I have watched you minister to someone stricken with grief, and you are wonderful, and yet when my mother and father were taken from me, you acted as though I should be able to brush it aside and continue on as if nothing had happened. I was devastated, Lucius! I needed you!" she cried.

Lucius stared, open-mouthed. "You didn't need me," he sputtered. "You rebuffed my every attempt to comfort you. You even refused my touch!"

"And instead of understanding the depths of my grief that provoked that behavior, you fled in self-pity to the arms of another!" Mariaerh shot back.

Lucius gasped and his eyes widened.

"Oh, I knew, Lucius," Mariaerh said bitterly. "I knew about them all."

Lucius rubbed his face with his hand. "I thought you blamed me for Marh's and Jochim's deaths. You said if you had been there you might have saved them, and I was the one who insisted that we live in Jerusalem."

"I never held you at fault," Mariaerh said sadly. "I think you held yourself at fault."

"Then why wouldn't you allow my touch if not to punish me?"

Mariaerh was dismayed. She tried to explain. "Grief knows no logic or reason, only feelings. I've thought long about this and I think somewhere deeply embedded in my mind was the irrational notion that since the union between man and wife was life-creating, it would be unconscionable for me to be a party to that union when my parents had suffered such a horrible death."

Mariaerh's eyes and voice were pleading. "Can you understand that, Lucius? Even though I explain it so badly?"

Lucius took her hand, moved by the grief and pain he heard in Mariaerh's voice even after all of these years. "I think so, though such a thing would never have occurred to me. Perhaps you are right about my own unadmitted guilt. I needed your welcoming arms to expiate my sins and relieve me of responsibility for their deaths."

They were quiet for a long moment. Lucius played idly with Mariaerh's hand, and her nearness stirred his blood. He said quietly, musingly, "Do you remember the first time we made love on the Mount of Olives? We promised then to be open and truthful with one another. We never kept that promise, did we?"

Mariaerh turned to face him and said sadly, "How could we, Lucius? Even as you mouthed such high aspirations you were lying by omission. You should have told me then about Vesta and your sons."

Lucius dropped her hand, defensive. "And what would you have said? You can be sure there would have been no passionate embrace on that day!"

"No, probably not. I would have been hurt and angry. But I was so young, Lucius! I would have accepted it eventually, and all the following days could have been built upon honesty. I would have known that going to Laodicea meant meeting your sons. Think how you would feel if after sixteen years of marriage you were suddenly confronted with sons of mine you never knew existed! Would you have so easily forgiven me?"

Her reasoning escaped Lucius' understanding. "You are a woman," he said in disgust. "You can't use that analogy as a comparison."

"I can!" Mariaerh cried. "You belie your faith if you say otherwise! God is no respecter of persons. What is a sin for me is a sin for you. And what of Vesta! Why can she fornicate and still earn your love, where if I did the same you would have me stoned for adultery!"

Lucius was saved from answering by John's mother who came to invite them to the evening meal. The room had darkened without their notice. The light from the brazier threw long shadows against the wall and mercifully hid their anger from Salome's curious glance. They postponed their quarrel and followed Salome into another room where the rest of the household already reclined.

The Lord's mother greeted Lucius lovingly, causing his eyes to blur and his heart to flutter, for the emotion she evoked surpassed any other in depth and awe. Elizabeth enfolded him to her ample breast and bid him welcome, and he met for the first time John's aunt, Elois, an aging, angular woman who unabashedly studied him with amused curiosity until Lucius squirmed in discomfort and wondered what Mariaerh had told them all. Even Adahr attempted a rusty, crooked smile that seemed more like a grimace, then Mariaerh led him to his place at the table.

Lucius saw the cup and loaf on the table in front of him and hesitated to take that place. His quarrel with Mariaerh had reminded him of his many sins, and he was loath to perform the blessing with his soul in such disorder, particularly for the Lord's own mother! But Mary asked him to preside, and he could not refuse. His hands trembled as he reached for the loaf. His mouth was dry and his throat seemed to close. He took the loaf and closed his eyes, silently implored the Lord's forgiveness, then struggled to still his mind and body, to banish every thought and allow only that pure, innocent, spark of the Divine to speak.

He quieted. His body relaxed. His hands ceased trembling and his throat opened. His thoughts receded and his mind turned inward, waiting for that small, still voice to announce the Lord's coming.

A stillness pervaded the room. The angry sea and rushing wind seemed suddenly to calm. He raised the loaf and opened his eyes, meeting Mary's across the board, blue-gray eyes that were the Lord's own. His soul melted into peace. He blessed the bread, then the wine, ate and drank, then passed it on to the others. His spirit expanded, blending and mingling with those of the Holy Women until they became as one soul and spirit, the mystery of Soul communing with its Lord.

Lucius never forgot that first meal he ate in Mary's house. Gentle female voices caressed his soul. The Blessed Mother's love was ineffable, like wisps of mist, a fleeting touch, a penetrating shock, a healing, soothing bath of holiness that retuned every nerve and cell until he seemed to blend and flow as one with All. He was moved to his depths. A lump of unidentifiable emotion stopped his food in his throat and he toyed with the contents of his bowl. Heaven on earth, he thought, a holy place, and holy women, and Mariaerh is one.

He watched Mariaerh. She was at ease and happy. Her eyes were like deep, dark pools of bliss. Her olive skin glowed in the lamplight, and her laughter was like birdsong at first morning's light.

Lucius swallowed and turned his eyes away, shaken, humbled, then near to despair. Saul-Paul was wrong, he himself was wrong, all the men who believed that women were inferior and could not raise to the heights of sanctity like men were wrong. Jeshua knew! He loved the women, depended upon them, turned to them for comfort and ease. Who made a haven of rest for the Lord? Not men! By what channel did He choose to enter the earth? Not by man! The Lord gave strength and power to men, but women gave strength to the Lord.

Lucius was on the verge of weeping and it horrified him. What would these Saints of the Lord think if he were suddenly to burst into tears? He struggled to keep his composure and was losing the battle when he felt a gentle pressure on his arm and heard Mariaerh say, "Excuse us, please, Mary. Lucius' journey has tired him. See? He does not even eat. I will show him where he can sleep for the night."

The women murmured in consolation and bade him goodnight. Mariaerh took a candle and helped Lucius to his feet. He stumbled, blinded by unshed tears, and followed the flickering light to a tiny alcove in the back of the house.

Mariaerh lit a lamp with the candle, then made up the bed that was nothing more than a straw mat on the floor, saying as she worked, "It's a normal reaction to this house, Lucius. Weep. It will heal and refresh you. Jeshua knew the curative powers of tears. It is not unmanly."

She finished spreading a coverlet on the mat, then straightened and raised to her toes and kissed him fleetingly on the mouth, then quickly disappeared into the shadows.

Lucius collapsed on the mat. He sat doubled nearly in two, rocking back and forth. The tears flowed freely, seeping through his fingers that covered his eyes, running down the backs of his hands and soaking his beard. He tried not to sob aloud, but did not always succeed. His shoulders shuddered and his throat and chest ached to bursting.

When his wellspring of tears ran dry, Lucius fell back on the mat in weary exhaustion. He felt purged, renewed, and inexplicably happy. He was drained and empty and overwhelmingly sleepy. He sprawled on his back and his last thoughts were, "I was blind, and You opened my eyes. I walked in the stubbornness of my own heart, and You showed me my error. I slept, and You awakened my soul. Blessed be the Lord forever and ever." Then he slept.

# Chapter 37

The wind changed during the night, blowing across the Sea of Galilee from the desert lands to the east, warm and laden with moisture. The distinctive aroma of the harp-shaped lake seeped through the lone, loosely shuttered window of the small alcove where Lucius slept, and he stirred, straining to surface from a deep, leaden sleep.

He was hot and sweaty. He had fallen asleep fully clothed, even to his sandals, and some time during the night he had chilled and rolled himself in a thick coverlet without even waking. Now he panicked. He was disoriented and confused and for a moment thought he was bound head to foot. The coppery taste of fear flooded his mouth. He fought against the blanket, kicking his feet and flailing his arms until suddenly he was free and awake and ashamed of his senseless terror.

He staggered to his feet and moaned aloud as a sharp pain raced down his back, and every muscle in his body protested against sleeping on a thin, straw mat. His eyes burned. His mouth felt as if it were filled with fleece, and tasted the same. He stumbled through the dark to the window and threw open the shutter and gasped in amazement at the warm, moist air that rushed past his face.

Memory of the night before invaded his mind and he moaned again. The house was silent. He could hear the lap of the waves against the shore, and wondered if he could find his way out of the house without causing a disturbance. He stank and wanted a bath, and the last thing he wanted was to see Mariaerh. He ran his hands along the window frame, measuring the opening, then hoisted himself up to the sill and squeezed through, praying to God that he would not get stuck and be forced to call for help, then dropped to the ground with a muted thud.

The gray pre-dawn provided more than enough light to see by, and Lucius slipped easily through the grove until he emerged on the shore where he stripped and plunged into the sea, crying aloud at the shock of icy water that assaulted his flesh. He swam into the waves, forcing his muscles to unknot and stretch and forget the hard mat, until he began to tire and headed back to shore.

He stumbled from the sea shivering and covered with gooseflesh. He dried himself with his shirt, then put it on, even though it was damp and offered scant protection from the chill. He pulled on the remainder of his clothes, trying to keep his balance in the sliding sand, then sat on the sand and pushed his bare feet deep into its warmth. He felt wonderful, refreshed and clean and mentally alert.

Lucius breathed deeply of the fresh sea air. Tiny flashes of silver danced on the water. A faint blush of pink stained the far horizon, deepening to lavender and mauve as it seeped across the sky, followed by vertical shafts of gold until the first brilliant view of the sun emerged from the sea.

Lucius squinted his eyes into narrow slits and saw the first of the fishermen putting out to sea. He thought of the days in his youth when he too had gone to sea at dawn's first light, back-breaking work that his young body had relished, and now, he thought ruefully, that same body complained of a night spent on a straw mat!

His stomach rumbled, reminding him that he had not eaten the night before. The east wind had deceived him, warm only when compared to the northerly gale of the day before, and he was beginning to shiver again. He wanted food, and shelter from the cold, but he was reluctant to go back to the house and face Mariaerh.

The memory of their quarrel made him wince and he

tried to push it out of his mind, but the look in Mariaerh's eyes when she had cried, "I needed you!" persisted in haunting him. He had expected to quarrel. He had been prepared for anger, tears, and recriminations over Vesta, but the pain and despair and heart-rending sorrow Mariaerh had laid bare at his feet had completely undone him. How could he have been so blind to another's need? His affair with Vesta had only been the last of a long chain of failures in regard to his wife, and if he had so failed her, how many others had he failed? The image he held of himself as one who like the Master served as a shepherd to his flock was shattered.

When Lucius could not bear his thoughts any longer, he got up from the sand and started walking down the shore, carrying his sandals by the latchets. He could not stay sitting on the sand forever, and he could not go back to the house, but the day stretched out before him, and he had to find some way to occupy the time. Perhaps he would seek out Cephas and offer to help in the Capernaum church. The Elect were always delighted to receive visiting dignitaries, and as a newly-named bishop, his welcome was assured.

Lucius stopped in mid-stride. Bishop! He had forgotten! He dropped his head back and laughed at the sky, a rueful, bitter sound. How he had longed to hold a position of prestige in the church! He could still feel the sharp disappointment he had felt when the Jerusalem church had passed him by as a deacon, and now at long last when he had achieved his heart's desire, it meant so little that he had completely forgotten it!

He turned and looked back toward the grove. He had not even told Mariaerh! He began to hurry toward the house, then stopped again.

Mariaerh would not be impressed. Bishop or Elder or the poorest of the poor made no difference to her; they were all one and the same. "God is no respecter of persons," she had said.

Lucius ran his hand through his hair in a gesture of despair. If only he could turn time back and begin again! But where to begin? In Antioch by telling her of

Vesta and his sons? In Jerusalem when first they had met? Or even before when Merceden had signed the marriage contract between a pubescent boy and a babe in arms?

He shook his head at the last. For all their misunderstandings, their assumptions made about one another's motives and thoughts, their many quarrels and unrealized expectations, he would not wish never to have known nor wed Mariaerh. Seeing her last night, happy, carefree, basking in the unconditional love of the Holy Women had moved him so deeply he had thought his heart would break with the burden of knowledge that never had he evoked such happiness in Mariaerh.

Lucius bent and put on his sandals and continued walking toward Capernaum. His shoulders were hunched and his eyes were focused on the sand. He was despondent and struggled to keep from falling into a morass of self-pity. The sound of human voices caused him to raise his head and he saw Cephas' house in the distance and veered direction, no longer wanting to see or speak to anyone. He let his feet take him where they might, entering the town and wandering through the marketplace. The booths and shops were already opened, and luscious odors tantalized his belly and made it roar, but he had left his money-pouch in his room and could buy nothing to appease his hunger. The closely huddled houses shaded the street from the warmth of the sun, and he slipped into the synagogue for a respite from the cold.

The two-storied synagogue faced the sea, with the roof extending out over the massive double doors to form a covered porch where God-fearers and curious Gentiles gathered to listen. The windows were high and narrow, and those to the east were behind the women's balcony and shaded by the porch roof. Lucius paused to let his eyes become accustomed to the gloom, then walked beneath the balcony into the men's cavernous hall.

It was eerily quiet. The early-morning worshippers had gone about the business of earning their daily bread and the synagogue was deserted. Lucius' footsteps echoed in the silence, and his nose wrinkled at the acrid smell of burned candles and incense. His eyes swept the soaring ceiling, the thick stone walls, across the wrought-iron balcony rail, then to the far end where burning lamps cast their flickering light on the Ark of the Torah.

Lucius had been there before in those long-ago days when first he had come to Capernaum and had heard Jeshua preach in this very hall. He could almost hear Him now, His clear, authoritative voice ringing out over the angry voices of dissension that murmured "blasphemer!" It was here that Jeshua proclaimed Isaiah's prophecy to be fulfilled. It was here that He had healed the man with a withered hand and had called a demon to come forth from another. It was here that the tide against Him may have begun.

Lucius was suddenly struck with the same foreboding sense of doom that he had felt in Jerusalem, a crushing burden of sorrow as if a massive weight had dropped upon his shoulders. He broke out into a cold sweat. His heart pounded and the blood rushed to his head. He fled to the street and let himself be borne along by the press of women making their daily trek to the market. He was shaking and sickened, gripped by cold dread. What would happen to his mother's people? Why did he feel with such certainty that he walked in a nation doomed?

He retraced his steps, hurrying, almost at a trot back toward the house in the grove, assailed by an overpowering need to see Mariaerh, the Holy Women, to be reassured of hope and the future. He arrived at the gate breathless, gasping for air and trembling from exertion. He leaned against the gate until he regained his composure, then went in search of his wife and something to eat.

Mariaerh greeted him as though nothing unusual had occurred the night before. Their quarrel was not mentioned, and Lucius' emotional collapse was ignored. She served him his meal as she had always done, and no one who did not know better would ever have guessed they had been separated for months.

They did not talk privately for a number of days. Judith and John came home from Jerusalem. Jude was in and out of the house on a continual basis to visit his mother, and all of the Apostles who spread the Good News throughout Galilee came often to confer with John and Judith and the Lord's Blessed Mother. Lucius quickly learned that the serenity of the house was not due to a lack of activity. Cephas and Naomi made almost daily visits, and Elizabeth and Adahr seemed to divide their time between John's house and Naomi's. Messengers arrived regularly with letters and news from every outpost, and Saints throughout all of Palestine came to sit for awhile with Mary of John, praying with her and for her, knowing that soon she would sleep in the Lord. The head of the church might be in Jerusalem, but the heart and soul was in the house by the sea.

It was just as well that Lucius and Mariaerh found no time to be alone. Lucius needed time to think, to examine his feelings and to ponder the lessons he learned while living in that house. For the first time in his life he was free of responsibilities. No one made demands on his time. No one insisted that he plan, organize, solve their problems, judge their disputes or ease their griefs, and he used that time to further his own spiritual growth. He kept a daily account of his thoughts, examining his feelings and motives in the harsh light of the written word. He entered his dreams, trying to learn from the depth of his being just where his true self lay. He had long talks with Judith that he recorded in the journal, talks that humbled and moved him to tears as she taught him the mysteries, the pearls that Jeshua warned not to be thrown to swine, and sometimes he would be so overcome that he fled to the sea in sheer wonder and joy as his heart cried aloud the words of the prophet, "O God, what is man that you should be mindful of him?"

Each morning Lucius went to the sea to enter the silence and commune with his Lord, and never before had his meditations borne such fruit. The expanse of the sea and the gentle lap of the waves on the shore would lull him into a deeper state of silence than ever before, and it seemed that his entire body responded in joy. One morning he had emerged from his closet of prayer and saw Mary standing far down the shore with her arms upraised and her face upturned to welcome the day. He watched, awed by the picture she made, then the mist rising up from the sea played tricks on his eyes, and he imagined he saw two figures outlined against the sky, two red-gold heads that caught the rays of the rising sun, but no doubt it was only an illusion, a mirror effect in the magic of dawn.

As Lucius turned ever inward, his sense of closeness to the Master increased with each passing day. At first he attributed that sense of nearness to the fact that he was in Jeshua's beloved Galilee, treading the same sand that the Master had trod, looking over the sea that He had so loved, wandering through the town where He had lived and preached and begun the long road toward His destiny. But Lucius slowly came to understand that it was not the place, it was his own soul that drew nearer to Christ. He could see it by reading his journal. He could see the subtle changes in attitude and thought taking place. His feelings were changed. His outlook was different. Things that had once mattered so much to him now seemed inconsequential, and things that he had formerly overlooked or considered of little value, he now began to cherish. It was exhilarating but also frightening to watch the old, familiar, comfortable self slowly fade away and a new, unknown, unpredictable self emerge.

Old habits of behavior were not so easily discarded. Lucius would spontaneously react to Mariaerh in his former manner, even though her words and actions no longer evoked the same emotions and thoughts. While his heart and mind urged a new response, his tongue and body stubbornly refused to obey.

They were awkward with one another. Lucius fumbled to express his new opinions and feelings, and Mariaerh warily wondered if he employed some new ruse only to win her confidence and then, when she had conceded, to once again dash all her hopes and dreams.

They were fearful of provoking a quarrel and so often retreated into the safety of silence, strained, uncomfortable moments when each wondered what the other was thinking but both were too timid to ask. They skirted subjects that they feared might give rise to the other's anger, until the tension and frustration became unbearable and exploded into the very quarrel they had tried so hard to avoid.

"You were never a wife to me!" Lucius shouted. "You cringed every time I came near you and when I turned to another for warmth and comfort, you called me adulterer!"

"You only came to me out of lust!" Mariaerh cried. "You didn't want *me,* you only wanted a body, any body, and I was just convenient!"

"That's not true!"

"Then why didn't you give me some indication of your feelings? The only time you ever spoke to me was to criticize, to show your disapproval of everything I did and said. The only time I ever felt as if you cared for me was at Naomi's wedding, and then you spoiled it all by flaunting your lust for Celicia!"

The quarrel was vicious. Each dredged up every hurt and resentment they had nursed for years, flinging accusations and insults at each other, shouting and flailing their arms until sheer exhaustion brought the battle to an end. Mariaerh was in tears. Lucius was sickened, shocked by the bitterness they had both revealed, and nearly despairing that they could ever right the many wrongs they had imposed upon each other.

Mariaerh's tears moved him to pity, and he laid his hand on her head and caressed her hair from her brow to the heavy coil at the nape of her neck. When she did not jerk away, he sat beside her and put his arm around her shoulders and drew her close to his side.

"Ah, Mariaerh," he said sadly, "what injuries we have inflicted upon one another. We must love one another, for how else could those wounds prove so mortal?"

Mariaerh rested against him and dried her eyes.

"Sometimes I loved you. Other times I hated you. I think I loved you when I was not near you, but as soon as you entered my sight, I was angry and hurt again. I missed you so much here in Capernaum, and when Adahr told me you were here, I was faint with joy. But then we quarreled and I wished you had stayed away."

Lucius winced. "Do you still wish so?"

"I don't know," she answered wearily. "It's so peaceful here, so void of any conflict that it's easy to be lulled into complacency, but I've also felt a vague uneasiness, a restlessness as though I knew this was only a respite, that eventually I'd have to go back and face the world. You are an abrupt reminder that I must finish what I have begun, and it fills me with dread. I feel like a child who is forced to make its first venture out of its mother's house, alone and afraid, not knowing what lies in wait out of view of the house. You are the danger that lurks around the corner, and yet you are also the haven where I can run for safety." She turned pleading eyes to him. "Please, Lucius, be one or the other, but no longer be both."

Lucius tightened his grip and laid his cheek on her hair. He had no words to answer her plea.

Mariaerh and Lucius struggled throughout the winter to build the long overdue foundation beneath their marriage. Their quarrels were frequent and bitter. They slogged their way through a jungle of misunderstanding, uprooting all their old assumptions, cutting down every preconceived notion they held of each other, blindly groping their way through a maze of hiding emotions and unvoiced resentments until every thought and sentiment lay exposed and vulnerable to scrutiny.

It was a frightening process. Years of distrust, fear of censure, rejection, and belittlement had to be overcome and vanquished before desires and needs could be disclosed and shared. It was a long, uphill, painful endeavor, and the pathway was strewn with shattered pride and crushed vanities. It was a purging of self, a regeneration of the very fabric of their natures, and they often despaired and nearly abandoned it as hopeless.

The first indication that the battle could be won occurred when the subject of Vesta arose. For weeks, both Lucius and Mariaerh had avoided the question of Vesta, each fearing that once her name was spoken, all would be lost, but it was inevitable that Vesta's ghost would arise to confront them, and when it did, the debate took a surprising turn and led to the core of Mariaerh's misery.

It was like a breach in a dam that had held back every hurt and anguish that had assailed her soul, and once breached, Mariaerh was powerless to stem the flood. She poured out her heart to Lucius, a heart-rending cry of desolation and loss.

Lucius did not interrupt with protestations in his own defense, but listened, really listened, and for the first time heard and understood Mariaerh's torment.

"I felt so ugly, so used and unclean, like a leper kicked to the side of the road ignored by passers-by out of embarrassment. You told me once that Merceden knew of Philippi's dalliances with other women, but she was secure in his love for her, and could overlook them. You gave me no such security, Lucius. I saw only reproval and distaste and regret in your eyes when you looked at me.

"You gave Vesta children! I could have endured your faithlessness, but you spilled your seed in another womb while mine went dry and empty!"

Mariaerh's voice broke. She hugged her body and rocked back and forth, keening, a tearless, terrible wail of grief that tore at Lucius' heart. He knelt before her, sitting on the heels of his sandals with his arms around her thighs and hips and his head on her knees. When she quieted, he raised his head and said gently, "Go on, Mariaerh, tell me all."

Mariaerh's voice was tremulous, hesitant. "To be a woman and not have a child, people think she is not well thought of by God. Remember how Jeshua cursed the barren fig tree? Oh, how I suffered each time that story was told!"

Lucius bit his lower lip to keep from protesting.

Mariaerh managed a weak smile. "I know, Lucius.

Now I know. The Blessed Mother taught me to understand. But until now I did not. I know my barrenness is not your fault, nor is it even mine. I was so jealous of Vesta! She was beautiful and exciting where I was plain and dull. She had your love and your child and I was bereft.

"How can I make you understand what it is for a woman to go childless! It is a hunger that is never satisfied, a longing, yearning, aching that goes on and on. I felt like only half a person, without a child, incomplete, unfinished, an abnormality among females. It is bearable only when understood by one who loves you despite all, who shares the loss and fills the void by his constant reassurance that the woman is needed and vital to his life, like Jonas with Susane.

"But you had children by another and publicly proclaimed my failure. You bared my deformity to the world and made me an object of ridicule and shame. They showed compassion for Jonas and Susane, forgiveness for you, but only contempt for me. Then Saul came and preached chastity as if it were a direct command from the Lord. I might have borne all the rest, but to think that Jeshua shared their opinion of me ..."

Mariaerh's voice again broke. Her chin quivered and emotion again threatened to overwhelm her.

The heels of Lucius' sandals bit into his buttocks. His knees ached and his lower legs had gone numb. He stood and flexed his legs to restore circulation, and his voice was harsh when he spoke.

"You must know better than that! Remember the first night I spent here? Why did I weep like that? Jeshua spoke to my heart. He opened my eyes and made me see you in the light He sees you, beloved in His sight, a Holy Woman more precious in His eyes than all the jewels in the earth, and He charged me sorely with neglect, for walking in the stubbornness of my own heart. Sins of commission are forgiven, while sins of omission are called to mind, even by the Master."

Lucius turned and strode down to the water's edge, so filled with remorse he could not bear to look at Mariaerh any longer.

Mariaerh watched him go, stunned. Her impulse was to run after him, to ease his guilt with words of forgiveness, but something held her back and she waited. After a few moments Lucius came back and took her hands.

"I have no excuses. There is not one thing I can do or say to erase the past. I can only promise to try not to make the same errors again, but I cannot promise to succeed. Even to ask your forgiveness seems pompous, but I do ask it, and beg you for another chance."

Whatever force restrained Mariaerh from running to him before, restrained her now from flying into his arms. She only squeezed his hands and said, "Let's go back to the house. I'm cold, and it's time for me to help with the evening meal."

Lucius released her hands and nodded. "You go. I'll be there soon."

He watched her walk away from him, then sat on the rocks and stared out over the sea.

Once all the old attitudes and misconceptions had been excised, new attitudes and impressions had to be formed, for as Jeshua warned, once a house has been swept clean of old demons, it must be refurnished or they would return again. The exorcism of the old had been excruciatingly painful, fraught with anguish and near despair. They had ended as strangers, stunned by the fact that even though they had lived together those many years, they really did not know one another at all. They were bashful, ill at ease with each other, as two people who had only just met, yet were attracted and eager to know more of each other.

For the rest of the winter, the activities in the house revolved around Lucius and Mariaerh without their notice. They were consumed by each other, oblivious to everyone else as they basked in the joy of discovery. They came to trust each other, and as trust grew, they found they could discard their old pretensions and tear down all the protective walls they had built and just be themselves. It was a heady sensation to be free to say and do and look just as they wished without fear of disapproval, and they seemed to float on the wings of euphoria.

Lucius discovered that Mariaerh still had the sense of humor she had displayed in Martha's class as a girl. He delighted in her witty quips, and pretended shocked outrage when her humor was boldly irreverent. He teased her as he used to tease Nimmuo, and exploded in merriment when in response she went him one better. He was amazed when she revealed to him some of her escapades. He laughed uproariously when she told him how Celicene had called Saul an "ugly little fanatic," and chortled with glee when she related her embarrassment at being caught by his sons hiding behind a tree.

Mariaerh was no less delighted. Every fantasy she had entertained about Lucius seemed to come true. He was affectionate and complimentary. He discussed with her at length his plans for the church, sought out her advice, listened intently to her suggestions, then voiced his approval and gratitude. She glowed with happiness and felt as a young girl ardently courted by a coveted suitor.

Mary of John died on the first day of spring, a spring that stole across Galilee during the night and bloomed into life with the morning sun. Mary was buried before sundown according to Law, in a tomb carved into the hills that faced the sea so the sun's first rays would remember her every morning.

The funeral procession was long. Hired mourners wailed and gnashed their teeth and pounded their breasts in anguish, but those who loved her were silent. A bitter-sweet day. A day of quiet joy that Mary's time of suffering was over, but of sadness and loss, that the beloved of Jeshua and then of her husband, John, no longer walked in the earth.

By nightfall the house was quiet. The Saints had gone home and John and the women had gone to their beds. Lucius lay on his mat, listening to the deepening silence when he heard what he thought was a muffled sob. He crept through the dark to Mariaerh's room, and she raised up her arms to embrace him.

# PART IV
# THE END
# TIMES

# Chapter 38

### At Home in Laodicea

"Brother will hand over brother—children will turn against their parents. Because of my *name* you will be hated by everyone."

Jeshua's prophecy has come true. The Jews of Rome have risen up in anger against The Way. Jewish-Christian homes are vandalized and their market booths razed. Their children are persecuted in the synagogue schools and their women subjected to verbal abuse in the streets. It was not to be borne. The Christians retaliated and the Jewish quarter has become a battleground of Jew fighting Jew.

Too often that beloved, unschooled fisherman from Galilee thinks with his heart instead of his head. His faith is such that he innocently believed that the Holy Spirit could miraculously open men's hearts and ears to the Gospel of Truth, and that uncircumcised Gentiles could be brought into the synagogue.

He should have known better. He forgot that Man must turn willingly to God, that God's own gift of free will forbids Him to force His creation to love Him.

I know Peter well and understand the purity of motive behind his actions. The synagogue is the life-blood of his existence. Every important event in his life has taken place in the synagogue, even after he followed The Way and Jeshua named him "The Rock." It would seem natural to him for Gentile Christians to be brought into the synagogue and to proclaim them as equal brothers to the Jews.

Beloved Apostle! A minimum of rational, objective thought would have shown him otherwise. He need only have considered the Idumeans. That race was forcibly circumcised and considered Jews for years before Herod, called The Great, became king of Judea, but the Jews never accepted him, never considered him a true Jew.

Not even a year has passed since we adjourned the council with high hopes, infused with enthusiasm to bring as many souls as possible into the fold while Jeshua delayed His return. We scattered to the ends of the earth to do the Lord's work. Thaddeus ben Alphaeus, Thomas and Andrew are in Persia, Matthias and James ben Alphaeus in Armenia and Matthew in Syria.

Paul, Barnabas and John Mark went back to Antioch with Pathos for a time, then planned another journey together, but quarreled over John Mark and each has gone his separate way, Barnabas with John Mark and Paul with Silas and Luke. Nathaniel and Philip have settled in nearby New Hierapolis and Jude, the Lord's brother, is with John in Ephesus. Peter returned to Rome with high expectations that the Lord would purify Gentile hearts by the means of faith and they would be welcomed into the company of Saints with peace and goodwill. God willing, peace will soon return to the church in Rome before the temperament spreads and we are all engulfed in persecution.

\* \* \* \* \*

### Entry

Vesta brings word that Claudius has expelled all Jews from Rome. I convened the Elders and set forth a plan to receive any Brothers and Sisters who seek refuge with us. It is all that we know. We await word from the church to know how our people fare. Mariaerh has given me a son.

\* \* \* \* \*

### Entry

At last! A messenger arrived this evening from Rome and the news is dire. Claudius has put a price on Peter's head. He and a group of his devoted followers have fled west, heading for Gaul and possibly Britain.

Our aging Emperor Claudius was too preoccupied with his writings and his own burgeoning palace intrigues to give time and thought to mediating a dispute between Jews. He chose an easy solution and simply ordered all Jews expelled from Rome, never considering the vast economic upheaval his off-handed edict would cause to the city, or the consequences of thousands of Jews wandering homeless and hungry throughout the Empire.

His troops descended upon the Jewish quarter without warning. They herded the people out of the city like cattle, with no time to dispense with their goods or plan for a journey. They snatched up what they could and, stripped of all their worldly goods, were set adrift beyond the city's boundaries. Roman authority makes no distinction between Jewish-Christians and Jews, thus only the Gentile Christians were spared, but every man, woman and child of Jewish blood is exiled from the city. Our own flock will fare better than others, for the church everywhere is ready with aid.

*     *     *     *     *

## Entry

As I feared, this new persecution has spread throughout the Empire. I tremble with dread as I wonder if I witness the first of the woes that Jeshua warned would usher in the end times.

Our enemies rejoice that Jews are again out of favor, and the Chosen of God face peril from every side. They are cheated and robbed while authorities look the other way. The synagogues are debased and Jewish businesses boycotted. The civil rights they had previously enjoyed under Claudius are now disregarded and their freedom of movement is vastly curtailed. Our own messengers take particular care.

In Judea some Galileans traveled through Samaria to Jerusalem to celebrate a feast and were set upon and slaughtered by the hostile Samaritans. The Elders appealed to the procurator, Cumanus, for protection, but were ignored. Desperate and frustrated, they turned to the infamous robber, Eleazar, for protection and vengeance, and plunged the land into civil war.

John ben Zebedee abandoned the house in the grove and has brought the Lord's mother to Jude in Ephesus. Judith has retreated to Mount Carmel. Cephas and Naomi and the remaining Holy Women have fled to the City of Salt. The sign of the fish is again drawn in the dust.

Cumanus finally had no choice but to interfere, but fought on the side of Samaria, slaying hundreds of Jews and taking twice as many prisoner. In Jerusalem, the city leaders feared Cumanus would take vengeance upon the Temple and pleaded with the Galileans to cease the fight, but they would not. Quadrates, the proconsul of Syria, at last intervened. He sent Cumanus and the principal men of both the Samaritans and Jews to Rome for Claudius to settle the matter. The Jews went without hope, knowing the Emperor's recent temper, but young Agrippa made a passionate plea in their behalf and Cumanus was banished. Felix, an old friend of the Emperor's, has been sent in his stead.

The Jews had little time to celebrate their victory. Eleazar, emboldened by the friendships he has made in Galilee, overran Judea, looting, killing, instilling terror and tyranny throughout the land. The Jews hoped that Felix would bring order, but their hopes were dashed when the procurator persuaded Agrippa's sister to divorce her husband and marry him. The Jews could not let pass such a blatant transgression of the Law. Their leaders cried out against the infamy and, to punish their daring, Felix allows the robbers to do as they will.

The Jews blame us Christians for their grief. Matthias was stoned in Armenia and might have died of his injuries if Andrew had not gone to his aid.

Only here, in Laodicea, has the church remained unscathed, but not without cost. Compromise, duplicity, cunning distortion of facts and sometimes bribery and outright dishonesty has been the price we pay for peace. I deplore such practices and my conscience allows me no rest, but my church survives where many have not.

\*     \*     \*     \*     \*

## Entry

Cornelius and Philoas have asked Pebilus to aid them in Peter's absence, and while my heart grieves to have my son removed from my sight and quakes in terror at the danger he may face, it also swells with pride.

\* \* \* \* \*

## Entry

Our beloved mother, Mary, now rests in the Lord. The church throughout the Empire mourns.

\* \* \* \* \*

## Entry

Claudius is dead, murdered more likely. Some say poisoned by his wife, Agrippina. Her young son, Nero, is now Emperor of Rome. Please God that he shows more mercy than his predecessor.

\* \* \* \* \*

## Entry

Every messenger brings news more dire than the last.

We hoped Nero would bring relief and, for a time, it was so. He lowered taxes, fed the poor, and if his parties and entertainments were somewhat excessive, the people forgave him because of his youth. But in less than a year the more sober, thinking men of Rome have begun to fear that a madman reigns as Emperor.

Nero indulges in every form of sexual debauchery. His appetites know no limits as he seduces young boys, rapes married women and vestal virgins. He committed incest with his sisters and even his mother! The whole Empire recoils in disgust and revulsion.

Sexual perversions have made way for a lust for blood. Now murder is Nero's new entertainment, exquisite tortures, grizzly, ghoulish fantasies made reality. He has slaughtered his entire family, including Agrippina, and the Empire is paralyzed with fear.

Nero considers himself a god and is determined to live as one. He paves walls and ceilings in gold, shoes his mules with silver and commits other extravagances until he has beggared Rome into bankruptcy. Hysteria rules. The most innocent act or statement is twisted into an act of treason until the people live in terror of the hellish punishments in store if an accusing finger should point their way. Scapegoats are sought and, as always, the lot falls to the hapless Jews and, consequently, to Christians.

Laodicea is the only safe haven. I remember the days of my youth when I so desired to provide a haven of rest for weary Saints as Martha and Lazarus provided in Bethany, but not for this cause!

Vesta, as much as any other, protects us from harm by her parentage and influence with government officials. She is one of us, brought into faith by the faith of our sons. She aids the Apostles and Elders by her knowledge of the surrounding lands and their political temperament. She plots their routes through the least dangerous passes and writes letters of passage to give them more freedom of movement. The Elders hold her in such high regard that John has appointed her a deaconess.

The Apostles and Elders often rest here to renew body and spirit as they travel back and forth through the persecuted lands. With throngs of merchants and caravans passing through each day, they can easily slip into the city without notice. They stay in my father's house and are free to come and go as they please for the authorities give pause before questioning a guest of Philippi's.

I have come to dread the call of a courier. This account was interrupted by a message from Jerusalem. Paul was arrested in Jerusalem and is being held for trial in Caesarea.

\* \* \* \* \*

Entry

Grief heaped upon grief has stayed my hand from keeping this journal. I pray for courage to put this account to paper, for what I must write is more than my heart can bear.

Nero has a new favorite pastime. He pits man against wild beasts in the arena to the delight of the rabble who revel at the sight of spilled blood. It does not matter who—senators, beggars off the streets, prostitutes, priests, anyone who catches his attention. Friends betray friends, relatives condemn relatives, servants their masters and masters their servants in a desperate hope to win Nero's favor and elude such fate for themselves. Rome is insane and her insanity has spread across the face of the earth.

Of late, Christians are his choice for victims. He rounds us up like beasts of the fields. Our beloved Marcia of Barnabas! A woman of such sweetness, such light! Carried into that infamous arena. To meet such an end! Barnabas, thank God, did not live to witness his loved one's suffering, for they crucified him first in Cyprus. My kinsman, my friend, my comrade in Christ. John Mark buried him with his own hands. May our Lord keep watch over John Mark.

Jude, the Lord's brother, and John ben Zebedee have both suffered prison and stripes in Ephesus, but were released through Philoas' influence. John has sent Jude to Athens, hoping he will be safe there. Paul languishes still under house arrest in Rome. Word has come to us that Judith has died at Mount Carmel, reportedly from the persecution she endured, but I think, no doubt, from grief. Thomas has been run through by a lance in far off Hindu lands.

My grief for the church is overburdened by my own loss. I have buried my beloved father, and hardly had I risen from weeping over his tomb, when Merceden followed him to sleep in the Lord. My second son has been called to Rome, accompanied by my beloved Nimmuo. Only my youngest son and good wife yet by my side give me courage and will to live.

\*     \*     \*     \*     \*

### Entry

James, the brother of the Lord, has been stoned in Jerusalem! That Saint! That godly man, called "The Just" even by the Jews, tried and condemned by an illegal court as his Brother before him, held up for ridicule on a high precipice on the Temple wall, humiliated, jeered upon, then cast forth into the Kidron Valley below where he writhed in agony until a kindly fuller put an end to his suffering by a merciful blow to his head. Lord, Come!

\*     \*     \*     \*     \*

### Entry

Peter has returned to Rome. He will watch over my sons.

506

*　　*　　*　　*　　*

Entry

Rome burns! Where are my sons?

*　　*　　*　　*　　*

Entry

Gehenna has risen up from the bowels of the earth and has spread like leprosy across the surface. Some say the fire in Rome was started by accident, some say by Nero himself, a new entertainment, watching his city burn, a funeral pyre for hundreds of citizens. He shifts the blame to The Way who are rounded up like cattle and forced under torture to confess they are Christians. He has them brought to his new palace which he calls "the Golden House" and orders them wrapped in animal skins to tempt starving dogs. Some he lathers with pitch and impales them upon pikes, then sets them aflame to provide light for his guests. Our women are cast into whoredom to satisfy pagan lusts and his garden decorations are crucified Saints.

Never before has creation known such infamy. Man has fallen to depths so low that the only solution can be his extinction. How long will God endure?

Our people have gone under ground. They inhabit the catacombs, a labyrinth of tunnels and caves that form a maze in the rock beneath Rome. For His name they have become moles, insects scurrying beneath the earth in darkness. My sons and my sister reside there. It is not to be borne.

They are not without aid. Even non-believers are revolted by Nero's fiendishness. They secrete food and clothing into the burrows. They hide our people by day and slip them into the passageways by night, always mindful that once caught, they will share in their fate. The Jews, too, give us aid, ever mindful of their own history of persecution.

*　　*　　*　　*　　*

## Entry

The Jews of Judea are in revolt. Samaria seethes in unrest. Caesarea has become a city of peril and risk. The streets of Jerusalem are a battleground of drunkenness, thievery, assault and murder.

Nero has appointed Florus as procurator over Judea, a man whose lust for wealth and power is surpassed by few. Florus uses every means of bribery and extortion that he can bring to mind, has even raided the Temple treasury, a sacrilegious act that provoked a riot in Jerusalem. He then took vengeance by crucifying the leading citizens and handed the city over to his troops for plunder. Young Agrippa pleaded for peace, but was jeered and driven from the city.

The captain of the Temple has persuaded the priests to stop offering sacrifice for the Emperor's welfare. Roman law is ignored, tax monies are withheld. Galilean youth join the dreaded Sicarii in droves. Jerusalem, Jerusalem!

\* \* \* \* \*

## Entry

My son! My son! Thaddeus, my son! My hand will not write of the means of your death, nor my mind think it.

\* \* \* \* \*

## Entry

The courier arrived this day with the death roll, for that is what every missive has become.

The sons of Alphaeus, all dead. Thaddeus and Simon crucified in Edessa in Persia and James in Syria. Matthew, stoned in Alexandria. Praise the Almighty One that the father does not live to grieve for the sons.

Matthias has been stoned in Jerusalem. Philip and his daughters lie buried in Hierapolis, five tombs, five martyrs to Christ.

Marcus and Josie were trampled in the streets of Jerusalem and have succumbed to their wounds. Beloved aunt of the Lord who followed Him, even on the way to the cross.

\*     \*     \*     \*     \*

### Entry

Black days! Evil days!

Those two foremost pillars of the church! Cut from our breast!

Peter, crucified! Always the humble fisherman, he asked to be hung head down as one unworthy to die as Jeshua had died, or, perhaps, it was his last way of atoning for having once betrayed Him. I cannot, as yet, write of Peter, for tears blur my vision and memory causes my heart to falter.

Paul beheaded, his Roman citizenship buying him an honorable execution.

Saul. That ugly, unlikeable boy whom I allowed to win at our boyish games out of pity for his weakness and deformity. Saul, the enemy of the church who became her most stalwart protector. Could anyone ever understand him, know him? A man who evoked such love and devotion in others that once he was forced to admonish his admirers that it was Christ they followed, not he. The same man who evoked hatred and fear and distrust, even from the church, even from The Twelve, but allowed nothing to deter him from his chosen path.

I did not know him. He is my kinsman and I have known him all of my life, but I did not know him, or, God forgive, love him.

\*     \*     \*     \*     \*

### Entry

The end times draw to a close. The era of chaos looms near. Of The Twelve only John and Andrew remain. Jude, the Lord's brother, is slain in Athens, Nathaniel in Derbend. John Mark, like a son to me, dragged to his death in Alexandria.

Judea is finished. Nero sent the commander, Vespasian, to quell the revolt and the might of Rome has swept through the land. The valiant Jews fought heroically, but the effort was futile. All of Judea lies waste beneath Vespasian's heel and only Jerusalem and the fortresses of Herodium, Masada and Machaerus remain in Jewish control.

The church has fled Jerusalem, warned by the Holy Spirit to flee. The City of Salt is abandoned, the records and scriptures sealed into jars and secreted in caves above the Salt Sea.

*     *     *     *     *

Entry

Nero has ended his miserable life. Too late. Vespasian has called a halt to the war until a successor is chosen. Whoever it is, he will be the last Roman emperor the world will ever know. Vespasian will destory Jerusalem, then rage across the earth until at last Rome devours herself and the world will revert to chaos.

I am as one who watches in the night and records what he sees. I am old unto death, but fated to witness the end. Lord, have mercy.

*     *     *     *     *

# Chapter 39

Lucius was surrounded by flames. Behind him the Lower City was a raging inferno; before him yellow, red and blue tongues of fire hungrily licked at the Temple walls. The heat was agonizing, searing his skin and sucking out the air from his shrinking island of safety. He labored for breath. His heart pounded and his eyes bulged with terror.

He flung his head back, casting his eyes upward, searching for any avenue of escape. Great billows of black smoke obscured the sky, filtering the sunlight into an ominous glow. Frantically he looked down to the Temple wall, hoping against hope to find a break in the fire, and then his belly revolted in horror.

An obscene row of crossed beams stood planted along the wide walkway at the top of the wall, starkly outlined against an indifferent brilliant blue sky which rose up beyond the holocaust. Mercifully the flames distorted the faces of those hanging there. He did not know them, he did not know the crucified, he could not know them. He tried to tear his eyes away, not wanting to see, not wanting to know, but his eyes remained riveted, would see, would know.

Insidiously the flames crawled upward, casting an ever brighter glow until he saw the faces clearly and opened his mouth wide, screaming a long, terrible scream of denial. The sound was lost in the roar of the fire.

He did know them! He knew them all! His eyes caressed each face, his sight become tactile, feeling each dip and hollow and blemish and mound, meeting each pair of sorrowing eyes, caught and held until he wrenched them away and passed on to the next.

Marh and Jochim, Martha and Thelda and Stephen and Sylvia and Celicia, Philas, Sara, Veronica, on and on, The Twelve but for John, the Lord's brothers James and Jude, His uncles Alphaeus and Zebedee, and last of all Luke.

He heard a sound like a faraway tinkling of breaking glass and knew it to be his heart and soul shattering to miniscule pieces.

He could bear no more. His body lurched into mobility. He ran this way and that, panicked, frantic to find a breach in the flames, but found none. He was trapped, doomed to watch the Temple and its infamous burden of crucified Saints collapse in the funeral pyre.

Lucius came awake with a cry and sat bolt upright. He was drenched with sweat. His heart pounded dangerously and he was fighting for breath. He flung off the heavy coverlet and leapt from the bed, staggering drunkenly to the tall windows where he flung back the draperies and threw the shutters wide and gulped at the cool, dawn air.

He breathed deeply, forcing his heartbeat and breath to return to their normal rhythm, but he was weak and shaking and his heart and spirit were as heavy as stone. He groped his way to a divan and sank down. He studied the room, letting his eyes rest upon each familiar object, trying to banish the phantoms of dreams with solid reality.

The bedsilks and window coverings were faded by years and the sun. The heavy brocade sofas too, frayed and splitting with age. The once luxurious Persian rugs were worn to the backing. The objects of art were gone, sold. The once gloriously gleaming woods in the bed and desk were dull and dry and roughened by lack of care.

No monies had gone into the great house in years. All revenues from Philippi's vast holdings had gone to provide sustenance for the Laodicean church since normal avenues of commerce had closed, first to the Jews and later, as the tribe of Christians became recognized, to them as well. With Philippi's lands, the Saints could raise sheep and grain, maintain vineyards on the rocky, terraced hills and, although Gentiles were leery of trade with Christians, at least they could eat and clothe themselves.

The room smelled musty. Cobwebs adorned the high corners and dust gathered on the shelves. The tall windows were cloudy and filtered the sun, and the walls were dingy with neglect and age.

There were few servants in the house these days. The peasants feared to work for a Christian and only a cook, a gardener and two young maid servants who followed The Way remained to care for Philippi's huge house. Lucius still thought of it as Philippi's house, though his for years since his father and mother had gone to God.

Lucius closed his eyes and let his head rest on the back of the divan.

The dream. Each time a messenger came bearing news of another loved one martyred, the nightmare recurred. He knew the dream's meaning, Jerusalem was doomed. The Temple would be no more. The old worship of sacrifice and incense, the grandeur of the feasts with all the exaggerated pomp and glory was finished forever.

Lucius' eyes came open. No messenger had arrived of late, thank God, why now the dream?

His train of thought evaporated as Mariaerh came through the door, smiling, happy to see him awake and out of his bed. She bent and kissed the top of his head, her clean scent pleasing and familiar, her touch a comfort.

"Our son awaits you for the morning meal. Will you be long?"

He shook his head. He had no appetite for food any more, but to refuse to eat caused the women distress. He wondered why women placed such emphasis upon food. Merceden had been famous for her persistence that the family eat well, and now Lucia was as bad and Mariaerh growing more like them with each passing day. If he consented to eat, Mariaerh would leave him in peace for the rest of the day.

Mariaerh prepared him a tepid bath, then left as he lowered himself into the scented water. He lay back in the copper tub and closed his eyes, relaxing as the scent cleansed the stench of fear from his flesh. When revived, he pulled himself up and stepped onto the tiled floor, drying himself with a length of rough linen until his skin was red and tingled. Still naked, he shaved, scraping the hollow cheeks above his gray beard, then wound a fresh toga around his torso.

The atrium was awash in sunshine when Lucius arrived. Lucia was placing a smooth board of hot loaves in the center of the table, slapping at two young girls' hands as they reached for the loaves. Her grand-daughters, but which ones Lucius did not know for he could never remember who was who in Lucia's large brood.

Sylvius bounded toward him and planted a kiss on his father's cheek then flung himself down on a wide couch with a hand reaching into a bowl of figs before he even landed.

Lucius took his place and waited for his grand-nieces to suppress their giggles before he gave thanks for the meal.

They were only six. Jesua had succumbed to fever just after his youngest child had wed. Now with all of Lucia's children married, they had their own homes, though some of her grandchildren forever invaded his house.

Lucius ate sparingly, paying little attention to the prattle around the table. He could not comprehend the chatter of youth. They had no regard for decorum. How old were these young females who giggled so and called him "Uncle"? Thirteen years? Fourteen? About the age when Susana ran away.

Lucius rubbed his face as though to wipe away the memory of his only daughter, but it persisted.

He would never understand why Susana had run away with a passing caravan! It shamed him still, that last ugly scene when she had accused him of hypocrisy and fraud, when she had spewed forth all that jealous rage over Sylvius. The embarrassment, the scandal she

had caused! Was it his fault that the church preferred
Sylvius over her? Was it his fault that she was female
and Sylvius male and thus naturally he would
personally tutor his son and send her to school with
other young females?

Lucius squirmed and quaffed a glass of wine.
Probably, somewhat, but not so dire a transgression as
to warrant the action she took.

Susana had always been difficult, caustic and strong-
willed like Vesta but without Vesta's wit and
passionate nature to temper her abrasive humor. There
was a bitterness in Susana, a petulance that did not
elicit affection, and Lucius rejected the thought that it
was born out of her illegitimacy. Thaddeus and Pebilus
had overcome that stigma, why had she not? She had
accused him of not loving her. He sighed. It was true. He
had never loved her, even when she was a babe. God
knew he had tried, and endured boundless guilt when he
did not succeed.

He turned his attention to Sylvius, who was teasing
the girls, and his heart melted with love.

Not so with his son. He had preened with pride at
Sylvius' birth, dandled him on his knee and lavished
him with baubles and playthings, then taught him
himself when he reached the age of reason.

Lucius smiled, remembering the pleasure and pride
he had felt at the ease with which Sylvius had
progressed in his lessons. He learned his numbers
quickly and had no trouble conquering difficult
mathematical problems, but it was letters that had
fascinated the child, words strung together to create a
tale. History, philosophy, science, tales of the Roman
and Greek goddesses and gods, the lore of the Jews,
Sylvius had absorbed them all like a sponge,
demanding more and more, devouring the library at the
medical school, wanting to know everything man had
been given to know.

The meal had ended and Lucius was free to escape to
his rooms. He was weary, as though it were the end of
the day instead of the beginning, and knew it was
caused by the dream. It drained him each time it

occurred, sapped his strength, left his thoughts disorganized and his spirits despondent. Particularly so this time, unsettled, nervous, as though something were amiss, a difference that he could not detect. He shook his head and settled at his desk to work with his papers. No doubt it was that, this time, the dream had occurred without provocation.

It was noontime when he heard Mariaerh's quiet knock on the door and looked up to see her white, stricken face. Fear froze his heart. He half rose from the stool and his hands gripped the desk's edge. His own face grew pale, slack, his mouth drooped agape.

Mariaerh saw his thought and quickly approached him. "Not Pebilus," she said, "not Pebilus."

Lucius sank back upon the stool, weak with relief, his eyes questioned.

Mariaerh nodded. "A messenger has come."

Lucius turned his head toward a sound he heard from behind Mariaerh. Sylvius was there, his strong arms bearing a large wooden trunk, and beside him a stranger.

Lucius could not speak, but gestured them forward.

Sylvius' mouth worked and his eyes were red. The man cleared his throat, but it was Sylvius who spoke. "It is Luke, father, and Andrew. They were crucified at Patmos."

Lucius cried out and tore at his toga. His head dropped onto his arms. The dream! Luke and Andrew had never before been in the dream. Why had he not seen it!

Mariaerh bent over his back, weeping and holding him close to her breast. He broke her hold and straightened, saying to the courier, "Tell me all."

The man again cleared his throat. "There is little to tell. They were arrested as Christians, tried and condemned." He held out a scroll. "It is here, the details. I bring Luke's possessions. They are in the trunk." He nodded toward Sylvius. "Andrew's I have for his daughter."

"Take them to her. Give her my love and my blessing and God go with you."

The messenger took his leave and Sylvius deposited the trunk at Lucius' feet. "Shall I open it for you, Father?"

Lucius nodded and waited while Sylvius worked at the stiff, leather thongs that held the lid fast.

When it opened, Sylvius gasped. "It is scrolls! And books and journals!" He was lifting them out, one by one, handing each to his father until the desk was filled to overflowing. Empty leather pouches lay scattered about Lucius' feet, worn, water stained, some stiff with age, the thongs frayed from being tied and untied again and again. Some scrolls were wrapped in silk, some linen, some of matted, rough wool. Lucius carefully unwrapped one, blinking back tears that shot to his eyes as he recognized Luke's bold, firm hand.

Sylvius and Mariaerh were eagerly waiting to hear what was written, so Lucius read aloud, "Paul arrived first at Derbe; next he came to Lystra, where there was a disciple named Timothy, whose mother was Jewish and a believer, and whose father was a Greek. Since the Brothers in Lystra and Iconium spoke highly of him, Paul was anxious to have him come along on the journey. Paul had him circumcised because of the Jews of that region, for they all knew that it was only his father who was Greek."

Lucius laid the scroll aside, saying, "It is Paul's second journey, when he had still not forgiven John Mark and took Silas and Luke."

He chose another which looked very old and opened it slowly, his hands trembling. He read, "Some were speaking of how the Temple was adorned with precious stones and votive offerings. He said, 'These things you are contemplating—the day will come when not one stone will be left on another, but it will all be torn down.' They asked him, 'When will this be, Teacher? And what will be the sign that it is going to happen?' He said, 'Take care not to be misled. Many will come in my *name* saying: *I am he* and *the time is at hand.* Do not follow them. Neither must you be perturbed when you hear of wars and insurrections. These things are bound to happen first, but the end does not follow immediately.'

"He said to them further: 'Nation will rise against nation and kingdom against kingdom. There will be great earthquakes, plagues and famines in various places—and in the sky fearful omens and great signs. But before any of this, they will manhandle and persecute you, summoning you to synagogues and prisons, bringing you to trial before kings and governors, all because of my *name*. You will be brought to give witness on account of it. I bid you resolve not to worry about your defense beforehand, for I will give you words and a wisdom which none of your adversaries can take exception to or contradict. You will be delivered up even by your parents, brothers, relatives and friends, and some of you will be put to death. All will hate you because of me, yet not a hair of your head will be harmed. By patient endurance you will save your lives.' "

Lucius could read no more. Mariaerh and Sylvius were weeping openly. He rolled up the scroll and wiped his eyes. "Our Lord's own words. Written in Luke's hand."

Lucius unrolled the scroll which contained the details of Luke and Andrew's death. It was as the messenger said, brief and expected except for one thing. Andrew was not nailed to the beam, but lashed, and his instrument of torture formed into an "X" instead of a cross.

Lucius laid the scroll aside, gently, reverently, then passed his eyes over the host of scrolls and books and journals heaped on his desk and spread at his feet.

"They must be read, sorted. Then—" he made a gesture of helplessness.

Mariaerh knew Lucius' need to be alone, to contend with his grief in private. She said to Sylvius, "Go into the city and inform Jehul while I carry the news to Lucia."

When the door closed behind them, silence and sorrow bore down upon Lucius. He bent over the desk, gathered the writings in his arms and wept.

In the following weeks, Luke's writings took precedence over everything else. Lucius stayed at the desk from dawn until long into the night, sorting, reading, cataloguing; often weeping, often gnashing his teeth in anger and helplessness at the tale which unfolded from Luke's bold hand. He was awed, humbled, filled with pride and sometimes borne on the wings of ecstasy by what he read. He slept little and ate less, only when Mariaerh insisted, too obsessed with his task to think of anything else.

When the last journal had been read and recorded and stored in its proper order on a shelf in a cupboard, a suffocating crippling desolation settled down upon Lucius. He withdrew into himself, seldom spoke, and seemed unaware of his surroundings.

Mariaerh hovered over him, her eyes dark with concern. Sylvius stayed near him, bewildered, afraid, even he unable to penetrate the wall of despair. Lucius seemed to grow old before their eyes, frailer each day, more uninterested each day, until Mariaerh reconciled herself to the fact that Lucius was willing himself to die.

So he was. His black, despairing thoughts told him that he had outlived his usefulness. His purpose, if ever there were one, had gone unfulfilled. His work, his efforts, his reason for being had all been for naught, for the world would end and who would remember?

Each morning Sylvius would lift him from bed, bathe him and shave him, then carry him out to the atrium to sit in the sun. Mariaerh would cover his knees with a throw, tempt him with sweets, urge him to sip a bit of wine, try in every way she could to spark in him an interest for living.

They were there one morning when Jehul burst into the atrium, his face pale, his hands shaking and his voice breaking and stumbling over his rushed, clipped words.

"Vesta has just given us word. Vespasian is Emperor! He sails to Rome. His son Titus is commander of the legion and has laid seige to Jerusalem!"

Lucius was surrounded by flames. Behind him the Lower City was a raging inferno; before him yellow, red and blue tongues of fire hungrily licked at the Temple walls. The heat was agonizing, searing his skin and sucking out the air from his shrinking island of safety, but he was not afraid, only weary, forlorn that again he must witness the dream.

Suddenly he was in Caesarea. A cold, driving rain pitted his face and an icy wind whipped his cloak at his knees. He shivered with cold. His eyes were closed against the pelting rain and his thoughts were a turmoil of longing and fear. A sudden break in the clouds allowed the sun to shine through and he opened his eyes and saw Mount Carmel rising in the distance above the sea as a beacon calling him forth. He saw Judith at the crest, Judith the record-keeper, calling his name.

But it was not Judith. It was Mariaerh, on her knees at his feet, tears streaming down her face, clutching his hands, crying out his name over and over again.

He wondered what was wrong with her? He looked at Sylvius who was white with fear, staring, rigid, as one who has seen a ghost. Had they suddenly gone mad? No matter. He had no time for hysterics now. There was work to be done.

He brushed aside Mariaerh's clutching hands and flung away the constricting lap robe. He looked at his son and wife and the gaping Jehul, and shook his head in wonder.

"Sylvius," he commanded. "See to your mother. Discover the cause of her distress and do what you can to help her." He looked toward Jehul. "And get Jehul a glass of wine. I have much to do."

They stared in amazement as Lucius strode from the room with a gait of a man of forty. His eyes were bright and clear and his face animated. He made for his rooms and there began pulling scrolls and journals from the shelves, selecting each one with care, then went to the old secretary he had used in his youth. He rifled through the shelves and drawers until he found what he was looking for, a stack of scrolls, small, yellowed with age, the ink faded.

He took the scrolls to his desk and read them, remembering the man in his prime who had spent a sleepless night wrapped in a sheet as he wrote them. He laid them aside, then brought his own carefully kept journals to the desk, his own account of the events he had witnessed.

"When you see all the things happening of which I speak, know that the reign of God is near. This generation will not pass away until all this takes place."

This generation was nearly gone. Who was left? Himself, John, Jehul, Philoas, a few more, all old men whose days were numbered by the gray on their heads. Jerusalem lay under seige, soon to be crucified as surely as the Lord and His martyrs. The old world was coming to an end, but a new world would emerge, a new world and a new generation, and generation upon generation.

The Remnant. Each time the Chosen of God were threatened with extinction, God preserved a Remnant, a handful of men and women who remembered the One.

A record must be made of the old and what happened here, a record that he, Lucius, must make before Jeshua returned to claim His own. The record, the purpose for which Lucius of Cyrene had come into the world!

Lucius took a quill and dipped in it ink. He paused a moment to pray, "Lord, come," then put the quill to parchment.

*"And it came to pass in those days that an edict went out from Caesar Augustus that all the world should be taxed, and Joseph also went up from Galilee, out of the city of Nazareth, into Judea, unto the city of David which is called Bethlehem, to be taxed with Mary his espoused wife, being great with child . . ."*

The End

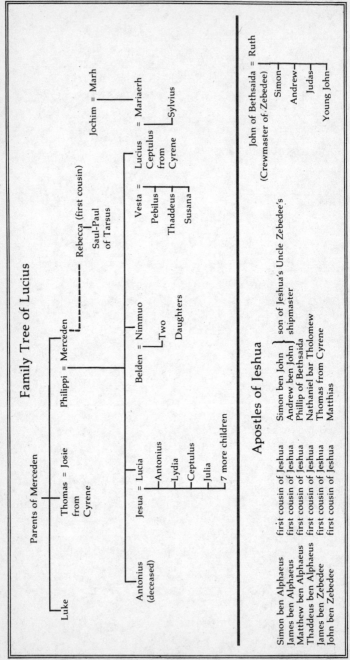

## Family Tree of Lucius

Parents of Merceden

Luke

Antonius
(deceased)

Thomas = Josie
from
Cyrene

Philippi = Merceden

Rebecca (first cousin)
Saul-Paul
of Tarsus

Jochim = Marh

Jesua = Lucia

Belden = Nimmuo

Two
Daughters

Vesta =

Pebilus
Thaddeus
Susana

Lucius = Mariaerh

Ceptulus
from
Cyrene

Sylvius

Antonius
Lydia
Ceptulus
Julia
7 more children

John of Bethsaida = Ruth
(Crewmaster of Zebedee)

Simon
Andrew
Judas

Young John

## Apostles of Jeshua

Simon ben John
Andrew ben John
Phillip of Bethsaida
Nathaniel bar Tholomew
Thomas from Cyrene
Matthias

son of Jeshua's Uncle Zebedee's
shipmaster

Simon ben Alphaeus        first cousin of Jeshua
James ben Alphaeus        first cousin of Jeshua
Matthew ben Alphaeus      first cousin of Jeshua
Thaddeus ben Alphaeus     first cousin of Jeshua
James ben Zebedee         first cousin of Jeshua
John ben Zebedee          first cousin of Jeshua

# Family Tree of Jeshua*

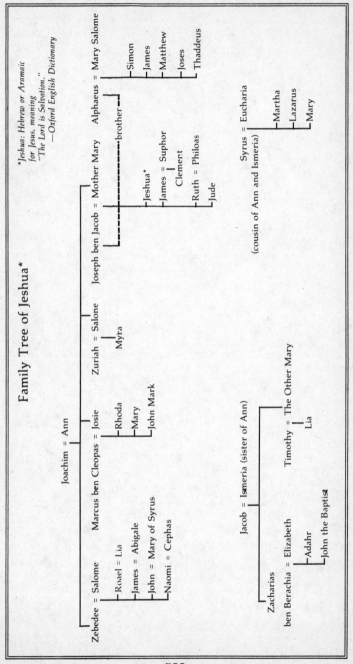

*Jeshua: Hebrew or Aramaic
for Jesus, meaning
"The Lord is Salvation."
—Oxford English Dictionary

Joachim = Ann

Zebedee = Salome

Roael = Lia
James = Abigale
John = Mary of Syrus
Naomi = Cephas

Marcus ben Cleopas = Josie

Rhoda
Mary
John Mark

Zuriah = Salone

Myra

Joseph ben Jacob = Mother Mary

brother

Jeshua*
James = Suphor
Clement
Ruth = Philoas
Jude

Alphaeus = Mary Salome

Simon
James
Matthew
Joses
Thaddeus

Syrus = Eucharia
(cousin of Ann and Ismeria)

Martha
Lazarus
Mary

Jacob = Ismeria (sister of Ann)

Timothy = The Other Mary

Lia

Zacharias
ben Berachia = Elizabeth

Adahr
John the Baptist

523

# Alphabetical List of Characters

ABIGALE — wife of Apostle James ben Zebedee

ADAHR — daughter of Elizabeth; sister of John the Baptist

AGNOSTA — another member of the early church

AGRIPPA — King of Judea; grandson of Herod the Great

ALPHAEUS — brother of Joseph; uncle of Jeshua; husband of Mary Salome; father of Apostles James, Matthew, Simon, and Thaddeus

ANDREW BEN JOHN — Apostle; brother of Apostle Simon Peter

ANNAS — former High Priest; father-in-law of Caiaphas

ANTONIUS — brother of Lucius (deceased)

ANTONIUS — son of Lucia; nephew of Lucius

ARCHAR — deacon of the early church

ARDOEN — son of Apostle Andrew ben John; husband of Paula

BARNABAS — husband of Marcia

BARRIAN — Roman captain

BELDEN — husband of Nimmuo; brother-in-law of Lucius

CAIAPHAS — High Priest

CALIGULA — Emperor of Rome

CARVETTE — another member of the early church

CAPITO — Roman procurator

CELIA — another member of the early church

CELICENE — daughter of the Roman centurion, Cornelius

CELICIA — another member of the early church

CEPHAS — brother of Naomi

CEPTULUS — son of Lucia; nephew of Lucius

# LIST OF CHARACTERS

| | |
|---|---|
| CERECEA | another member of the early church |
| CLAUDIUS | Emperor of Rome |
| CLEMENT | son of James ben Joseph; nephew of Jeshua |
| CLEO | wife of Apostle Simon Peter |
| CLEOPAS | father of Marcus; grandfather of John Mark |
| CORNELIUS | Roman centurion |
| CUMANUS | Roman procurator |
| DORA | daughter of Apostle Andrew ben John |
| DOROCHEN | another member of the early church |
| DUORS | deacon of the early church |
| ELEIZA | sister of Apostle Nathaniel bar Tholomew |
| ELIZABETH | cousin of Mother Mary; mother of John the Baptist |
| ELOIS | aunt of Apostle John ben Zebedee |
| EX-ELOR | wife of Roman centurion, Cornelius |
| FLORUS | Roman procurator |

| | |
|---|---|
| GAMALIEL | renowned teacher of the Mosaic Law |
| HELENE | another member of the early church |
| HEROD ANTIPAS | Tetrarch of Galilee and Perea |
| JACOBEAN | deacon of the early church |
| JAMES BEN ALPHAEUS | Apostle; brother of Apostles Matthew, Simon, and Thaddeus; cousin of Jeshua |
| JAMES BEN JOSEPH | brother of Jeshua; husband of Suphor; father of Clement |
| JAMES BEN ZEBEDEE | Apostle; brother of Apostle John ben Zebedee; cousin of Jeshua; husband of Abigale |
| JEHUL | husband of Rhea |
| JESEUHA | wife of Sylvia |
| JESHUA | The Messiah |
| JESUA | husband of Lucia; brother-in-law of Lucius |
| JOCHIM | father of Mariaerh; father-in-law of Lucius |

# LIST OF CHARACTERS

| | | | | |
|---|---|---|---|---|
| **JOHN BEN ZEBEDEE** | Apostle; brother of Apostle James ben Zebedee; husband of Mary of Syrus | | **JUSTIN** | husband of Essene leader, Judith |
| **JOHN LOUIE** | nephew of Apostle Simon Peter | | **LAZARUS** | cousin of Jeshua |
| **JOHN MARK** | son of Josie; nephew of Jeshua | | **LIA** | wife of Roael (deceased); daughter-in-law of Zebedee |
| **JONAS** | husband of Susane | | **LONGINUS** | Syrian proconsul |
| **JONATHAN** | High Priest | | **LUCIA** | sister of Lucius; wife of Jesua |
| **JOSEPH BEN CAMAS** | High Priest | | **LUCIUS CEPTULUS FROM CYRENE** | bishop of Laodicean church; husband of Mariaerh; nephew of Apostle Thomas from Cyrene; nephew of Luke; second cousin of Saul-Paul |
| **JOSIDA** | another member of the early church | | | |
| **JOSIE** | sister of Mother Mary; aunt of Jeshua; wife of Marcus ben Cleophas | | | |
| **JOSIE** | wife of Apostle Thomas from Cyrene | | **LUKE** | brother of Merceden; brother of Apostle Thomas of Cyrene; uncle of Lucius |
| **JUDAS ISCARIOT** | disciple who betrayed Jeshua (deceased) | | | |
| **JUDE BEN JOSEPH** | brother of Jeshua | | **LYDIA** | daughter of Lucia; niece of Lucius |
| **JUDITH** | leader of the Essenes | | **LYDIA** | another member of the early church |
| **JUDITH** | prostitute | | **MARCIA** | wife of Barnabas |
| **JULIA** | daughter of Lucia; niece of Lucius | | **MARCUS BEN CLEOPAS** | husband of Josie; uncle of Jeshua; father of John Mark |
| **JUNIE** | daughter of Lucia; niece of Lucius | | **MARCUS** | Syrian proconsul |

# LIST OF CHARACTERS

| | | | |
|---|---|---|---|
| MARH | mother of Mariaerh; mother-in-law of Lucius | NATHANIEL BAR THOLOMEW | Apostle; brother of Eleiza |
| MARIAERH | wife of Lucius; mother of Sylvius | NERO | Roman Emperor |
| MARTHA OF SYRUS | sister of Lazarus; cousin of Jeshua | NICHOLAS | another member of the early church |
| MARTHA | wife of Nicodemus | NICODEMUS | husband of Martha |
| MARY OF SYRUS | sister of Lazarus; cousin of Jeshua; wife of Apostle John ben Zebedee | NIMMUO | sister of Lucius; wife of Belden |
| | | OTHER MARY | sister of Elizabeth; cousin of Jeshua; wife of Timothy |
| MARY SALOME | wife of Alphaeus; aunt of Jeshua | PASQUARL | another member of the early church |
| MATTHEW BEN ALPHAEUS | Apostle; brother of Apostles James, Simon, and Thaddeus; cousin of Jeshua | PATHOS | husband of Ulai |
| | | PAULA | wife of Ardoen |
| | | PEBILUS | son of Lucius and Vesta |
| MATTHIAS | Apostle | PETER | see SIMON PETER |
| MERCEDEN | mother of Lucius; sister of Apostle Thomas from Cyrene and Luke; wife of Philippi | PETRONIUS | Syrian proconsul |
| | | PHILAS | another member of the early church |
| MOTHER MARY | mother of Jeshua; mother of James, Ruth, and Jude | PHILIP | another member of the early church |
| NAOMI | daughter of Zebedee; cousin of Jeshua; wife of Cephas | PHILIPPI | father of Lucius; husband of Merceden |
| | | PHILLIP OF BETHSAIDA | Apostle |

# LIST OF CHARACTERS

| | |
|---|---|
| PHILOAS | husband of Ruth; brother-in-law of Jeshua |
| PHOEBE | another member of the early church |
| PONTIUS PILATE | Roman procurator |
| REBECCA | cousin of Merceden; mother of Saul-Paul of Tarsus |
| REBECCA | daughter of Nicodemus |
| RHEA | wife of Jehul |
| RUTH | daughter of Mother Mary; sister of Jeshua; wife of Philoas |
| SACHET | another member of the early church |
| SALOME | wife of Zebedee; aunt of Jeshua |
| SALOME | another member of the early church |
| SALONE | sister of Mother Mary; aunt of Jeshua; wife of Zuriah |
| SARA | innkeeper's daughter |
| SAUL-PAUL OF TARSUS | leader of the early church; second cousin of Lucius |
| SHUGARD | Roman general |
| SILAS | another member of the early church |

| | |
|---|---|
| SIMON BEN ALPHAEUS | Apostle; brother of James, Matthew, and Thaddeus; cousin of Jeshua |
| SIMON PETER | Apostle Peter; brother of Andrew ben John; husband of Cleo |
| STEPHEN | another member of the early church |
| SUPHOR | wife of James ben Joseph; sister-in-law of Jeshua |
| SUSANA | daughter of Lucius and Vesta |
| SUSANE | wife of Jonas |
| SYLVESTA | another member of the early church |
| SYLVIA | husband of Jeseuha |
| SYLVIUS | son of Lucius and Mariaerh |
| THADDEUS | son of Lucius and Vesta |
| THADDEUS BEN ALPHAEUS | Apostle; brother of Apostles James, Matthew, and Simon; cousin of Jeshua |
| THELDA | aunt of Mariaerh |

# LIST OF CHARACTERS

| | |
|---|---|
| THOMAS FROM CYRENE | Apostle; brother of Merceden and Luke; uncle of Lucius; husband of Josie |
| TIMOTHY | husband of the Other Mary |
| ULAI | wife of Pathos |
| VERONICA | mother of Stephen |
| VESPASIAN | Emperor of Rome |
| VESTA | companion of Lucius; mother of Lucius' children, Pebilus, Thaddeus and Susana |
| VITELLIUS | Syrian proconsul |
| YOUNG AGRIPPA | son of King Agrippa |
| ZEBEDEE | brother of Mother Mary; uncle of Jeshua; husband of Salome; father of Apostles James and John |
| ZURIAH | husband of Salone; uncle of Jeshua |

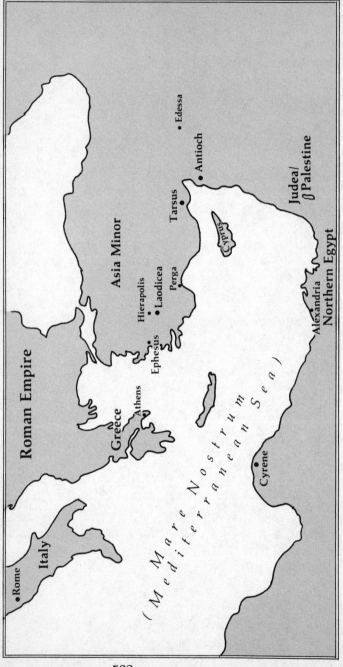

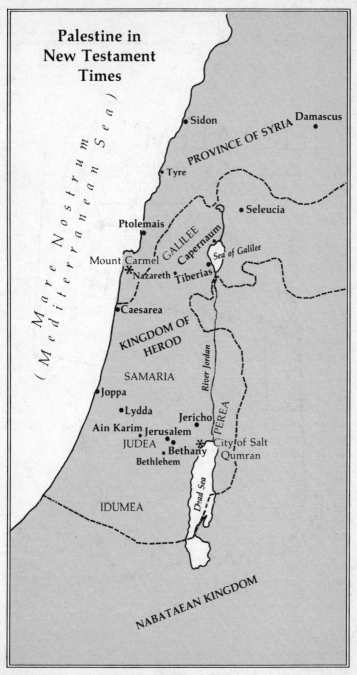

Palestine in
New Testament
Times

*Mare Nostrum*
*(Mediterranean Sea)*

• Sidon

**PROVINCE OF SYRIA**

Damascus •

• Tyre

• Seleucia

Ptolemais •

GALILEE

Mount Carmel

Capernaum •

*Sea of Galilee*

Nazareth • • Tiberias

• Caesarea

**KINGDOM OF
HEROD**

*River Jordan*

SAMARIA

• Joppa

• Lydda

Jericho •

**PEREA**

Ain Karim • Jerusalem

JUDEA • • City of Salt

• Bethany    Qumran

Bethlehem

*Dead Sea*

IDUMEA

**NABATAEAN KINGDOM**

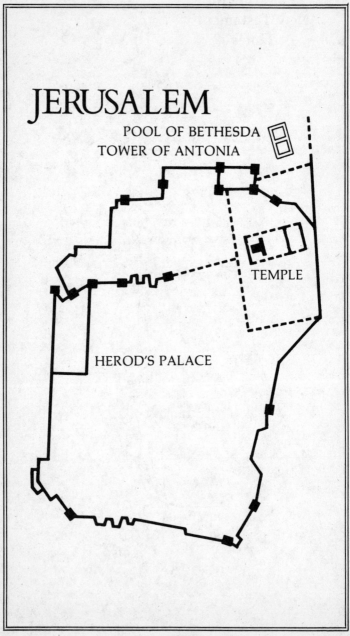

# JERUSALEM

POOL OF BETHESDA
TOWER OF ANTONIA

TEMPLE

HEROD'S PALACE

# Scripture Index